ACTIONS AND PASSIONS

BOOKS BY PATRICK ANDERSON
The Presidents' Men
The Approach to Kings
Actions and Passions

ACTIONS
AND PASSIONS

A NOVEL OF THE 1960s

Patrick Anderson

DOUBLEDAY & COMPANY, INC.
GARDEN CITY, NEW YORK
1974

Excerpt from *The Unquiet Grave* by Palinurus
(Cyril Connolly). Reprinted by permission of
Harper & Row, Publishers, Inc.

Lines of lyrics from "High Hopes" by Sammy Cahn
and James Van Heusen. Copyright © 1959 Maraville
Music Corp., New York City. Reprinted by
permission of Maraville Music Corp.

ISBN: 0-385-00369-2
Library of Congress Catalog Card Number: 73–83610
Printed in the United States of America
First Edition

FOR ANN AND LAURA

I think that, as life is action and passion, it is required of a man that he should share the passion and action of his time at peril of being judged not to have lived.

Justice Oliver Wendell Holmes
Memorial Day Address, 1884

ACTIONS AND PASSIONS

BOOK I

HIGH HOPES

We've got high hopes,
We've got high hopes,
High apple pie
In the sky hopes
    Kennedy campaign song, 1960

Only by avoiding the beginning of things
can we escape their ending.
                      Palinurus

1

JANUARY 1961

Charles and Carol Pierce arrived at the Senator's office at eleven and stayed until noon, drinking champagne and talking with the politicians who drifted in and out. It was a dozen degrees below freezing outside, but Senator Hugh Pierce's office was warm and comfortable, and the talk there flowed as freely as the Senator's French champagne. Hubert Humphrey was there, laughing and talking exuberantly, and Stu Symington and Scoop Jackson and John Sherman Cooper and one non-Senator, Clark Clifford. Their host, Hugh Pierce, moved among them easily, an elegant, silver-haired man of fifty-five whose female constituents often said of him, "He *looks* like a Senator." The talk that morning was of politics, mostly, although there was precious little talk of Jack Kennedy, whose day this was. These men had Kennedy stories, but they were sharp, sometimes bitter stories, not the mellow kind that went with midmorning drinking and reminiscing. There was more talk of Lyndon. "A toast to our departed leader," one Senator said, and another added, "May he rest in peace."

Charles Pierce drank the champagne, which was dry and nutty and quite good, and he smiled and nodded and said as little as possible. He had been a Senator's son for roughly half his thirty years, he had been his father's "executive assistant" for the past year, and he knew that the secret of success in this company was to be a good listener. These men loved above all else the sound of their own voices. It was agony enough for them to suffer interruption from a peer, a "distinguished colleague," much less from Charles, an able but rather brusque young man who seemed to have inherited precious little of his father's political sense.

So Charles Pierce listened well, hoping as always that an attentive manner would conceal his distaste for politics and politicians. He was a handsome man, slender and possessed of his father's fine features, and like his father he was expensively and tastefully dressed. Yet, to those few who knew him well, Charles Pierce was at thirty a curiously unformed man. He had drifted through life with the advantages of intelligence and looks and wealth, never tested by adversity. He knew this, and he was vaguely troubled by it, vaguely envious of men his age who had scrambled up from nowhere to success. Charles had grown up knowing how many men hated him for his advantages, and it had instilled a certain reserve in him, one that set him apart from the professional politicians around him, who always seemed to be giving something of themselves, even when they had long since ceased to give anything at all.

Charles's wife Carol, standing beside him, glowing in the dark room, was more the politician. Carol was twenty-seven and very pretty, and she possessed the gift for small talk that her husband lacked. She possessed, too, a gay smile, a jaunty, cheerleader's body, a pleasing Southern voice. The Senators, men twice her age, clustered about her like schoolboys. That was fine with Charles. He listened while Carol chattered. Soon he was a little high, and he felt that this was one of those rare times when he could accept the Senate on its own terms: the rich wine of its traditions, the spice of cynicism, the enveloping cloak of power, possessed and possessing, the occasional hint of accomplishment, even of honor. In such moments he could regard his father not as a vain and superficial man who had destroyed his family in a quest for glory, but as a charming, flawed, essentially decent man who on balance had probably done more good than harm.

Senator Pierce had been reading aloud, with glee and malice, a report in the morning's *Post* that the Architect of the Capitol had, in the previous night's blizzard, sent his men out to fire their guns into the air to drive away starlings that threatened to embarrass the day's solemnities. Just as the Senator finished reading the story, the Architect of the Capitol himself wandered in, an aging gentleman who was no architect but whose connivance on various matters was useful to the Senators.

4

"George," Hugh Pierce said solemnly, "I understan[d] forces have routed some troublemakers."

The Architect of the Capitol accepted a glass of cham[pagne,] nodded gravely. "I'd have used Roman candles on the little devils," he said, "but I was afraid of setting the grandstands on fire."

Charles Pierce winked at his wife and poured them both more champagne. The Architect left after a few minutes and the party drifted on. It reminded Charles of one of the bloody mary parties his college fraternity used to have on the mornings of football weekends, the kind that started at eleven and seemed to go on forever. And this was a kind of fraternity party, except that the fraternity was the most exclusive in the world.

"He'll be all right if he'll just stand firm with the Russians," Senator Pierce was saying. "Stand firm, right from the first. Over there in Southeast Asia, that Laos, that might be the first test, mark my word. But Jack'll be all right. He's got some fuzzyheads around him, but he's his father's son, mark my word."

Several heads nodded agreement, and Charles glanced at his watch, then chatted with Clark Clifford for a moment.

"Well, Charles, will you be answering the call of the New Frontier?"

"I haven't heard any call."

"Oh, I suspect the Administration could find a place for a young man of your abilities."

Charles studied Clifford's handsome, reassuring, inscrutable face. Because Clifford and Senator Pierce were old friends, Charles had known this man well, as well as you knew anyone in Washington, for a dozen years. Yet Clifford was a political person, a most political person, and thus at certain moments he was a total mystery. Charles knew that Clifford had been advising the Kennedys on appointments. Did his comment mean he was sounding Charles out about a job? Or was it just idle chatter? With someone like Clifford you could never be sure, and that was what Charles disliked about politics, the deception, the game-playing, the sense of being a pawn on someone else's chessboard. Charles Pierce was not a simple man, but he longed for a simple life, a life free of the complexities and evasions of his father's profession. He had set himself one of the most difficult of life's goals—he wanted to be honest.

"I don't particularly want them to find a place for me," he told

Clifford. "I want to go back to Louisville and hang out my shingle and make some money."

His remark was slightly barbed, since Clifford was in no position to fault a young lawyer for wanting to make money, but the older man only smiled pleasantly and said, "Well, Washington's loss will be Louisville's gain," and his measured tones made the cliché sound deeply profound.

Clifford looked at his watch—its golden needles pointed straight up. "Ladies and gentlemen," he said, and paused while the dozen people in the room turned toward him, "I propose a toast." He raised his glass high and all the others did the same. "To the President of the United States."

Charles watched as the older men repeated the words and emptied their glasses. At least three men in the room, his father among them, had dreamed of becoming President today, had dreamed that great dream and then seen their bubble burst on the hard rock of Kennedy money and Kennedy glamor and Kennedy hustle. But if there was anger or bitterness or even hesitation in their hearts as they drank to the man who had bested them, Charles Pierce could not find it in their faces, and he was watching closely.

When Charles and Carol left the Old Senate Office Building a few minutes past noon it was like stepping out of a cave, and they stopped for a minute, blinking into the sun. The clouds had parted and the bright sunlight glistened on the Capitol. A huge platform called the President's Stand had been erected over the Capitol steps and thousands of people were standing before it, bundled in bright blues and reds against the bitter January cold.

"How many people are there?" Carol asked.

Charles studied the crowd for a minute. "Forty or fifty thousand," he said. "There'd be twice that if it wasn't so damn cold."

"It's so exciting," Carol said. "Can't you feel it?"

Charles shrugged and took her arm and led her through the crowd toward the VIP grandstand. His wife's enthusiasm annoyed him, yet she was right. The air was electric. He had tried to resist it, for the Kennedys were no heroes of his, but he had lived in politics too long not to feel the sharp knife of history cutting across this day.

"Carol, Charles, let us get a picture of you." It was a society reporter from the *Star,* with a photographer in tow.

6

"Are you starting to remember all your Democratic friends, Cissy?" Charles said.

"I've always remembered you two darlings," the woman said as the photographer snapped his pictures.

"What a lot of crap," Charles muttered to his wife, and they nodded good-by to Cissy and pushed on. Despite the cold, the crowd was cheerful, even festive. Hand-painted signs bobbed about, saying things like "We Love Jack and Jackie" and "Let's Go, New Frontiers." They passed one cluster of Texans—men in Stetsons, women swathed in yards of mink, one big fellow waving a defiant sign that said, "All the Way with LBJ." It was almost twelve-thirty when Charles and Carol arrived at the grandstand reserved for senatorial families.

"Wasn't it supposed to start at noon?" Carol asked.

"They always run late," Charles said. "Legally, Kennedy became President at noon, wherever he was."

"Charles—it's me!" It was a girl's voice, excited and familiar. They turned and saw Charles's sister Beth pushing through the aisle toward them. She was a short, slightly plump girl, not pretty but with a pleasant, intelligent face that now was flushed pink with the cold.

"We thought you had exams," Carol said.

"Oh, I worked it out," Beth said. "How could I miss this?"

Beth glowed. Unkind acquaintances sometimes quipped that unfortunately Charles Pierce had inherited his father's good looks and Beth Pierce had inherited his good sense. But if Beth was not beautiful, she had a vivacity that made her the center of any group. It was only after Charles and Carol had hugged Beth that Charles noticed the Negro girl standing behind her.

"Charles and Carol," Beth said, "this is Sharilee Hunter, from school."

"Hello, Shirley," Charles said, and extended his hand to the girl.

"Sharilee," Beth corrected.

"We're so glad you could come," Carol said.

"Sharilee spent last summer organizing sit-ins in the South," Beth said.

Carol's eyes widened. "You must be very brave," she said.

Sharilee, who was thin and very black, smiled faintly and spoke for the first time. "Not brave," she said. "Just stubborn."

There was a great cheer and they turned to watch Kennedy and Eisenhower march onto the President's Stand.

"Oh, he's so beautiful," Carol said.

"You used to say that about me," Charles whispered.

"You're beautiful," she said. "But you're not President."

"Thanks." He was standing with his hands jammed in his overcoat pockets, with his wife hugging his left arm and his sister his right.

"Charles," his sister whispered as the band played "Hail to the Chief," "there's something I wish you'd do for me while I'm here."

"What's that?"

"I want to know about this new program, the Peace Corps."

"What about it?"

"All about it. I think I might join."

"Are you crazy? You want to go live in a mud hut somewhere? I thought you were talking about law school."

"Law's so *dull*. I think it's so exciting, now that Kennedy's President and he's going to get the country moving, and I want to do something, something to help people."

"Be a lawyer. You can get people out of jail."

"Oh, you're too cynical to live."

"Listen, don't call me cynical. The Kennedys are the most cynical people alive. You think any of them are going to live in mud huts?"

"You know what it sounds like, Charles? It sounds like you're jealous because Kennedy got the nomination and Daddy's campaign never got off the ground."

"I did my bit for Kennedy's campaign—I don't have to love him," Charles said. "As for him getting the country moving again, I'm not sure it needs so much movement. That old soldier up there didn't do a bad job."

"Don't let Sharilee hear you say that," Beth said. "She spent last summer being thrown in jail for trying to eat lunch in dime stores. Is that what you call a good job?"

"We're making progress," he said. "It takes time."

"Oh, God, you sound like Daddy," Beth cried. "Anyway, will you find out about the Peace Corps for me?"

"You can do it yourself," he said. "Call Sarge Shriver's office and tell them who you are and what you want. They know the name."

Charles frowned as Marian Anderson sang "The Star-Spangled Banner." Well, he thought, at least it's not Sinatra. He felt the same vague annoyance as the ancient Robert Frost read a poem—it was all so slick, so show biz. Yet he saw the Negro girl's eyes sparkling

8

as Marian Anderson sang and he guessed that if it was show biz it was still more good than bad.

Cardinal Spellman began an interminable prayer, droning on even when an electric heater at his feet began to billow smoke.

"It's a sign," Charles said to his wife. "God's telling Spellman to cut out the crap."

"Hush," Carol whispered.

Finally the new President stepped up to speak, and the four of them leaned forward—a world leaned forward—to hear him.

"Let the word go forth from this time and place, to friend and foe alike, that the torch has been passed to a new generation of Americans. . . ."

Carol Pierce tingled. That was it—that said it all. They were a new generation and it was their turn now. Carol was not political—a Southern education had taught her little of politics and most of that wrong—but all that was young and exuberant in her responded to the excitement of the Kennedys. Washington had been so dull before but now the brightest people and the best parties and the newest fashions would all be here and she hoped Charles would change his mind about returning to Louisville. Her life had for several years centered on her two small children and now she felt it was time for her to have some fun, perhaps to get a job, and she felt that Washington was the place to do all that. She would try to persuade Charles to stay in Washington, for she sensed that somehow the coming of the Kennedy era would change their lives.

"If a free society cannot help the many who are poor, it cannot save the few who are rich."

Yes, yes, oh, Lord God, yes, thought Sharilee Hunter, who could not quite believe where she was and what she was seeing. Sharilee Hunter had picked cotton in the blazing Mississippi summers to pay her way through Tougaloo College, and then she had won a scholarship to the Eastern university where she had met white girls like Beth Pierce, who now had brought her to this amazing ceremony, this inauguration. She barely breathed as she watched John Kennedy speak. His words were so beautiful—he was so beautiful—and she wanted desperately to believe him. Yet an instinct as painful as an open wound warned her against believing any white man. She had

9

seen too much. There were blurred memories of childhood nights when white men would kick down the doors of black men's shacks and drag them away to unknown punishments for unexplained crimes. There were the still fresh memories of a year of sit-ins in Nashville and Greenville and Birmingham, memories of insults and beatings and jails. Try to understand us, Mr. Kennedy, Sharilee prayed. Try to understand how hard it is to be non-violent when they spit on you and call you a black whore and burn your skin with cigarettes and knock you down and kick you and then the police throw you in jail. She looked at the new President and she thought, Try to understand us, Mr. Kennedy, try to understand how my people have suffered, how long they've waited, how patient they've been, how good they are. Try to understand that we need your help, we've suffered all flesh and blood can suffer, done all we can do when our enemies have the guns and the law and all we have is our bodies and our dreams and our prayers. Try to understand us, Mr. Kennedy, she pleaded to the man who stood on a platform a hundred feet away, so near and so far, but even then she felt a shudder run through her body and suddenly, in the midst of this multitude, Sharilee Hunter felt immeasurably alone.

"Now the trumpet summons us again—not as a call to bear arms, though arms we need; not as a call to battle, though embattled we are . . ."

Bull*shit,* Charles Pierce thought. Come on, Jack baby, what is this "trumpet summons us again" crap? Maybe you meant "the strumpet summons us again"—that's more like the Jack Kennedy I knew. But it wasn't Kennedy, it was politics. It took a decent guy who liked to drink and screw and raise hell and it made a posturing fraud of him. Politics, Charles Pierce thought—screw it. I've been there and now I'm getting out. When the *Star* photographer took his and Carol's picture that morning he had thought of all the times in his youth when photographers from the Louisville and Washington papers had taken pictures of the Pierce family ("Senator and Mrs. Hugh Pierce and their two lovely blah-blah-blah posing in their lovely blah-blah-blah . . .") and after the photographers had left the lovely Pierce family would take off its smiles and return to its reality, the parents not speaking, the father as unreachable in private life as he was charming in public life, the son sullen and resentful, the daughter desperately carving out an identity of her own amidst the chaos. . . . No, Charles had had his fill of politics. When his father got the presidential bug, Charles had finally agreed to come and spend a year aiding his vain quest, but that year was over and Charles was going back home and practice law and drink a lot and screw a lot and make a lot of money and if he never saw Washington, D.C. again it would be too soon.

And yet . . . and yet . . . Charles had been in politics too long to be immune to its call. He had seen power up close and he knew it could be as seductive and as satisfying as a woman; he had felt his nerves tighten that morning when Clark Clifford seemed to be hinting that the new Administration wanted him. Well, damn them, they ought to want him. After Kennedy was nominated, Charles had worked hard for them as a co-ordinator in the border states. They owed him at least the courtesy of a job offer. Oh, to hell with them, Charles thought. I'm going back home to practice law. . . . And yet, as he watched Jack Kennedy chop the icy air with his forefinger, he knew that his mind was far from made up, that in truth he was much like the girl who was just waiting to be asked.

"And so, my fellow Americans, ask not what your country can do for you; ask what you can do for your country."

That's it, Beth Pierce thought, that's it exactly. I've been given money and an education, and now I want to give something to someone else. She had thought of law school or social work but now they seemed inconsequential compared with this new idea of a Peace Corps, this wonderful idea that her generation might go forth to share its skills and its dreams with all the peoples of the world. Beth was not naïve—she was, after all, Hugh Pierce's daughter—but it seemed to her that with the Kennedys in power, with this great nation now being led by its best and wisest people, there were no limits to the good that might be done. "Let us go forth to lead the land we love," John Fitzgerald Kennedy implored, silhouetted boldly against the white wall of the Capitol, and Beth Pierce's heart went out to him. Oh, God, she thought, it's like the beginning of the world, and she burst into tears of joy.

The speech was over, the moment was gone, and the fifty thousand people who had for a brief time been united were individuals

11

again, shoving and shuffling through the snow and slush toward cars and offices and homes.

"You guys want to come to our place for a drink?" Charles asked his sister and her friend.

"We're going to watch the Inaugural Parade," Beth said. "Aren't you?"

"It's too cold," he said. "Have you got badges for the grandstand?"

"No," Beth said. "Should we?"

"Sure. Take these. They'll get you in the grandstand across from the White House. But you might as well wait a minute, until this crowd thins out."

"I don't think I ever saw so many people at one time," Sharilee said.

"How'd you like the speech?" Charles asked her.

"Well, I *liked* it," Sharilee said. "But all he talked about was foreign policy. What about civil rights and housing and unemployment?"

Beth frowned. "I see what you mean. But . . . I still think it was a wonderful speech. I think we'll remember it the rest of our lives."

"So do I," Carol said. "What about you, Charles? What did you think of it?"

"Oh, I thought it was grand," Charles said. "Best thing Sorensen ever wrote."

The two girls left to watch the parade, and Charles and Carol joined the stream of people moving past the Library of Congress toward Pennsylvania Avenue.

"Let's go over to Jimmie's for some lunch," he suggested.

"Great," she said, and they jay-walked across the avenue to the little hole-in-the-wall restaurant.

People were lined up inside the door, but Charles caught a waitress' eye and she called out, "Come on through, Mr. Pierce, your table's ready." They followed the waitress to a booth in the back room and Charles handed her a dollar as they sat down.

"Thanks, sweetheart. How about two bowls of chile, two meatball sandwiches, and two Buds?"

"Sure thing," the waitress said. She was short and plump and had henna-colored hair. "You been over hearin' the speech?"

"Yeah," Charles said. "Did you go?"

"Nah, we watched it on TV. Boy, that Kennedy is a good-looking man. I could go for him. I never could stand that joker he ran against. The beady-eyed one—what was his name?"

"I forget," Charles said. "How about those beers?"

Two Congressmen passed by, pink-faced from the cold. "A great day, huh, Charles?" one of them said. He had a silver flask in his hand and he was weaving a bit.

"Yeah, a great day for the Irish," Charles said, and the Congressmen grinned automatically and slipped into a booth with two young girls.

The waitress brought their beers and Charles poured them. "A toast," he said. "New Frontiers. Sis-boom-bah."

"I heard Mr. Clifford asking you about a job," Carol said.

"He was just talking."

"But shouldn't you think about it? Don't you think it'll be exciting here?"

"I don't want to work for the Kennedys."

"Why not?"

"Because I know them. Because I was there the day Steve Smith charged in and started telling Dad and Pat O'Neal how to run a campaign in Kentucky—the bastard had never *been* in Kentucky before."

"Oh, Charles, you'd have done the same thing. It was their campaign."

"Well, it's my life, and I want to get back home and enjoy it. Okay?"

"Okay," she said. "But I still think you ought to consider it."

They walked the six blocks to the town house they rented on E Street. The children were with friends for the day and soon they were in bed.

"Ask not what your husband can do for you," he said as he slipped her panties down her lovely legs, "ask what you can do for your husband."

"You're awful," she said, but she didn't mean that and soon they had forgotten the speeches and the politicians and found the best of their day.

The winter dark had fallen when they finally left the bed. Charles poured two drinks and Carol put some soup on the stove.

"You're sure you want to go to this thing?" he asked.

"Of course I do."

"It won't be like in the movies, with people waltzing and saying witty things. It'll be like Grand Central at 5:00 P.M., but with everybody drunk."

"I don't care. It may be the only Inaugural Ball I'll ever go to."

Charles shrugged and poured himself some soup. "Okay, but don't say you weren't warned."

They got to the Mayflower at nine and fought their way into the ballroom just as the Kennedys and Johnsons arrived. The band's "Hail to the Chief" was lost amid the cheers and rebel yells and the din of hundreds of people pushing and shoving to get a glimpse of the new President and First Lady. Men and women stood on folding chairs for a better look. Some fell off. Charles saw one woman's gown ripped in the melee and then her escort got into a fist fight with the man who'd allegedly ripped it. All this went on while the new President, looking glum, cut a five-tiered cake that the bakers' union had contributed to the festivities. Then the Kennedys went to their box and the band played dance music.

"Why doesn't anyone dance?" Carol asked.

"They're politicians," Charles said. "Politicians don't dance."

"The President dances," Carol said. "He and Jackie do the Twist, don't they?"

"Not tonight, they don't," Charles said. "Come on, let's go over to Dad's box and have a drink."

The Senator was telling a story to two men as they arrived: ". . . so this other boy, he says, 'boss man, we usta have chiggers 'round here, but now Dr. King, he says we got to call 'em Che-groes!"

The Senator's two guests, a banker and a union president, laughed appreciatively as the Senator turned to greet his son and daughter-in-law.

"Hello, my dear," he said, and kissed Carol on the cheek. He shook Charles's hand as if they hadn't met in months.

"You both know Mr. Trabue and Mr. Higgins, don't you? My son and his lovely Alabama belle. Good, good, now how about some champagne?"

Carol accepted a glass of champagne, then went to greet her mother-in-law and the other women. Emily Pierce was tall and stately. She was wearing a simple white gown which, Carol guessed, must

14

have cost five hundred dollars. Emily Pierce only rarely made an appearance in Washington, and when she did she did it right.

"Carol dear, so good to see you," she said. "I want you to meet our guests from Kentucky."

Carol offered her hand to each of the women, but their words were lost in the roar that went up when Bess and Harry Truman entered the ballroom. There were shouts of "Give 'em hell, Harry," and the band began "The Missouri Waltz."

Charles watched it all with amusement. After a while a tall, balding man came by their box and greeted the Senator. He proved to be the new Secretary of State, Dean Rusk, and he chatted for a few minutes with the Senator and his guests.

"What a charming man," the banker's wife said when Rusk had left.

"Seems like a sensible sort," the Senator said.

"They tried to give you that job, didn't they, Hugh?" the banker asked.

"Oh, now, I'm not *that* crazy," the Senator said with a wink. In fact, Charles knew, the Kennedys had floated the Senator's name for a couple of cabinet posts; they knew he'd never leave the Senate, so it was harmless flattery.

"I must say I'm encouraged by the new Administration already," the Senator continued. "Rusk seems like a sound fellow, and the President's speech today was absolutely first rate. Served notice on the Russians right off the bat that they can't push him around."

The banker and the union president nodded their agreement and the Senator poured them all another glass of champagne. The band was playing and a few middle-aged couples were dancing.

"Excuse us," Charles said. "We've got to meet some people."

They said their good-bys, then left the box and started across the ballroom floor.

"Who do we have to meet?"

"Nobody," he said. "But when Dad starts his speech about standing up to the Russians, it's time to leave."

"I was having fun. Mr. Higgins was telling me all about the minimum wage."

"What he was really doing was looking down the front of your dress. That's got to be the lowest-cut dress I've ever seen. The banker was getting his eyes full too."

"Well, let the boys have their fun," Carol said. "Why don't we dance?"

"I don't want to dance. I want a drink."

"Oh, come on, grumpy. One dance, then we'll have a drink. Listen, they're playing 'The Tennessee Waltz.' "

"Well, that's about my speed. Okay, just one."

He took her by the hand and they joined the middle-aged couples on the dance floor. The music was slow and she was light in his arms and he felt good, glad they'd come. He thought of their love-making that afternoon and he thought how good it would be to go home tonight and make love again. But this was good too, to feel Carol warm against him and to move in easy circles to the music, to be content like this, to put politics and the Kennedys and all that far from his mind.

"You're lovely," he whispered.

"Ummm," she said, pressing close against him, nibbling his ear, "I could go home right this minute."

"Good God, stop that or I'll attack you right here on the dance floor."

"Ummm, new thrills," she said.

The music stopped and she looked up at him, her round child's face glowing with delight.

He squeezed her hands and looked around at the people staring at them, smiling at them.

"You're the belle of the ball," he said.

"Do you want to go now? Whatever you want to do is fine."

"Oh, let's have that drink first. There's a bar up by the lobby."

"Far from the madding crowd," Carol said.

"Don't bet on it," he warned.

As it turned out, the bar was crowded and noisy. There was a piano and eight or ten Kennedy people, men and girls Charles remembered from the campaign, surrounded it, drinking and laughing and singing. Charles got two drinks and found them a table in the corner. The people at the piano were singing a loud, garbled version of "McNamara's Band."

"Drunken Democrats everywhere," Charles said. "Well, cheers."

"Who are they?"

"The tall one is Joe Clayton. The dark-haired one is Ken O'Don-

16

nell. The girl in the red dress is called Fiddle, or maybe she's Faddle."

"She's what?"

"Salinger has two secretaries, one called Fiddle and one called Faddle. I think that's Fiddle."

"Who's Joe Clayton?"

"He's Joseph Sidwell Clayton III. He's a New Frontiersman. Maybe he's *the* New Frontiersman. He was Harvard's basketball captain. Then a Rhodes scholar. Then he flew jets in Korea. Then an academic career—he's been teaching international relations at Princeton. Except he took a year off to work on the campaign. He was on Bob's staff, and I talked to him a few times there."

"What's he like?"

"An impressive guy."

"Well, don't look now, but he's waving at you."

Charles turned and saw Joe Clayton coming toward them. He was a tall, graceful man with sharp features and blond hair cut short and neatly parted.

"Charles, great to see you," he said. "Isn't this a terrific night?"

"Yeah, it's great," Charles said. "Sit down. This is my wife Carol."

"Hi, Carol," Clayton said, and grinned at her. Carol smiled back. Joe Clayton spoke in quick, staccato bursts and he had an air of tremendous confidence about him. She liked him immediately.

"Listen, Carol, this husband of yours did a terrific job for us in Kentucky. If it hadn't been for the religion thing we'd have carried that state."

"We did our damnedest," Charles said.

"You must be awfully excited tonight," Carol said.

"You bet I am," Clayton said. "Listen, I've played in the Olympics and I've flown jets and I've spent a year on a presidential campaign and it's all exciting as hell, but there's nothing like this, like knowing that finally you've got your hands on the power and if you work hard you can change this country. Change the world."

Charles was growing impatient with Joe Clayton's enthusiasms. They'd go soon, as soon as they finished their drinks.

"What will you do for the Administration?" Carol asked.

Clayton grinned again, an infectious, winner's grin. Carol could imagine him as a basketball star, posing for pictures with a trophy

17

under his arm. She wondered how old he was. Not much older than Charles, probably, thirty-four or thirty-five.

"I've been playing politician for the last year, Carol," he said. "But my real field is international relations. Asia, in particular. So I'm going to work on the NSC staff."

"NSC," Carol said. "Is that a football league?"

The men laughed. "It's the National Security Council," Charles said. "It's a cabinet committee that's supposed to co-ordinate foreign policy, and it's got a big staff to do the co-ordinating."

"Correction," Joe Clayton said. "It *had* a big staff. We're trimming away the fat."

"Bundy's in charge, isn't he?" Charles asked.

"Right, with eight or ten first-rate guys under him. I'll handle Southeast Asia, and there are a couple of guys for Europe, a guy for Africa, and so on."

"Sounds exciting," Carol said.

"It will be," Clayton said. "Listen, Charles, do you mind if I bring up a little business? I was going to call you tomorrow."

Charles shrugged. "Fire away."

"We've got a job you'd be terrific for."

"I've already got a job I'd be terrific for. I'm going home and practice law."

"In Kentucky? Listen, the action is here. A sharp guy like you could write his own ticket."

"My ticket's already written, Joe." He was annoyed. If Clayton had a job to offer him, he shouldn't do it in a noisy bar at midnight.

"Will you hear me out?"

"Sure. But what would I do for the NSC? I don't have any foreign-policy experience."

"We want one guy to be a liaison man with the Pentagon. A generalist. Kind of a trouble shooter. And I happen to know you were assigned to the Pentagon when you were in the army. So you know something about the place."

"Yeah, I know enough about it that I don't want to be anybody's ambassador to it."

"And you know the Senate too, and that'd be a big plus. Maybe you'd brief Senators on foreign-policy stuff. Maybe you'd brief the President. The job's as big as you can make it."

Charles finished his drink. He was interested. But he wasn't ready to admit that to Clayton.

18

"What about Bundy?" he said. "Shouldn't he be the one making offers?"

"Don't worry about that," Clayton said. "So what do you say?"

"I don't know what to say. I'll think about it."

"Terrific," Clayton said. "I'll call you on Monday. Okay?"

"Okay."

Joe Clayton got up, grinned good-by to Carol, and returned to the circle of New Frontiersmen at the piano.

"Well, that was sudden," Carol said. "What do you think?"

"I don't know. It could be an interesting job, depending on how Bundy and Rusk and McNamara and a lot of things work out."

"He's an attractive man," Carol said.

"Yeah, I guess so. He's really brighter than that jock-strap front he puts on. He's written some book that everybody's supposed to read."

"What about?"

"I don't know. The future of Asia, I think."

"Maybe you ought to read it."

"Screw Asia. I'm worrying about the future of Charles Pierce."

She squeezed his hand and they finished their drinks. As they left the bar they passed the piano where the Kennedy people were singing their campaign song:

> "We've got high hopes,
> We've got high hopes,
> High apple pie
> In the sky hopes"

Charles smiled as he passed them, smiled and felt a tremor of something like envy. They had fought a long battle and they had won. He did not envy them their victory or their power, but he did envy their optimism, their high hopes. It would be good to feel that way, but he could not. He had been too close to politics for too long. These people pouring into the city now from places like Massachusetts and Nebraska and California saw Washington with fresh eyes, saw it as a city of challenge and hope. But Charles had known Washington too long; he knew too much of its compromises and its deceits and its defeats. There was cynicism deep in his bones and he was sorry that there was, and as he passed the joyous people at the piano he envied their high, glittering hopes and he smiled at them a little sadly and he wished them well.

2

APRIL 1961

He took the job, of course.

He took it and was plunged into a political world unlike any he had ever known. Charles knew the Senate well enough, knew its rhythms and ceremonies, knew how its real decisions were finally made by proud old men whispering and sipping Bourbon in hideaway offices deep in the Capitol labyrinth. But the Kennedy administration in those first months was a different sort of world. It was a world being born, a world of flux, a world where jobs were up for grabs and reputations were made and unmade in a day. Charles loved it, loved the excitement and challenge and intrigue, loved it and wondered how he could ever have hesitated.

The thing he loved most about his job was the sheer multiplicity of the problems they faced—inertia at State, duplicity at Defense, the endless policies that needed to be changed, rules that needed to be broken, questions that needed to be answered. It was stand-up fighting; you were in the middle of the ring and the decisions flew at you from all directions and most often you had no precedents to guide you. You had only your energy and your instincts and your judgment—he thought sometimes of those chess masters who play a score of games at once; it was like that—and if you were tough enough and smart enough you'd win most of your battles. The bureaucrats he dealt with hated that, of course; they always wanted to sweep any new problem under the rug, to hope it would go away, and Charles and the men he worked with had only scorn for their nine-to-five timidity. The Kennedy administration in those days was a place for can-do people, people who met problems head on, and that was the way Charles Pierce saw himself and he savored every moment of it.

But the Administration was not all work. You worked hard and you played hard, and thus on a bright Sunday near the end of April Charles was lying on his back in the grass at Hickory Hill, resting after a hard set of tennis, enjoying the warm spring sun on his face, sipping from a Dixie cup of beer, half listening as his wife and Joe Clayton and Joe's wife Muffie chatted nearby.

"This is the day you change the clocks," Muffie Clayton was saying. "I can never remember which way you change the clocks."

"Spring forward, fall back," Carol said. "That's how I remember it."

"But why change them at all?" Muffie demanded. "Why can't it just stay the time it was? Why, Joe?"

Joe Clayton was watching a tennis match. "Ask Charles," he said. "Charles is our expert on domestic questions."

"Well, *why*, Charles?" Muffie said. "Why do we change the clocks? What is it you said, Carol? Spring up, fall down?"

Charles groaned. He was happy on the grass. His eyes were shut, and he could hear the cries of the children playing softball across the lawn, could hear the faint chirping of birds in the trees, could hear the steady thump-thump of the tennis ball on the clay court. As he sat up, for an instant he saw only green—green grass, green trees, green hills, as if the whole world had turned a rich Virginia green. Then he saw Muffie, who was fine to see. Muffie was a relic of Joe's All-American days, a fine All-American girl, willowy and rich and empty-headed.

"It's all politics, Muffie," he said. "We couldn't expect your husband, the renowned expert on Asian affairs, to grasp it. But what it boils down to is a brilliant compromise. You and Joe get an extra hour to play tennis on summer evenings, and the American farmer gets an extra hour of light to do his chores on winter mornings. Good government triumphs again."

"I thought it was politics," Muffie said. "I hate politics."

"Why?" Carol Pierce asked. "Why do you hate politics?"

"Because it's dull," Muffie said, "and because that's all anybody ever talks about in this city, like people in Grosse Pointe talking about their stupid automobiles. Let's talk about something fun. Have you seen *The Alamo?*"

"No," Carol said. "Is it good?" Charles looked at her and liked what he saw. Carol was wearing sneakers and Madras Bermudas and a sleeveless white blouse. She was as pretty as Muffie, he thought, and she had ten times as much sense.

"It's super," Muffie said. "John Wayne's just terrific." "Terrific" was one of the Kennedy words. Like "key"—everything was "the key thing." And jabbing the air with your index finger when you talked, the way the President did, and now dozens of others did in conscious or unconscious imitation.

While Muffie told Carol about John Wayne and the Alamo, Charles looked past them at the people spread out across the lawn. Thirty or forty men and women were scattered about, and at least that many children were running about or playing ball. Charles knew most of the men, at least casually. They were young men like himself who worked at the White House or Justice or Defense, and they were all sufficiently well regarded to be invited for a Sunday afternoon at Hickory Hill.

"Do you know what this reminds me of?" Carol had said to him earlier.

"What?"

"A fraternity party. A very good fraternity party, like going to the Phi Delt house at Sewanee or the KA house at 'Bama, where you know everybody is super something. Super rich or super smart or a super athlete or something."

And she was right, for to be on this lawn today was to belong to a most exclusive fraternity, one whose hundred-odd members were running the executive branch of the American government. Charles thought you could have made an interesting list of the men who were there that day and how they had gotten there—this man had won a Pulitzer for exposés of Jimmy Hoffa; that man was a Supreme Court Justice's son; two or three had been Rhodes scholars, one had been a football All-American, and probably eight or ten had been editors of their law reviews.

"Put me down, you fool, stop it, put me down!"

Halfway up the lawn to the house, Ollie Hines had picked up someone's wife, slung her over his shoulder, and was spinning her around in circles. The woman was trying to hold her skirt down with one hand, was beating at his head with the other hand, and all the while was screaming at the top of her lungs. People turned to watch, but no one intervened.

"What is that madman doing?" Carol asked.

"That's Ollie Hines," Charles said. "It's okay."

"Why is it okay? He's scaring that girl to death."

"It's okay because he was on the PT boat with the President," Charles said. "He's kind of a court jester."

"He's a maniac," Carol persisted.

"No, I think he's from Illinois," said Muffie.

Ollie Hines finally put the woman down, kissed her on the cheek, shook her husband's hand, and strolled away. He was a short, husky man wearing baggy red Bermudas and a T-shirt with "West Side Warriors" on the front. Suddenly Ollie Hines snapped to attention, shouted, "Ten-hut!" and threw a smart salute up toward the house. A black Mercury had just arrived and a general was climbing out of it, the stars on his shoulders glittering in the sunlight. Instinctively, he returned the salute. Then, his gaze focusing on the stocky man in the baggy Bermudas, the general reddened and marched quickly toward the house.

Charles Pierce watched the exchange with grim amusement. The general would undergo worse than Ollie Hines's ribbing before the day was over. The Cuban fiasco was just past, and Bob was in charge of an investigation of it. He and Mac Bundy and Max Taylor were up there at the house now, grilling people from the Pentagon and the CIA. Heads would roll. That had been Joe Clayton's first comment when the bad news started coming in from the Bay of Pigs: "Charles, my friend, the Pentagon's stock is falling and ours is rising." That was the way it was, inevitably. You talked about co-operation and co-ordination but the reality was rivalry and suspicion and hostility.

When Charles had presented himself to the Joint Chiefs as a liaison man from the NSC, the generals had been civil to him—less, he thought, because he was from the White House than because he was Hugh Pierce's son. But when he started trying to get specific answers to specific questions—about germ-warfare tests, about cost overruns on the RS-70—the runarounds began. He expected that to change now, in the wake of the Bay of Pigs. The generals would never be quite so smug again. You could feel the power shifting, away from the Pentagon and the CIA, into the White House, into the hands of the President's own men.

"Tell me more about your job, Joe," Carol said. "I mean, exactly what do you do?"

"I worry about Southeast Asia," Clayton said.

"What *is* Southeast Asia?" Carol asked. "What countries?"

"Well, there's Vietnam," Clayton said. "And Cambodia."

"What's that other one?" Muffie interrupted. "The one you divided up—the one with the funny name?"

"Laos," he told her.

"Louse," Muffie said. "I always think of louse, like loused up."

"Well, what about a country like Laos?" Carol persisted. "I mean, what are you *doing* about it?"

"The past few weeks," Clayton said, "I've mostly been worrying about General Phoumi."

"Foo-me?" Muffie said. "Foo-you."

"Who's he?" Carol asked.

"General Phoumi," Clayton explained, "is the anti-Communist general we're backing in Laos. Except he's a general who doesn't much like to fight battles. So we've got to decide whether or not to get rid of him."

"Do we just hire and fire generals in Laos like that?" Carol asked.

"We hire more than we fire," Clayton said.

"But what right do we have to do that?" Carol protested.

"We have commitments there," Clayton said. His boyish face was dead serious now, his voice firm and confident. "We're bound by the SEATO treaty. And beyond that by our determination not to lose Southeast Asia to Communism."

"It all seems so far away," Carol said uncertainly.

"The world is very small today, Carol," Joe Clayton said gently, "and our responsibilities are very large."

There was a moment's silence, with Clayton's words hanging in the air, and he savored the moment. It was fine to kid around, fine to charm a pretty girl like Carol Pierce, fine to indulge yourself in wit or irony, but Joe Clayton was increasingly aware of the seriousness of his role and it did not hurt to remind others of it now and then. He wondered how many of the people here today had the slightest idea of the importance of what was happening in Laos and Vietnam—a handful, at best.

When Joe Clayton looked around him, looked at the people scattered across the lawn, he was struck not so much by how much he was like the rest of them—and they did have much in common, a lifetime in common—as by how much he increasingly felt different from them. Already, as he settled into his job, he could feel himself chang-

24

ing, growing away from them. For most of these people were inno-
cents, tough enough where politics was concerned, but naïve about
the world they lived in. They had no sense of the evil of the world,
no feeling for the interrelatedness of events, no understanding of
the dark passions that moved men and nations. They thought the
Communists were just a Russian ADA, thought the President could
charm Khrushchev into co-operation. But Joe Clayton knew better.
He had fought against the Communists in Korea, he had studied them
for a decade, and now it was his job to help the President of the
United States stand firm against them. And he had faith in the President. Cuba had been a fiasco, of course, but the President had
learned from that, had toughened, and the next confrontation would
be different.

Joe Clayton had his frustrations, of course. Right now, as he sat
on the lawn bantering with the Pierces, he yearned to be up at the
house, where the people who counted were making the decisions
that mattered. In the wake of the Bay of Pigs, the entire foreign-
policy apparatus had come unglued, and Joe Clayton wanted desperately to help put it back together. But he had not been included
in today's meetings because they were on *Cuba* and he was an expert
on *Asia*. As if the two were not interrelated, as if what happened
last week at the Bay of Pigs would not influence what would happen next week in Asia. But Joe Clayton, if not content, was confident. He had had his share of the President's and Bob's time in the
past month or two. He was on top of events in his part of the world,
more so than any other man in the government, and he knew that
those events would soon demand major decisions, and he would help
shape those decisions. So he sat on the grass, enjoying the tennis
and the horseplay, yet feeling apart from it too, a man with a mission,
a man confident that his time would come.

"Hey, you guys, come on over," someone called. "Let's play
touch."

Joe Clayton jumped up quickly, glad for the diversion. Charles
Pierce rose more slowly. He thought touch football an idiot game.
But if you came here you played and that was that. It was a kind of
religious ritual.

They chose up sides quickly, nine men to a team. Joe Clayton was
the captain of one team and a fellow from Justice who'd been an All-
American at Penn State was the other captain. Charles was on the

All-American's team—he couldn't remember his name, so he was just the All-American. The wives and children watched from the side lines. It was only as the game started that Charles noticed that some of the men had changed into cleats. He'd never played at Hickory Hill before; he guessed he had a lot to learn.

Charles took the opening kickoff and ran it back to mid-field, where a whiz kid from Defense crashed into him and sent him sprawling. Charles picked himself up and walked over to the fellow.

"I thought this was touch," he said.

"I touched you, didn't I?" the whiz kid said, and the game went on.

A few minutes later Charles got a chance to cream the whiz kid in return, and after that he began to enjoy the game. He caught a couple of passes from the All-American, but before his team could score, Joe Clayton intercepted a pass. Clayton was the other team's passer and his star receiver was Ollie Hines, who raced about in his red Bermudas, making up his own rules, knocking people down, generally enjoying himself and outraging his opponents.

It was a tight game. Joe Clayton hit Ollie Hines for a touchdown, then the All-American hit Charles to tie it up. Soon all the players were caked with dirt and sweat and some were bleeding from scraped elbows and knees. The worst injured was a lawyer from Mayor Wagner's staff who was in Washington for the weekend. He'd made some caustic remarks about the Bay of Pigs, too many caustic remarks, and on one play Joe Clayton let him catch a short pass, then blind-sided him, smashing him to the ground, leaving him to wobble uncertainly to his feet with blood trickling from his nose.

"What the hell are you doing?" the New Yorker demanded.

"Just playing the game, pal," Joe Clayton said.

"Game, hell. Whatta you mean, hitting me like that?"

"What do you mean coming to Bob's house and bad-mouthing the President?" Clayton replied. "Come on, play the game if you're going to."

The visitor from New York wobbled back to his team's huddle, where no one offered him any sympathy. A few plays later, Ollie Hines twisted his ankle, thrashed about on the grass for a moment, then hobbled to the side lines, where he stretched out on the ground. But on the next play he jumped to his feet, raced down-field, and caught a long pass from Joe Clayton that put their team ahead by a touchdown. At that point Ollie Hines announced that the game was over. Charles's team argued for another series of downs, but to no avail, and everyone wandered off in search of beer. Except the man from Mayor Wagner's staff, who went to his car and drove away alone.

"Good game," Clayton called. "You were really hitting."

"Yeah," Charles said. "It was terrific." He was sore all over. He thought a beer would help and he looked for their cooler. He found it, and Carol, and the children with her.

"You were *good,* Daddy," Liza said. Seeing her made him feel better, as it always did. Her blonde hair blew loose around her face, and her cheeks were flushed with excitement.

"Thanks, sweetheart. Where have you been?"

"We were up at the house," his son Hugh explained. "They've got all these swell toys. Can we come back here?"

"We'll see," Charles said. "You want a beer, Carol?"

"No, thanks. We ought to go pretty soon."

"Okay, after a while. Bob's supposed to come down before long. You may as well meet him."

"Oh, that'd be terrific," Carol said with a wink.

But Bob didn't come down. Instead, he sent for Joe Clayton to come join the meetings. Clayton set off for the house at a trot. Charles watched him go. Clayton was an impressive man, moving easily from a game of touch to a policy meeting, yet there was something bothersome about him, something that Charles could never quite identify. Charles shrugged and joined a group of people sitting by the tennis court. It was a lazy, timeless afternoon, with people drifting here and there as casually as the tattered clouds that moved from west to east above them. Children played tag and kicked a soccer ball. Carol had a long talk with a producer for a local television station. Charles talked to a fellow from Justice about the voter-rights cases being filed in the South. A young man named Jim Samuels sat against a tree strumming a guitar and singing Kingston Trio songs. A society writer from the *Post,* a dumpy woman in a flowered hat, wandered from group to group, scribbling things in her notebook, and once was heard to exclaim, "Oh, Gawd, you're all so *beautiful!*"

Charles didn't feel particularly beautiful, but he felt content. He was glad to be here with these people—this was the *place* to be. He well remembered how he'd felt about the Kennedy crowd only a few months before, but he wrote that off now as sour grapes, the feelings of an outsider looking in. Now he was on the team, he played the game as well as they, and it was a damned exciting game. These people were bright and they worked hard and they had the right goals. And they were practical, pragmatic men, not the wild-eyed radicals his father and others in Congress had feared. Charles sensed that great things were about to happen in America, in large part because of the men here on this lawn today, and he was glad to be part of the unfolding drama.

It was past five when they left Hickory Hill. Hugh and Liza were asleep in the back seat by the time their car crossed Chain Bridge.

"You're all skinned up from that crazy football game," Carol said. "What's the matter with those men?"

"I think they wanted to prove their manhood. Or maybe they wanted to impress Bob."

"He wasn't even watching."

"Bob's always watching."

"I think it's crazy," Carol said. "Did you meet the television fellow I was talking to?"

"Briefly. What were you talking about?"

"A lot of things. One of them was a job."

"A job for who?"

"A job for me."

"You don't need a job."

"How do you know I don't? You're not there all day. Maybe I do need a job. Maybe a job is just what I need."

"What about the kids?"

"They'll be in nursery school this fall. So I could work mornings. And in a couple of years they'll be in school all day and I could have a real job."

"Aren't I providing for you? Do you need a new mink or something?"

"Charles, that's not the *point*. You're just like the Kennedys. I was talking to a girl today, this really bright girl with a master's degree who worked on the campaign and now she's a secretary in Bobby's office. She says the Kennedys just won't give good jobs to women. Down deep, they don't think women should work. They think women should just be *wives*."

"Oh, hell, Carol, there are plenty of women with important jobs in the Administration."

"Name two."

"Well, there's . . . well, Esther Peterson."

28

"That's one."

"There's lots more. Mrs. Lincoln. She's important."

"Yeah, she's an important *secretary*. Charles, I'm talking about *me*. I want to *do* something. The kids go off to school and I read the paper and do the breakfast dishes and there I am, all by my lonesome."

"What kind of a job did you talk about?"

"Did you ever see the 'Eleanora Kirby Show'?"

"An interview show? Yeah, I think Joe Clayton was on it once. They want you to replace Eleanora Kirby?"

"No, but they need somebody to be her assistant. To set up interviews and things like that."

"Doesn't sound very exciting."

"Sitting at home isn't very exciting."

They were driving along Canal Road. Down on the canal they could see a barge full of teenagers being pulled along by a team of mules. Charles didn't want to argue with her.

"Talk to the man, then," he said.

Carol scooted across the seat and kissed him. "Your nose is sunburned," she said.

"So's yours."

They drove on past the Lincoln Memorial, along Independence Avenue, past the National Gallery, and up the Hill. The first wave of the spring tourists dotted the Mall. Charles was thinking about Carol's wanting to work and he was confused by it. His instinct was to oppose it, yet he hardly knew why. Somehow it seemed like a challenge, an affront. Did it suggest that they needed money? Or that she wasn't happy at home? Or didn't care about her children? Or was asserting her independence from him? His mother had never worked—he was sure his father would not have allowed it. Nor did he recall the mothers of any of his boyhood friends working. His aunt Molly had worked but that was because her husband had run off and left her and she had to support herself and her son. In Charles's mind, women working was associated with poverty and husbands who were sick or dead or shiftless. He had always assumed that if you worked hard and gave your wife a good home she would be happy to stay in it and take care of it. Carol's unexpected wish confused him, but his instinct was to wait and see, to avoid a fight. Perhaps she would forget about it, or change her mind, or not get the job. In any event, he didn't want to argue now. It had been too good a day to end like that.

3

OCTOBER 1961

"I must say, it's perfectly clear to the rest of us," Joe Clayton was saying to the Weary Diplomat, "that these men would serve primarily as a symbol, a gesture—"

"A shot in the arm," the Curt Colonel injected.

"Exactly," Clayton said smoothly, hanging onto the ball, still running with it, "a shot in the arm."

"They may seem like a symbol from here," the Weary Diplomat replied, "but over there they're real men, getting fired at, eventually firing back, and then damned hard to get out of there."

"Ah, but that's the beauty of this flood," Clayton said. "If the men are sent in explicitly for the flood-relief project, they can be withdrawn easily, with no loss of face."

It's an ill flood that blows no good, Charles Pierce thought, and shifted restlessly in his chair. He didn't want to be at this meeting; he was here only because Joe had insisted that he come. Things were going to hell in Vietnam. Diem was asking for U.S. troops and there was a proposal to send in 5,000 men under the cover of a flood-relief program. The President's decision would come within a week, countless bureaucratic battles were being fought over it, one of them here in this meeting of VIG, the Vietnam Interdepartmental Group, a new committee that was supposed to co-ordinate things at the second level, a committee that would soon send up a recommendation that might or might not have any impact on the final decision.

Clayton wanted the troops sent in. So did the Curt Colonel. The

30

Suave Spook was non-committal. Only the Weary Diplomat was protesting, and he was having a hard time. Charles Pierce watched the debate without great interest. Berlin was his main concern these days, and he was involved too in the bomb-shelter mess, and he couldn't get excited about Vietnam. As he saw it, Vietnam was a fluke. We'd taken a drubbing in Laos, then the President had a rough time at Vienna, so now we were taking a hard line in Vietnam. We'd hang tough there for a while, let the generals have their jollies, then get the hell out. Charles wished he could get the hell out of this meeting. It was almost noon and he'd promised to meet Carol for lunch at Sans Souci at twelve-thirty.

"This flood-relief thing is a rather flimsy excuse for sending in 5,000 men," the Weary Diplomat was saying. He was slender and fortyish and had on horn-rimmed glasses and a cord suit; he looked like hundreds of those lost souls you saw wandering about the corridors at State.

"Oh, I couldn't agree to that," the Suave Spook said. He was an old-shoe-looking fellow, wearing a tweed jacket and a regimental tie. "As cover stories go, it's quite acceptable. A cover story needn't be airtight, just plausible."

"It would, of course, be a blatant violation of the Geneva Agreements," the Weary Diplomat said, but his voice no longer carried any force; he was just reciting facts.

"Which Hanoi has blatantly violated for months," the Curt Colonel injected angrily.

"Has it?" the Diplomat replied. "The intelligence reports I've seen show no significant infiltration from the North."

"Just what are you arguing?" the Curt Colonel asked.

"What I'm arguing," the Weary Diplomat replied, "is that our military power will prove ineffective in South Vietnam. If we send in men, the other side will send in more men. So we start to escalate, one step at a time . . ."

Escalate, Charles thought. A much-favored word of late. He was keeping a list of the bureaucrats' pet words. Finalize. Expertise. Conceptualize. Panacea. Catalyst. Jesus, real Americans didn't talk like that. Someone had a joke about Lyndon thinking a catalyst was a livestock expert.

". . . until we have God knows how many men over there. Then

31

we have to consider the intervention of the North, or even the Chinese."

"I wouldn't worry so much about the North," the Colonel said. "And as far as the Chicoms are concerned—"

"You have a new study on that, I believe?" Clayton said.

"We do," the Colonel said, like a man playing the ace of trumps. "It shows that a maximum of 40,000 men would be needed to clean out the VC, and that with 128,000 we could handle the North Vietnamese *and* the Chicoms."

"You see," the Weary Diplomat protested. "You start talking about 6,000 men in the delta, then it's 40,000 or 100,000. When does it stop?"

"It stops when we've defeated the Communists," Clayton said with finality.

Joe was such a bug on Vietnam, Charles thought. A case of a little thing but mine own. Yet he was fascinated to watch Joe in operation. In a meeting like this you saw a side of Joe you would never guess at if you only knew him socially. Then you saw the handsome, charming guy, the basketball captain, the tennis whiz, and it was all very disarming. You forgot that Joe Clayton had been a Rhodes scholar, a professor, a respected author, and now was deeply involved in the most serious affairs of state. But at a meeting like this you saw a new glint in his eye, heard a new edge to his voice, you realized how all that energy and self-confidence could be translated into bureaucratic victories, perhaps global victories.

"Have you ever studied guerrilla warfare?" Clayton asked. He got up and stood behind his chair, the professor again. Oh, God, Charles thought, here comes the Hearts and Minds of the People lecture.

"I've made rather a specialty of the subject," Clayton continued, "because I happen to believe the future of civilization won't be decided by H-bombs and D-days, but by face-to-face encounters in jungles and forests."

"You can't turn back the tide of history with the Green Berets," the Weary Diplomat protested.

"Can't you? What if the Green Berets *are* the tide of history? The fact is that any insurgency starts with only twenty or fifty or a hundred guerrillas, and if we can get a hundred of our counterinsurgency troops onto the scene early enough, we can win, because our men can march farther and shoot straighter and are backed up by our technology. Don't talk to me about the tide of history. Castro could have been eliminated if we'd sent a hundred men into the Sierra Maestra in 1957. So could Mao, for that matter, if we'd gone after him early enough."

Joseph Sidwell Clayton III conquers the world, Charles thought. He daydreamed for a moment about the new girl in their office, a divorcee named Amanda—or was it Annabelle?—twenty-five or so with long brown hair and dimples and the sweetest little ass you ever saw. That morning she'd brought him the bomb-shelter report after she'd typed it. She stood beside his chair and when he'd pointed out a typo she had leaned forward until her arm rubbed against his shoulder.

She'd asked a question about the report and he'd kept her in the office a few minutes, joking about the bomb-shelter mess, telling her about the generals and their plan to move America underground—Operation Mole, he called it. She had a good laugh, and when she laughed her eyes stayed fixed on his. He thought back over the encounter. Did she have in mind what she seemed to have in mind? Maybe not. Maybe she was just friendly. Maybe she was nearsighted and had to rub up against him to see the paper. Maybe she was a Pentagon spy sent to seduce him.

"We haven't heard from you today, Charles," Clayton said abruptly. "We're faced with three alternatives. The Pentagon proposal to send in twenty-five thousand men to close off the Laotian border. The proposal to send in five thousand men on the flood-control mission. And, finally, our colleague's proposal for, ah . . ."

"Disengagement," the man from State said wearily.

"Capitulation," the Colonel snapped.

"Given these alternatives, Charles, which seems most viable to you?" Joe asked.

Charles hesitated. Joe had no business putting him on the spot like this.

"Well, I'm no military expert," he said, stalling.

"We understand that," Clayton said, "but you *are* a student of domestic politics, and we'd like your reading at that level."

Charles looked at the men around the table. The Curt Colonel looked like he wanted to leap across the table and throttle the Weary Diplomat. The Suave Spook was unruffled, uninvolved, bored. The

Weary Diplomat looked very, very tired, like a man who thought his next assignment might be Denmark or Sierra Leone.

"I don't think the public or the Congress is prepared to surrender South Vietnam to the Communists," Charles said. "I suspect the President will support some measured show of force, one that leaves our options open, perhaps something like sending in this flood-relief project."

Joe Clayton nodded, pleased. "Yes," he said, "I suspect that's exactly how the President will see it. Let me just say this in closing, gentlemen. Whether we're talking about an individual or a nation, you can't win if you don't *think* you can win. And I think we *can* win in Vietnam; I believe . . ."

He went on with his pep talk for a minute or two more, and Charles thought of lunch with Carol. She would be the prettiest woman in the restaurant and they would have a bloody mary and some good wine and she would tell him excitedly about her new job, about the people she'd met and the jokes she'd heard and the ideas she'd had. She'd only had the job a month but he'd decided it was a good thing. She was happy; she glowed with enthusiasm the way she had when he'd first known her. When her first pay check came, she'd insisted on treating him to dinner at Rive Gauche. That had taken half her pay check but she'd loved it. She's such a lovely girl, he thought. What are you doing playing grabass with some damned secretary? Are you out of your mind? Madness, he thought, madness, madness, madness. Just then the VIG meeting broke up and Charles left behind its muddled problems and hurried off to lunch at Sans Souci.

4

OCTOBER 1962

The yellow mini-bus arrived for the children promptly at eight-fifteen. Hugh was ready, as he always was, his books in one hand and his lunch pail in the other, and after a formal peck on each parent's cheek, he marched out the door, a solemn, dark-haired boy of five who was, his parents agreed, too good to be true. Liza, of course, was late. Liza was blonde and lovely and chaotic. This morning, as every morning, her shoe was untied and her snack was mislaid, and while the mini-bus honked a second time she climbed onto Charles's lap.

"Where are you going today, Daddy?"

"To the sunny Southland, dear."

"On the airplane?"

"Yes, dear."

"Will you miss me?"

"Sure I'll miss you. But I'll be back soon."

"I'll miss my daddy," she said, and threw her arms around his neck and hugged him tight.

"*Come on,* Liza, the bus is waiting," Carol cried. Charles hugged the child, kissed her soft cheek, and held her close, and as he did he heard the voice of a news announcer on the radio and he did not think he could let her go. But he did, finally, and Carol took her by the hand and led her out to the school bus.

"Do you have time for more coffee?" she asked when she came back inside.

35

"Yeah, please."

"Must we have the radio on?"

"I want to hear the news."

"Nothing's happening, is it?"

"A lot could happen if they try to send a ship through our blockade."

"I don't understand it," she said. "One minute everything is just hunky-dory, and the next minute we've got this big-deal crisis."

"It's because they're putting offensive missiles into Cuba. You understand that, don't you?"

"Of course I understand it. I just don't think it's something to blow up the world about. Don't they already have a jillion missiles pointed at us from inside Russia?"

"That's not Cuba, ninety miles from Florida."

"If a missile is pointing at you, what does it matter where from?"

"Oh, hell, Carol. Pass the sugar."

"Well, I think the trouble is that those Kennedys *like* to have crises, and I don't appreciate it at all. It's me and my children who'd get blown to kingdom come, not them."

"Nobody's been blown up yet."

"Yet," she repeated angrily. "Charles, what do you really think is going to happen? I mean, some people are taking their children and leaving town, just in case."

"Is that what you'd like to do?"

"I *know* it sounds stupid. But you just don't want to take chances where the children are concerned."

"Carol, here's what I think. I think we're sane and they're sane so nobody's going to blow up the world. I trust my government, so I'm just going on about my business. Okay?"

"Okay," she said unhappily. "What is this trip, anyway? You never told me."

"Didn't I? Oh, this is a great one. It all started when a Negro sergeant stationed in South Carolina wrote the President—yes, sir, went right to the top—and said the landlords around his base would rent to white non-coms but not to him and he'd complained through channels and gotten nowhere. So this letter somehow makes its way to my desk and I call the Pentagon and after the usual runaround they told me that couldn't be true because it was against policy. So, either the

36

sergeant is lying or the Pentagon is lying, and I've got a sneaking suspicion it ain't the sergeant."

"So what do you do about it?"

"First I go down and visit the base and talk to the Negro non-coms and to some landlords and to the base commander. Then I'll come back here and raise hell with the brass. Those bastards. They'll sit there and look you in the eye and tell you black is white and think that if you're a civilian you're dumb enough to believe it."

His cab honked out front and they got up and went to the door. She smiled and raised her face to be kissed.

"Which reminds me," he said. "That sure was good last night."

"Well, with the bomb hanging over us and all, I guess we'd better get it while we can."

He laughed and kissed her again. "You're too much," he said. "See you tomorrow."

If there is a tomorrow, she thought, suddenly and bitterly. She waved as his cab pulled away from the curb, her eyes stinging with tears, and she thought how handsome he looked, with his face freshly shaved and his hair still wet and shining. She wondered for an instant if she might never see him again, and her mind conjured up a blurred vision of fire and falling buildings and screaming children, then she forced that from her mind and went back inside to get ready for work.

Her job as "associate producer" of the Eleanora Kirby Show had turned out to be a disappointment. Mostly she lined up guests for the show and briefed Eleanora on them, and it had all gotten pretty boring after a few months. But she had hung on, hoping it might lead to something better.

This morning, as most mornings, Carol sat down with a second cup of coffee and skimmed through the *Post,* looking for stories that might suggest guests for the show. The best she did this morning was an article about a Baltimore doctor who denounced the ill effects of the new birth control pill. Carol wrote his name in her notebook, then she slipped on a jacket and walked over to Pennsylvania Avenue to catch a cab to the station.

The morning was more hectic than most, as Carol revised the week's schedule to focus on the missile crisis. She had been on the phone for an hour when Eleanora burst in.

"Good God, Carol, what a week! The whole world about to be

blown up and nobody wants to talk about it. What have you dug up for today?"

Eleanora was buxom, permanently blonde, and pushing sixty, although she admitted only to forty-eight. She had in decades past been a minor film actress, and the wife, then widow, of an air force general; now she was a minor but tenacious local television celebrity. Sometimes, when in her cups, she called herself "the last of the troopers," and Carol guessed that was true.

"I've got a retired admiral who can talk about the blockade and a Cuban exile who knew Castro in college."

"How's his English?"

"As good as the admiral's. Here're their bios."

Eleanora glanced at the bios for a moment, then tossed them aside. "Mrs. Dean Rusk," she cried. "Have you tried her?"

"She never gives interviews."

"She's a dowdy little thing but, my God, what a coup. 'How I Handle Dean in a Crisis.' The network'd snap that up in a minute. See if she'll have lunch with me. Or just a drink. Girl to girl. Okay?"

"Okay," Carol said, but she didn't intend to call Mrs. Rusk. Eleanora usually forgot these brainstorms in a few hours.

The admiral and the Cuban arrived and the two women chatted with them a few minutes. Then, just before noon, Eleanora and the men took their seats before the cameras. Carol watched the first few minutes of the interview, then started back to her office.

As she walked along the corridor, it seemed that a radio was playing in every office. Everyone was awaiting news from the Caribbean. The jangle of loud music and excited voices annoyed Carol, angered her. She wanted privacy, peace. She shut her office door, sat down at her cluttered desk, and lit a cigarette. Soon she felt her anger fading into depression. It was not the missile crisis that caused her moodiness. That was too vast, too impersonal to touch her in this personal way. Her depression, rather, was one that had seized her more and more in recent months, one that had its roots in her here and now, in her life as she found it in her twenty-eighth year, in the sudden barriers to happiness she had encountered after so many years of effortless success.

Carol's had been a special youth, a sweet and golden Southern girlhood. She had been a latter-day belle, not the belle of the twenties who danced on table tops and swigged bathtub gin and was rumored

38

to be "fast," but a belle of the fifties, "popular," more conformist than rebel, elected to school offices by respectful classmates, probably as "fast" as the twenties belle but more discreet about it.

Carol had barely entered her teens when she embarked on a decade of spectacular social success. She had not owed her success to money, nor did she owe it entirely to good looks, although she had been a lovely child, with a round, gay, almost perfect face, bright green eyes, golden curls, and a lithe, cheerleader's body. But Carol had more than looks; she had an inner balance, a sense of self, an instinct for people that she took for granted until she realized one day how few people possessed it, men or women. She guessed she had been born with it.

Her father was an army officer, a south Alabama farmer's son who worked his way to West Point and a different kind of life. Carol's mother was the daughter of an Episcopal clergyman in Birmingham, one whose lineage could be traced back to the American Revolution and some generations beyond. Carol's father had seemed destined for a brilliant army career when he was killed by a sniper on a tiny, nameless South Pacific atoll in the war's final week. Carol could dimly remember his funeral amid the sultry Alabama summer, as she could dimly remember his golden eagles gleaming on his broad shoulders. But what she more vividly remembered, in years to come, were her fears and doubts in the weeks after the funeral. For Carol was eleven and was beginning to sense the subtleties of the world around her, to sense some of the distinctions it drew between people, and particularly between young girls. Not the simple distinctions between black and white, Yankee and Southerner, good Negroes and bad Negroes, respectable whites and white trash—she had learned those in her sandbox, like all Southern children. No, at eleven Carol was concerned with the more complex gradations that had to do with money and occupation and "family," which could mean what one's great-grandfather had done in the past or what one's father did in the present or both. And Carol had no father; that was the overwhelming fact that confronted her as she gazed out at the world that would soon receive her.

In Birmingham, as in most Southern cities in those days, the social order largely let children alone through their first six years of schooling. The neighborhood school system tended to divide the poor from the rich—and of course Negro children were totally excluded, unknown, unseen—but beyond that a kind of rough democracy of the playground existed. It was in the seventh grade, as children started junior high, rich and poor and middle class together, that a process of social selection began, and its instrument was the sorority-fraternity system.

The system was more rigid for girls. It was possible for poor boys with athletic skill to scale the social heights, at least for a few heady years, but few girls could rise above their economic class, only those who were very pretty, or very popular, or very clever.

In the junior high Carol entered at age thirteen, there was a "best" sorority, Phi Mu. Another sorority existed, but only as a consolation prize. To "make" Phi Mu was of excruciating importance, for it was a steppingstone toward the best high school sorority, which was a steppingstone toward one of the Big Four college sororities, which were of course themselves steppingstones to the right marriages, the right country clubs, the right lives, and the final satisfaction of one day seeing one's own daughters repeat the process.

In Washington, in later years, Carol met women to whom the sorority system was as strange and unfamiliar as a Jewish girlhood or life on welfare would have been to her, women who found her explanations of it puzzling or amusing or distasteful. But to girls of Carol's time and place, the system was ubiquitous and all-powerful. It was accepted as the first great challenge of their lives, and if they were pretty enough or clever enough, they met the challenge.

Carol was not without resources as she went through the summer rush parties that preceded the seventh grade. Through her mother, she was of "good family," and her father's profession was an honored one. Moreover, Carol proved herself at the summer's series of rush parties to be a bright, polite, cheerful girl, one who was surely destined to be popular, one who exhibited no cynical or unwholesome thoughts. So when Phi Mu's members met for their annual blackball session and the long night's shouting and crying and bargaining were finished, Carol was among the dozen girls selected to join the sorority's 1947 pledge class.

At that point, as a Phi Mu pledge, Carol was guaranteed at least minimal social success, barring blatant misbehavior on her part. But her instinct was not to settle for that; rather, sensing her momentum, she reached out immediately for other prizes. As she knew, as every seventh-grade girl knew, the greatest honor open to them was to be elected a cheerleader. So, one morning in October, Carol was one of a dozen nervous seventh-grade girls who appeared before the student body, each with a chance to show how gaily she could smile, how high she could leap, how exuberantly she could twirl her skirt, how willingly she would "show some leg," as the boys put it. Carol did all those things quite well. Equally important, she had been busy in the weeks before the election, bestowing a smile and an excited "Hi!" on each unknown and pimply face that bobbed into her view in the school's crowded corridors.

So she won the election, not simply because she was the prettiest candidate but because she was the one who cared the most. After that, success bred more success. It became a matter of deciding what honors she wanted and which ones she should leave for the other popular girls. Senior high was a repeat performance—cheerleader, Homecoming Queen, sorority president—and by the time of her graduation Carol had become bored with honors and elections. By then, however, she had become interested in boys, and boys almost never bored her.

In the South in those days, courtship centered about the institution known as "going steady." A popular girl like Carol might go steady with two or three boys a year. As each couple "broke up," the partners would soon be going steady with someone else from the same crowd, and would almost always remain "real good friends." It was a pleasant, placid social life, filled with dates and dances and football games. Not much sex was involved. A lot of necking, a little petting, but very few of the girls went all the way in their junior-high years.

Not until Carol entered senior high did she begin her first real love affair. In her first month at Stonewall Jackson High School, she began dating the most popular boy in school, Hank Bailey, who was both the ROTC battalion commander and the football captain, a lanky, broad-shouldered, good-natured youth with a cowlick and sleepy brown eyes. As the romance bloomed, Carol entered upon a glorious year, one she would later recall as the best year of her life. Each Friday night Hank would lead the Jackson Tigers to victory while Carol led impassioned cheers from the side lines. After the game there would always be a party at somebody's house, and after that an hour or two of increasingly heavy petting in the back seat of Hank's old Plymouth. Late one Friday night in November, a few hours after Hank had led the Tigers to the district championship, Carol yielded up her virginity to him, amid much pain and many promises, and there followed a busy year of love-making that ended only the next fall when a lucrative football scholarship lured Hank away from Alabama to the playing fields of Ohio State.

They parted sadly but with finality. There would be no long-distance romance. In their world, Carol and Hank were celebrities and, as such, realists; even though they were in love, neither could imagine a year apart in which they didn't date other people. Still, that fall, as her junior year began, Carol was not much interested in the boys in her high school. Instead, she began to accept the invitations she was receiving to football weekends and fraternity parties at the Phi Delt and Kappa Alpha and ATO and SAE houses at the University of Alabama and Auburn and Vanderbilt and Duke and Sewanee and Georgia Tech.

Carol entered upon no serious romances in her travels, although there was some heavy petting one night after a "gin-din" at the Phi Delt house at Sewanee. That had been a hectic day, with bloody marys in the morning and a beer bust in the afternoon, before the football game, and someone's silver flask in constant circulation during the game, and finally the gin-din in the evening, with huge cups of gin and grapefruit juice being served and all the boys and their dates sitting around drinking and laughing and singing:

> "Oh, it's gin, gin, gin
> That makes you want to sin
> On the old Phi Delta lawn."

Carol laughed and sang until she thought she would burst with happiness. She often felt that way in the next few years, felt that in the splendid isolation of the fraternity houses she and the other young people had created a special, joyful world that was all theirs, a world far removed from the world of Eisenhower and Stevenson and Senator McCarthy and all the dreary things you read about in the newspapers. She loved the parties and the laughter and the crazy things the boys did, and when this boy or that would late some night solemnly offer her his fraternity pin, she would kiss him sweetly and turn him down. Why be pinned to one boy when you were being pursued by a score of boys on ten campuses in five states?

So Carol had her fun. She was one of those special, sought-after girls of whom it was admiringly said along Fraternity Row: "She'll drink with you on Saturday night and go to church with you on Sunday morning." Carol would do those things, and she could do other things too. She was a first-rate cook, she played a decent game of tennis and a good game of bridge or poker, and through it all she managed to keep her grades up to Honor Roll standards. She did things well because her self-esteem demanded it, because she thought herself a special person, with a duty to excel. She was, everyone agreed, a remarkable girl.

In times to come, Carol would sometimes recall each of the years of her youth in terms of the boy, or boys, with whom she had shared it. Her sophomore year in high school had been Hank, all Hank, unforgettably Hank. Her junior year had been the first year she had stepped into the college whirl. Her senior year in high school belonged to a very wealthy classmate named Cliff Tolbot, who became her second lover, who on the night of their graduation asked her to marry him and said his parents had agreed to put them both through college if she accepted. Carol kissed him and wept and then said no, a reply that reflected her self-confidence at seventeen. For by then Carol took for granted that there would always be the heir to some fortune or other seeking her hand, and she had no intention of letting marriage keep her from the fun of college.

So Cliff went off unhappily to Princeton and Carol enrolled expectantly at 'Bama, the University of Alabama, where she pledged Pi Phi and spent her freshman year in a pleasant blur of boys and parties. Not until her sophomore year did she begin to date one boy exclusively again, and that boy, James Fairchild, was quite different from her other beaux. To begin with, he wanted to be a writer.

"You're a Fitzgeraldian heroine," he told her the first time they met, at a party at the ATO house.

"A what?" she ingloriously replied.

"You're the last of the belles."

"I hope I'm not the last of anything," she said with a just-pretend pout, but she liked him and when he asked for a date she accepted.

James entered Carol's life at the right time. She was tiring of athletes and fraternity parties and sorority-house politics, and James opened new vistas for her. Instead of fraternity parties, they went to lectures and foreign movies, or to James's apartment where sometimes he'd read to her. The schools of the South in her day rarely ventured into the literature of the twentieth century, and it was only

43

when James Fairchild took her education in hand that she discovered the modern writers who were his favorites, Hemingway and Fitzgerald and Joyce, Eliot and Yeats and Cummings. Her favorite discovery was Edna Millay—Carol wept the first time James read her *Renascence*. She thought she had never heard such a lovely poem and she was stunned that it could have been written by a girl no older than herself.

Under James's guidance, she changed her major from elementary education, which a lot of the girls majored in because it was so easy, to journalism, which was easy too but which seemed more exciting and would give her a chance to learn to write. Carol was beginning to wonder about her life after college. At twenty she had won all the prizes that all the girls she knew desired, yet none of it meant anything to her any more. Except for her times with James, she was bored by college and she wondered if she'd spend the rest of her life being bored.

She loved James, but she was soon to lose him. James's problem was that, while he wanted to be a writer, his father expected him to enter law school the next fall and join the family law firm. James agonized all spring over whether he could defy his father, then, abruptly, the matter was settled on the night before James's parents were to arrive for his graduation ceremonies.

James and Carol had been to an open-air showing of *The Red Shoes* and he was depressed when they returned to his apartment.

"It was that movie," he explained. "I mean, I don't give a damn about ballet, but it was about people who were *doing* things with their lives, people who were *creating*. Carol, I'd go crazy being a lawyer and writing people's wills and all that. I'd always think I could have made it as a writer."

"Of course you could."

"Maybe not, but how can I find out if I don't try? Listen, the most fantastic thing has happened. I got a letter today from Jay Burton, my friend in California, and he's offering me the chance of a lifetime."

"What on earth is it?"

"His grandmother left him some money, and he's starting a literary magazine. He wants me to come out and help him run it."

"Gosh, are you going?"

"I honestly don't know. My father would blow his stack. I'd never see another dime from him."

"Poor James," she said.

"What do you think I ought to do?" he asked.

Carol thought for a long time before she answered, and then the words seemed to come out involuntarily.

"I guess if you really want to be a writer," she said, "then you ought to go to California and try to write. I mean, people ought to do what they want to do with their lives, shouldn't they?"

"Yeah," James agreed, and sat in troubled silence. Carol was half surprised at what she had said. What she had advised James was not the sensible thing. She suspected that James's prospects for success were greater as a lawyer in Mobile than as a writer in California. And yet she believed what she had said. A person should do what he wanted with his life. Or her life.

James left for California the next morning. They exchanged a few letters, then lost touch. A few years later she saw his by-line on an article in *Esquire,* and the "editor's note" said he was a reporter for the Los Angeles *Times* and that he lived in Burbank with his wife and son.

Yet James had left his mark on Carol's life. He was the first boy with whom she'd ever discussed anything more serious than football plays and fraternity-house politics. He had introduced her not only to new books but to a new kind of relationship, one in which ideas were exchanged as well as kisses and Christmas presents. After James was gone and she began dating the usual boys again, she became aware of a new, difficult choice she faced. She could be what she had always been—vivacious, jaunty, undemanding—and her success was assured. Or, and this was the harder choice, she could follow her new instinct to express ideas, to ask questions, to assert herself, but she soon found that when she did these things her friends were puzzled, annoyed, even angered. It was far easier to play her old, accustomed role, but she would never again be content with it. She would thereafter be increasingly torn between what the world expected of her and what she expected of herself.

As her junior year began, she felt lost, adrift. Two more years of college seemed unendurable, yet she saw no alternative. As the memory of James faded, she felt uncomfortable without a man to anchor her life, and so she entered another romance, with a most eligible and most conventional young man. By winter, she was drifting toward the most obvious solution to her malaise, marriage.

The young man's name was Stu Brantley. He was blond, broad-shouldered, an SAE, captain of the golf team, and the heir to a Memphis fortune that had something to do with barges on the Mississippi.

Carol was not sure she loved Stu, but he was solid and attractive and there was much to admire about him. They were pinned in the fall, became engaged in the spring, and the wedding was set for August. It was to be in Birmingham, but Carol agreed to spend July in Memphis so the Brantleys and their friends could meet and honor her.

It was a lavish month, much chronicled in the papers, much appreciated by the city's caterers and gift shops. Night after night the city's leading families gave dances and dinners honoring the young couple. By day there were luncheons with Stu's mother and bridge or swimming with Stu's sister and other young married women who would be her friends in Memphis. Carol and Stu barely had time to speak—they were like strangers being rushed through an extravagant, slightly mad bacchanalia.

When Carol returned home on August 1, three weeks before the wedding, the first thing she did was walk in astonishment through her mother's small house, packed now with a king's ransom of china, silver, linens, appliances, antiques, paintings—the gifts, her mother coolly estimated, had a total value near twenty thousand dollars and more were arriving every day. The next thing Carol did was to go to her room and cry for an hour.

That night she told her mother she couldn't go through with the marriage. Pressed for an explanation, Carol could only reply, "I don't love him," which her mother regarded as no explanation at all. Carol had other reasons, but not the kind that would make sense to a mother who had spent twenty years preparing her daughter for marriage to a Stuart Brantley. Carol's reasons were vague. That Stu's mother had been too insistent about Carol's quickly learning all her friends' names. That Stu's sister was maddeningly dull. That Stu was more interested in discussing golf than the books and movies she wanted to talk about. That she had spent too many afternoons at Stu's country club watching young women with beautifully arranged hair and expensive bathing suits that never got wet lingering over long lunches and gossiping and watching their children swim. Carol wanted desperately not to be like those properly married, bored young matrons. Carol's mother could not understand these feelings, for Carol herself only half understood them, only half sensed that for her, as for James

Fairchild, a better life was waiting somewhere, if she could only find it.

The next morning she called Stu. He might have talked her out of it, perhaps she hoped he would, if he had been patient and understanding, but instead he was outraged and their talk ended with the wedding off.

She went away, leaving her mother to send back the wedding gifts, and spent three weeks with a girl from school who had a cabin on the Gulf Coast, near Biloxi. They drank beer and fished and read and listened to Dave Brubeck's "Jazz Goes to College" album and to Erroll Garner's "Concert by the Sea." Carol felt sorry for herself for a few days and then the news came of the Grand Canyon crash and Carol did not feel sorry for herself after that. Two huge airliners had collided over the Grand Canyon, killing everyone aboard, more than a hundred and fifty people, and one of the planes had been carrying thirty Pi Phis who were returning from a national convention in Los Angeles, a convention Carol would have attended had it not been for her engagement. When she and Kay heard the first fragmentary reports on the radio they were numb with disbelief. They got on the phone and called friends and newspaper offices until they had the full, terrible story. Four of the dead girls were sorority sisters of Carol's and Kay's at 'Bama, and Carol had known ten of the girls who attended other schools. Carol could not imagine them suddenly dead, their bodies tossed like broken dolls across the burning desert. Carol and Kay wept uncontrollably for hours, and when finally that night they fell silent, Carol lay upon her bed sleeplessly, overcome by an emptiness of spirit such as she had never known before. For the first time she thought she understood life, understood that it is terrible and tragic, understood that all the things she had lived for, the boys and the parties and the honors, were less than nothing, a joke, a delusion.

In the days ahead, as Carol began to pick up the pieces of her own life, her broken engagement, which had seemed so tragic, began to seem a trifle, a trifle and an opportunity too. She was haunted by the thought that she might have been on the death plane, and she felt somehow a sense of rebirth, of having been given a second chance with her life. The first question that faced her was what to do about college. She did not want to return to the university. It was not simply that she was embarrassed about the broken engagement. That was part of it. People would whisper and Stu's friends would hold a grudge. Yet she could have survived the episode—more people would take her side than that of the departed Stu. Her reason for wanting to leave 'Bama was more basic. Her instinct told her that in breaking with Stu she had also broken, however uncertainly, with a way of life, and that it would make no sense now to return to 'Bama and become engaged to another Stu. She needed a change, she needed privacy and time to think. She could not imagine doing anything so radical as dropping out of college without her degree, but she decided she must not return to 'Bama. So she did the best thing she could arrange in the few weeks before school began. She enrolled at Duke, whose registrar stretched the rules and said she could take her B.A. degree on schedule that June.

She knew no one at Duke. She took a dormitory room and spent her first weeks on the new campus in almost total solitude. She studied hard, read novels, and if she wanted a break she would go for coffee in the student union, where the jukebox kept playing a song called "Heartbreak Hotel" by a new singer with a sexy voice and a funny name.

She began reading the newspaper regularly, something she'd never found time for before, and it was in her first week at Duke that she read of the disturbances at 'Bama when a Negro named Autherine Lucy had tried to register. Carol did not understand politics. It was far from her life, something you read snatches about in newspapers sometimes, or heard someone's father talking about. The only politician she really knew much about was their Governor, Big Jim Folsom, Kissing Jim, and he was sort of a joke. Sometimes she had looked at Westbrook Pegler's column in the Birmingham paper and he was always saying how terrible Mrs. Roosevelt was or how the labor unions were full of Communists. Sometimes the paper carried cartoons showing Senator McCarthy defending a frail-looking woman labeled "Individual Rights" and sometimes they showed President Truman, who was always pictured as an absurd, popeyed little man jumping up and down in frustration.

Carol began reading the New York *Times* at Duke and it seemed to view politics quite differently than the Birmingham paper, but she was less interested in its politics than in the advertisements it carried for movies and shows and clothes, and she began to think of going to New York after she graduated. It was nice to sit alone in the student union, reading the New York *Times* and dreaming about working in New York City. Sometimes boys would come by and try to strike up a conversation but she would discourage them. She wasn't ready for boys yet. Better to sit in the coffee shop, anonymous, almost invisible, and watch the boys and girls come and go, strangers yet so familiar to her, strangers she had known all her life. They gathered between classes just as the kids at 'Bama did, to drink coffee and gossip and flirt and talk about tests and parties and football games. She knew them all by sight—the football stars, the campus politicians and the campus clowns, the grinds and the oddballs and the rich kids. Carol even spotted the local version of herself, the campus belle, the one toward whom all the most eligible boys gravitated each morning, and when Carol recognized this girl she had a crazy urge to rush up to her and seize her by the hand and warn her.

But warn her of what? Carol wasn't sure she could put it into words. Only that something was wrong with the wonderfully sweet lives they had led, that it could all go sour so quickly and completely, that there ought to be something more, more to learn, more to aspire to, but Carol did not know what it was or even how to look for it.

One Saturday afternoon in October she was in her room reading Yeats and she heard the roar of the crowd from the football stadium where Duke was playing its first home game, and she laughed aloud with joy. Good-by to all that, she thought, good-by, good-by, good-by.

The next evening two pretty young women came to her room. They introduced themselves as the president and vice-president of Duke's Pi Phi chapter. They spoke gently, almost apologetically. They knew about her "difficulties," they said, and they understood her wish for privacy, but they wanted her to know they considered themselves her sisters and they wanted to be of any help they could. Carol was touched. When the girls left, she thought it was the first time since she'd joined Phi Mu in the seventh grade that the sorority system had made any sense to her.

The next weekend she went by the Pi Phi house for a Sunday brunch, and it was there that she met Charles Pierce.

He was in his final year at the Duke law school and he was a popular, somewhat controversial figure on the campus. He was a favorite along Sorority Row. The girls all liked to date law students because it was assumed they'd be rich someday, and because Charles was a Senator's son it was assumed that he'd be rich sooner than most.

He sought her out at the brunch and steered her away from the girl she'd been talking to.

"I hear you're a mystery woman," he said.

"No mystery. Just an Alabama girl trying to get her B.A."

"I hear you almost got your M.R.S."

"Almost. Not quite." Carol felt very good. Her status as a woman was different now. She wasn't just Susy Co-ed any more.

"Do people call you Chuck?" she asked. "Or Charlie?"

"Only once."

"I guess that's right. I guess you are a Charles."

"Look, how about dinner tonight?"

Carol was delighted. "You work fast," she said. "Is that because you're a politician?"

"No, it's because you're beautiful."

"I'm not beautiful. My face is too round and my nose is funny."

"You'll do," he said. "What about dinner?"

"I can't," she said. "But thank you."

"Have some of the inmates of this institution been telling you what a son of a bitch I am?"

"No. Should they?"

"Then why no dinner?"

"I've got to finish reading the *Four Quartets* tonight for a class tomorrow."

"Shot down by Tom Eliot! Okay, what about tomorrow night? Or are you starting *Paradise Lost* tomorrow?"

"Tomorrow night would be fine," she told him.

Their romance started slowly. He was dating several other girls and he was also busy with Moot Court. But as winter came they were dating regularly. He was not like any other boy she had known. He was worldly and cynical and fiercely independent. He ran hot and cold —charming one day, moody the next. Some people found him stuck up or rude, but Carol simply saw in him a reserve, a vulnerability, a determination to preserve his privacy. He *did* have a hot temper. One day they'd been playing tennis with a couple they didn't know. Soon after they started, while Carol was playing net, the other man had smashed a shot that came straight at her; she'd managed to get her racket up or it would have hit her in the face. Charles had been livid.

50

He'd jumped over the net and grabbed the other man by the collar. "What kind of a man are you, hitting a shot like that at a girl?" he'd shouted. "I want an apology and I want it fast!" There'd almost been a fight before the two girls pulled them apart.

But he could be nice too. One night she told him the story of her broken engagement and he'd fully understood. "You were smart," he said. "You'd have gone batty married to some Babbitt and playing Junior League with all those Southern birdbrains."

"You used to say I was a Southern birdbrain."

"That was before I figured you out."

"Then why'd you keep calling me for dates?"

"Because I lusted for your plump little bohunkus. But then I figured out that you had a brain, too, you'd just been hiding it all your life so you wouldn't be ostracized. God, what a social system —it puts a premium on stupidity."

"You didn't have to go to school in the South."

"Well, why not? The weather is nice and I don't have to work as hard as I would have at Harvard and I can do a little missionary work among the native wenches."

"You're awful."

"I'm crazy. About you."

When he proposed that spring, she put him off. She was very fond of Charles, perhaps she loved him, but she wasn't convinced that life with a lawyer in Louisville would be that different from life with a shipping executive in Memphis. She didn't want to marry at all. She wanted to work for a newspaper. In the spring she wrote letters to the six New York daily newspapers asking about a reporting job; the one reply she got, from an assistant editor at the *Herald Tribune,* suggested that she get some experience on one of the good Southern papers. So, one weekend in May, Carol took a bus to Atlanta for an interview at the *Constitution.* The editor there told her the only job they'd consider her for would be in the society department and the salary would be fifty dollars a week. When she said she couldn't live on that, the editor, who was husky and about forty, shrugged and asked her how long she'd be in town and if she'd like to have a drink with him.

Carol went back to school depressed. She thought of going to New York without a job, just trying her luck, but in the end she lacked the courage—the thought of being alone and unknown in that vast city frightened her, overwhelmed her. The South was her country, yet the South seemed to offer her no choice but marriage. She could marry and live a life of comfort, even luxury, or she could go to work as a fifty-dollar-a-week society-page reporter. Her education seemed wasted—a four-year party that hadn't even taught her to type. There seemed, as her graduation neared, no middle ground, no way to live an independent life. So, angry and frustrated, she began to think of marrying Charles Pierce.

She was honest with him. She told him how she felt and they discussed it candidly.

"You ought to marry me because we both want a sensible life and I can provide it for us," he told her. "First, I have to get the military out of the way. But I'll be an officer and I can swing an assignment to the Pentagon, so it won't be so bad. Then back to Louisville to practice law. I'm a good lawyer and pretty soon I'll be making a lot of money."

"How much is a lot?"

"All I want. I'm not particularly greedy. We'll have a big house with some land, and a tennis court and a pool and horses if you like. I want two or three kids and I'll get you a nigger mammy to do the dirty work. I'll do some civic stuff—the bare minimum I can get away with. You can join things or not join things, as you please. We'll belong to the country club, for the golf course, but we can swim and play our tennis at home. And we'll go to New York a couple of times a year to buy clothes and see the shows."

"It all sounds lovely, Charles, but what does it add up to?"

"It adds up to living our own lives our own way. No bosses. No people we have to entertain or parties we have to go to or clubs we have to join or churches we have to go to."

"What about politics?"

"No politics. I've told you that. Politics screwed up my parents' lives and it's not going to screw up mine. If you're a politician other people own you, and I'm going to own myself."

"Are you sure there's room for a wife in this private little world of yours?"

"For the right wife, sure."

"Little me?"

"Yeah, little you. Because you're bright and you're great-looking

52

and you've got all the social graces without giving a damn about society. If you'd shape up your tennis game, you'd be perfect."

They were married in Birmingham two months later. Then he spent his two years as a lawyer at the Pentagon and they lived in a narrow little house in the Oldtown section of Alexandria. It was a pleasant time and when it was over they moved back to Louisville, right on schedule, and he entered a law partnership with two friends. Hugh Pierce II was born in the first year of their marriage and Liza in the third. They were about to buy the big house in the country when, late in 1959, something unexpected upset their plans—Senator Hugh Pierce got the presidential bug.

As the Senator saw it, a deadlocked convention was shaping up. Kennedy was too young, Humphrey too liberal, Johnson too Southern, and Stevenson too oft defeated. Inevitably, in the Senator's projection, the convention would turn to a compromise candidate, and who better than he?

The Senator implored Charles to come to Washington to help set up his national organization. Finally Charles agreed. He urged Carol to stay in Louisville, but she insisted on bringing the children and taking a house in Washington. It was as well she had, for once Kennedy got the nomination his people recruited Charles for the duration of the campaign, then came the NSC job, and now the six months had become an indefinite stay.

Charles was happy, caught up in his work, fascinated by it, and now it was Carol who dreamed of returning to Louisville. Washington had not turned out as she expected. Everyone was so *busy*. You might go to the White House or Hickory Hill once or twice a year, but your reality night after night was your husband working until nine, then coming home and working some more. They had rented a town house on Capitol Hill, in a racially mixed neighborhood, and the longer they were there the more Carol realized that the Hill was impossible, it was dirty and noisy and dangerous and no place to raise children. Already, Hugh and Liza were riding a bus each day to and from a good preschool in northwest Washington. But at least they were in school, gone from eight-thirty till past one, and that had made it possible for Carol to think about a job, at least part time. She had talked to editors at the *Post* and the *Star* and found them unimpressed by her five-year-old journalism degree from Duke. Jobs for a woman with children were almost non-existent. So when the offer of the television job came, she jumped at it. Now she wished she'd waited, for she was sick of her piddling salary and her piddling responsibilities and the whole thing. She'd applied for better jobs, such as reporting on the local news show, but she got no encouragement.

Carol was angry and bitter—for the first time, she thought she knew how Negroes felt, for she saw that she would forever be a "girl" to the TV executives just as a Negro in the South was forever a "boy." She wanted to think that society somehow mistreated women like herself, yet she had met women in Washington who had good jobs as economists or scientists or lawyers. What had she been doing when those women were getting an education? Leading cheers. Dating half-backs. Going to rush parties. Her girlhood now seemed a hoax, a cheat, a lie. You grew up accepting the values of the people around you and then, too late, you discovered they were the wrong values, or no values at all. She had been a Phi Mu and a Pi Phi and a Home-coming Queen and all that and now it didn't make a damn; she was twenty-eight and a college graduate and she had no talent that was worth a hundred dollars a week. Her social function was to be an orna-ment, like the silver woman on the hood of a Rolls-Royce. Carol remembered reading in school that in China the wealthy people bound and stunted their daughters' feet because they thought small feet were ladylike. How strange, how barbaric that had sounded. But now she thought that the South had been even worse, because in the South it was your mind they stunted to make you a proper lady.

It would be different for her daughter. Liza would go to the best schools, would be encouraged to go to graduate school, maybe in law or medicine. Naturally Charles scoffed at the idea of a daughter in law school, but that was just too darn bad—he didn't know what it was like to find yourself socially useless at twenty-eight. But plotting Liza's future didn't ease Carol's present. She was sick of her job but she wouldn't leave it until she found something better. Charles would be delighted if she quit working. He had a funny ha-ha routine about how her job actually cost him money because of the tax loss and her clothing and transportation and the nursery school expenses. Maybe it did, but that wasn't the point. "I think it'd be pretty nifty to sit home all day," he'd say. Well, it wasn't, and if he didn't understand it, she couldn't explain it to him. She didn't know if the fault was hers or society's or what; all she knew was that something was ter-ribly wrong. Let them have their missile crisis, Carol thought, let them blow up the world, it's all screwed up anyway. All her and Charles's plans and dreams were somehow going wrong. It made her feel empty and helpless. She had been so happy for so long and now she could not see where it all had gone.

5

MAY 1963

Senator Hugh Pierce spent the morning talking with a lobbyist for the American Medical Association, who was concerned by reports that the Medicare bill might be revived. "We're dug in on this one, Hugh," the lobbyist said. "We'll fight this one all the way." The Senator knew that already. He had voted against Medicare the previous year, but with misgivings. His vote pleased the doctors but it prompted almost a thousand angry letters from old people—"senior citizens," they now called themselves. The Senator hoped he would not soon have to vote on Medicare again, because it was very hard to choose between the AMA, with all its money, and the senior citizens, with all their votes. He thought Medicare would pass eventually, but he wouldn't mind if Wilbur Mills kept it bottled up a few more years.

Promptly at eleven the Senator rose, shook the lobbyist's hand, and saw him to the door. He planned to have an early lunch and get out to Burning Tree for a round of golf. But as he returned to his desk he felt a sharp pain in his chest. He gritted his teeth and the pain passed. He lit a cigar and buzzed for his secretary, then the pain returned, much worse this time. When the secretary entered the office, she found the Senator slumped over his desk.

At the other end of Pennsylvania Avenue, Charles Pierce was meeting in his White House office with a most exalted general from the Pentagon. It was a meeting that Charles had been working toward for months, ever since the Negro sergeant wrote the President to complain about discrimination in off-base housing in the South. Charles had gone South and had discovered that the charge was true and then he had returned to Washington and discovered just how hard it was to do anything about it. The Pentagon demanded time for "field reports" and Charles, for his part, realizing the sensitivity of an issue involving both the military and race, had to get his ducks in a row, so he had talked to Sorensen and to O'Brien and to Yarmolinsky, and now, finally, he was talking to this suave and confident general, who was by no means in retreat.

"The thing you must understand," he was saying, "as I'm sure your father would understand, is that these things take time. Time and careful planning."

"General, it seems to me that all that is required is for Secretary McNamara to issue the order and for you to enforce it."

"But can it be enforced, Charles?"

"I don't see why not. The base commanders simply tell the landlords that either they rent to Negro soldiers as well as white soldiers, or they don't rent to anybody."

"Charles, precipitous action can cause terrible problems with the local communities . . ."

"They need us worse than we need them."

". . . and with certain Congressmen I could name . . ."

"General, you enforce the order and we'll worry about the politics."

"It will take time."

"How much time?"

The general frowned. "For the proper impact studies, for a solid community-relations campaign . . . a year, perhaps."

"General, the President doesn't want studies, the President wants action."

"If the President would only consider . . ."

"General, suppose you go back and work out a program of enforcement, and then you and I and Mr. Yarmolinsky meet here tomorrow morning—"

"I must protest . . ."

"And if we three can't come to agreement, we'll just have to sit down tomorrow afternoon with Secretary McNamara and iron things out—"

His telephone buzzed. He grabbed it impatiently. "Yeah?"

"It's Mr. Hendricks in your father's office," his secretary said. "He says it's urgent."

Charles frowned. "Ask him to hold a minute." He stood up and stuck out his hand. "Shall we say ten o'clock tomorrow?"

The general shook Charles's hand, nodded, and departed pleasantly enough. They both knew what he would do next. On the one hand, he would go through the motions of co-operation; on the other hand, he would soon be on the phone with Rivers or Eastland or some of the other Southerners, and there would be hell to pay on the Hill.

Then he remembered Hendricks' call and grabbed the phone.

"Hendricks?"

"Charles, I have very bad news," Hendricks began. Hendricks was his father's administrative assistant, a frail ex-newspaperman who had been with the Senator since his first campaign.

"What is it?" Charles asked, his recent victory suddenly forgotten, his nerves tensing now for the half-expected blow.

"The Senator died, quickly and painlessly, a half hour ago."

Charles shuddered, asked for details, then was all business. "I'll go home and break the news to Mother. You meet me there at two and we'll start on the funeral arrangements."

"Fine," Hendricks said. "Excellent."

"All right, I'll see you at two," Charles said.

"Charles, let me . . . let me extend my deepest sympathy. He was a . . . a very great man."

"Yes, he was. Thank you, Hendricks." Charles put down the phone with the thought that Hendricks was more grieved than he was. But that was understandable. The Senator had been a better boss than he had been a father.

He caught a cab to his parents' home in Georgetown and found his mother about to leave for a book-club luncheon. She took the news calmly and they sat down and had a drink together.

Charles hated funerals, but he spent the next forty-eight hours working hard to make his father's funeral all he would have wanted. To Charles, it was a challenge. There were people who would screw up a funeral like there were people who would screw up anything—in particular, he did not trust Hendricks; Hendricks was too shaken to make decisions now—so Charles took all the details into his own hands. The right bio and photograph to the papers. The right minister in the right church at the right hour. The flowers, the pallbearers. Finally, he was satisfied; his father's last hurrah would be up to his own exacting standards. There would be a memorial service in Washington, then burial at Raleigh, the little town west of Louisville where the Senator had been born. Charles did all he could to get the President to the funeral. He talked to Ken O'Donnell, had some heated words with him before it was over, but O'Donnell was adamant; the President had weekend plans at Hyannis Port that could not be changed. Finally it was agreed that Lyndon would go down as the President's official representative. Lyndon took down the vice-presidential plane, filled with Senators and Representatives, and carrying, too, two cabinet members whom Charles had persuaded O'Donnell to send with the official party. When these dignitaries landed in Louisville, limousines were waiting to carry them to the old Methodist church that Hugh Pierce had attended as a boy, and they milled about outside the church for a time, enjoying the sunshine and the dogwood. When Charles arrived at the church with his mother and his sister, he saw Lyndon charging around, wearing his most doleful expression and his most expensive suit, throwing his arms around the men and kissing the women. Lyndon is the last of the big-time funeral-goers, Charles thought. He thought, too: If that son of a bitch tries to kiss my mother, I'll knock him down. But Lyndon contented himself with pumping Emily Pierce's hand in both of his while he drawled his condolences. Then he spoke to Beth.

"Where'd you get that sun tan, little lady?" he asked.

"I've been in Ecuador with the Peace Corps," Beth said.

"Oh, ain't that fine," the Vice-President said. "America's mighty proud of you, honey, mighty proud."

Several photographers were taking pictures as the Vice-President greeted the Pierce family and Lyndon didn't seem in any hurry to leave them. He took Charles's hand in both of his and pulled him so close that Charles could smell the mixture of Rolaids and scotch on his breath.

"I'm figuring on seeing a lot more of you, boy," the Vice-President said.

Charles was prepared to make the standard replies to the standard condolences, but Lyndon's remark meant nothing to him, so he said nothing.

"You'll be a good'un, like your daddy was," Lyndon added, and squeezed Charles's hand before he ambled away to greet Governor Roark.

"What the hell was that supposed to mean?" Charles said, half to himself.

"I think we'd better go inside now," his mother said, and took his arm.

"That fool," Beth whispered scornfully, and they went into the church.

Beth had been one of the weekend's surprises. He had met her at the airport the day before and it had taken only a few minutes for him to realize how much she had changed. To begin with, she looked different. She had lost ten or fifteen pounds, lost all her baby fat, and there was a sharpness to her face now. Beth would never be pretty, but now, lean and tanned, she was an attractive young woman by anyone's standards.

But more had changed than Beth's looks. The night she arrived, after their mother was asleep, she and Charles sat down for their first talk in two years.

"Well, how was it?" he had asked her. "Did you save the world?"

"No, I didn't save the world. I didn't even save the one little village I was in."

"You must have learned a lot. Say, are you sure you don't want a drink?"

"No, I don't want a drink. But yes, I did learn a lot."

"Such as?"

"Well, I learned that the Peace Corps is a noble farce."

"It must do *some* good."

"Yes, it raises the hopes of a lot of people whose hopes are never going to be realized. And it opens the eyes of a lot of middle-class American kids. That's probably the most important thing it does."

"Opens their eyes to what?"

"To the fact that nothing is going to improve down there until our government stops letting our corporations and the local juntas exploit the people for their own profits."

"Beth, have you turned Castroite?"

"If I was a peasant in Ecuador I would. In a minute."

"What about the Alliance for Progress?"

"What about it? It's a joke. An obscene joke."

"Oh, come on, Beth . . ."

"I've *seen* it, Charles. Not the phony press releases. I've seen the people who get the money riding around in limousines while the people who need the money are begging for food for their children."

"We can't just drop the money out of airplanes."

"It would do more good if we did. This government is so screwed up. Our lovely diplomats make their lovely speeches and—"

"Beth, forgive me, but I don't want to listen to a lot of radical crap. I and all the people I work with have spent the last two years beating our brains out trying to do a little good in the world and finding out how God damned impossible it is to get *anything* done when you're up against the Congress we're up against, and then once in a while, just for comic relief, I pick up the *New Republic* or Izzie Stone's sheet and read how we're a bunch of spineless sellouts who— Beth, it's easy to snipe but it's not so easy to get things done in the real world."

"Kennedy could do more."

"Look, could we maybe get off politics and you just tell your reactionary brother what you were doing down there? Just day to day?"

"Day to day. Well, the first three months I taught school in Quito and it was a farce . . ."

"Why?"

"Because I was living in an air-conditioned apartment and teaching English to middle-class kids who could already speak English. So finally I complained until they sent me to Cuenca and Bill was there and I at least got to do some real work with real people."

"What kind of work?"

"Oh, God, Charles. I taught women about boiling food and bathing their children and I tried to teach them about birth control, which got me into a fight with the village priest that you wouldn't believe."

"How many of you were there in this village?"

"Just Bill and I. Bill was fantastic. He organized the only farmers' co-operative in Ecuador that even halfway worked. He doubled their corn crop and set up a chicken farm and even started a football team. You should have seen that football team."

"Sounds like quite a guy."

"He is. He'll be here in a few months. Maybe you can meet him."

"Be where?"

"Washington. We're going to start a CO project."

"A what?"

"Community organizing."

"Are you going to teach the Washington peasantry to boil their food?"

"We're going to teach them that the only way to improve their lives is through politics and that means through organization."

"How do you manage that?"

"You start by living with them and knowing them. We'll rent a house in one of the Negro slums. Then you just work face to face, door to door. Bill's great at that."

"What kind of radical is this guy?"

Beth laughed. "He's a Republican, I think. At least his family is. He's from Kansas and he majored in agricultural science and he's the most wonderful person I've ever known."

"Do I detect romance intermingled with all this social uplift?"

"You're so shrewd, Charles."

"Marriage?"

"We never discussed it. I don't see much point in it."

"Wonderful."

"Spare me your middle-class morality."

"I will. But go easy with this on Mother, okay?"

"Charles, I'm not a debutante any more."

"No, but you're still a person of a certain age and class and position."

"Have you ever seen a dead child?"

"Beth, I understand—"

"No, you *don't* understand. Charles, I was there in a little hut three weeks ago and this child was born dead. Maybe it was born dead because of the mother's diet and maybe it was born dead because she'd had three miscarriages before but her God damned husband and her God damned priest wouldn't let her use the loop, but this child was dead. And that wasn't the worst of it. The worst of it was that when the midwife held up the baby and slapped it and we knew it was dead and Bill was massaging its chest and trying to breathe life into it, while that was happening the midwife and the mother and the mother's sister were down on their knees before their little plaster Jesus *thanking God. 'Gracias a Dios. Un angelito.'* Do you know what *un angelito* is? A little angel. A child who's lucky enough to be born dead and to go straight to heaven and to escape the misery that they live their lives in. *They thank God for it, Charles.*"

He went to her and put his arms around her. "Beth, baby, please.

Please. I'm proud of you and I'm happy for you, and you and Bill are going to do good things."

She brushed away tears. "That's right," she said. "We are. You'd better believe we are."

"Dearly beloved, let us pray."

The church was full now, with folding chairs in the aisles to seat the overflow. Reverend Denton stood before them, tall and gaunt in his black suit and starched shirt. Charles could remember the old preacher from his youth, could remember countless of Reverend Denton's prayers, all blurred together now, prayers for love and prayers for peace, prayers of hope and prayers of thanksgiving, prayers for the living and prayers for the dead. But Charles was no longer interested in prayers. He heard Lyndon cracking his knuckles in the pew behind him, and he wished the organ music had gone on longer. It had been relaxing. But now there was only the old preacher's interminable prayer, and as it flowed on, Charles twisted in his seat and looked at the members of his family, lined up beside him.

His mother sat next to him, tall and dry-eyed, immaculate in black. "How good she looks," the women had whispered as Emily Pierce entered the church. Charles wished he knew what his mother was thinking, but he had never known that. He had understood his father without loving him and he had loved his mother without understanding her. "How brave she is," the women had whispered, but Charles had wondered whether his mother's calm reflected bravery or something closer to relief.

The night of his father's death, Charles and his mother had their first and last real talk about him.

"What was he like when you met him?" Charles had asked.

His mother had smiled. He had always thought of her as a cold woman, but when she smiled her face was soft, almost girlish.

"He was the handsomest man I'd ever seen," she said. "All the girls were crazy for him. He had that gentle manner, and those remarkable eyes—hungry eyes. You knew he'd get whatever he wanted. He'd just won his first important case, a ten-thousand-dollar judgment against the L & N Railroad. I remember my father saying that the L & N had better hire that boy before he bankrupted them. We all thought he'd be governor someday—we underestimated his ambitions.

He had his pick of the girls in Louisville. I guess he chose me because of my family. Not so much the money as the status."

"He always said you were the prettiest girl in Kentucky."

"Well, that may have helped, but Hugh certainly knew that marriage into the Tanner family wouldn't hurt his law practice or his political ambitions."

"But don't you think he loved you?"

"Of course he loved me. And I loved him. And we were very happy, in the early years. There was a lot I could do for him then. He was terribly sensitive about his origins. He wanted to know so much—which tie to wear, which fork to use—and I could teach him. But time passed, and he was elected to Congress, and that led to the separations and that led to the women. The women were inevitable, I suppose. He needed love so much, needed reassurance—the higher he rose the more he needed it. I don't know what Hugh would have done if he'd ever lost an election. I think it might have killed him."

"Would you like another drink?"

"Yes, dear, if you please. So, finally, I found out about the women. One of the discarded ones called me up one day and told me about herself, that was her revenge. Hugh would make promises, of course, but he could no more give up women than he could give up politics. So in time we reached an understanding, as I think you know. We kept up appearances, but that was all."

"Why didn't you divorce him?"

"For a lot of reasons. For you children's sake. For the sake of his career. Because there are certain amenities to being a Senator's wife. I could name you at least five Senators' wives who'd be divorced right now except for the possibility that their husbands might be President someday. And the final reason I didn't divorce him, Charles, is that in a way I always loved him. Or at least I loved the memory of that solemn, handsome young man who'd come sit on my porch and call me 'Miss Emily' and tell me that he planned to be President someday. With all his faults, Charles, he was a remarkable man, and with all its drawbacks, I've lived an interesting life, a better life, I think, than most of the girls I grew up with. I have no regrets."

"And He walks with me
And He talks with me
And He tells me I am His own . . ."

The choir was singing hymns that had been the Senator's favorites, and Charles looked past his mother at the others of his family. His own children, Hugh and Liza, were between his mother and his wife. He looked at Hugh, a dark-haired and solemn boy, who was growing and changing faster than Charles could comprehend. He had been amazed at how readily the child accepted his grandfather's death. "What did he die of?" he asked, and "Will they bury him or cremate him?" How much he knows, Charles thought, and how little I know him. And he thought, I didn't know my father and I don't know my son, and sorrow swept over him, the only true sorrow he had felt that week.

He had tried, on the flight to Louisville, to summon up memories of his father. He could dimly remember the time when he was six and his father had taken him to meet the President and he had sat on the lap of a jovial man in a wheel chair who had on his desk a model of a sailing ship; the sailing ship was all he remembered well from that visit. But he remembered well, all too well, a fishing trip he had taken with his father when he was eleven, a long-planned, long-delayed fishing trip, and he and his father had arrived at the lakeside camp on Saturday morning and set up the tent and fished in the late afternoon and fried their fish for dinner over an open fire, using Charles's Boy Scout equipment, and had talked for a long time before going to sleep. Then the next morning, just after breakfast, just before they were going out again, Hendricks had driven up, honking his horn, and even before he had rushed down the dock with the news about Pearl Harbor Charles had begun to cry because he knew their fishing trip was over and something more than that was over too, some hope that he and his father could ever share a private world.

He had been a boy who wanted heroes and in time his heroes would be men unlike his father, men who did not parcel out bits and pieces of themselves to other men, men who kept their souls whole, inviolate. Lindbergh had been one of his heroes. One weekend when he was fourteen he had spent two days in the public library reading the old newspaper accounts of Lindbergh's flight and his landing with a million people cheering and how that slender young man had amid that multitude kept his pride and his privacy—that had been Charles's boyish dream, to have the world's acclaim, but not at the price of your soul.

He had kept on wanting his father, but less and less as the years passed. He remembered the summer when he was sixteen and playing in the state junior tennis tournament. After each match he won he would hurry to the telephone in the country club locker room and call his father's office to report the score and the time of the next match. He wanted very badly for his father to come watch him play. But that was the summer of his father's first race for the Senate.

He played in the finals on Labor Day and he lost the first set because he'd lost his concentration—he was looking around after each point to see if his father had arrived. Then, suddenly, he thought, Can't you see he isn't coming? and To hell with him, and he returned to the court to play the best tennis of his life, furious tennis, winning the two final sets 6–3, 6–1. And the next day, when his father called from the coal-mining country, where he had been campaigning, and offered congratulations and apologies, Charles said, "Don't think anything about it." But in later years Charles thought of that as the time when he quit trying to please his father. At Christmas, when his father asked if he'd like to fly to Washington to see him sworn into the Senate, Charles had said he didn't think he could take the time away from school. And the next spring when his father spoke of Charles attending the University of Kentucky, Charles had said he was thinking about the University of Virginia. After that, after he went off to college, there wasn't much time for them to be close, even if they'd wanted to.

Charles thought of these things as Reverend Denton stepped forward to eulogize his father's virtues, and he looked at his own son, solemn and vulnerable and growing more distant each day. He thought how little time he had given the boy in the past two years, and he shut his eyes and thought, Oh, God, don't let it happen again.

"He was a man of the people . . . a son of the soil."

Charles looked down the row at his father's sister, his aunt Molly, Molly Pierce Atkins. It was hard for him to imagine his father and Molly growing up in this little village a half century before. They had been the only children of a big, brawling, hard-drinking tenant farmer called John Hugh Pierce. Molly had spent her whole life in Raleigh. She'd married a good-looking barber named Will Atkins who one day boarded a Trailways bus for Florida and never came back, leaving Molly to support herself and her son Eddie. Molly had taken a job as a waitress at Henry's, the town's only decent restaurant, and she still worked there.

66

Charles had visited her house the night before and she told him again the story of the time his father left home. "Hugh and Daddy, those two must've started fighting the day Hugh was born and they went on at each other until the day Hugh walked out," Molly told him. "Hugh was always smart as a whip in school and the old man would make fun of that. And Hugh hated farm work worse'n the plague and they'd fight about that. I recall one night when Hugh was twelve or so he was talking at the supper table about what he'd learned in school that day and the old man says, 'What you need all that book larning for? We're just country folks around here.' And Hugh says, 'You may be just country folks, but I'm not. I'm gonna be somebody important someday.' And the old man tanned his hide for that but Hugh wouldn't take back a word of it. Whenever the old man whipped me, I'd just beg and cry, 'cause I knew that's what he wanted to hear. But not Hugh. The old man could beat him till he was black and blue and he'd never let out a whimper. Not one. Lord, how those two hated each other. It was enough to break your heart.

"Well, the end came right after Hugh graduated from high school. He came home from town that Saturday afternoon, and the old man said, 'Come on, boy, we've got some postholes t'dig.' And Hugh just shook his head and said he wasn't digging any postholes that day. Well, the old man'd been drinking and he grabbed Hugh by the collar and says, 'The hell you ain't,' or something like that, and right then Hugh just knocked him flat. Ma was praying and I was crying and Hugh just hugged us both and said, 'I'm leaving now,' and he took off walking down the road with just the clothes on his back. He never even looked back.

"That was in June and we didn't hear a word, didn't know if he was alive or dead, till Christmas, when we got a card. It was from Louisville and all it said was, 'Dear Mother and Molly, I am well and working hard, Love from Hugh Allen Pierce.' No return address or nothing. And not another word until the next Christmas, when there was another card and this one says, 'Dear Mother and Molly, I am well and I am reading law in a law office here, Love from Hugh Allen Pierce.' Ma started crying like a baby, she was so happy for him. She'd've given her life to go see him, but I guess we figured that if Hugh wanted to see us he'd let us know. He was only twenty years old and we were his poor relations already.

"Anyway, the next Christmas came we didn't get a card and Ma's heart was about to break, when long about noon there was a frightful commotion out front of the house and we looked out and there was Hugh driving up in a shiny new flivver with half the kids in town tagging after him. He was wearing a black suit and had a string tie and a gold watch chain hung across his vest and he was proud as the devil. We ran out to meet him and he hugged us and all he said was, 'Ma, I'm a lawyer now.'

"All this time, the old man was up on the front porch, grumbling and growling, and I figgered, Oh, Lord, they'll have at it again. But Hugh just marched up to the old man and stuck out his hand and said, 'How you making it, Pa? You look mean as ever.' I guess it was right then that I knew we had us a politician in the family. Anyway, Hugh'd brought us all presents and he stayed for Christmas dinner, and then about four o'clock he said he had to drive back to Louisville, said he had to try a case the next day. The truth was, he'd swore he'd never spend another night in the old man's house. And he didn't. We didn't see much of him after that. He'd left us; I guess he'd left us a long while back, before we ever knew it. But he always tried to provide for us. When Ma was sick, he sent over the best doctor in Louisville to care for her. 'Course, the best medicine would've been a visit from him, but that wasn't Hugh's way. He was a strange man, Charles, a hard man sometimes, but he wasn't a bad man. I know you think he wasn't much of a father, but you got to remember *he* didn't have much of a father, either."

Charles sat in the church, looking at his aunt Molly and her son Eddie, who was eighteen now, a cousin whom Charles barely knew, a nice enough kid who'd graduated from high school and was talking of volunteering for the army. He looked at them and he thought of what Molly had said about his father, forty years before, walking away from his home, never looking back. That was how Charles would remember his father, as a man walking down a long road, a proud, lonely man who never looked back. Charles would never understand what dreams or demons had set his father on his journey, but it was finally over and Charles was suddenly pained to think of it. He could not love his father but he no longer hated him. He accepted him, wished he had known him better, wished he had been a better son. But it was too late now.

Charles had two appointments on the Monday after the funeral.

The first was at ten o'clock with Coleman Harris, his father's former law partner. Charles and his mother and Beth went to the lawyer's office to discuss the Senator's will.

"Emily, I want to keep this as brief and informal as I can," Harris said. He was a plump, solemn man, and he was said to be one of the richest lawyers in the state.

"Thank you, Coleman," Emily Pierce said. "Why don't you just go ahead and tell us whatever you're supposed to?"

"Fine, fine. Well, the gist of it is this. The Senator left an estate valued at about a half million dollars. Of that—"

"A half million dollars?" Charles said. "I don't see how that's possible."

"Oh, it's quite possible, I assure you. Now, to continue, there are two bequests of any consequence. One, of twenty-five thousand dollars, to his sister, Mrs. Atkins, and another, also of twenty-five thousand dollars, to his administrative assistant, Mr. Hendricks. Aside from that, the balance of the estate is to be divided as follows: one half to his widow, one fourth to his son Charles, and one fourth to his daughter Elizabeth, upon her reaching age twenty-five."

"I don't want it," Beth said.

"I beg your pardon, my dear?"

"I don't want the money. I didn't do anything for it and there's no reason why I should have it."

"Well, actually, you don't get the principle until you reach twenty-five, although the interest accrues to you in the interim."

"I won't take it."

"That of course is your decision. The money will be in the bank if you choose to make use of it."

"It's insane," Beth said. "People just shouldn't be *given* fortunes, when millions of people work hard all their lives for nothing. Excuse me."

Beth rushed out the door. The lawyer looked after her with raised eyebrows.

"No doubt she'll change her mind in time," he said.

"No doubt," Emily Pierce said. "Now, Coleman, as you know, I have my own means and I doubt that I'll touch this new money. Barring something unforeseen, I'd simply like mine to accumulate and to go to my children and grandchildren after my death. Can you work something out to that effect?"

"Of course, Emily."

"Then that should be all for now, shouldn't it?"

"Just a minute, Mother," Charles said. "There's something I want to know. Mr. Harris, how did my father acquire a half million dollars? He spent the past twenty-five years in Congress."

"Well, the estate is fairly complicated, Charles. There are investments and some real estate, and he had over the years retained an interest in this law firm, although he was not an active partner."

"He never mentioned that."

"We saw no need to publicize the arrangement. But his advice could frequently be quite valuable to us."

"I'm sure it was," Charles said dryly.

"I can assure you that your father's affairs were quite in order," Harris said.

"No doubt they were, legally."

"Legality is my area, not morality," the lawyer said, "and, if I may be so bold, let me ask you to consider your father's finances from his point of view. For most of his years in Congress, his salary was ten to fifteen thousand dollars a year. Your father could have accepted money from wealthy constituents. He preferred to earn money on his own. I suspect that some of the money your father made from his outside legal consultations put you through school."

"That's true," Emily Pierce said. "He would never touch a cent of my money."

Charles wondered if he was being absurd. Not many Senators lived on their salaries.

"Well, I'd like you to prepare me a detailed listing of his holdings," he said rather lamely, and the meeting broke up.

His second meeting that day was with Pat O'Neal, the state Democratic chairman, an old friend and backer of his father's. Pat O'Neal had started as a coal miner, had switched to selling insurance, and soon plunged into Democratic politics. Although an Irish Catholic in a Protestant state, he had become one of the state's leading Democrats because he worked hard, because he knew politics at the door-to-door, face-to-face level, and because his honesty was unquestioned. Charles liked him—and there were not many politicians Charles liked.

But Charles had not expected to be seeing much more of Pat O'Neal, and he had been surprised when the politician whispered at the funeral that he wanted to talk with him as soon as possible.

O'Neal was a wiry, nervous man who chain-smoked Lucky Strikes

70

and always wore a green bow tie. His office walls were covered with pictures of him and politicians—FDR, Truman, Barkley, Kennedy, Kefauver, Johnson, Rayburn, Stevenson, and many more.

"What's on your mind, Pat?"

O'Neal stubbed out one Lucky, coughed, and lit another. As an afterthought, he offered the pack to Charles, who shook his head.

"I thought you smoked," O'Neal said.

"I used to. I quit."

"Good boy. A terrible habit. Curse the day I started. Well, boy, how are you? A wonderful turnout for the funeral. A great tribute to your father."

"What's on your mind, Pat?" Charles said again. "I've got to get home to have lunch with the family."

"Of course, of course," O'Neal said. "Charles, what's on my mind is trying to see that Kentucky continues to have the high level of representation in the Senate that your father provided."

Charles nodded—someone had to replace his father, but he didn't want to get involved in the fight.

"What do they do?" he asked. "Call a special election?"

"No, not with less than two years remaining on the term. The Governor appoints someone to serve out the remainder of the term. In this case, some seventeen months, until next year's election."

"Okay, who's the lucky fellow?"

"I can't say that I know, Charles. But I have an idea."

"Maybe he'll appoint himself," Charles said. "He could, couldn't he?"

"He'd dearly love to, but he's worried about Baker's Law."

"What law?"

"You've run into Bobby Baker in Washington, haven't you? Well, Bobby made an important discovery. Governors who appoint themselves to the Senate usually get beaten when they run for the full term. People think it's unsportsmanlike, to get elected to one job and then appoint yourself to another."

"So they appoint someone to keep the seat warm in the interim. Like the President had his pal Ben Smith appointed to fill his Senate seat until Teddy was ready."

"Exactly," Pat O'Neal said. "That's what Roark will want to do."

"So who's his man? The Mayor? He's Roark's protégé, isn't he?"

"I wouldn't look for that. Roark knows he can't trust the Mayor. He'd get up to Washington and decide he liked it there."

"Well, he's got to trust someone, doesn't he?"

"Not necessarily. He could appoint someone who he thinks wouldn't run again, or wouldn't be a threat if he did."

"Like Judge Mayhew? He must be seventy by now."

"That's a possibility. Except the judge is as spry as a chicken. And what if he did decide to run next year, how would Roark look running against a fine old gentleman like that?"

Charles glanced at his watch; it was almost noon. "So where does that leave us, Pat? You said you had an idea."

O'Neal snubbed out his cigarette and searched through his desk drawers for a fresh pack.

"You know, Charles, there've been instances where a Governor appointed a member of the departed's family. Maggie Smith, for instance."

"Jesus Christ, you're not suggesting that Roark would try to appoint my mother? Believe me, she's not interested."

"No, I don't think he'd consider your mother."

It was stuffy in O'Neal's small office and the smoke was bothering Charles. He had a hangover, and he thought a bloody mary would help. He was ready to go.

"Then what are we talking about, Pat? Frankly, I don't give a damn who the Governor appoints. It's not my affair."

"It might be."

"What are you driving at?"

"Just this. Right now the Governor is sitting down to lunch with the Mayor. I expect he'll break the bad news to him that he isn't going to get the appointment. Then, this afternoon, I expect the Governor is going to call you, Charles, and ask you to come see him in the morning. And I expect he'll offer to appoint you to your father's seat."

"You're out of your mind."

"Well, maybe not. Just maybe not."

"Then he's out of his mind."

"That might not be so either."

"Damn it, Pat, I don't want to be in the Senate."

"You don't? You wouldn't take it?"

72

Charles twisted in his chair. "Hell, I don't know. But I don't think it could happen. I'm too young."

"You're no younger than Teddy or this fellow Bayh or some others I could name."

"But why should Roark do it? He can't trust me."

"He can't trust anybody. So he's trying to figure who he can beat if he has to run against his own appointee next year."

"And he figures I'd be easy to beat?"

"Let's look at it coldly, Charles. You're a young man who has never run for office. Who perhaps isn't . . ."

"The political type? Who'd probably put his foot in his mouth? Okay, I never claimed to be a politician."

"So, he appoints you and you choose to run on your own next year. What kind of opponent does that give him, as he sees it? A young fellow, one who's never run for office, and who's been up in Washington working for the Kennedys."

"Do you mean he thinks it'd hurt me to be associated with the Kennedy administration?"

"People are upset by all this civil rights business."

"Damn it, either we have a Constitution or we don't."

"All right, Charles, I agree. But let's get back to what you do if the Governor calls."

"I just can't see it happening."

"It can happen, believe me. And there's not many young fellows who'd hesitate two minutes. Can you turn it down, Charles, just because you've maybe had some problems growing up as a Senator's son?"

"I don't know. Damn it, I don't know." He only knew that he had both hated politics and been fascinated by it for as long as he could remember, and he didn't know if his hate or his fascination was greater.

"What's your interest in this, Pat? What do you care if I take it or not?"

O'Neal shrugged. "Your father was a good friend to me, Charles. More important, he was a good Democrat, as good as he could be. Maybe he didn't always vote right, but he'd been poor and he never forgot what it was like. John Roark's not fit to shine his shoes."

"If Roark calls, what should I say?"

O'Neal leaned forward eagerly. "Act surprised. Beat around the bush. He'll try to hint that you'd only be taking it for the unexpired term, that you wouldn't run next year. Don't make any commitment. Act like you don't understand."

"In other words, play dumb."

"That's right. Remember, he's not doing you any favor. If he appoints you, it's because he thinks you're a patsy."

"The son of a bitch could get surprised, couldn't he?"

"Indeed he could," Pat O'Neal said. "Indeed he could."

The Governor's call came that afternoon. Could Charles join the Governor for breakfast the next morning? Charles said he could. Then he went into the study and poured a drink and sat thinking for a long time. He didn't tell his mother or his wife what was happening. He would talk to them at dinner, but for now he thought this decision was his alone. He knew politics, knew its demands, knew how public life could destroy private lives. He had always said he wanted only a private life. Had he been kidding himself? Had he in truth hungered for the world of power? Yet there was more than power involved. There was good to be done—he had learned that in the past two years —and precious few politicians concerned with doing it. Could he reject a Senate seat, even for a year, and let it go to John Roark or the kind of politician he'd appoint? Charles knew the young men in the Senate, and he regarded none of them as more capable than himself. Perhaps it finally came down to ego. As he pondered his decision, as he thought of the good he might do and the losses he might suffer, one question kept coming back to him: Why not? Why the hell not?

6

SUMMER 1963

Charles Pierce took the oath of office as a United States Senator on the morning of May 22, 1963. After lunch with his mother and his wife, he returned to the Capitol for the standard briefing from the Secretary of the Senate. He learned, among other things, that his salary was $22,500 a year, that he was assigned two parking spaces in the underground garage, and that he was allowed 600 minutes of free long-distance phone calls each month. By the end of the day he was temporarily installed in the office that had been his father's, on the second floor of the Old Senate Office Building.

During those first days he was struck by the friendliness of the older Senators. Without waiting for him to make a courtesy call, the giants of the Senate—Dirksen, Humphrey, Kefauver, Douglas, even Russell—dropped by to welcome him. Each would sit and chat a few minutes, letting his eyes sweep around the huge, high-ceilinged old office, enjoying its spectacular view of the Capitol, talking warmly of Charles's father and of times past.

"It's wonderful how friendly they are," Charles said to Hendricks at the end of his first week as a Senator.

Hendricks grunted non-committally.

"Well, I think it's damn good of them to come by like that," Charles said. "They could just sit back and wait for me to call on them, couldn't they?"

Hendricks looked up from the papers he was signing.

"It's not entirely a matter of friendliness, Charles," he said. "You

75

see, this is one of the three or four finest offices in the Senate, and those gentlemen want to look it over, to decide whether or not to put in for it."

"Oh."

"As a matter of fact," Hendricks continued, "I just had a call about your permanent office assignment."

"How bad is it?"

"Well, it's a nice enough little office. Of course, it's on the top floor and at the back, but that has its advantages. You don't have so many constituents dropping in on you."

"You mean they can't find us back there?"

"Well, it does require some effort."

The next day Senator Charles Pierce and his staff moved to a five-room suite with a fine view of Union Station, and after that the giants of the Senate did not come calling any more.

He saw Capitol Hill with fresh eyes in those first weeks. He was glad he had come to the Senate in the spring, when Washington was its loveliest. He rarely took the subway from the Senate buildings to the Capitol. He preferred to walk through the bright gardens and flowering trees of the Capitol grounds, then to jog up the high marble steps and to pause at the top and look back, at the Senate buildings on his left, the House buildings on his right, the circular sweep of the Capitol grounds before him, and beyond them the glistening white marble of the Supreme Court. The scene from the Capitol steps was bright and lovely and it was good to enjoy it for a moment, then to turn and march briskly into the Capitol, where he would be met by a respectful "Good morning, Senator," from the pages and guards and elevator operators and secretaries and clerks he passed. The Senate was a small town and, before, Charles had seen it as an outsider. He remembered how he had resented it as a boy, had hated it sometimes for what it had done to his family. Now he began to understand his father a little better, to see that for all those years his father had had another family, and he began to realize how easy it would be to love this place.

"Only two chillen?" Senator Tom Montrose was saying. "Come on, Charles, you got to have you a couple more. Ain't nothing in the world like chillen. See that little rascal there?" He pointed to a picture on his desk. "That's my oldest grandson. Going on ten, and mean as the devil. Lord, I wouldn't take the world for that boy! No, sir! Pour yourself a little more of that Johnnie Walker Black, Charles, just he'p yourself. Might even pour me another drop while you're up."

Charles poured the drinks dutifully. He had come to call on Senator Montrose to seek a seat on the Senator's Health and Welfare Committee, but so far all they had done was drink whisky and talk about the Senator's grandchildren.

"I tell you, Charles, it's for these young folks that you'n me have got to do our jobs. Hell, it don't matter what happens to an old fart like me, whether I get blown up or shot up or what. But these kids is the hope of the future. Yes, sir!"

"I couldn't agree more, Senator," Charles injected.

"Bright young feller like you, he's gonna do a lot fer this country. Hell, you'll probably be President someday."

Charles laughed with what he hoped was becoming modesty. "I don't want to be President, Senator Montrose."

"That's 'cause you just got here. You ain't caught the bug yet. But you will. They all do. Hell, boy, I'se seen 'em come and go."

"I know you have, Senator," Charles said. "You know, I'll be getting my committee assignments soon—"

"You know the secret of gettin' ahead in this place, boy?"

"What's that, sir?"

Senator Montrose leaned forward. He was a short, plump man with tiny eyes and a rubber nose. "The secret, boy, is to stay right on the issues. Yes, sir! You take this nigger issue. There's some folks been kissin' a lot of black ass lately. Thinking that was smart politics. But let's just wait an' see. Folks in this country don't like mobs an' they don't like threats an' they don't like for things to change too fast, neither. You understand?"

"I think I see what you mean," Charles said.

"I knew you would," Montrose declared, and jumped to his feet. "Let's have another little drop." He seized the bottle by the neck and filled both their glasses. "Ain't that fine stuff?"

"It sure is," Charles agreed.

Montrose reached into his liquor cabinet and pulled out an unopened bottle of Johnnie Walker. "Here, take this along with you," he said. "I like a man who appreciates good whisky. Good whisky an' good women an' good politics, too. Your daddy, he appreciated good things. Yes, sir."

"Well, thank you, Senator," Charles said, and put the bottle on the floor beside his chair. Senator Montrose sat down heavily in his big leather chair.

"I'll tell you another issue that can make or break a man around here—oil!" Montrose said. "Yes, sir! An' I happen to know right much about that one, being as I'se from an oil-producing state myself. So if you ever got any questions about oil, you bring 'em to me."

"I'll do that." You bet your ass I will.

"Good! Now, what about them committee assignments?"

"I'm supposed to see Senator Mansfield about them tomorrow, and I'm going to tell him that your committee is my first choice."

"Ain't Mike a fine feller?" Montrose asked. "Kind of an old maid, sometimes, an' ain't got much practical sense, but I wouldn't take the world fer him." He paused, as if reflecting on the Majority Leader's virtues.

"I don't know if you can make room for me on the committee or not," Charles said. "But I want you to know that if I get on it I'll hold my end up."

Charles waited for Montrose to reply. The older man was loudly sucking on an ice cube. Charles was angry and getting angrier.

"I reckon it might be possible, boy," Montrose said. " 'Course, I'd hafta pull a few strings, to open up a spot for you."

"You know I'd appreciate it."

"Heck, boy, I owe it to your daddy. What kinda feller would I be if I didn't help out an old friend's boy?" Senator Montrose stood up, rocking back and forth a bit, and pulled a huge wad of keys from his pocket. He began to sort through them, squinting at each one in the dim light.

"I reckon you're strapped for money," he said. "I reckon you've got a campaign debt that'd break a mule's back."

This son of a bitch is either drunk or crazy, Charles thought. Or both. "Well, not really," he said. "You remember, I was appointed, so there wasn't any expense."

"Yes, sir, we all got our money problems," Montrose said. He found the key he was looking for and unlocked one of his desk drawers. "That's why I always try to help you young fellers out. Come around here, boy."

78

Charles got up and walked around behind the desk.

"There," Montrose said, "he'p yourself. Take a handful, boy."

Charles looked down and saw that the drawer was filled with money, twenties and fifties mostly.

"Go ahead, boy, take some. You gotta pay off them debts, don't you?"

"You see, Senator, I don't really have any debts."

"What's the matter, boy, don't you like money?"

"Sure, I like it. But I just don't need any."

"Don't need any, huh? Boy, you don't think I'm putting you up to anything crooked, do you?"

"No, sir, not at all. But I really don't need your money."

Montrose scowled at him and slammed the drawer shut. "To heck with you, then. Trouble is, a boy like you, he's born with a silver spoon in his mouth. Me, I'se out in the fields when I'se twelve years old, doing a man's work, an' I reckon I know what a dollar is. You, you're a bright boy. But you better remember, it takes more'n that to get along around here. To get along you gotta go along, boy. Yes, sir!"

He locked the desk drawer and put the keys back into his pocket. Then he came around and took Charles's arm. "But I wish you the best, boy. We need your kind around here. You come see me any time, you hear?"

He picked up the bottle of scotch and stuck it under Charles's arm and hustled him out the door.

Charles deposited the scotch at the first door he came to—Senator Dirksen's office, it happened to be—and walked quickly out of the building. He did not feel like returning to his office, where he might be called upon to make some rational decision. Instead, he crossed Constitution Avenue and wandered for a minute in the dusk on the Capitol grounds. A young couple was sitting on the grass with a small child. Their dog, a cairn terrier, was racing around them in great circles. Charles fastened his eyes on them, for they seemed sane enough, and the world had begun to seem quite insane to him. He shook his head, thinking about the scene with Montrose, not sure whether he should laugh or cry or just mark it off to experience. He wasn't really shocked at the morality of the thing; everyone knew that Montrose was the oil industry's man—Petroleum Tom, they called him. But he wondered if he might have handled it better. He didn't see how. If you took his money you put yourself in his pocket and if you didn't you offended him. Either way, you lost.

He sat down on a bench and after a while he began to laugh. What a way to run a country. It had been a funny scene, if you wanted to see it that way. A kind of seduction—Montrose had done everything but chase him around the desk. Charles wished he could tell someone about the episode. But no one would believe it.

He went to see Mansfield the next day and the Majority Leader sucked on his pipe and quizzed him the way a department head might quiz a bright graduate student. When Charles said Senator Montrose's committee was his first choice, Mansfield said, "Oh yes, he called this morning and said he'd make a place for you." And that was that. Charles thought perhaps he hadn't handled the old bastard so badly after all. Or perhaps it didn't matter. He'd never know.

Pat O'Neal came in and settled himself across from Charles's desk. He lit a Lucky and balanced the manila envelope carefully on his knee.

"How is everything, Charles?"

Charles frowned a little, both at the delay and at the "Charles." He was a Senator now and Pat could damn well call him by his title. He'd been annoyed with Pat ever since an article appeared in the *Courier-Journal* describing him as the master mind behind Charles's political career. Was that how other people saw him? Was that how Pat saw himself? Damn it, it was time people gave him credit for some sense of his own.

But Pat was useful.

"Everything's all right, Pat. I'm working like hell. Now let's see those polls and see if it matters."

Pat O'Neal took the manila envelope off his knee and handed it across. "I warn you, Charles, they're not real good."

Charles tore open the envelope and began to read the papers inside. He read them twice, then tossed them aside.

"Not real good?" he said. "I'd say they're devastating. Most of the people in Kentucky have never heard of me, the ones who have don't think I'm qualified for the Senate, and if the election were held now Roark would beat me two to one. I feel like I've been sandbagged.

80

What's the use of entering the primary next year if it's going to be that bad?"

"Well, now, wait a minute," Pat O'Neal said. "It says 47 per cent would vote for Roark, 23 per cent would vote for you, and 30 per cent were undecided. That's not so bad. If he's been Governor twice and less than half the people say they'll vote for him for the Senate, he's got problems."

"Damn it, Pat, I make speeches every weekend, I send out a press release every day, I see my constituents, I answer my mail, I kiss babies and shake their daddies' hands and pat their mamas on the fanny—I do everything I know to do—and 23 per cent of the idiots say they'd vote for me."

"They don't know you yet. It takes time."

"Time? It'll take a miracle."

"Miracles do happen," Pat O'Neal said. "But mostly you'd better count on hard work."

The rain had started when they took off from Washington, and as their plane soared over West Virginia Charles could see thick dark thunderheads drifting beneath them. The rain was even worse in Louisville, washing out the horseback ride his mother had planned for Carol and the kids. Charles built a fire in the study and spent the afternoon working on the speech he was to deliver the next day at a UMW Labor Day picnic. He finished the speech at six, poured himself a scotch, and just as he took the first sip there was a knock at the door.

"Come in."

One of the maids, a young Negro girl, opened the door. "You have a telephone call, Senator Pierce," she said. "It's Mr. O'Neal."

"Okay, thanks." He took another sip of his drink and picked up the phone.

"Pat, what's up?" He felt good. The first of the scotch was tingling in his stomach.

"I'm calling about this rain, Charles," Pat O'Neal said.

The remark struck Charles as funny. He laughed, thought about it, and laughed again. "Pat, I'm sorry," he said. "But I can't do a blessed thing about the rain. Maybe you'd better call the senior Senator. He's closer to God than I am."

"Have you heard the reports from over around Hazard?"

"No, what's happening?"

"It's flooding bad. Bridges are down and houses are being swept away."

Charles saw what was coming and he didn't like it. He wanted to stay right where he was, with his fire and his drink and his family.

"Sounds bad," he said.

"I think you better get over there," O'Neal said. "Right now, tonight."

Charles sipped at his drink. "Wouldn't that be a bit of a grandstand play?"

"It's no grandstand play. You're those people's Senator and they're in trouble."

Charles was getting tired of Pat O'Neal's lectures. "My father wouldn't have gone slogging around in something like this," he said. "He'd have said the smart thing was to keep an arm's length away. If I go, and the relief program gets screwed up, people blame me."

"There were plenty of times when your father did go slogging around floods and mine cave-ins and all the rest. If he wouldn't have gone tonight, it would be because he wouldn't face the problem you face in being elected next year. And I happen to know that Governor Roark is in Florida and his staff's been on the phone begging him to fly back. But he's not. So if this flood's as bad as it looks, plenty of people will be asking where Johnny Roark was. And it might be a big plus for you if you were on the scene."

Charles looked at his watch. "I can be ready in fifteen minutes," he said.

In half an hour Charles was in the back seat of a state patrol car, speeding east through the rain. Pat O'Neal was beside him, and a young reporter from the *Courier-Journal* named Burris was in the front seat, along with their driver, a patrol sergeant named Whitt.

"The last report we had, there were seven dead," the reporter said.

"They're saying twelve dead now," the sergeant added.

"Good thing you being in the state, Senator," the reporter said.

"Well, I want to do all I can."

"Did you hear about the Governor?"

"What about him?"

"He's down in Florida at a Governors' conference and not coming back until tomorrow. What do you think of that?"

Charles felt Pat O'Neal jab him in the ribs.

"Well, I guess the Governor knows what he's doing."

This reporter made him nervous. He was crew-cut and intense and he kept writing things in his notebook, even when no one was saying anything.

Charles watched the evening turn from gray to black. Rain clouds hung low like ghosts over the little shacks and stores beside the road. He read some of the signs they passed—"Wonder Bread," "Nehi Cola," "See Rock City"—that hadn't changed since years ago when he would drive through this country on the way to school or to Washington. That was all this country had ever been to him, a place to be gotten past on his way to a better place. His Kentucky was the center of the state, the bluegrass country around Louisville and Lexington. But Charles felt no special attachment to the state as a whole. It was a good enough place to be from. It had a vaguely aristocratic aura about it, and almost no one had ever been there. You mentioned Kentucky and people mumbled something about the Derby or the Bourbon or the basketball teams, then dropped it. But Charles didn't really know the state and as he raced through the rain toward a small town in eastern Kentucky, he felt like a stranger in a foreign land.

The rain came down as if it would never stop. Fields had become lakes and the low parts of the highway were flooded. The power was out in the little towns they passed, and only the occasional flicker of a candle or a lantern challenged the eerie darkness that covered the land.

They entered Hazard in silence, parked on the dark, deserted courthouse square, and saw a man with a lantern waving at them from the steps. They splashed through the puddles and up the steps, where the man led them inside. He grinned and stuck out his hand.

"Senator?" the man said. "I'm Jim Lunsford, the sheriff hereabouts. I reckon I'm your host for the evening."

Charles and the other men shook the sheriff's hand and went into his office for coffee.

"Well, Senator, what can I do for you?" Lunsford asked. He was a tall, lean man of about forty-five.

"I wish you'd start by telling us what's going on," Charles said.

"I'll tell you what I know. I was on duty till two last night, and the rain was just starting when I got home and went to bed. The thunder woke me up once, about five in the morning. I went on back to sleep, till about 10:00 A.M., when one of my deputies called and said we was losing cars on highway 7—they was just being swept off the road. And then we started getting calls from people who said their houses was flooded.

"I got on down to the office and this is the first time I've sat down since. I've never seen nothing like it. A lot of them new houses, the little bungalows that've been built on low ground—they're just gone. Nothing left but the foundations. And people gone with them. Eight or ten people missing, mostly kids. It's real bad, Senator. It's the worst thing I ever saw."

"What's the situation right now?" Charles asked. He saw the reporter, Burris, taking notes.

"Well, we've got a roof and a hot meal for all the people who've had to leave their homes," the sheriff said. "Most of them are right down the street at the Methodist church. I thought we might go by there."

"Fine," Charles said. "Let's get started."

The Methodist church was the best-lit building in Hazard. A dozen lanterns had been placed around the large meeting room where now almost a hundred people were sitting and standing, including two dozen Negroes who huddled in one corner by themselves. As they entered the church, Charles felt their eyes and wondered how he looked to them—young and smooth-faced and snugly dressed, a man from another world. There was a deathly silence, even the children were quiet, and you could hear the steady drumbeat of rain on the tin roof. Charles was a dozen feet from the nearest of the flood's victims—he could see the stubble of the man's beard, the mud on his boots, the dirt under his square-cut fingernails—but suddenly he felt himself a hundred yards, a hundred miles, a lifetime removed from these people.

"I better introduce you," the sheriff said.

"Yeah," Charles said. "Go ahead."

"Folks, this here is Senator Charles Pierce, Senator Hugh Pierce's boy, who's come to try to help us. I think he'd like to say a few words, so how about you all coming up here a little closer?"

Charles watched them move toward him—not so quickly as to seem anxious, not so slowly as to give offense. He studied their faces as they studied his. Most of the men were miners and their faces had the pallor that came from work beneath the ground. The women all seemed old—even those with small children looked more like grand-

84

mothers than mothers. Charles watched as these people formed a semicircle around him and he wondered what in God's name he could say to them. Their problem isn't the flood, he thought, their problem is their lives.

How to begin? Ladies and gentlemen? My fellow citizens? My friends? These people weren't his friends and he knew it and they knew it. He wondered if they hated him.

But he felt something else too. If part of him recoiled from the hundred pairs of eyes fixed upon him, another part of him was challenged by them, and savored the challenge. He felt the way he had felt once before a tennis tournament, another time before a fight; his blood ran fast.

"I've come to see this flood first hand," he said, "and to see that you get help from Washington. I'm sure Governor Roark will see that you get all possible state aid."

"Then where is he?" someone muttered.

"There's no use me making a speech," Charles said. Brief, keep it brief. "You want to know about individual cases—what kind of help you can get if you lost a home or lost livestock or something else. I don't have all those answers. But I'll have a man from my staff here tomorrow to talk to each of you. And I'll talk personally with the President himself if that's what it takes to get help. Beyond that, I want you to know that my door is always open to you. That's all I can say. Thank you."

He stopped and there was silence. Did I blow it? Was I too brief? Did they want more emotion? Then the sheriff began to applaud and all of them applauded. Charles moved to the nearest man and put out his hand. "I'm Charles Pierce," he said. "Would you tell me what happened to you in the flood?"

"My name's Earl Settles," the man said. His teeth were rotted. "We ain't so bad off. We got a foot of water in our place, but we all got out all right. There's those whose houses was plain swept away."

"Mine was," a man in overalls said. "I lost ever'thing 'cept what's on my back—house, car, furniture, ever'thing. You reckon there's any help for us, Senator?"

"I think so. If there is, I'll see that you get it."

He felt a hand on his arm. "It's time for us to go, Senator," Pat O'Neal said.

"All right," he said. "Just a minute." He walked over to the knot of Negroes at the side of the room and put out his hand to the first man he came to. "I'm Charles Pierce," he said, "and I want you to know I'll do everything I can."

"God bless you, Senator," a woman called out.

"We was for your daddy and we're for you too," another woman said. The Negroes held out their hands and Charles shook them one by one.

"Senator, would you do us one special favor back in Washington?" a woman said.

"What?" Charles asked.

"Would you tell President Kennedy we're praying for him? Tell him we said God bless him."

"I'll tell him," Charles promised, then hurried out of the church.

"Damn good," Pat O'Neal whispered as they climbed into the sheriff's car. Charles didn't answer. He knew it had been good.

"Now what?" he asked the sheriff.

"Just out of town, there's a place where we're putting down sandbags, trying to keep Goose Creek from flooding a little hollow. We might see how they're doing."

"Fine," Charles said. "Let's go."

"Where'd you find the sandbags?" the reporter asked.

"We found a couple of thousand of them in the National Guard armory," the sheriff said. "But we can't find the National Guard."

"How many houses are down in the hollow?" Burris asked.

"Oh, eight or ten. The bad thing is, there's an old lady, Miz Frye, in one of them and she won't leave. She says her people moved there in eighteen-ought-seven and she reckons she'll just stay there till the Lord takes her away."

"Maybe you ought to carry her out," Charles said.

"Maybe so, except she's got a shotgun and she might blow my head off."

They came to a place where a dozen men were working, illumined in the beams of a huge searchlight. A creek ran on one side of the road and on the other side the land fell off sharply toward a long hollow. The water was up atop the road now and at its lowest spot only a wall of sandbags kept it from sweeping down into the hollow. The row of sandbags was three feet high and the floodwaters were only inches from its top. Charles and the others got out of the sheriff's car and watched for a minute as a dozen men trudged back and forth, carrying sandbags from a row of trucks down to the wall they had built.

"Who are those men?" Charles asked.

"The fellow in charge, the one in the yellow slicker, is my deputy, name of Sisk. Most of them are men who live around here. They been at this for six hours now and I reckon they're about to drop."

The deputy, Sisk, came over. He held a tin cup of coffee in his hands.

"How is it?" the sheriff asked.

Sisk shook his head. "It's still rising but not as fast as it was. I give it two hours. By then either it'll give out or we will. We sure could use some more men, Sheriff."

"I been calling for the National Guard," the sheriff said, "but the commandant says they got bigger problems somewhere else."

They stood for a moment watching the men struggle with the sandbags. Beyond the men, as far as the beams of the searchlight reached, was the water—Goose Creek, a raging river now. You could feel its power even before you saw the debris it swept along—fence posts, dead animals, firewood, a piece of a barn, a barrel, even a telephone pole, bobbing like a cork.

One man stumbled climbing up the muddy bank. Another man helped him up and together they walked up to the truck. They stopped beside the searchlight to smoke a cigarette. "It ain't no use," one of them said. Charles looked past them, down at the wall of sandbags. The water was still only inches from the top. It seemed so useless. Charles's elation was gone. He had made a good talk and scored a few points but all that meant nothing.

"What's the matter with you, mister? Your arm broke?" It was the man who had fallen down and he was looking at Charles.

"Hold on, Roy," the sheriff said.

"No, he's right," Charles said. "I ought to help."

"You don't need to do that, Senator," the sheriff said.

"What else can I do? Go around shaking hands? Come on, Sheriff, are you game?"

"Sure, I'm game if you are," the sheriff said.

"What'd he call you, mister?" the first man said.

"Senator. I'm Charles Pierce, one of your Senators."

"No shit?" the man said incredulously.

"No shit," Charles said. "Come on, Sheriff."

They swung a sandbag off the truck and started down the muddy bank with it, walking sideways, each man holding one end. Charles had gone only a step before he dropped his end, and only a few more steps when he stumbled for the first time. The bags weighed eighty pounds and there was no good way to grasp them. With gloves, they slipped, without gloves, the burlap rubbed your hands raw. Walking sideways, crab-walking down the slick muddy bank, was awkward and they fell often, until their clothes were caked with mud. After five trips Charles began to feel the pain; after ten trips he thought he could not go on; after twenty trips the pain was forgotten, replaced by the rhythm of the work, and he felt good, challenged, exhilarated. Up and down, up and down, lifting, carrying, stacking, the work became all-consuming, became the only reality for the men who moved in their slow circle up and down from truck to water's edge. They rarely spoke, there were no greetings or introductions, and yet they were united by the mud that sucked at their feet, by the roar in their ears, by the river that surged past them, threatening to overcome them. As they worked, they watched the water, watched and measured its rise by quarter inches, watched their wall slowly outstrip the water, until it was chest high, a foot above the water.

"It's stopped rising," the sheriff said. "I do believe it's stopped rising."

"We've beat that old river," a young boy said. "He ain't gonna mess with us no more."

"Let's ever'body carry one more bag down," the sheriff said, "then we'll take us a good break."

"How do you feel, Senator?" the reporter asked when Charles got back up to the truck. Burris had been sitting in the state patrol car all night drinking coffee with Pat O'Neal.

"Tired, Burris, tired. Why haven't you joined the fun?"

Burris shook his head. "A reporter can't get involved in the story he's covering," he said.

"God forbid," Charles said. "Come on, Sheriff, one more."

They hoisted the final sandbag between them and slid down the bank and tossed it atop the wall. Then they paused, catching their breath, gazing out over the dark swirling water.

"What's that?" Charles cried. "Right out there."

Something small and white was floating past them a dozen feet out in the slow-moving currents near the edge of the water, caught momentarily in the milky rays of the searchlight.

"Is it a doll?" the sheriff asked, squinting into the night.

"It might be a child," Charles said. "My God, I think it is."

"They've got a boat up there."

"There's not time for a boat," Charles said. He threw himself over the sandbags into the water and stumbled forward. The water was chest high and icy cold, but he barely felt it. He pushed through the water as fast as he could, because if he was to get to the object, whatever it was, he would have to get it soon, before it reached the place where the water became deep and the current fast. He stumbled once and went under, came up sputtering, and just as the water became neck high, just as he could feel the current beginning to grab, just then his outstretched hands closed over the bobbing white object and he saw that he had been right. It was a child, a girl, Liza's age, eyes fixed open, small body stiff and cold, blonde hair spread out around her head like a halo. He took her and held her above the black water and carried her back. The sheriff came out and helped him the last few feet and over the sandbags. Charles kept the girl in his hands, held her close against his chest, and for a moment he put his mouth on hers, and tried to breathe life into her body, but it was too late, far too late, her mouth was ice, and he slipped to the ground and sat against the sandbags rocking the dead child in his arms.

He had been numb before but now he felt the opposite of numb. He could feel everything, everything in the world. His fingertips could feel the child's bones beneath her skin and his face could feel each needle of rain that fell upon it. Huddled there against the sandbags, he felt that the starless sky above him was a vast dome that united them all, him and the dead girl and all the people who had lost their homes and lives that night and all the people everywhere whose losses he could not imagine.

"Poor baby," he whispered, pressing the child tight against his chest. "Poor baby, poor baby."

"Let me take her, son," the sheriff said, and knelt beside Charles and lifted the child gently into his arms.

It was past dawn when he arrived back at his mother's house. He slept until midafternoon, when Carol came into the bedroom and spoke his name. He opened his eyes and saw her beside the bed, smiling, holding a cup of coffee in one hand and a copy of the *Courier-Journal* in the other.

"What time is it?" he asked sleepily.

"About three. How do you feel?"

"Tired."

"I wouldn't have awakened you, but Pat O'Neal has called twice."

"About what?" He took the coffee and began to sip it.

"About this," she said, and spread open the newspaper. It had a banner headline: TWENTY FEARED DEAD IN EAST KENTUCKY FLOOD. Beneath the headline were two pictures, side by side. One showed Charles and Sheriff Lunsford struggling with a sandbag. The other showed Governor Roark playing tennis at a Miami Beach resort.

"Pat O'Neal's so excited he can hardly talk. He says the Governor will never live this down."

"Yeah, Pat thinks he's got a winner."

"Charles, aren't you excited?"

"I didn't do what I did for publicity."

"That doesn't mean you don't deserve the publicity."

"Anybody would have done the same thing."

"No, they wouldn't. The Governor didn't—he wasn't even there. Charles, read that story there."

There was a side bar to the main story. It had Burris' by-line, and it began:

"When Charles Pierce got up yesterday morning he expected to spend a quiet day at his mother's plush estate outside Louisville. Instead, he was to spend three exhausting hours fighting a flood last night, an ordeal climaxed when the young Senator plunged into a cold, dangerous river in a vain attempt to save a drowned child's life."

Charles dropped the paper to the floor and put his head in his hands. He saw the child floating on the dark water, with her hair spread out around her head. He began to sob.

"Charles, what's the matter?" Carol sat down beside him and took his hand.

"I held this child in my hands and she was dead and other people are dead and they've lost their homes and now I'm scoring points in the newspapers against John Roark. It's cheap."

"Charles, everyone is proud of you. People have been calling all day."

90

"If you could have seen them. People who'd lost everything they ever had."

"Don't think about it, darling. Go back to sleep."

"I've got to think about it. It's my job to think about it."

"All right, darling," she said. "All right. But go back to sleep for a while."

Two days later the *Courier-Journal* carried an editorial cartoon that pictured Charles struggling with a sandbag, the Governor playing tennis—and below it the jingle:

> Where was Johnny when the big flood came?
> Down in Florida in a tennis game!

Pat O'Neal came to see Charles that afternoon.

"Well, Senator, it's a new ball game."

"I don't think you ever called me that before, Pat."

"Didn't I? Well, things are looking better."

"People forget. They'll forget all this."

"Not that jingle. 'Where was Johnny when the big flood came?' You can't buy that kind of publicity."

"You just have to luck into it, huh?"

"You earned it. You did a fine job that night."

"I wouldn't have even gone if you hadn't twisted my arm."

"It was your decision."

"Pat, how would you like to come to work for me? I've got to get rid of Hendricks."

O'Neal grinned. "Thanks, Charles, but no, thanks."

"Why not?"

"I've found that if you go on a politician's payroll he starts telling you what to do. I like it this way, where I tell politicians what to do."

"Well, I hope you'll keep telling me, because I need the advice."

"I've got some for you right now."

"Shoot."

"Your political career began this week. Before, you were just a name. Hugh Pierce's son. A rich kid who'd been appointed to an office that was probably too big for him."

"Alas, all true."

"Maybe, maybe not. But that doesn't matter any more. Now there's a new Charles Pierce. The one who went to the flood while the Governor played tennis. The one who hauled sandbags half the night. The one who jumped into a river to try to save a kid who could have been anybody's kid. A fellow who's young and aggressive and who cares about ordinary people."

"A God damned prince."

"A darned fine Senator."

"Okay, Pat, what do I do? Keep looking for floods where I can haul sandbags? Or maybe mine cave-ins?"

"What I want you to do is not make jokes like you just made. Not to reporters. Not in speeches. People don't want their politicians funny. You've got an image worth a million dollars. Don't play around with it. When you're in public, you've got to be—"

"Young and tough and aggressive and solemn as a judge."

"That's right. Listen, two weeks ago I wouldn't have given a nickel for your chances of getting the nomination next summer. Now I'd say they're fifty-fifty. But you've got to work. You've got to show some discipline."

"It's just such crap, Pat. Playing a role. Building an image. I like being me."

"You like being a Senator, too, don't you?"

"Yeah."

"Well, then you're going to have to play the game a little. Maybe you can't be you as much as you'd like to."

Charles didn't reply because there wasn't anything to say.

He flew back to Washington the next day and the aftermath of his flood episode continued. His mail was fantastic. Letters came from all over the country.

But the most interesting reaction was in the Senate.

He had found in his first weeks there that he had almost no social contact with his fellow Senators. The first day or two, the younger ones clustered around his desk on the Senate floor with smiles and handshakes, saying things like "Great to have you here" and "This place is changing fast, you watch," but after that first flurry there was no follow-up. No one asked him to lunch or for a drink or home to dinner. He was lobbied on votes, of course, and he got big smiles in the corridors and waves across the Senate floor, but that was all. After a month or so it occurred to him that his colleagues were very busy men and they'd decided that he wasn't worth cultivating, at least not until he'd shown some signs of permanence.

And yet he had enjoyed those first months. He spent as much time as he could on the Senate floor, trying to learn the basics of parliamentary procedure, trying quite simply to figure out what the hell was going on. Charles was fascinated by the younger Senators, his contemporaries. He took the older Senators for granted; they were his father's friends; they had always been there and presumably always would be. But he felt differently about the younger men. Instinctively he found himself studying them, measuring himself against them, running imaginary races against them. Charles wished he knew them better. His mother had once said that every Senator she'd ever known had been somehow twisted inside, crippled, driven to prove himself or to escape his past, that a normal man would never enter politics, or, if he did, would never succeed. If these things were so, Charles could not tell it as he watched his new colleagues from his seat in the back row. He was impressed by them, by their power and their poise and their self-confidence, even if they weren't much impressed by him.

But all that changed after the flood. His star began to rise. His colleagues gathered around him again, shaking his hand, congratulating him, telling him what a hell of a fellow he was, inviting him for lunch or for a drink. Most seemed not so much impressed by what he had done as by the amount of publicity he had reaped from it, but their attention was nonetheless pleasant and he didn't question anyone's motives very closely.

7

NOVEMBER 1963

Carol had decided to quit her job. She hated to admit defeat, but she'd waited and waited and finally realized she would never get promoted. She'd talked to the station manager, Ken Holton, a dozen times about reporting or working on documentaries and he would always smile and say, Oh, Carol, you're a great girl and we love you but all the good jobs are for men.

Ken put it more nicely than that, of course, for Ken was a smoothie, a charmer, the old-shoe type with tweed coats and a pipe and hair graying just so at the temples. He was always pleasant and he was even more pleasant to Carol now that she'd advanced from being a Senator's daughter-in-law to being a Senator's wife. So now that Carol had decided to quit she would be equally pleasant. She had invited him to lunch. She would explain why she was leaving. Perhaps, faced with losing her, he would offer her a better job, but she wasn't counting on that.

They left the station a little before one and Ken hailed a cab. It was a cool, cloudy afternoon.

"How about Chez François?" Carol asked as they settled into the cab.

"That's fine," Ken said. "But, Carol, this one is on me."

"No, Ken. *I* invited *you*."

"But I'd been *meaning* to invite you."

"Well, you'll just have to act more quickly. This is *my* treat."

Ken gave an exaggerated shrug. "Well, all right. I know better than to argue with you."

Carol liked Ken. She'd always felt a slight moral advantage over him since the time at the Christmas party when he'd made a tipsy, halfhearted pass at her. Sometimes she thought that making passes at her was the new national sport. Most of the male guests on their show did, visiting firemen who didn't even know who she was, just that she was pretty and pleasant and perhaps could be induced back to their hotel rooms. The most recent one had come from a stock boy at the station, a lad of eighteen, who'd hung around her office for several days and finally blurted out, "Mrs. Pierce, would you like to come to my apartment sometime?" She certainly didn't want to go to his apartment, but she did take him to lunch the next day and listen to his long tale of adolescent woe, feeling quite motherly. Well, she had thought, I've got them all falling at my feet, from the general manager to the stock boy, and it's a shame I can't translate that into a better job.

Chez François was crowded, but Ken knew François, who personally led them to a table in the back. Ken held Carol's chair, waved across the room to some friends, sat down, and ordered their martinis. He did all this gracefully, for he was a man who took pride in the way he managed life's smaller amenities. And women too, Carol thought, we're one of the little details he likes to manage. Okay, Mr. Smooth, let's see you manage *me*. You've got a little surprise coming there.

"Well, Carol, I hardly know where to begin. You and Charles have moved to Georgetown, haven't you?"

"That's right. His mother has moved back to Kentucky, and we're leasing her house."

"So how is the life of a dashing young Senator's wife?"

Carol made a wry face. "Overrated, if you want the truth. I mean, your husband doesn't grow ten feet tall or anything. He's still the same lovable lad who snores and won't pick up his socks. Except now you've got all these impossible demands on your time. Believe me, if you've seen one embassy party, you've seen them all."

"My, aren't we world-weary?"

"Washington-weary, maybe. Oh, I'm proud of Charles and happy for him and all that. But just for myself, sometimes I wish we were back in Louisville."

"You'd be bored stiff in Louisville and you know it."

"Would I? We had dinner at Joseph Alsop's house the other night and I was bored stiff *there*. I guess the food was better than Louisville. But, my Lord, all that ponderous talk about the Pentagon budget and who shot Diem. I could do without that, thank you."

"How did Charles hold up?"

"Oh, Charles can be pretty ponderous when the occasion demands. He's not in Mr. Alsop's league yet, but he's got potential."

They smiled at that and Carol thought how much more she could have told him about the dinners she'd been attending recently, except it was too unpleasant to tell. She'd learned that the more important the men were at a Washington party the less important the women were. When you dined with Senators and cabinet members and the super-journalists, you were tolerated during dinner and then sent packing afterward, to chitchat upstairs while The Men had their cigars and brandy and Deep Conversations in private. She'd learned that her dinner partners would usually begin with polite inquiries about the age and sex of her children; occasionally one might even express awareness of the curious fact that she had a job in television. But soon the dinner conversation would become Profound, with the ladies expected to venture no more than brief compliments on the food. At one dinner Carol had expressed a serious opinion on a political issue and the men had stared at her as they might at a bright child who talked about nuclear science. There had been a long silence and then the host, a very senior Senator, had smiled indulgently and declared that her view was indeed an interesting one and the conversation had flowed on as if she had never opened her mouth. It became almost a relief to get to the after-dinner phase when the women were safely segregated and could say a word or two to one another. At the most recent dinner she'd attended, Carol and another young woman, the pretty wife of an Assistant Secretary of Something-or-other, had exchanged a silent, sympathetic glance, and proceeded to down all the brandy they decently could, both aware that their true function for the evening was still an hour or so away.

"Well," Ken said, "ponderous or not, Charles is certainly getting a good press. He's a real comer."

Carol smiled to herself, wondering if she had a dirtier mind than Ken. "The flood thing helped," she said. "And he's young and handsome and photogenic and all. And he works hard, too. He's up till midnight lots of nights, getting ready for committee hearings."

"He seems to be lining up with the Administration a lot. Is that good politics for a Senator from Kentucky?"

"Who knows? The thing you have to understand about Charles is, whatever his faults, he's honest. And he's stubborn. He says he just doesn't see how an honest man can be against civil rights and open housing and all. I guess we'll find out next year whether it's good politics or not."

The waiter took their order and Ken ordered a bottle of their best white wine.

"In the meantime, Ken, you'll forgive me if I don't want to talk exclusively about my husband's job. I was hoping we might talk a little about *my* job."

"By all means, Carol. I've been thinking about your job."

"Thinking what?"

"The obvious thing. That you're too bright to go on being Eleanora's assistant."

"Then you've got a reporting job for me? I'd heard there might be an opening coming up."

Ken frowned. "Yes, there may be, but we've got some problems there. Still, there are other possibilities."

"Such as?"

"Let's talk about Eleanora's show."

"What is there to talk about? It's *her* show. She's got a five-year contract with three years to run on it."

"Let's talk about it anyway. It's an important slot and I'm not pleased with it. The ratings are off. I'd like some ideas on how it could be improved."

"I don't want to criticize Eleanora."

"I understand, Carol, and believe me, I appreciate loyalty. But just give me your professional judgments, in total confidence."

Carol was annoyed. He'd been a long time getting around to asking her opinions on anything. But she'd give them to him anyway, as a farewell present.

"The basic problem with Eleanora's show, Ken, is that Eleanora is out of touch with new people and new ideas. Here we are in this tremendously exciting Kennedy administration and she's still living in the New Deal. She's only comfortable with her own generation, so she keeps on having retired diplomats and all those actresses who are, shall we say, past their primes. She misses all the new things that are happening."

"Such as?"

"Oh, there're so many things. I was reading about these Black Muslims and I'd like to know who they are and what they want, but Eleanora would never consider having one on the show. And Kennedy is trying to start a domestic Peace Corps and we could find out what it would do. And I just read a book about poverty in America—Ken, nobody *knows* about it. And there're conservation and consumer issues and a million things. It could be such an exciting program. It's really very frustrating."

Ken Holton studied her with interest. "Carol, may I ask a personal question?"

"Why not?"

"Do you really want to keep working? In the next few years, aren't you going to feel an increasing obligation to assist Charles in his career, and isn't that going to make it impossible for you to keep working? You don't need the money, so why bother?"

"Why not just be a good little Senator's wife and go to the teas and fashion shows? Is that it? That's what Charles wants to know."

"That doesn't sound so awful."

"Doesn't it? Ken, it all has to do with wanting to do something on your own instead of just being an appendage of your husband. Does that make any sense to you?"

Ken Holton looked perplexed. "I suppose so, Carol. I know *my* wife has never complained about being an appendage. Between the children and all her charities, she keeps quite busy."

"Fine. I'm happy for her. But I wouldn't be satisfied with that. Which brings me to the point of this luncheon, Ken. Which is to tell you that I'm not satisfied with my job and I just can't keep on with it any more. So I'm giving you a month's notice and then I'll look for something else."

To her surprise, Ken Holton only smiled. "I won't let you quit," he said.

"Well, you really can't *stop* me."

"I think I can."

"*Really,* Ken . . ."

"Carol, it's time for *my* little surprise. Eleanora is leaving the show and I want you to replace her."

"Leaving?" she said so loudly that people looked around.

"Yes. Marrying some wealthy retired diplomat."

98

"I can't believe it. I don't know what to say. Oh, Ken, I'll work so hard."

"For heaven's sake, don't cry. Drink some wine. Let's talk about the show."

"I'm sorry. Let's *do* talk about it."

"I agree with everything you said. Eleanora *was* getting out of touch. We *do* want to attract a younger audience. We *do* need to be alert to new ideas. Which is not to say we can let the show become a soapbox for every crackpot who comes down the pike. We must use judgment."

"Of course."

"That book about poverty you mentioned. It's by a fellow named Harrington, isn't it?"

"Yes."

"Did you know he's a socialist?"

"Well, no."

Ken Holton smiled indulgently. "You see what I mean? We must be careful. Responsible."

"Oh, I will, Ken, I promise you."

The waiter brought their food. Carol tasted her quiche. It was delicious but she wasn't hungry any more.

"Ken, would you forgive me if I do something awful? I know we've got a million things to talk about, but could they wait until Monday? I've just got to tell Charles about this. I'd like to take a cab down to his office right this minute. Do you mind?"

"No, my dear. I'm glad to see you so happy. I don't make many people happy in my job."

She kissed him on the cheek and dashed out of the restaurant.

As her cab passed the White House, then moved up Pennsylvania Avenue toward the Hill, Carol barely saw the people and the traffic and the familiar buildings. Ken's news had left her in a daze. She had broken through. To be Eleanora's assistant was nothing, but to have her own show was everything. People in Washington were carefully graded, everyone knew that. The military had its ranks and the civil service had its GS ratings and the Hill had its elaborate pecking order. And now Carol was making a leap toward the top. Soon she would be just as well known as Charles, would be known for herself and what she could do. And there was so much she could do. There was no reason why the show couldn't be syndicated; the country cared about Washington now, with the Kennedys here and all the excitement they generated. A nationally syndicated show, that was her goal now.

Her cab stopped in front of the Old Senate Office Building. The fare was a dollar and Carol handed the driver a bill and was debating the tip, when the driver switched on the radio and an announcer said President Kennedy had been shot in Dallas.

The cab driver, a middle-aged Negro, cried out as if *he* had been shot. Carol was startled for a moment, then she saw it was just a hoax. She remembered the famous invasion-from-Mars radio show. It was something like that. But the man on the radio kept talking about the motorcade and the shots and the hospital and Carol gasped and threw the money down and began to run up the steps that led into the building. No one was on duty at the elevator, no one was in sight anywhere, so she raced up the wide marble stairway, the click-clack of her heels echoing like gunfire in the silent building. As she ran along the fourth-floor corridor toward Charles's office, she could hear radio bulletins coming from many offices—the metallic voices seemed to pursue her down the long corridor and she thought of the radios during the missile crisis and she wondered if it would be like this the rest of their lives, with some new crisis or tragedy pouring out at them from their radios and television sets.

She stopped in the doorway to Charles's reception room. They were all there, no one moving. A transistor radio was on one of the secretaries' desks. Three secretaries, young girls, had drawn their chairs up close to the desk. Two were crying and the other kept biting her knuckles so that they were bleeding. Hendricks was sitting at his desk, his face white, his hands trembling. He looked a hundred years old. Charles was leaning against the wall in his shirt sleeves, his head down, his arms folded. Carol stood in the doorway, hearing the pounding of her heart, and no one even noticed her. She felt invisible. Perhaps it's I who's dead, she thought. Or crazy. Or dreaming. She felt detached from reality, outside it, like someone looking in a window at the world. She wanted to scream but she knew no one would hear her, for they were still there motionless listening to the announcer say that no one knew whether the President was alive or dead.

You idiot, Carol thought, of course he's alive. It'll be a tiny injury and maybe he'll wear a bandage for a few days or use a cane and then he'll be fine again. He was such a beautiful man. That summer he'd gone swimming on a beach in California and there'd been pictures of him with people crowded around him and he'd looked wonderful, strong and well built. When had there ever been a President before who could be photographed in a bathing suit? The others were all potbellied old men but President Kennedy was young and handsome, and how stupid it was to talk of him being dead when it was only a scratch and he'd soon be out walking in the Rose Garden again and playing in his office with Caroline and little John-John. Oh, what a beautiful man he was.

And he was dead. The announcer said so. One of the secretaries, a tall girl with red hair, began to scream and the others tried to comfort her. Carol ran to Charles and put her arms around him. She could feel him trembling and after a moment he led her into his office. They stood at his window where they could see the little park, growing brown and bare with the coming of winter, and above it jagged white clouds swept past by the wind.

Carol was surprised that she was not crying. She felt weak and broken inside, but no tears came. Somehow this was too vast, too terrible for tears. Tears were too easy.

"It's like the end of the world," she said.

"It is. It's the end of one world."

"How do you feel?"

"I don't feel anything," Charles said. "Just numb. I guess it hasn't really sunk in yet. Maybe I'll start to feel something after a while."

"Is Johnson the President now?"

"Yes."

"It doesn't seem right. It seems like if somebody has to take President Kennedy's place it ought to be Bobby."

"Well, it's not." He turned away from the window and put on his coat. "Come on, let's start home."

In the outer office, the girl who had been sobbing was typing a letter despite her tears. Charles went over to her.

"Why don't you go home, Joan?"

"I've got to keep on working," she said. "He would have wanted me to keep on working."

Charles touched her hair, then he turned and took Carol's arm and led her out of the office.

They got the car and started up Pennsylvania Avenue. The car

101

radio was tuned to WGMS. Duruflé's Requiem was playing. The music filled the car, heightened her sense of unreality. Carol looked out at the people on the sidewalks and they seemed to be moving like sleepwalkers. The streets were thick with cars, yet no horns honked, no tires squealed, no fists waved. The cars moved slowly, silently, like a vast cortege. Carol wanted to cry out to the strangers around her, to say, "It isn't true," or "God help us," or "We must love each other," but all she could do was stay huddled in her seat, listening to the Requiem, numb and sad and increasingly angry, feeling sorry for Charles and for Jackie and for all of them.

Ellen, their housekeeper, burst into tears as soon as they came in. "Oh, Miss Carol," she cried, "he was the best man that ever was, and now the Lord has took him up to heaven. Oh, I loved that man, Miss Carol, I did love that poor man." Charles went into the study and tried to call a cab to take Ellen home, but he couldn't get a dial tone, so he went out onto the street and flagged one down.

When the children arrived home, Charles took them into the study. "Hugh, Liza," he began, "President Kennedy died today."

"Our teacher told us," Hugh said. "A bad man shot him in Texas."

"A cowboy?" Liza asked.

"No, just a bad man," Charles said. He wondered if he was expecting too much of them. Hugh seemed saddened, subdued by the news, but Liza's blue eyes looked back at him with perfect innocence. Liza was all life; death had no reality for her.

"There'll be pictures of President Kennedy on television after a while and I want you to watch them with us. He was a good man and a good President and I hope you both will remember him all your lives."

"The President is like the principal of our school, isn't he, Daddy?" Liza asked.

"Yes, dear."

"Will he go to heaven like Grandfather?" Hugh asked.

"I think so," Charles told the boy. "Now, I want you both to go upstairs and play until dinner."

The children went out, subdued, hand in hand. Charles fixed himself a drink, turned on the television, learned that the assassin had been captured, and turned it off again. He went into the kitchen and watched while Carol fixed the children's dinner.

"Life goes on," she said. "In the kitchen, anyway."

"Can I get you anything?"

"Maybe some Dubonnet."

"Coming up."

After the children had eaten, they all watched television. One station was showing Kennedy's news conferences. Kennedy cracked a joke, then the camera showed a close-up of his grin. Liza clapped her hands in delight.

"He's a *funny* man," she cried, and Charles held her close and felt worse than he had all day.

Hugh asked a question or two about Kennedy, then they talked about schoolwork and Liza's Christmas play, and soon a kind of normality settled over the evening. A President was dead, but there were still baths to be taken, pajamas to be put on, stories to be read, an evening to be gotten through. When the children were finally asleep, Charles and Carol settled down in the study. He leafed through an anthology of poetry; she looked at the new *Show* magazine. It was nine o'clock before, quite suddenly, she remembered her new job and excitedly told Charles about it.

"My God, that's great," he said. " 'The Carol Pierce Show.' "

" 'Carol Pierce Presents,' " she corrected.

" 'Carol Pierce Triumphant,' " he said. "You'll be fantastic. How about me as your first guest?"

"I was thinking of maybe Lyndon B. Johnson," she said, and they laughed and talked of her plans for the show.

Beth called at ten. She and Bill Hall had rented a house near Du-Pont Circle that they were making into some sort of a settlement house—Charles didn't really understand it. She had called Charles the day they leased the house and she had been filled with enthusiasm, the way she had always been, but tonight she was different.

"What is *wrong* with this country?" she kept asking. "What in God's name is *wrong* with it?"

"It's not this country," he protested. "It's . . . I don't know. It's life. The human condition."

"This country killed him," Beth insisted. "He was too good for them so they killed him."

"It was one nut, Beth. One left-wing madman."

"I don't believe that. Not in Dallas. Those oil millionaires had something to do with it."

Her words hit him hard, hurt him worse than anything else that day. He shut his eyes, trying to think what to say to her.

"Beth, listen to me. Kennedy's dead, but the country has to go on and the country needs people like you. You've got to have faith in the country, Beth, and if you cared about Kennedy, then you've got to keep working for the things he was working for."

"I guess you're right," she said finally. "Charles, we were talking about calling our community center Kennedy House. Do you think that'd be good?"

"I think it'd be great," he said. "How about you and Bill coming to lunch tomorrow and telling us all your plans."

"I'll ask Bill."

"Okay, call me. Good night, Beth."

"Good night."

Their talk had depressed him. He didn't want to see Beth's generation lose its optimism. He thought they were a wonderful generation, brighter and better than his had ever dreamed of being; he thought they would be Kennedy's real legacy to America.

He poured himself and Carol another drink. He was half drunk, and he saw that Carol was getting that unfocused look that she got when she was high.

"You've never liked Johnson, have you?" she asked.

"He can get things done. That's what we need now. Kennedy started things moving in the right direction, and maybe Johnson's the man to finish what Kennedy started."

"Will Johnson, you know, be nominated next year?"

"Probably. Unless he really screws up he will."

"How will that affect you when you run?"

"It depends. He might run stronger in Kentucky than Kennedy would have. But let's let Kennedy be buried before I start figuring how his death will advance my career. There's plenty of others doing that tonight. Let's us just get drunk like decent people."

She squeezed his hand. "You believed in him, didn't you?"

"I guess so. Didn't you?"

"I don't believe in much, Charles. When I was a girl I believed in too much, so now I don't believe in anything very much."

"You know how skeptical I was at first," he said. "But I was wrong. He did something intangible that no one else could have done.

He made things seem . . . seem *possible*. We mustn't lose that now. Damn it, we *mustn't*."

She took his hand and kissed it. "Let me tell you something, Charles," she said. "Don't ever love anything too much. Not me or your children or your work or anything. Because it's only when you love things too much that you lose them."

He looked at her in surprise. "You've never lost anything."

"Haven't I? That's what life is, Charles. Losing things."

"I've never heard you talk like that."

"No, of course not. Not Carol, the little optimist. Do you know that joke? 'With all this shit around, there must be a Shetland pony somewhere.' Ha-ha. But I'm not really an optimist, Charles. I'm a realist. By thirty a woman gets to be a realist. The real optimist in the family is you, my tough two-fisted politician husband. You pretend to be so tough but you're a real softie underneath. That's part of why I love you. But just don't expect too much from life. Don't expect too much because what happened to Kennedy happens to everybody someday, one way or another."

He was confused by what she said, and troubled, but he loved her and he wanted her close beside him, for this was no night to be alone. His thoughts were hopelessly mixed; he felt grief and hope, loss and challenge, sorrow and exaltation.

"Maybe I am an optimist," he said. "This has been so damned exciting, to see this country start to come alive, start to keep its promises. What happened today just means that we're all going to have to work harder, to give more, and help Johnson every way we can. We can keep things moving. Damn it, we *have* to."

She pressed close against him. "I hope you can," she said. "For your sake, I hope you can." She began to cry for the first time that day and he put his arms around her and held her close until they went finally up to bed.

BOOK II

THE STATE OF
THE UNION

*This, then, is the state of the Union
Free and restless, growing, and full of hope.*
                    Lyndon B. Johnson, 1965

1

AUGUST 1964

Central Airlines was holding its ten o'clock Louisville–Washington flight while Senator Charles Pierce held a news conference. The lights and the cameras had been set up in the airport lobby and Charles faced them eagerly, fresh-shaven, tanned by a summer of campaigning, smiling his best TV smile.

"Senator," called a tall, handsome, deep-voiced fellow. Charles took him for a TV reporter because TV reporters were mostly tall, handsome, and deep-voiced, whereas newspaper reporters were generally average-sized and disheveled.

"Senator," the man repeated, "I'm Randy Porter of WLEX-TV, and my question relates to the President's announcement last night." Randy Porter paused and looked at his notes. Of course it relates to the President's announcement last night, Charles thought, why the hell else would we all be here at this hour?

"The President announced bombing strikes against North Vietnam," the man continued in his best Huntley-Brinkley voice, "in retaliation for their attacks on two U.S. destroyers. My question, sir . . ."

Get to it, buddy, my plane is waiting.

". . . is whether you support the President, especially since you've opposed U.S. bombing in the past."

Charles smiled at the nearest TV camera. "Well, Randy," he began, "that's a pretty complicated question." He paused for the ripple of laughter from the reporters and the passers-by who were gathered

109

around. He was learning how to play an audience, how to make people laugh or applaud or cheer. It was mostly a matter of timing.

"Well," he said, serious now, "first and foremost, I want to see an end to this war. So does the President. He says this bombing is a limited action. I support that."

"Another question, Senator," said another tall TV man. "Governor Roark said last night you are, and I quote, 'a nice kid who doesn't know the first thing about standing up to the Communists.' What's your response to that?"

Charles flashed his best grin. "Well, I'm glad he thinks I'm nice," he said. That got a big laugh. This was going well. Charles wished he could drag it out, enjoy it a bit, but there was that damned plane waiting at the gate and all those people aboard.

"I'm glad he thinks I'm nice, but I don't think he's shown any understanding of world affairs. He takes the Goldwater approach—if we don't like something, we'll drop some bombs. But the world isn't that simple. Frankly, I think the Governor ought to worry less about the Communists and more about those scandals in his highway program."

More laughter. Quit when you're ahead. Charles waved and started toward the boarding gate, with Pat O'Neal beside him.

"How'd I do?"

"First class."

"When'll those new polls be out?"

"Next week. I'll call you."

Charles glanced up the ramp at the stewardess, who was straining to maintain her frozen, professional smile. She wasn't bad-looking, not as good as you'd get on a coast-to-coast flight, but not bad at all for Washington to Louisville.

"Have a good flight," Pat O'Neal said.

"I will, if the other passengers don't lynch me for holding them up."

"Oh, I spoke to the airlines fellow about that," O'Neal said. "He had the pilot say there was a mechanical problem."

"You're too much," Charles said. "You ought to be the Senator."

"If I was, who'd I get to advise me?" Pat O'Neal said, and Charles pondered that one while he hurried up the ramp to the plane.

In midafternoon, two days later, Charles left his office, walked thirty feet down the corridor, and entered Rip Horton's office. It was always a pleasure to enter Rip Horton's office because Rip maintained, by common agreement, the most stunning secretarial staff in the Senate. There had been rumors of a new one, and when Charles entered the reception room he saw her, perched behind the receptionist's desk, a tiny, honey-haired, ripe-bodied Southern belle of eighteen or so, smiling up at him with an expression of pure innocence.

"Kin Ah hep yew, suh?"

Could you ever, he thought, but the words that came out were: "I'm Senator Pierce. Is the Senator free?"

"He ain't free," Rip Horton called from the doorway, "but he can be had cheap. Come on in, tiger, take a load off your feet."

The walls of Rip's office were covered with photographs, not only of the usual Democratic leaders, FDR and Truman and Kennedy and Johnson, but also a gallery of his Southern colleagues—Russell, Byrd, Stennis, Talmadge, Sparkman, Ellender, Ervin, Long. Rip, more than any of the young Southerners, had managed to walk the tightrope between the national and the Southern wings of his party.

"Okay, where'd you find her?" Charles demanded.

"Ain't she a sweet little thang? Plumb edible. Sit down, sit down."

"I was on the way over to the floor."

"Hell, they ain't doing nothing but talking. They'll ring them damn bells if they need us. Sit down, Ah got something on my mind. Want a little drop of Bourbon?"

Charles settled into the overstuffed chair beside Rip's desk. "No, thanks. What's on your mind?"

Rip was sitting straight in his chair, his elbows resting on his desk, his hands clasped under his chin. He had on his serious face, the one that meant you'd better keep one hand on your wallet. Rip Horton, raconteur and wheeler-dealer, son of the Old South and spokesman for the New. A showman, with some of the early Lyndon Johnson in him, and perhaps some of the late Huey Long, but in his way a more subtle man than either. For Rip did not intend to be written off as a regional figure. Rip had learned early in the game how to deal with the Yankees, how to talk to the big-city reporters and the Harvard professors, just as smoothly as he talked to the dirt farmers back home. Charles had watched once as Rip addressed the Women's Press Club and he had been a different Rip, the "ain'ts" and the "thangs" were gone, and he was a very polished, very attractive man of forty, lean and self-assured, opening with some funny stories, closing with some ringing generalities, fielding their questions as smoothly as a Kennedy.

"What's on my mind?" Rip said. "Hubert's on my mind."

"What about him?"

"He's looking like Lyndon's boy for Vice-President."

"So?"

"Hubert's too damn radical."

"Oh, hell, Rip. Hubert's a great Senator. He was magnificent on the civil rights bill. He even got you to vote for it."

"Yeah, Ah voted for it, after him and Lyndon might' near twisted my arm off. And it passed. And next thing you know, our black brothers start showing their appreciation by burning down cities. Don't think Ah haven't been hearing about that, buddy boy."

"What are you saying, Rip?"

"Ah'm saying it'd be damned hard for Lyndon to blow this election, but he just might manage it if he puts Hubert on the ticket and then our black brothers spend September and October burning down cities."

"Rip, according to the polls, the President could run with Mickey Mouse and be elected."

"Mickey Mouse ain't known as a radical."

"Okay, just for conversation, who could it be if it wasn't Hubert?"

"Who do you think?" Rip shot back.

"Bob's the obvious one, if the President would take him."

"He'd take Bobby like Ah'd take rat poison."

"Okay, what about Shriver? There've been trial balloons for him."

"Shriver's too pretty. Lyndon'd never pick anybody prettier than him. Which narrows the field considerable."

"Okay, Rip, let's have it. Who's your man?"

"How about Tom Dodd?"

"Get serious."

"Ah am serious. Tom's a good man. Ain't got a radical bone in his body."

"Come on, Rip."

"Okay, maybe Tom's a little old, so you scratch him. And maybe you scratch Hubert for being too radical, and Shriver for being too pretty, and Bobby and Gene McCarthy because the President can't stand 'em. That still leaves one other possibility."

"Which is?"

"For the President to find hisself a younger fellow."

Charles was beginning to catch up with the conversation.

"Any particular younger fellow, Rip?"

"Well, there's Bayh, except Ah reckon he's *too* young. Or Abe Ribicoff, if he wadn't a Jew. Or Ed Muskie—except he and Lyndon had a fight back in '58 and Lyndon never got over it. Or there's our pal Pete Wilson, who'd be great except'n that he ain't much of a campaigner. And there'd be you, except as Ah recall you ain't quite thirty-five yet."

"Which would seem to leave only you, Rip."

Rip's eyes widened. "Me? Shitfire, Ah ain't in the runnin'—Ah'm a Southerner."

"Maybe that's what the President needs to woo the South. A dynamic young Southern statesman like Richard P. (Rip) Horton."

"You're just bullshittin' me now, pal," Rip protested, but Charles was intrigued. Perhaps Johnson would pick a dark horse. Perhaps Rip *was* a contender. Stranger things had happened.

The bells rang, announcing a roll-call vote, and as they did the little receptionist came in with a message. The message went unread as they watched her exit from the office.

"Lord, Lord, wouldn't you like to put skates on her ass?" Rip whispered.

"I don't want to talk about it," Charles said.

They took the elevator to the basement and caught the subway over to the Capitol. "What's this vote?" Rip asked.

"This Vietnam resolution," Charles told him. "The Gulf of Tonkin resolution, they're calling it."

Rip nodded without much interest. "Ah guess old Lyndon is showing folks he can be as hardass as Barry."

"I guess so."

"They all love that stuff," Rip said. "The Churchill bit. Sending the planes out and making speeches about fighting the bastards on the beaches and not having anything to give but blood, sweat, and tears. They eat that shit up."

"You're not against this resolution, are you?"

"Ah'm not gonna *vote* against it. But zapping the Chinks ain't helping mah folks back home any."

They walked through the cloakroom together, nodding at the Senators who stood about in little groups of two or three. When they walked onto the floor of the Senate, two of their younger colleagues were standing together near the speaker's rostrum, deep in conversation.

"Ah believe Ah better join that conference," Rip said. "You better come too. Looks like a big one."

Charles shook his head and walked toward his desk. He glanced up at the gallery and saw the reason for the conference—a good-looking redhead sitting with her legs crossed at a revealing angle. But Charles wasn't in the mood for the thigh-watching game, so he took his seat and waited for the vote to begin. He wished he knew more about this resolution. He guessed Rip was right, and the President was just hanging tough, protecting himself from Goldwater's "soft on Communism" attacks. But whatever the President was up to, the resolution was a godsend for Charles. With one vote he demolished John Roark's charge that he didn't stand firm on Communism.

"Charles, can I talk to you for a minute?"

Peter Wilson, Charles's fellow back-bencher, was standing beside his desk, a tall, slender man with thinning hair and a worried look. Pete had a bunch of papers in his hand and he looked rather like an absent-minded professor. He was, in fact, a lawyer who had practiced in Portland before a reform group drafted him to run for the Senate.

"Sure, Pete, what's on your mind?"

"Charles, what do you think of this resolution?"

"I think I'm going to vote for it."

"Have you read it? Listen to this: '. . . all necessary force to repel any armed attack . . .' That's a blank check, Charles."

"Isn't it just to retaliate against these attacks on our destroyers?"

"Morse is saying there may not even have been any attacks, or if there were we might have provoked them with secret raids."

Charles threw up his hands. "Pete, I don't know anything about secret raids. All I know is that Fulbright is sponsoring the thing and Mansfield is for it and I don't see how I can be against it."

"It's just too fast," Peter Wilson said. "Why does he suddenly need a declaration of war?"

Charles shook his head helplessly. The roll call was starting and he wanted to get the whole thing over with. Peter was making him uncomfortable. For Peter was right, this thing was too sudden. But what could you do?

114

"Are you going against it?" he asked. He worried about Pete Wilson, for Pete was a soul-searcher, an agonizer. Sometimes in this business you just had to do things without thinking about them too much.

"I don't know what I'm going to do," Peter Wilson said. "All I know is there've been two hundred Americans killed over there, Charles. Two hundred. I don't think the country will stand for much more of this."

He turned and walked slowly back to his desk, frowning, his hands in his pockets, his shoulders hunched forward, a troubled question mark of a man.

Slowly the roll call progressed down the alphabet. When the clerk reached the *P*s there had been only two "nays," Gruening and Morse.

"Mr. Pastore."

"Ay."

"Mr. Pearson."

"Ay."

"Mr. Pell."

"Ay."

"Mr. Pierce."

"Ay," Charles said, loud enough to be heard from his back-row seat, then, frowning a bit, wishing there were more time to study things, he left the chamber. He was halfway back to his office when Peter Wilson cast the final "ay" and slumped down in his seat like a man stricken.

Word of the Senate vote reached Joe Clayton's office in the White House only minutes after Peter Wilson cast the final "ay." The Senate vote followed closely the unanimous House vote, and once Joe Clayton heard the figures he put the telephone down gently, as if fearful of breaking a spell. After a moment he called Valenti to make sure the President had the news. Assured that he did, Joe Clayton began to pace the floor of his office, growing more excited by the minute.

The figures echoed in his mind. 416 to 0. 88 to 2. Even the two opposition votes in the Senate pleased him—two puny votes by two cranky old men, just enough to make all the opposition look ridiculous. Joe Clayton leaned against his desk and began to laugh, and he laughed until tears filled his eyes. It was such a stunning, total victory, almost unbelievable. Yet it was by no means an accidental victory. No one knew better than Joe Clayton how carefully planned it had been.

The first steps had been taken almost nine months before, in those uncertain December days when the new President was settling into office. It was a time of despair, of departures, of shifting alliances, and at the center was the new President, an unknown factor, uncommitted, unpredictable, a novice in world affairs. They had feared then that he would pull back from the unknown, concentrate on the domestic legislation, carry the nation toward neo-isolationism. But he had not. He had listened. He had questioned and grumbled and learned and finally he had accepted the challenge they put before him.

For Joe Clayton, of course, the first question had been his own status. Would the new President keep a Kennedy man? But Joe Clayton no longer thought of himself as a Kennedy man. He was a man with a mission, the mission of freedom, and he would serve any President who shared his commitment. If Johnson would accept him, he would accept Johnson. And Johnson had. He liked the tall, confident Ivy Leaguer who seemed to have every fact, every answer at his fingertips. So Clayton's status rose. There were more and more of his lengthy, late afternoon talks with the President, more and more opportunities for him to press for the clandestine strikes against the North, for the secret bombing in Laos, finally for the provocation strategy he and his allies at the Pentagon had developed. And it had worked. The provocations had increased, week by week, until inevitably Ho had responded with these gunboat attacks, and after that events had followed Joe Clayton's scenario to perfection. The first open bombing raids on the North. The resolution quickly sent to Congress. And now this stunning legislative victory. 88 to 2. 416 to 0. Who now could protest the bombing of the North, in the face of that congressional carte blanche?

Yet some would protest, both in and out of government. Joe was not concerned with the cranks who marched outside the White House with their hand-lettered signs. But he was concerned about dissenters within the government, the little men who could not see the Communist menace or, seeing it, lacked the stomach for battle. Such men were an enemy within, and they must be found, discredited, removed. He knew what they would be saying now. Stop the bombing and negotiate. But negotiations now would be a disaster. So the bombing must continue, until the North was crippled and ready to make peace on acceptable terms.

Joe Clayton was confident. He felt the momentum moving his way. History was being made, this week, this day, part of it right here in his office. He was proud, yet he sought no credit. He sought only victory for his country, victory for the forces that would free the human spirit over those that would enslave it. Mao had said the East wind would prevail over the West, but Joe Clayton knew Mao was wrong. The battle now was joined. Vietnam was the test case. If the Communists could be stopped there, the tide could be turned, and no man could say what battles the forces of freedom might win in the final third of the century. Joe Clayton was thrilled by the magnitude of the struggle, awed by it, finally humbled by it.

He called in his secretary and dictated a memo to the President. He might have called, but at this moment that might have seemed presumptuous. A memo could be more carefully worded, and could have the formality, the permanence, appropriate to the event. The President would understand. So he dictated the memo, he praised the man no less than he deserved, and sent his secretary to type it. Then, finally, he thought of the evening ahead. Muffie was at the Cape for the summer. He had spent most evenings working. But this evening cried out for celebration. He thought a moment, then called Valenti back.

"Jack, you said something about a party tonight."

"Yes, that's right. A fund-raiser at the Hollingsworth estate."

"Is the President going?"

Valenti laughed. He was a pleasant little man. Above all he was loyal. "Who knows, Joe? Who knows what that man will do? But you should go. It ought to be fun."

Joe Clayton smiled into the phone. "Perhaps I will," he said. "I deserve a little fun, don't I?"

"My Lord, who are all these people?" Carol asked as they rounded the corner of the mansion and stepped onto a stone terrace that overlooked the wide, now crowded lawn of the Hollingsworth estate.

"Democrats," Charles said. "Loyal Democrats with twenty-five bucks to contribute to the cause." Faces on the lawn turned up toward them, hands waved in greeting; he took Carol's arm and led her down the wide stone steps.

117

"Do we get to see Himself for our fifty dollars?" Carol asked.

An Assistant Secretary of Labor to whom Charles didn't want to talk raised his hand in greeting; Charles waved and turned toward Carol as if deep in conversation. "Nope," he told her. "In the first place, our tickets were freebies. In the second place, Himself doesn't bother with twenty-five-dollar affairs."

"Look," Carol said. "There're the girls."

Charles looked and it was true. The Johnson girls, clad in bright summer dresses, were standing with John Bailey near a rosebush, granting smiles, handshakes, and an occasional autograph to a long line of admirers.

"Which one is Lynda Bird?" Charles asked.

"The tall one. Should we go over and say hello?"

"We should," Charles said. "But let's go get a beer instead."

He took her arm and they crossed the lawn, enjoying the smiles and stares that followed them, stopping a few times for hellos, listening to the Western band playing "Yellow Rose of Texas" and "Foggy Mountain Breakdown," moving in no great hurry toward the long table beneath an oak tree where draft beer was being served in big Wing-Ding cups.

"God, smell that barbecue," Charles said. "I take back everything I ever said about Texas."

"Charles, I think I'll go meet the Johnson girls."

"Oh, hell, let's don't be social."

"I'm not. I might could get one of them on my show."

"Oh. Okay, I'll walk over with you."

"No, you get a beer and I'll be back in a minute."

"I don't mind."

"That's not the point. This is business."

"Maybe I could help."

"Charles, I am capable of dealing with the Johnson girls *without* your help."

"Okay, okay."

She started toward the receiving line. He sighed and got himself a beer and stood under the tree for a minute looking out at the two or three hundred people gathered on the lawn. He knew many of them and could guess the identity of many others. They were Democrats, of course, a cross section of the party as it came together on the eve of a great election, some from Washington, others come from around the nation, like an army gathering for battle. There were perhaps two dozen Senators and Representatives scattered about, aristocrats of the party, accepting homage as their due, men like Charles who thought this gathering might provide a pleasant end to a hectic day. There were two cabinet members, one of whom, a Kennedy appointee, was worried for his job and hoped that by attending parties like this, by shaking the right hands and speaking the right words, he might shore up his crumbling status. There were Texans, many Texans, new to Washington, recognizable by their clothes and their twangs and their self-confidence, men and women who spoke casually of the Ranch and the Pedernales and of Juanita, the President's secretary, and Zephyr, the President's cook, and Blanco, the President's dog. There were Negroes there too, two generations of Negroes, the older ones light-skinned and mustached and dressed like morticians, talking proudly of the civil rights bill, the younger ones, more casually dressed, more argumentative with whites, discussing whether the summer's riots would trigger massive federal aid to the slums, which they now were calling the ghettos. There were sociologists and urban theorists from the poverty program staff, excitable men in cord coats and brown shoes who huddled together and spoke earnestly of upward mobility and indigenous leadership and cultural deprivation. There were a great many young men at the party, bright young men who worked on Capitol Hill or for the Administration or for the great Washington law firms, alert and talented men in their late twenties and early thirties, each trying to understand the mysterious process by which certain of Washington's bright young men go on to be wealthy middle-aged men and in time certain of those go on to be powerful old men. There were political operatives at the party too, quick-eyed men in wash and wear suits, advance men and money men and precinct men and media men, all converged on Washington now like pickpockets at the state fair.

There were union men standing on the Hollingsworth lawn, not the Meanys and Reuthers but second-level men, tough old labor skates who had come up with their fists but now fought their battles with money, men who knew what power was and knew that their power would outlast the professors and the reformers and the whiz kids who came and went every four or eight years. There were three or four Grand Old Ladies there, widows of men who had served in the Roosevelt and Truman Cabinets, regal women in white gloves

119

and flowered hats who sipped soft drinks and smiled toward the horizon and retold tales of Franklin and Eleanor, Harry and Bess. There were, finally, a great many attractive young women who proved on inquiry (and many inquiries were made) to be secretaries to politicians and lawyers and lobbyists who had dutifully bought tickets to this affair and then given them away, vivacious young women in the prints and pastels of summer who in time paired off with the young men and the not so young men who vied for their attentions in the dappled summer dusk.

All these people were gathered in the late summer of 1964 at the estate of a Washington real estate broker named Hollingsworth, and as Charles Pierce watched them group and regroup he was struck by the endless differences between them, between labor leader and academic, between Southerner and Negro, between Kennedy men and Johnson men, between farmer and city dweller, between Protestant and Catholic, between almost all of them on one point or another. Yet despite their differences, perhaps because of their differences, theirs was a great political party, arguably the greatest in history, and their differences with one another were less than their differences with Barry Goldwater. Tonight they would come together, an unspoken truce declared, to drink and swap Goldwater stories and discuss polls and make predictions, savoring the sweet scent of victory in the air, buoyed up by it, united by the certainty that after November they would have a four-year lease on America. After that there would be time enough to fight among themselves.

Carol appeared out of the twilight.

"Standing there all by yourself?"

"Thinking deep thoughts. How'd it go?"

"I had a good talk with Lynda."

"About what?"

"Politics, mainly. She's bright."

"She ought to be. So what happened?"

"I think she's going to be on the show. She's got to check with headquarters."

"Good work."

"A girl's got to hustle."

He squeezed her hand and got them two beers and they stood for another moment looking out at the people coming and going.

"Quite a gathering, isn't it?" said a voice behind them.

They turned and saw Peter Wilson, a cup of beer in his hand, a thin mustache of foam on his upper lip.

"Democracy in action," Charles said. "You've met Carol, haven't you?"

"Of course," Peter Wilson said, "I'm one of her fans."

"And I'm one of yours," Carol said. "Is Susan here?"

"She and the children are spending the month at Rehoboth Beach."

"I love Rehoboth," Carol said. "We used to go there, before Charles got so important. We'd always end up at Whiskey Beach, where everybody drinks all day and never goes near the water."

Peter Wilson smiled, but not very well. His long, melancholy face was even sadder than usual.

"I guess the ays had it today," Charles said.

Peter nodded unhappily. "I started to vote against it," he said, "but it seemed such a futile gesture. But I'm frightened, Charles. Where is he leading us?"

"To victory," Charles said. "Ask anybody. Come on, let's get some barbecue before those damned Texans eat it all up."

They got into line and emerged with paper plates piled high with barbecued ribs, baked beans, and cole slaw, served up by men in Western shirts from the back of a chuckwagon with "Walter Jetton's Famous Texas Barbecue" painted in big red letters on its side.

"That was Walter Jetton himself carving up the ribs," Charles said. He led them across the lawn to a table with four folding chairs beside it.

"How do you know?"

"I know all these important Texans," he said. "Besides, he had 'Walter' stitched on his shirt pocket. You want to see another important Texan? Look over there by the steps, the guy with the red tie. That's Melvin Holmes of Joy, Texas, the President's new man Friday."

"Is *that* Holmes?" Peter asked.

"That's him. A good man to know. Or maybe not to know. Yesterday he quietly axed a dozen Kennedy people from the DNC staff— zap, just like that. Little Melvin, silent but deadly."

"He called me last week about something," Peter Wilson said. "He sounded rather unimaginative."

"He's what they call literal-minded," Charles said. "Around the

White House they're saying that when the President says 'shit' Melvin reaches for his belt buckle."

They laughed and bit into the spicy ribs, washing them down with beer, listening all the while to the Western band playing across the lawn.

Carol drank the cold beer and listened to the music, letting it carry her back into the past while Charles and Peter talked shop, talked about Medicare and the gun control bill and Charles's primary campaign.

Carol enjoyed the spectacle of the event—politicians were fun, if you didn't take them seriously—yet she felt a vague, nagging sadness, and for a while she couldn't remember why. Then it came back to her. That morning's paper had carried an obituary of Flannery O'Connor. Carol had read it with a pang of sorrow, then hurried into her day's activities and forgotten it. But now the fact of O'Connor's death came back to her—a woman not much older than herself—and with it memories of the year she dated James Fairchild and how he would scan new editions of the *Sewanee Review* and *Mademoiselle* and other magazines for the latest O'Connor story and they would read them together, James awed by the writing, Carol simply awed that someone so young, a *woman,* could have created such strange and beautiful tales out of the dusty little Southern towns and the weird country people who lived in them. Carol had always thought of those towns and people as things to be avoided, not to be written about. And now O'Connor was dead and her death had a special poignance for Carol, as she sat lonely and brooding amid three hundred politicians, for if Flannery O'Connor was dead, at least she had left much behind her, had accomplished much, had fulfilled herself, and her passing reminded Carol of her youthful dreams, of all that she had once hoped to do, and of how little she had in fact accomplished.

She was gloomy, and it pleased her when she saw Joe Clayton walking toward their table. She gave him a gay smile. It was hard to believe that anyone so young and attractive could be as important as Charles said he had become.

He nodded to the three of them. "Carol. Charles. Senator Wilson," he said. "No, please, don't get up—I just wanted to thank you for the support you gave the President today. You'll never regret it."

"Join us, Joe," Charles said.

"No, I mustn't intrude."

"No intrusion," Peter Wilson said. "In fact, I'd like very much to talk to you."

"Of course," Joe Clayton said, and slipped into the empty chair between the two Senators. "What's on your mind?"

"This resolution today," Peter said. "I voted for it but I don't see why it was necessary."

"It was necessary to show the enemy this country is united behind the President," Joe Clayton said.

"Yes, but united for what?" Wilson asked.

"For whatever is necessary to save South Vietnam from the Communists," Clayton said in his smooth, reassuring voice.

"But what do you mean 'whatever is necessary'? An air war against the North? An invasion of the North? Mining the harbors?"

"I don't think any of that will be necessary," Clayton said.

"But you think they're authorized by this resolution?"

"The language is quite clear. But again, I don't think those things will be necessary, because I think the threat of massive bombings will force Ho to the conference table."

"But what if it doesn't?" Wilson asked.

"That's up to the President, of course," Joe Clayton said. "But I imagine we'd just keep turning the screw."

"Oh, God," Peter Wilson said. Charles got up and nodded to Carol to do the same. He was sick of talk about Vietnam. To hell with Vietnam.

"You guys ponder the fate of the world if you want to," he said. "We're going up and listen to the music. See you later."

He took Carol's hand and they walked up toward the bandstand. The band was playing "You Are My Sunshine," amid whoops and rebel yells, and people were starting to gather around for the promised entertainment. The Western band finished its song, took a bow, and its members began to drift toward the chuckwagon. Up on the bandstand, Jim Samuels was taking over as MC for the evening's entertainment.

Jim Samuels was a well-known young man-about-Washington, a lawyer, the son of a Democratic leader in the House, a singer and stand-up comedian whose routines had made him the life of the party at many Democratic gatherings. Charles could remember him singing at Kennedy rallies in 1960, could remember him singing at Hickory Hill in 1961, but this was 1964 and now he was wearing a cowboy hat and a red, white and blue jacket with an outsize "All the Way with LBJ" button on the lapel.

"Howdy, pahdners," he said, and winked, and strummed his banjo and began to sing the new campaign song.

> "Well, hello, Lyndon!
> Yes, hello, Lyndon!
> It's so nice to have you here
> Where you belong . . ."

He sang the song through once, then waved to the audience. "Come on, everybody join in," he cried, and slowly, in uncertain, off-key voices, the people gathered before the bandstand began to sing "Hello, Lyndon," self-consciously at first, then loudly, exuberantly, cheering and clapping and singing until their voices were a mighty wave crashing across the lawn and echoing off into the night.

Charles, standing with Carol in the middle of the crowd, mouthed a line or two, then fell silent. He felt alone, depressed, trapped. He wanted to flee. He could not have explained his mood, except that in the midst of this celebration of Lyndon Johnson he had thought of Jack Kennedy, of how quickly he had come and gone, and how quickly they all had gone from singing one man's songs to another's. His mind had slipped for a moment from the political context to the personal and he felt a sharp pain, a sense of loss, somehow a sense of dishonor. He took Carol's arm and led her out of the crowd. They passed Joe Clayton, standing a head taller than the people around him, his face bathed in light, singing loudly and solemnly, like a crusader marching to battle. Somehow, seeing him made Charles feel even worse.

"I talked to Beth today," Carol said to him as they drove home.

"Yeah? What's she up to?"

"All sorts of things. She's starting a day-care program and Bill is organizing welfare mothers for some kind of a protest against the welfare regulations. The whole thing is fascinating."

"Yeah, it's great. My sister has gone from Vassar to the Peace Corps to shacking up with some guy in the middle of a slum."

"Charles, really. We shacked up, as you so delicately put it, before we were married."

"We slept together. We didn't move in together."

124

"Well, maybe kids aren't so hypocritical today. If more people lived together first, there'd be less divorce."

"Okay, okay. But I don't like her living in that neighborhood. It's dangerous."

"Oh, Charles, first you say you're worried about her morals, then you say you're worried about her safety. If she survived in a village in Ecuador, she can survive three blocks from DuPont Circle."

"It's just no place for her."

"Charles, she's an idealist. She wants to help people."

"She wasn't raised to live in a slum," he persisted. "If she wants to help humanity, I'll get her a job at the U.N. or somewhere."

"She doesn't *want* a job like that. She wants to be out where things are happening. Her generation is different from ours. Stop worrying about her and be proud of her."

"I am proud of her, damn it. I just don't understand it. A girl like Beth living in a slum and a bright guy like Bill who could get a good job is out there organizing welfare mothers. It's like that damned incomprehensible music they listen to—I just don't understand it."

She smiled and took his hand. "You know what?" she said. "Even Senators aren't supposed to understand everything."

He laughed and squeezed her hand, but his sense of unease stayed with him, all the way back to Georgetown.

2

JANUARY–JUNE 1965

The new year came with a rush. Suddenly the holidays were past, the snow and slush had gone, the dogwoods and cherry blossoms were out, and the glorious Washington spring surrendered to the long, humid Washington summer. In later years Charles Pierce would think of 1965 as the fastest year of his life. He would see it in memory as a kind of speeded-up movie, its chronology confused, its highlights blurred. And when he looked back on it, to try to understand how so much could have happened so fast, the memory that would come to his mind was the ringing of bells.

They rang and rang and rang. They filled the Capitol and they echoed through the offices and corridors of the Senate. The bells rang from morning to night, calling Charles Pierce and Rip Horton and Peter Wilson and all the rest of them like Pavlov's dogs, telling them to pull on their coats and hurry across to cast their votes, adding their names to the lopsided majorities that were passing Medicare and the rent supplements and the education bills and the voting rights bills, passing higher Social Security benefits and more job-training programs and new money for Appalachia, passing new programs by the dozen, virtually anything the White House asked for. No one knew quite what was happening. Charles tried for a while to study each new bill but there were too many, so he studied those that came before his committees and took the rest on faith. He saw older Senators shaking their heads in disbelief; he saw one great Senator weeping openly as federal aid to education passed easily one afternoon, a bill for which that Senator had battled in vain for twenty years.

Charles gave his job all he had, for it was *his* job now. He had been a fluke before, but he was a full-fledged Senator now, elected in his own right. He had been lucky, of course. He had won his primary because his opponent, John Roark, had been overconfident, had learned the hard way what happens to arm-waving old politicians who debate polite young opponents on television. After that, running against a Goldwater Republican in the general election, Charles had coasted to victory on LBJ's coattails, as so many others had. But there had been more to his campaigns than luck and television. In the final days, when there was no doubt that he would win, he had gone before the voters not in supplication but in triumph. The crowds had grown larger, their cheers louder, until those last days had been like a dream. He had thrown away his prepared speeches and talked to them of a new era, of justice and equality, of schools and hospitals to be built, of laws to bring a better life to men who worked in mines and tilled the soil. He told them those things and they had answered him with cheers that roared louder from day to day, from town to town, cheers that each night would echo in his mind like thunder. When it was over, he had felt humbled, and immeasurably fortunate, for it seemed to him that the best of his life and the best of his country's life were coming together, that there was nothing he could not do and nothing his country could not do.

If his election had been a dream, the Senate in that next spring was reality, a new reality of legislation such as Congress had never seen before. Day after day, month after month, the bells rang, calling them to vote, ringing in a new era. That was how Charles Pierce would remember 1965.

Carol Pierce would remember it differently. For 1965 was the first time that she had been acutely aware of Charles's absence, his physical absence from her. She had accepted his constant travels during his campaign, but she had thought that after his election they could return to something like a normal family life. But that was not how it had worked out. Charles said there were too many ex-Senators who were ex-Senators because they had spent five years ignoring their states and one futile year trying to mend fences. So he was back in Kentucky two or three weekends each month, attending civic dinners, presiding at picnics and ox roasts, crowning queens and princesses of this and that, umpiring Little League games, marching in parades and judging livestock, speaking to the 4-H and the

Hi-Y and the Allied Youth and the Lions and the Elks and the Grange and the Future Farmers and all the others. Carol went with him sometimes, but not much. It was too hard on the children and there was something else, too, something that she had learned during his campaign—that she could not share whatever it was that happened to Charles when the crowds gathered and the cheering began—and rather than be jealous of a lover with whom no woman could compete, she chose to stay at home.

And it wasn't just Kentucky. There were speaking invitations from all over the country, and he usually accepted one of them each month and that always meant another night away from home. She wondered about those nights away sometimes. She guessed he met his share of liberal ladies who'd be glad enough to go to bed with a handsome young Senator, and she doubted that Charles would turn down *all* the offers. Charles was not the soul of morality. But he was at least discreet, and that was the next best thing. God, some of the men in the Senate were notorious, their sleeping around was a public joke —Carol didn't see how their wives stood it. She didn't think Charles would ever be like that, and if he wanted to bed down with some sex-starved Democratic lady in Dallas or Toledo, Carol could live with it. Not that she *knew* he did. She didn't *want* to know. If you didn't know, it didn't bother you. And one night's sex wasn't that big a deal. God, aren't I modern, she thought. Miss New Morality of 1965.

But that was how she felt. She couldn't even honestly say she minded his being away a few days a month. It had its advantages. Not having to fix dinner for him. Not having to listen to his incomprehensible tales of Senate intrigue. Being able to get in bed with a book and read as late as she wanted to and not having to make love if she didn't want to. No, she could survive without Charles a few nights a month. It was for the children's sake that she minded his travels. For Liza's sake, really, Liza who was six now and vulnerable and who loved her father as only a six-year-old can. Hugh was no problem. If Hugh minded that his father was away—if he even *knew* his father was away—you never knew it. Hugh was like his father; he kept things bottled up. But Liza was different. Liza could be hurt —she *was* hurt by Charles's absence. He saw only the joyous homecomings and didn't see what went before them, the bedwetting, the bursts of temper, the notes from her teacher. Carol had talked to their doctor and he had assured her it was normal, Liza would outgrow it—easy enough for him to say, but he had never had the child cry herself to sleep in his arms.

Carol had never really told Charles how bad it was. She'd started to a hundred times but . . . but perhaps the doctor was right, and Liza would outgrow it. And if she had spoken to Charles, he would no doubt have reminded her that she worked too, that she was gone from nine to four each day and it was Ellen—Ellen who was wonderful, Ellen who gave you her heart and soul for a dollar fifty an hour —who greeted the children each afternoon and who cared for them if they stayed home sick. Charles would have equated her hours away with his days and nights away; that was how he would see it, it was another kind of double standard that men believed in.

Men, men, men. Sometimes she thought men were driving her crazy. Charles was an angel compared to the ones she dealt with at the station—the station manager, the fools she interviewed, the empty-headed announcers and the filthy-minded cameramen and all the rest of them. Her interview show had not worked out as she had hoped. Somehow that too had gone wrong. She had dreamed that it would be a showcase for all the bright and important people in Washington, that in time it would be syndicated. But none of that had happened, for a lot of reasons. One reason was money. The station manager wouldn't hire her an assistant to help her screen her interviewees, so she had to do it herself and there wasn't time and inevitably some bores and frauds got onto the show. And she had run up against the Washington pecking order. The really important people made their annual appearances on "Meet the Press" or "Face the Nation" and they didn't bother with local interview shows—"women's shows." Oh, a few young Senators would come on as a favor to Charles, or a few Administration officials who wanted his favor, but she needed ten or fifteen people a week and so she was forced to take the second-raters, the minor bureaucrats and the first novelists and the unknown actors in town for a tryout and the retired diplomats who had written their memoirs—and once the floodgates were opened the hope of syndication flew out the window. It was a vicious circle. To get better people you needed a national show, and to get a national show you needed better people. Carol found herself in such a crazy position. People told her how lucky she was to have such an exciting job, to meet such interesting people, all that, but she found herself endlessly frustrated, spending most of her time asking dumb ques-

129

tions of dull people, sometimes having a good interview with an interesting guest, and then wondering if anyone was watching out there. And in truth not as many people were watching as should have been. Their audience was off from Eleanora's heyday and so advertising was down and Cy Hollenbeck, the news director, had been frowning and grumbling more than usual that spring and Carol did not know what he intended to do about the show and she was not sure she cared any more.

It all came to a head one weekend in June; a lot of things came to a head, more than she would ever have imagined possible, things past and present and future all converging on her from out of nowhere.

It began on Thursday evening when she came in from a shopping spree and found Charles in the study reading the paper. When she entered, he glanced up, then put the paper on his lap and whistled.

"Hey! A new skirt. A *short* skirt."

"They're called miniskirts, dear."

"That's pretty darn mini."

"Oh, it's not, really. Young girls are wearing them a lot higher than this. Or had you noticed?"

"Me? Notice short skirts? Nonsense."

"Ha-ha. Well, how do you like it?"

"Turn around."

She turned around.

"It looks great," he said, and returned to his newspaper.

"You don't like it."

"I said it looks great."

"In a tone that meant you don't like it."

"I like it fine."

"What's wrong with it?"

"Nothing, damn it."

"Your tender morality is outraged, is that it?"

"Oh, bullshit. If I don't object to those peekaboo necklines of yours, why would I object to a short skirt?"

"Then what is it you don't like?"

"Well, if you must know, I think if you're going to wear skirts like that you could lose a pound or two."

"My legs are fat, is that it?"

130

"I didn't say that. Your legs are fine. I just said you could lose a pound or two."

"Charles, I'm not eighteen any more. I'm thirty-one and I've had two children and sometimes women gain a few pounds."

"Okay, but you might lose a few if you'd give up bread and desserts and things."

"So I'm a glutton."

"Oh, for Christ's sake."

"If my legs are so offensive to you, you don't have to—"

"Oh, shut up, will you? Let me read the paper in peace."

"Don't tell me to shut up!"

He put down the paper, looked at her a minute, then crossed the room and put his arms around her.

"Why are we arguing? I like your skirt. I like your legs. I hope to remain on the most intimate terms with your legs."

She pressed against him, not wanting to argue. "It's my fault," she said. "I had a hard day and my period is starting and . . . well, it wasn't a good time for you to tell me I'm overweight."

"You're not overweight," he said. "You're perfect."

"Charles, you're going to have to realize I won't always be as pretty as when you married me. I'll gain weight and I'll get lines in my face and—"

"Kiddo, I'm doing all those things already."

"It doesn't matter in a man. Men get more attractive as they get older."

And women get less attractive, she thought, but she couldn't bring herself to say it. It was something she'd been thinking about this past year, for when she looked in the mirror she could see the lines beneath her eyes and the puffiness around her chin and she knew that all the diets and cold creams in the world could not reverse them. It was so damned unfair. When she was forty she'd be finished as far as her looks went and Charles would be more attractive than he'd ever been. At least that was how they taught you to think of it, taught you so early and so completely that when you saw a man and a woman of fifty you thought she was ugly and he was distinguished when in fact there was no real difference between them. But they had taught you to see things differently. A beautiful couple was a fifty-year-old actor and an actress half his age. But that was not the way the world was. You married a boy your own age and they worshiped you for a few years and then you began to lose your youth and your looks and they began to have their fun with young girls. Damn them, she thought, damn them, damn them. And yet she could not blame Charles, could not hate him. He was more understanding than most men and whatever was wrong was wrong with all of them, was wrong with the world they lived in.

The next morning, Friday morning, everything went wrong. Charles left early to catch a plane for Louisville. As soon as he left, Liza cried for a half hour. She made herself late to school and made Carol late for work. Carol's period had started and she had cramps. And finally there was the fiasco with the novelist.

It was a mistake to have a novelist on the show at all, of course. Novelists as a group were the worst interviewees of all, worse even than retired generals or bureaucrats from HEW. Because novelists could never *talk*—probably that was why they became novelists in the first place. Of course there were exceptions. It was fine to have a Wouk or a Drury because they'd had best sellers, learned to talk, learned to behave like celebrities, but your average, garden-variety novelist was about as interesting as a doorknob.

So Timothy Platt would never have been on the show at all, except for Cy Hollenbeck, who mumbled something about his being the nephew of the wife of somebody important with the network. Thus, when Carol arrived at the studio that morning, he was standing in her office, arms folded across his chest, a dark-visaged man with lots of bushy black hair, scowling at her.

"I'm terribly sorry to be so late," Carol said, taking a copy of his book from her secretary.

"Humph," said Timothy Platt.

Carol sat down in her chair before the cameras and hastily skimmed the jacket copy on the novel. It was called *The Lambs of Spring* and the blurb said something about ". . . a sensitive and compelling portrait of a vanishing America, as seen through the eyes of . . ." Carol flipped impatiently through the book. The paragraphs were long and there wasn't much dialogue. Someone named Hawkins seemed to turn up often.

She guided Timothy Platt into his chair and hooked the microphone around his neck and then the red light blinked and they were on the air.

132

"Good morning." Carol smiled at the nearest camera, behind which a potbellied technician was scratching himself. "I'm Carol Pierce and I have several fascinating guests today, beginning with a fine young novelist named"—she smiled and glanced quickly at the book in her hand—"Timothy Platt, who's written a novel called *The Lambs in Spring*."

"*The Lambs* OF *Spring*," Timothy Platt corrected.

"Yes, of course, *The Lambs* OF *Spring*. Now, Mr. Platt, tell me, is this your first novel?"

He glared at her. "It is my fifth novel."

"Oh, well. You look so young to have written five books."

"What does age have to do with it? Some days I'm twenty, some days I'm a hundred."

"Yes, I know the feeling," Carol said, and gave him a big smile, but Timothy Platt only scowled. "Ah, now, Mr. Platt, can you tell us a little about your novel?"

Platt ran his fingers through his bushy hair. "I don't know where to begin," he said angrily. "A novel defies summary. A novel simply *is*."

"Well, perhaps you can tell us what the critics have said about it."

"There are no critics in America. Only reviewers."

"Well, what have the reviewers said about it?"

"Reviewers are idiots. What they say doesn't matter."

"Well," Carol said. Her mind was an absolute blank. She wanted to tell this madman to get out of her sight. Just then she saw the red light blinking and she forced a smile at the camera. "We'll be right back with Timothy Platt, author of *The Lambs in Spring . . .*"

"OF *Spring!*"

"*The Lambs* OF *Spring*, right after this word from your neighborhood People's Drug Store."

They went off the air and Carol decided to take a hard line with Timothy Platt, no matter whose favorite nephew he was.

"*Mister* Platt," she said frostily, "if we're to conclude this interview, you simply must open up a little and talk about your book."

"I don't care whether we conclude it or not," the novelist said. "Do you have any idea how insulting it is for you to presume to discuss my book with me when you haven't even read it?"

"Mr. Platt, I sometimes interview five authors a week and it just

133

isn't possible to read everyone's book. But if you'll just summarize the plot it might interest people who'd want to read it."

"Ha!" Platt barked. "People who read my books don't watch programs like this."

"Then why are you wasting your valuable time being here?" Carol asked with as much irony as she could summon.

"I don't know," Timothy Platt admitted. "My publisher arranged it. I must have been out of my mind to accept."

I must be out of my mind, Carol thought, but the red light was blinking again and they were back on the air. "Welcome back with Timothy Platt," she smiled, "the author of"—she could feel his furious scowl—"*The Lambs* OF *Spring*. Now, Mr. Platt, you have a major character in the book named Hawkins. Can you tell us something about Hawkins?"

Platt frowned, scratched, coughed, spoke. "He . . . he . . . he is a man with a rare sensitivity to, and understanding of, sheep."

"Sheep?" Carol said blankly.

"Yes, sheep," Platt said, as if that exhausted the subject.

"He, ah, he owns some sheep?"

"Of course."

"How many sheep does he own?"

Platt looked at her as at an idiot. "I don't know," he said. "I never counted them."

That brought laughter from the cameramen, which was not easy to do.

"Well, Mr. Platt, in a sense you created them, didn't you? I mean, they're your sheep too."

Timothy Platt scowled and twisted in his chair—for an instant she thought he was going to get up and leave. "Oh, all right. Maybe he has a hundred sheep. Maybe five hundred. The point is, he *communicates* with them."

The cameramen were roaring. Dirty-minded bastards. Carol knew what they were thinking because it was what Charles would have been thinking too.

"You mean he talks to the sheep?"

"Talks, talks? Of course he doesn't *talk* to them. How could he *talk* to sheep?"

"Then how *does* he communicate with them?" She was struggling

134

to keep her voice down. She'd find out about Hawkins and those damned sheep or die trying.

"They simply understand each other. *He is sensitive to sheep.*"

"A kind of telepathy . . ." Carol began.

"What is that dog doing there?" Platt cried.

Carol stared at him in confusion. What dog? Was a dog chasing his sheep?

"I don't want him near me," Platt said. "I'm allergic to dogs."

Carol followed his gaze, then she understood. The next guest was an animal trainer and he had arrived in the studio with a little white poodle that reputedly could dance and count to five. Someone moved the poodle back a few feet, and the interview with Platt dragged on. Finally a viewer called in who said he was writing his thesis on Platt's work and wondered if Platt could comment on the influence of D. H. Lawrence's novels on his own. Platt warmed to the question and Carol let the two of them chat on to their hearts' delight—their discussion was incomprehensible but at least it used up the remaining minutes. Carol kept an eye on the poodle. Come on and pee on his stupid leg, she was thinking, but the dog never did and finally Platt was off and the animal trainer was on and the show lurched to a conclusion.

As soon as they were off the air Carol headed for Cy Hollenbeck's office. She found him sitting behind his cluttered desk, eating an apple.

"Want one?" he asked.

"Cy, I have had it," she said. "Don't you ever tell me I've got to have anyone on my show again. That damned writer . . ."

"Ah, it wasn't so bad," Cy said. "A lot of laughs. People probably liked it."

"Well, I didn't like it. It made me look like an idiot."

Cy Hollenbeck took a final bite out of his apple and tossed the core into the wastebasket. "Sit down, Carol," he said. "I've been wanting to talk to you about the show. I've got a couple of ideas."

Carol looked at him suspiciously and sat down.

"I've got some ideas too, Cy," she said quickly. "I was thinking we might could get the cabinet members, or at least some of them, if we'd give them the full half hour with no interruptions."

Cy began to pick his teeth with his middle finger, examining the fragments of apple peel he found before flicking them toward the wastebasket. He was an ex-newspaperman, the gruff and cynical type. Carol hated him.

"Damn it, Carol, the show goes on at noon, the women are ironing, doing their hair, maybe fixing lunch. They want a few laughs, a little fun, not W. Willard Wirtz, for Christ's sake."

"Cy, I meet people all the time who say how they'd like more good public affairs programing."

"Yeah, and those people never see the show. Who sees the show is a lot of housewives and what those little ladies want is some fun."

"Those little ladies! Listen to you. The trouble is, you think all women are idiots."

"I think anybody who watches daytime television is probably an idiot, regardless of sex."

"What's more, I need an assistant. I can't screen fifteen or twenty people a week by myself. Eleanora had an assistant."

"It was in her contract," Cy said.

Carol's anger was fading. She just felt tired. She had lost too many arguments with Cy that year. In April, when some young people had a demonstration against the war in Vietnam, she'd wanted to have one of them on the show, but Cy had vetoed that. Too controversial. A bunch of cranks. Just cause problems. Forget it. So Carol went on having the retired generals and the first novelists and the dog acts. And now she felt too tired to argue any more.

"I'll tell you, Cy, something's got to be done. I've done my best but the show isn't what it should be."

Cy lit his pipe, sucking and puffing until it began to smoke up the room. "Let me tell you my idea," he said. "You know Eddie Waters?"

"Yes, I know Eddie Waters," Carol repeated, not seeing what he was getting at. Eddie Waters was a big, loud buffoon who was the weather announcer on the evening news show and had drawn a lot of attention by telling jokes, dancing jigs, reciting poems, and otherwise making an ass of himself while he told people whether or not it was going to rain the next day.

"Eddie's a talented boy," Cy continued. "He's built himself a following on that weather spot and he's ready to move up to bigger things."

Carol listened in confusion, then horror, as she began to see what was coming.

136

"I've been kicking it around, and everybody agrees Eddie'd be great for a variety show. So I think the obvious thing—"

"No, Cy!"

"Wait a minute. The obvious thing would be for you two to co-host a show. The Carol and Eddie Show. We could expand it to an hour—"

"No!"

"And you could have an assistant to help out. And there'd be a nice raise in it for you."

"I don't care—"

"Just think about it, Carol. Think about the chemistry. The two of you might make a great team. You're serious, you ask the probing questions, all that, and Eddie raises hell. You might be one hell of a combo."

"He's an idiot."

"He's a personality. He's got something. People watch the whole God damn news show just to see Eddie's weather report."

Carol sat and looked at Cy for a moment. The smell of his pipe was making her sick and her cramps were returning. She didn't know what to say. What happened if she said no? Maybe it would be a better show. Maybe it was all her fault for not giving out more of the giggles and the tee-hees that Cy wanted from a woman interviewer. All Carol really knew was that she felt like hell and she wanted to go home and have a drink and do nothing for a while. She was sick of hearing men tell her what was wrong with her—sick of Cy telling her she was too serious and Timothy Platt telling her she hadn't read his stupid book and Charles telling her she was overweight, sick of all of them.

She stood up. "I'll think about it," she said. "Let's talk about it Monday."

"Fine," Cy said. "Fine. Maybe you and me and Eddie can have lunch together."

Carol went back to her office and sat down for a minute. She took some pills for her cramps. She had missed lunch and it was too late to go anywhere, so she sent her secretary down to the cafeteria for a carton of milk and an egg salad sandwich. She ate the sandwich and drank the milk and she began to feel better. She was just getting up to leave when her secretary buzzed.

"There's a Major Bailey on the phone," she said.

137

"What about?"

"I don't know. He said Hank Bailey, from Birmingham."

Carol sat back down, stunned. Hank Bailey. She shut her eyes and she saw the tall, gangling quarterback of fifteen years before.

"Mrs. Pierce, do you want to talk to him?"

Her mind was racing in several directions at once. What was the protocol with ex-boy friends? Ex-boy friends who had been your first lover. Should she talk to him? See him? Could you have a polite conversation with someone with whom you'd shared such a year as she'd once shared with Hank? She hadn't any idea what he was doing now. She wondered if he was still a big country kid like he'd been then, with a lock of hair always falling into his eyes. But she'd changed since then, and probably he had too. She realized she wanted to know, that she was curious. Why not? Why not be polite to an old school friend? Polite. That was all.

"Yes, Lynn, put him on."

"Carol?"

"Hank? How in the world are you?"

"No complaints. Listen, this is a crazy coincidence, but I'm in town and I happened to have the TV on in my hotel room and I saw your show. And I thought, By God, I'll call her. So, hello."

"I'm glad you did. What are you doing now?"

"I'm in the army. A career type."

"You like it?"

"Love it."

"What do you do? I bet you fly."

"That's close. That's what I started out to do. But something better came along."

"What?"

"What we call special forces."

"Is that the Green Berets?"

"Right."

"That's . . ." She tried to remember. "That's Fort Bragg, isn't it? I remember when President Kennedy went down there."

"Right again."

"Is that where you're stationed?"

"I'm in and out of Bragg. For the past year I've been in Saigon."

"Saigon? You mean you're over there in the war?"

"We've got a saying, 'Don't knock it, it's the only war we've got.' "

138

"Oh, Hank, there's so much I'd like to ask you. You're married, aren't you?"

"Negative. I was, but it didn't take."

"Oh. I'm sorry."

"Nothing to be sorry about. I know *you're* married, of course. Did pretty well for yourself."

"I've been very fortunate, Hank. I've got Charles and two wonderful children and I'm . . . well, I'm very happy."

"Nobody could deserve it more."

Carol was moved; she *was* so damned lucky to have Charles and the children and the life she had. She remembered once when she and Hank had come within an inch of eloping and she wondered what insane life that might have led her to.

"Well, I've got a meeting to get to," Hank said. "It's been great talking to you."

"I'm so glad you called," Carol said. And she was. It was nice to remember a life she'd almost forgotten, the year with Hank, the year of football games and cheerleading and slumber parties and sweet madness in the back seat of his old Plymouth. Lovely memories, of another girl in another world.

"Listen, Carol, this meeting of mine should break up around four. Is there any chance you'd meet me for a drink?"

Naturally he would ask. And naturally she would accept.

He had said his meeting was "over near the White House" so she suggested they meet in the bar downstairs at the Hay-Adams. When she entered the big dark room a few minutes past four, there were several people at tables having drinks, but no Hank. Then she looked in the smaller room at the back, where the bartender was, and she saw him, sitting at a table, staring into his drink, and she stood for a moment in the doorway just looking at him. She almost hadn't recognized him. He had filled out, he was a tall, rugged-looking man of thirty-four.

"Sorry, miss. Men only in this room," the bartender called.

Hank jumped to his feet. "The lady's meeting me," he said sharply, and hurried across to Carol.

"I'm sorry, Carol," he said. "I didn't see you come in."

"You must have been thinking about Saigon."

139

He smiled, a big, easy smile. "As a matter of fact, I was. Come on, let's get a table in there."

She led the way to a corner table and he held her chair for her. The waitress came and Hank told her exactly how he wanted his martini and exactly what gin and what tonic should go into Carol's G & T.

Carol looked at him and almost laughed. It all seemed so strange. "You've . . . you've changed," she said.

"How so?"

"Oh, I guess I expected you to still be in jeans and a letter jacket and tossing a football around."

"It's been a long time, Carol. I got a little education at Ohio State, and I've gotten a lot more in the service. So I guess I have changed. But you haven't. You looked great the last time I saw you and you look maybe just a little bit greater today."

The compliment made her feel happy, warm. "Tell me where you've been," she said.

"Oh, everywhere. London for a few years. Then Africa for a while."

"When all that Congo stuff was going on?"

Hank hesitated. "That'd be a good guess."

"Oh, goodness, are you super-secret?"

"We're taught to be careful."

"Then I guess I shouldn't ask what you're doing in Vietnam."

"It'd be hard to explain."

"I always think of the Green Berets building bridges and giving out medicine to the villagers and all."

"There's some of that," Hank said. "Tell me about Birmingham. What's happened to all those people? I've completely lost touch."

Carol thought. "Well, I guess the most exciting story is Alice. You remember Alice?"

"Vividly."

"That's right, you went with her, didn't you? Well, maybe you won't be so surprised then. But she was at 'Bama, and she married this boy whose family practically owns this town in South Alabama. And they lived on the old plantation and Alice had four children and then—wham!—one day at a party in Mobile she met this Jewish writer and the next day she packed up the children and drove off to California with him."

"Then what happened?"

"Nothing. I mean, she's still in California with the writer and every-

140

body assumes they're living off her money and there's a big legal battle about the children and I guess there'll be a divorce."

"It doesn't surprise me," Hank said. "Alice liked excitement. Well, tell me another."

"That's the only very exciting story. Claire Hamilton married Bill Rush and he's a lawyer. Suzy Napier married Fred Wofford and he's a dentist and they've got twins. I go back and everybody's got a lot of kids and they play tennis at the club and do all the charities and cuss the government—they think Charles, my husband, is practically a Communist. I guess everybody's pretty content."

"But you wouldn't be."

"Down there? No. When I heard about Alice, I thought, There but for the grace of God go I."

Hank nodded. "You were smart to get out. You were always meant for better things than Birmingham had to offer."

"I guess I always felt that way."

"I felt that way too. I wanted excitement and I wanted to see the world and the army's let me. I'm the luckiest man I know."

"You really like the military?"

"It's not just that. It's that right now I'm part of the most important struggle in the world."

"You mean . . . ?"

"I mean Vietnam. I mean freedom versus Communism."

Carol frowned. "I wish I knew more about the war," she said. "It's hard to know what to believe."

Hank leaned forward, his face intent. "There's nothing hard about it, Carol. It's like if ten men walked in that door right now with guns and took everyone's money and shot down anybody that protested. That's all the VC is, a bunch of terrorists. Murderers. I've seen things they've done that I wouldn't even repeat to a woman. All the people want is to be left alone. And all the government needs is another year or two to get itself together. And that's where we come in. To give the people there a chance for peace and freedom."

"It's good that you feel that way," Carol said. "That you believe in what you're doing. I guess my father felt that way. He was killed in World War II."

"I remember," Hank said. "And it's the same thing today, Carol. Stopping the Communists in Vietnam will be like stopping Hitler in Poland would have been."

141

Carol nodded and took a sip of her G & T. Mostly she was confused by Vietnam, but she thought what Hank said made sense. She didn't like the war but it seemed to her that we were in it and we'd just have to keep on until we'd won. She was impressed by Hank's intensity—after all, he'd been there, so he ought to know what he was talking about.

"Well, this is a surprise."

Carol looked up and saw a very tall man standing by their table. Hank jumped up and the two men shook hands.

"Hello, Mr. Clayton."

"For Christ's sake, Hank, call me Joe. I'm not a general."

"This is Mrs. Pierce," Hank said.

"I know Carol," Joe Clayton said. "I didn't know *you'd* had the honor."

"We're old friends," Carol said. "How are you, Joe?"

"Oh, not bad. Busy."

Joe Clayton had aged since she first met him at Hickory Hill. He was still slender and boyish, but you could see the lines on his brow and around his eyes. He looked very tired. His name was turning up in the news more and more these days. There had been a story that he had broken with the Kennedys because of his loyalty to LBJ. There were stories about his increasing influence on Vietnam policy. There were stories too that he and Muffie were separated.

"Can you join us, Joe?"

"No, I've got to get back to the office. Listen, Hank, if you could come by a half hour early in the morning, we could kick things around before the meeting starts."

"Right. I'll be there."

"Fine," Joe Clayton said. "See you guys later. Best to Charles."

Carol smiled and wondered if Joe Clayton was thinking nasty thoughts about her meeting a handsome Green Beret for a drink. Well, he could just think them. She was having a good time—just as good a time as Charles, wherever he might be.

"You must be very important if you have meetings with Joe Clayton," she said.

"It's not that I'm important," Hank said. "It's that he's the kind of man who really wants to know what's happening in the field."

"You like him then?"

"Like him? Listen, I'm just a dogface doing his bit out in the bush, but Joe Clayton is someone who sees the big picture, someone who's shaping how the world's going to be for the next century. Right now, Joe Clayton is doing as much to defeat Communism as any man in the world."

The religious fervor was back in his eyes. Carol was impressed but a little frightened too by his intensity.

Hank, as if reading her thought, sat back in his chair and relaxed. "Excuse me. I didn't mean to make a speech. Maybe that's what being in Washington does to people."

"I guess Washington is pretty dull to someone who's used to London and Saigon."

"It's not so bad. Last night I hit a couple of the discotheques in Georgetown and they were lively enough."

"What're they like?" Carol asked.

"You haven't been?"

"Charles isn't a dancer."

"Well, the music is loud and the dance floor is the size of a postage stamp."

"Who was your dancing companion?" she asked, and immediately was sorry she had. It was probably just some stewardess or something like that.

"Oh, just a girl I met here," Hank said. "You might know her."

He mentioned the name of a divorcee who was a friend of Jackie Kennedy's and was much discussed in the local society columns. Carol felt a twinge of jealousy.

They talked a little longer, of Birmingham and of Washington and of the war, pleasant talk, interesting, made all the more pleasant by how very attractive Hank Bailey was. He had certainly come a long way from Birmingham—Carol remembered, not without amusement, that her mother had once declared that Hank would never amount to anything. Well, from the way it sounded, he'd be a general before too long.

She looked at her watch. It was five-thirty.

"Goodness, I've got to fly."

Hank got up, pulled back her chair, tossed some bills on the table, and walked up to the lobby with her.

"Do you need a ride?" he asked.

"I'll get a cab right out front. Can I drop you anywhere?"

"No," he said. "I'm staying here at the Hay-Adams."

143

"Oh." And she thought: How easy it would be for you to ask me up to your room for another drink or to show me your war trophies or something. But there had been none of that, not even a hint. He had been a perfect gentleman.

"Well, you certainly travel in style."

"I might as well enjoy myself when I can," Hank said. "I'll be back in the boonies soon enough."

"How long will you be here?"

"Until Tuesday, I think."

She smiled at him. It was time to go. Perhaps she'd never see him again. She thought of giving him a kiss, just an old-friend kiss on the cheek, but he had been very proper and she didn't want to do anything that might be misunderstood. So she put out her hand and he took it.

"Good-by, Hank," she said. "I can't tell you how much I've enjoyed it."

"It's been a thrill for me, Carol, to see that a lovely girl has become such a lovely woman."

Now she felt tears stinging in her eyes and she wished she had kissed him. "Good-by, Hank," she said, "good luck." And she turned and pushed her way out the revolving door.

She kept him from her mind until quite late that evening. She fixed hamburgers for the children and they watched "Car 54, Where Are You?" and finally she read them their stories, a chapter of *Huckleberry Finn* for Hugh, a chapter of *Charlotte's Web* for Liza, and put them to bed.

She had been edgy all evening and when the kids were finally down she poured herself some cognac and sat down and after a few minutes she realized why. She was waiting for the phone to ring. She saw his game now. He was a big ladies' man—that was obvious enough —and he'd expected her to throw herself into his arms. Plenty of women probably did. But she hadn't, so now he'd call her back and suggest that they meet again.

And then what do you do?

That depends on him. If he's crude, if he just says, "Hey, why don't you drop by my room?" then I'll tell him to go peddle his papers. But if he's more subtle about it, if he suggests lunch or maybe a drive . . . well, that'd be something else.

What would it be?

Well, let's just wait and see. Let's just keep cool and wait and see.

And while she waited, she thought of that year with Hank. She remembered the year in a kind of haze, a year when she floated through classes and sorority meetings and football games and the only reality had been Hank and the hours they'd spent discovering each other in the back seat of his Plymouth. Or on a blanket on the ground. Or in a bed if one was available—it didn't seem to matter then. In memory, that year had been one long wonderful orgy—God, what madness, two children at play. It was a miracle she hadn't gotten pregnant. But what a year it had been. Even now, all these years later, she remembered how good he had been, how her body had been warm for hours after they made love, how they could just go on and on forever.

He'd still be that good, wouldn't he?

What an awful thing to think.

Well, you *are* thinking it. And you're hoping *he's* thinking it too.

Well, why not? Yes, he's probably *better* now, if that's possible. He's surely had plenty of experience. Probably that's why he hasn't called. I'm just one of a hundred to him.

No. You and he shared something special. You still do. Why else would he have called in the first place?

Then why hasn't he called back?

Because you blew your chance. There were a dozen times when you could have said something or touched his hand or just given him the slightest encouragement, and he'd have taken it from there.

It's his responsibility to make the first move. He called me and he can say something. Just the slightest little something. And if he's really interested, he'd better call back, and do it pretty soon.

You idiot, he's not going to call at ten o'clock at night. He's out at some discotheque with his little jet-set divorcee. And she can just have him. To hell with him!

Just then the phone rang.

She ran to it.

Don't answer it too fast. It'll look like you were sitting there waiting for it to ring.

You idiot, if you don't answer it, it'll wake the children.

She caught it just before the third ring.

"Hello?"

"Hi, beautiful. I'm stuck at the airport in Paducah so I thought I'd check in. Everything okay?"

"Charles!"

"Well, who did you expect? Richard Nixon?"

"Oh, Charles, Charles . . ." She began to sob.

"What's wrong? Are you crying?"

"Oh, Charles. I . . . it's just that I've had the most impossible day. Cy Hollenbeck wants to change the show around and put me on with Eddie Waters, the weather man, and I've had cramps and there was this idiot I interviewed and—"

"Look, I could probably come home tomorrow if it's really serious. I've got the strawberry festival on Monday but . . ."

"No, no. I'll be all right. Go to the strawberry festival, I'll be all right. I'm just . . . tired."

"How're the kids?"

"They're fine. Hugh thinks Huck Finn is a jerk and Liza wants a bicycle."

"In Georgetown she wants a bicycle. Listen, why don't you take them to the zoo tomorrow? I've been promising them for a month."

"Okay. That's a good idea."

"Swell. Good night, baby. Sleep tight."

"Good night, darling."

She put down the phone, rinsed out her cognac glass, and went quickly to bed.

The next morning was bright and a little cooler than it had been. Carol recalled briefly her thoughts of the night before, dismissed it all as madness, and took the kids to the zoo. They had lunch at a Hot Shoppe and it was past three when they got home.

Well, he probably called while you were out, she thought. Of course, that's the real reason you spent the morning out. It's much simpler that way. Avoid any complications. You had an interesting talk with him, and that's the place to end it.

She took the kids to a Walt Disney movie that evening and when she got to bed that night she slept very soundly and dreamed not at all of Major Hank Bailey.

It was on Sunday afternoon that she began to think of calling him.

Why not? she asked herself. It'd be fun to see him once more, to talk some more, to get to know each other better.

146

Do you want to go to bed with him?

Well, what's so wrong with that? Why shouldn't I have a little fun? Charles wouldn't waste five seconds searching his soul if he'd run across an old girl friend who wanted to go to bed with him.

He's a man.

Well, what's the difference? They all say, "Don't be a girl." Okay, I won't be a girl. I'll do just what I want to do, just like they do.

What about your period? That's a lovely complication.

Well, it's almost over. We'll just play that one by ear. If he wants it . . .

Don't be vulgar!

Well, why not? Why can't I even *think* like I want to? God, how can you live in this world and not be vulgar?

You can try. What about the children? Won't that be just lovely? You hire a baby sitter for them and go off to screw some soldier in a hotel room. Oh, you're a fine little mother.

Good God, what am I? A person with a life to lead or just somebody's mother? Can't I do what I want to do just once in my life?

How do you think you'll feel the next day?

Ha! Pretty good, probably.

Really?

Okay, maybe I'll feel guilty. But I *shouldn't*. Nobody should feel guilty for doing what they want to do. Damn them, they mold you and shape you with their schools and their rules and their sermons and their traditions until you don't know who you are or what you're supposed to be. They give you a conscience and don't bother to give themselves one. They brainwash you from the day you're born and try to make you into a little ninny. But I won't play their game. I'm going to do what I please. And if I want to go to bed with Hank, then I'll just go to bed with him.

You could at least wait for him to call you.

He *did* call. He called and asked me for a drink and I sat there like a bump on a log waiting for him to beg me to go to bed with him. I could have at least showed a little interest. What an idiot he must think I am.

He might think you're a lady.

A lady! That's just what I need. As my dear husband would say, bullshit.

All right, are you going to call him or not?

Yes. Yes, I am. Why shouldn't I?

Carol dropped her cigarette into an ashtray and went to the kitchen telephone. She could see the children at play in the back yard. She looked up the number of the Hay-Adams. She studied it a moment, then underlined it with a ballpoint pen.

Do you really want to do this? Or have you just got yourself all worked up over nothing? Maybe you should think about it some more. Wait till tomorrow. She picked up a newspaper and began to read it at random. Sandy Koufax had pitched a no-hitter. She threw down the paper. Good Lord, I'm going mad. Over one phone call.

She seized the telephone and dialed the number.

"Major Bailey's room, please."

There was a click, a silence, three rings, then another click.

"One mo-ment, puh-leeze."

"What's the matter, Operator?"

But the operator was gone.

"Hello?" a man's voice said at last.

"Hank? It's Carol. I just . . ."

"This is Mr. Bowen, the desk clerk. Major Bailey checked out about an hour ago."

"Checked out?"

"Yes. If you like I can—"

"No, no. Thank you." Carol put the phone back on the wall and looked out the window at the children at play on the swing set, Hugh hanging by his knees from the crossbar, Liza swinging high, her skirt flapping in the wind, her long legs straight out before her, her toes skyward, a golden girl-child, as her mother once had been. Then Carol sat down at the kitchen table and put her head on her arms and cried bitter tears until all her tears were gone.

3

JULY 1965

It was early on a hot Saturday morning and Charles Pierce had a hangover, the all too usual Saturday morning hangover that followed the all too usual Friday night unwinding, but he was nonetheless one of the handful of Senators present on the Senate floor. He was on duty. Most of the Senators wanted badly to adjourn for the midsummer break, to flee the Washington heat like sensible men, but a dozen Democrats, Charles among them, were filibustering the Social Security bill. A coalition of Republicans and Southern Democrats had cut eighty million dollars in welfare funds from the bill, and the liberals were determined to stall its passage until they could get the money restored. That was why Charles was on duty this Saturday morning. If the conservatives brought up the Social Security bill, his job was to start filibustering.

But he assumed it wouldn't be brought up as long as he was on hand, so he glanced through his mail while the other Senators droned through some routine business. His mail was routine too. A tobacco farmer protesting the bill to regulate cigarette advertising. A World War I veteran who wanted to bomb Hanoi. A letter from his aunt Molly, who said her health was good and her son Eddie was joining the army.

Charles looked up and saw Al Kline, his new AA, coming toward him. Kline was small, dark, quick, alert even at this ungodly hour.

"What's happening?" Kline asked.

"Just routine stuff," Charles told him.

Kline looked skeptical. "Just now, as I was coming in, they were passing something. Wait a minute, I'll check."

He walked rapidly to the clerk's desk at the front of the chamber. He spoke quickly to the clerk, the clerk gave a more leisurely reply, and Kline slapped his hand down on the desk. Charles jumped to his feet and joined them.

The AA was white-faced. "Senator, they just passed it."

"Passed what?"

"The Social Security bill."

"What?"

"That's correct, Senator," the clerk drawled. "Senator Montrose made the motion and the bill passed without objection."

"What do you mean, without objection?" Charles said, his voice rising. What had happened was just beginning to sink in.

The clerk, a plump old Alabaman who'd been there forever, looked at Charles blankly.

"What's the trouble here?" Tom Montrose asked.

"The trouble, Senator," Charles said angrily, "is that you just passed a bill without notifying me. You knew why I was here."

"Boy, you was sitting right there and didn't say a thing. You think we send out engraved invitations?"

"I want that bill called back up."

"Called back up?" Montrose repeated. "Ain't you learned the rules yet, boy? The bill has done passed."

Charles wished he could grab Tom Montrose by the lapels and shake his teeth out. *These bastards have made a fool of me.* The realization was sinking in and it made him feel physically weak.

"I thought this was a gentlemen's club," Charles said coldly.

"Oh, it is, it is," Tom Montrose said, his little eyes sparkling. "It's just that some gentlemen is smarter than others."

Charles turned on his heel and left. It was that or hit him.

"Well, there's old Charles," Rip Horton said that afternoon. "Screwed, Jewed, and tattooed."

"Those sons of bitches," Charles said, sinking down into Rip's easy chair. "They're gonna get theirs."

"They've been getting theirs for a long time."

"I'm pissed, Rip. Really pissed. I thought they at least played the game fair."

"They play the game to win, just like you and me."

Charles managed a grim smile. "What do you mean, 'you and me'? You didn't give us any help on that one."

"Ah stayed clear of that one," Rip agreed. "Ah had friends for it and Ah had friends against it, and Ah always help mah friends."

Charles lapsed into silence.

"Ah wouldn't worry so much about it if Ah was you," Rip said. "It was just a Bobby bill, anyway."

"It wasn't a Bobby bill. He was one of the group, that's all."

"Yeah, and he was the one who'd've got all the publicity if you'd won."

"Well, I don't know what to do about that."

"Stop helping him, that'd be one thing."

"Rip, sometimes Bob and I are going to be for the same things. Maybe he'll get more publicity. I don't see any way around it."

"Ah'll tell you this," Rip said. "Ah'm sick of that little bastard thinking he can come in here and take over. Hell, if he farts he gets on Huntley-Brinkley with it."

"He's been making some damn good speeches. And when he talks about the Indians and the migrants, he gets publicity for the problems that the rest of us could never get."

"Publicity for hisself, you mean. Ain't you figured it out yet, pal? The son of a bitch is running for President!"

Charles waved his hand impatiently. "Okay, damn it, let him run. I can't help it."

Rip leaned forward, his face colder than Charles had ever seen it. "Listen, buddy, you and me are gonna be sucking hind tit to Bobby the rest of our lives unless we get together and take him down a few notches. He figgers he gets his eight years, then Teddy gets his eight years, then God damn maybe it's Caroline and little John-John's turn."

Rip leaned back in his chair and lit a cigar. Charles stared silently out the window. He was wondering if the papers would pick up how Montrose had tricked him that morning. It was bad enough for the Senate to know he had been made a fool of, but far worse if the whole world heard about it.

151

"You know, Rip," he said after a moment, "you say Bob's running for President, but I don't see where he's got anything to run for until '72, and that's a long way off."

"There's a little election scheduled for '68," Rip said. "Or had you heard?"

"I'd heard. And there's also a fellow named Johnson I figure will be running again."

"That's three years off," Rip said. "A lot could happen."

"Like what?"

Rip shrugged. "Like the Man's got a bad heart."

"He's too mean to die."

"A lot else could happen."

"Such as?"

"Such as this Vietnam thing. Lyndon still thinks he's gonna win him a glorious victory over there and Ah ain't so sure he is."

"They say the bombing has the other side on the ropes."

"Yeah, that's what they say. But Ah heard some news the other day that don't quite agree with that."

"What?"

Rip leaned forward. "This has got to be confidential, old buddy."

"I understand," Charles said. Rip loved to play these games. It was annoying as hell, but most of the time his information was good.

"Well, Ah was having a little talk with Uncle John yesterday," Rip said. Uncle John was Senator Stennis, who ranked very high on the Armed Services Committee. "Ah was having a talk with Uncle John an' he told me"—he lowered his voice—"he told me Big Daddy is about to send a hundred thousand combat troops over there."

Charles looked at Rip blankly. "A hundred thousand men? I don't believe it."

Rip shrugged. "Maybe Uncle John made it up."

"Do you belive it?"

"Ah've been trying to tell you, Lyndon's got a wild hair up his ass on this Vietnam thing."

Charles was stunned. He had been so busy on legislation that year that he had not tried to think about Vietnam. He didn't want to think about Vietnam. Bill after bill was passing, legislative history was being made, and he just kept hoping that Vietnam would go away.

"Jesus Christ," he said to Rip. "We've had our advisers over there and all that, but what happens if we send in a hundred thousand men?"

Rip sucked on his cigar and blew a perfect smoke ring, one that rose slowly above his head like an improbable halo. "Old buddy," he said after a moment, "Ah'd say that's when the shit hits the fan."

4

AUGUST 1965

They arrived at Lafayette Park at noon and stopped for a moment to study the crowd.

"How many are there?" Beth asked.

"I'd say six or eight hundred."

"More are still coming in," Beth said. "And it's not all kids. There're some people in coats and ties and everything."

"I wish there were more blacks," Bill said. "I talked to them but it's hard to make them understand."

"It's a good start," Beth said. "Come on, let's go up by the speaker's stand. I see some TV cameras."

They sat down in the shade of an oak tree and waved at friends and watched the crowd grow larger. Beth let her eyes scan the buildings around the park, the lovely old Federalist buildings along Jackson Place, the Peace Corps building, the huge fortress of the Chamber of Commerce, the lovely yellow-walled St. John's Church. Most of all her eyes were drawn across Pennsylvania Avenue to the White House. That was why they were here, to reach the people inside the White House, to make them listen, to make them understand. Beth thought of a spring day when she was eight or nine and her mother had taken her to the White House for an Easter-egg roll that Bess Truman had given. She tried to imagine herself a child rolling eggs on that lawn but the image eluded her.

The program began at twelve-thirty with a half hour's silent vigil. Beth didn't care much for the idea of a silent vigil because she didn't think those men in the White House were going to be reached by silence but by shouts and numbers and marching feet. But she looked at Bill, sitting Indian style on the grass, his head bowed in prayer, and while he prayed she thought about him. They had been together for three years now and Beth had never regretted a moment of it. It had been wonderful to watch Bill grow and change, to meet each new challenge, to discover new sides of himself. He had come such a long way, from a farm in Kansas to where he was today. It was the Peace Corps that had opened new vistas to him, had shown him that he wanted to work with people, not with crops and livestock. So they'd opened Kennedy House and already it was a success. The SDS kids who were starting community-organizing projects around the country often came to talk to Bill and get ideas from him. The poverty program people were impressed too. Right now there was a grant pending that would triple the Kennedy House budget and make it a show place in the "war on poverty." Beth guessed that Bill's future—their future—lay in that direction. He would become a leader in the new social-action movement, eventually would become an administrator of some big anti-poverty agency, maybe would even teach and write books too. She smiled at the thought of his pending celebrity. Maybe they would even have to get married.

She smiled at that too, at the thought of how her marriage would please her mother. Not marriage to *Bill,* just *marriage.* Her mother had been outraged to learn Beth was living with Bill. But she'd quickly tuned it out, as she tuned out everything that she found unpleasant. She now told her friends that Beth was "living with some girls near DuPont Circle" and "doing social work." That was fine with Beth. She didn't want to hurt her mother; she only wanted to live her life her way. Sometimes she thought of how far she'd come in a few years, how she'd left behind her parents' world and discovered a new life in a new world. It had begun in Ecuador, when she met Bill and learned about the real world where people lived in fear and pain and ignorance. Beth had never known that before, never really known it; her very expensive education had never taught her about those things. But now she knew. Now her first twenty-two years, the schools and the boys and the dances and the luxuries, all that seemed unreal to her. She couldn't even despise it because she couldn't believe she had really lived that life. It was like a dream from which she'd finally wakened. She had left nothing behind in that other world that mattered to her. Bill had shown her the important things: love and friends and being honest and helping people. He had shown her that they could change the world if they would do their part and if all the others of their generation would do their part. And they would.

When the prayer vigil ended, songs and speeches began. Joan Baez sang and was wonderful and Beth wished there'd been more Baez and less speeches, because the August sun was beating down and soon all that they said about the bombing and the napalming began to run together in your mind. The only speech she cared about was Bill's and he was very brief and low-key. He welcomed the people to Washington and talked about the need for non-violent action to bring the government to its senses.

A. J. Muste was the last speaker. He was a very old, very frail man, and his voice was so weak you could hardly hear him. Beth didn't know much about Muste, only that he'd been a pacifist leader for a long time and that the New York people practically worshiped him. She listened to him respectfully, but still she was glad when he ended his speech and said it was time for the march to begin.

Slowly, they all rose up from the grass, stretching stiff muscles, smiling nervously at each other, and about half of them followed Muste across the street to the sidewalk in front of the White House. The other half stayed behind in the park, fearful of the rumored arrests. Beth and Bill crossed the street just behind Muste, hand in hand. Beth was proud and excited. No President could ignore this many people. She wished Johnson would come outside and meet with them and see how deeply they felt. They would treat him politely. There was still time for him to end the war and do all the good things he wanted to do. That was why they were here today, to make him think, to save him from himself or from his advisers or whatever incomprehensible madness was causing this war.

Muste stopped at the gate outside the West Wing and spoke to a guard.

"We have come to see the President."

The guard peered at Muste for a moment in disbelief, then shrugged and went inside the gatehouse to make a phone call. Muste waited at the gate, surrounded by reporters and photographers.

"Mr. Muste," a reporter called out. "Are the Communists in control of this demonstration?"

"No, they are not," Muste said.

"But you don't deny there are Communists in the crowd?"

"There might be," Muste conceded, and the reporters all scribbled in their notebooks.

You idiots, Beth thought. Ask him about the war. Ask him about napalm and bombing. Why did reporters never see what the real story was? There were more questions for Muste—stupid questions, insulting questions—and then the questions stopped as they saw the door of the West Wing swing open and a tall man in a seersucker suit start down the driveway with long, confident strides.

"Who's that?" Bill whispered.

"His name is Joe Clayton," Beth told him. "My brother knows him."

Joe Clayton felt good. He had not expected this assignment but he relished it. He thought himself a man of action, and he was happy to confront these demonstrators, this ragtag band of pacifists, kids, and kooks. Of course the confrontation was an uneven one, for the government held all the cards, had all the options. They had held a staff meeting that morning on this demonstration and, unable to agree, had taken the decision to the President. Some of them, citing FBI reports of Communist infiltration and possible violence, urged that all the demonstrators should be arrested. Others wanted a milder approach. Don't overreact. Don't make martyrs of them. If they want to sit down on the sidewalk, let them sit there till Christmas.

The President chose conciliation. The President had signed the voting rights bill that morning and his mood was expansive. So he chose the kill-them-with-kindness route and he chose Joe Clayton as the implementer of that policy. And Joe was proud to be.

Yet as he neared the White House gates, as he saw the faces of the demonstrators beyond the fence, he felt his pride turning to scorn, then anger, at the ignorance and the cowardice that had brought these people here. They were scum at best, traitors at worst. He bit his lip, determined to keep his temper down.

"Mr. Muste? I'm Joseph Clayton. I understand you have a petition."

"We have a Declaration of Conscience for the President."

"We can admit a small delegation to present the petition."

"How small?"

"No more than seven."

"Seven is not enough," Muste said.

"It is the maximum we can permit."

"For what reason?"

"For reasons of security."

"We are non-violent," Muste said. "It is the government that practices violence."

Joe Clayton felt his anger rising. Who was this old man to tell him of violence? What about the VC atrocities against helpless villagers? Why were these people here, encouraging Hanoi, telling the world that America was divided? He fought to keep his voice down. "Mr. Muste, this government is protecting the right of millions of Vietnamese to be free of Communist domination. You and your followers would do well to consider that." He saw the reporters scribbling and he was pleased with the exchange. But he was not here to debate. "Now, unless you wish to send a delegation inside, I'll get back to my work."

"No, no delegation will be sent."

"Then good day," Joe Clayton said curtly, and turned on his heel. He felt good as he marched back up the driveway to the West Wing. The record was clear. The White House had invited them in and they had refused. Now they could go to hell.

Behind him, on the sidewalk, Muste and the people around him, the ones who had vowed to commit civil disobedience, began to sit down on the sidewalk. Bill and Beth sat down. They had discussed it that morning and Beth had been skeptical about the civil disobedience. Why be arrested for nothing? But it was not for nothing, Bill had said. It was a statement of belief. It would impress the President and it would encourage others to take a stand. He had spoken with intensity, for there was a moralistic side to Bill that Beth was just coming to understand, a stubbornness, a determination to follow his beliefs wherever they led. Beth was more the pragmatist, the compromiser; she guessed she had inherited that much from her father. But when Bill sat down on the hot sidewalk Beth sat down beside him. Because she loved him. Because she guessed he was right. And because she had her pride, and if he was going to be arrested, she wasn't going to be left behind.

But there were no arrests. The people sat and they sang, and before long Beth was restless. She was ready to be arrested but she was not ready to sit on the sidewalk all night singing "We Shall Overcome." So she was glad when, after an hour or so, Muste got up and said he thought they had made their point, and with his followers slowly shuffled off toward Seventeenth Street.

Beth leaned over and whispered to Bill, "Let's go. My bottom's numb."

He grinned at her. "So's mine." They got up and stretched. As they walked away, Bill invited some SDS kids from out of town to join them for dinner at Kennedy House. Soon there were a dozen of them, marching up Connecticut Avenue, excited now, laughing and joking, unwinding from the tension of the confrontation.

"They were afraid to arrest us," someone said.

"No, they were smart," someone else said. "It would have been better if they'd arrested us."

"Man, I can do without another night in jail."

"It all depends on the publicity," Beth said. "If we get enough publicity this way, we don't need the arrests."

At Kennedy House they sprawled in chairs and on the floor. Bill brought out beer and a gallon of Gallo wine. The SDS kids from Newark and Cleveland told about the rent strikes and boycotts and police harassment. About seven o'clock Beth and another girl served a dinner of hot dogs and beans and after that they listened to Dylan and one boy produced a joint and passed it around the circle. When it got to Beth she passed it on without smoking. She was happy enough just to be here with Bill and their friends and to think of all they were doing and would do in the months ahead. The party was about to break up, around midnight, when someone brought in the first edition of the *Post* and they all gathered around to read the story on the day's demonstration. Their story had made the front page, which was good, and they were excited too by two other stories in the paper, one about a civil rights march in Mississippi and another about some kids who'd blocked a troop train in Oakland. Beth was thrilled. There were thousands of them now, all over America. Nothing could stop them now.

When everyone had gone, Beth and Bill went up to their bedroom. Bill yawned and slipped off his jeans and shirt and stood in his shorts, winding the alarm clock.

"What happens tomorrow?" Beth asked him.

"Workshops at the Washington Monument grounds."

"When's the march to the Capitol?"

"That's the last day, Monday. Nagasaki Day."

"Maybe we should have our own special march to my brother's office."

"Maybe we should. What's he say about the war these days?"

Beth shook her head. "I don't know. He just talks around it. He's so impressed by all the legislation that's passing that he just tunes the war out."

"Most people do," Bill said.

Beth slipped off her clothes. She always slept naked on hot summer nights. Bill was more modest. He would wear his shorts to bed, then slip them off when the lights were out and they began to make love—his Midwestern modesty, she called it. She looked at him now, lying in bed, leafing through the *New Republic,* and suddenly she wanted him, wanted him deep inside her, and it was just as she was going to turn out the light that she noticed the letter on the bureau.

"What's this?" she asked.

"Nothing," he said. "Come on to bed."

"It looks official," she said. "What *is* it?"

Bill sat up cross-legged in the bed and stared at her for a minute before answering. "It is official," he said. "It's from my draft board."

"What about?"

"About me being drafted."

"I thought you had a deferment."

"I thought so too. My board hadn't been drafting Peace Corps returnees. But now Johnson's upped the draft call and they want me."

"What will you do?"

"I don't know."

Beth wanted to cry out in frustration. How could he be so calm about it? What was happening?

"Well, what are the alternatives? There are a lot of ways to beat the draft, aren't there?"

"One alternative would be to do nothing."

"Nothing? How could you do nothing? They'd just come and get you, wouldn't they?"

"I guess so."

"Then how could you do nothing?"

"Because as soon as you do anything at all, as soon as you start talking about deferments, you're playing their game. You're admitting the legitimacy of the draft, of the government, but you're asking them to give you an easy out. Well, I don't admit the legitimacy of the government, not as long as the war goes on, and I don't recognize their authority to draft me to fight in this war. So maybe I should just ignore them."

"Bill, that just doesn't make sense."

"It makes sense. What you mean is it's not practical."

"Couldn't you say you're a conscientious objector and get deferred that way?"

"Maybe. But, like I said, I'd be granting the legitimacy of the system. Besides, I'm not sure I qualify as a CO."

"You're against the war, aren't you?"

"This war. Not necessarily all wars."

"I know. They give exemptions to married men, don't they? Or to fathers? We could get married and have a baby and that'd solve everything!"

Bill laughed silently. "Wouldn't that be a fine reason to be married? To beat the draft. Do I let the government into our bed? Into your womb? No. No, no, no. It isn't right."

"Then what do you do?"

"I don't know yet. But I know this. People are going to have to resist this war and that means resisting the draft. I may be one of the people who has to take a stand."

"Bill, they can put you in prison!"

"I know that. But they can't make a murderer out of me."

She threw herself down on the bed beside him. "Bill, I love you and I need you and we all need you and you can't just let them take you away."

He touched her hair, lifting it with his fingers, feeling how soft it was. He was sorry to have caused her tears, but he didn't know what he could say except what he had said. "Don't worry," he told her. "It'll be all right."

He turned out the light and they held each other close and Beth tried to take him so far inside her that he could never leave her, but when their love-making was over and he was asleep she lay awake for a long time. She was frightened and confused. He was so stubborn, so determined to do what was right. Sometimes you had to compromise to get what you wanted. She had to make him understand that. She didn't know how but she would find a way. She loved him too much to let him go. She would have to save him, save him from the government's madness, save him even from his own terrible pride.

161

5

It was supposed to be a special day but soon it was as screwed up as every other day. Charles's appointment schedule got blown out of the water just before noon when his secretary called with the unexpected news that his cousin Eddie was in the reception room.

"Oh, my God. Okay, call the tobacco guy and cancel lunch. Tell him my wife had twins or something. Send Eddie on in."

He entered a moment later, a tall, gangling, jug-eared boy in a Pfc. uniform.

"What brings you to Washington?" Charles asked, waving the boy into a chair.

"I just finished basic up at Dix and I'm heading home on leave and I just thought I'd stop off for a day."

"Well, it looks like the army agrees with you."

Eddie grinned his easy, country-boy grin. "Yes, sir. I put on ten pounds in basic. The army feeds you right good."

"Is that the sharpshooter's medal?"

"Yep. I was always right handy with a rifle. Lord, some of those city boys, they couldn't hit the broad side of a barn."

Charles smiled. "How about some lunch, Eddie? We don't want you getting hungry."

Eddie frowned uncertainly. "Well, I know how busy you are. I just meant to say hello."

"No problem," Charles said, and slipped his coat on. They walked over to the dining room reserved for Senators and their guests.

162

"Try the bean soup," Charles said when the waitress came. "And have a beer if you want one."

"I'll just have milk, please. And the soup and maybe a couple of hamburgers, all the way. And that chile sounds good too."

The waitress smiled and wrote down his order. Charles asked for a salad and iced tea—he was dieting, more or less.

"How's your time, Eddie? I can take you around the Capitol, and maybe we can get you into the White House this afternoon."

"I haven't got the time, Charles. My bus leaves at two. I walked around town this morning and looked at some of the monuments."

"How'd you like the big city?"

"Well, downtown there, it sort of looks like the colored people have taken over."

"Yeah, the District is about seventy per cent Negro."

"I saw this one colored boy walking along with a white girl, *holding hands,* right there on the street. Boy, they'd play heck doing that back home."

"Are you headed for Vietnam, Eddie?"

"Yes, sir."

"How do you feel about it?"

"I'll tell you, I'm all fired up. I didn't know much about Vietnam before, but they showed us these movies in basic that told how the Communists are trying to take over and if we don't stop 'em in Vietnam we'll just be fighting 'em later in Hawaii or someplace."

"Are most of the fellows that fired up?"

"Most of 'em. There was a few college boys who wised off but we could usually straighten *them* out pretty fast. Say, this soup is really good."

"How's everything back home, Eddie? How do people feel about the President now?" It was instinctive for him to pump people now. Most people liked to talk, were flattered to be asked their opinions.

"I guess everybody likes him pretty good. Except maybe for all this civil rights stuff. Molly's all shook up about that. She says all you see on TV any more is a bunch of colored agitators making a lot of threats. She says it seems like they don't let white folks on the news shows any more."

Their food came and Eddie made fast work on his chile and the first of his hamburgers.

"What are your plans when you get out?" Charles asked the boy.

163

"There's a fellow in Raleigh who's got a little garage I'd like to buy into. Then when I start to make some money I could get Molly out of that darn restaurant."

"Good luck. My father tried for years to get her into a better job, but she wouldn't hear of it."

"She's as independent as a hog on ice. But she's getting up in years and it's time I gave her some help."

Eddie was persuaded to have pie à la mode, and then Charles walked him over to Independence Avenue and pointed him down the hill toward the Greyhound station. He stood for a moment watching the boy march off with long, easy strides. He'd never known Eddie well, but he liked him. He thought the army was lucky to have Eddie; he'd make a good soldier. Yet as Charles walked back to his office he found himself disturbed by their talk. It seemed that Eddie's morale was higher than his own. Eddie was willing enough to go to Vietnam, but Charles didn't want him going there. Charles still supported the war, vaguely, with less and less enthusiasm, but he knew he didn't want Molly's son going off to fight, perhaps to die. The thought of Eddie dead was incredible. And yet there were more and more each week. Who the hell *was* fighting this war? No Senators' sons, that was for sure.

So Charles was not in the best of moods when Pat O'Neal came in that afternoon, and Pat's long-winded political gossip did nothing to improve his humor. Charles wondered how much he needed this man. How much did he know that Charles didn't know himself?

Pat O'Neal finally got to the point. "Charles, I was upset by this Hendricks business."

Charles waved his hand impatiently. "Look, Pat, I've got a small staff and I've got to have somebody in charge who'll run things right. Hendricks was screwing me up every time I turned around."

"And this Kline boy is better?"

"You're damn right he is. Hendricks was too set in his ways."

"You could have kept him on the staff."

"It wouldn't have worked. So I got him the subcommittee job."

"He could have got that for himself," Pat said. "And you could have eased him out more gently."

"I don't like to waste time, Pat."

164

"Sometimes, when you're dealing with people, you have to waste a little time."

Charles wondered just how much more of Pat O'Neal's free advice he could take in one afternoon.

"Hendricks has a lot of friends back in the state," Pat said.

"Kline'll make friends."

"Maybe not as fast."

"Okay, damn it, I know he's a Jew. But he's doing a tremendous job for me and if people don't like him because he's a Jew, to hell with them."

"It didn't help that he used to work for Bobby. You don't want people saying you're firing Kentuckians to hire Bobby Kennedy's rejects."

"Pat, as far as I'm concerned, the matter is closed. And unless you've got any urgent business, I happen to have one hell of a busy schedule today."

Pat O'Neal stood up. "Then I won't waste any more of your time." He started toward the door. Charles felt a pang of regret, but he didn't say anything. But when Pat got to the door he turned back. "Oh, I almost forgot, Charles. Happy birthday."

Charles grinned and crossed the room with his hand outstretched. "Thanks, Pat. It's good of you to remember."

"You planning a big celebration?"

"Not very big. Carol and I are going to the Jockey Club for dinner, that's all."

"How is Carol?"

"Oh, fine, fine. Big TV celebrity."

"She's a lovely young woman," Pat said. "Wish we could get her down to the state more. Well, order the best champagne. Thirty-five is a big milestone for a politician."

"How so?"

"Have you forgotten? Charles, as of today, you're old enough to be President."

Finally, at the end of the day, Bill Hall came in.

Charles looked across his desk at the young man and wondered why he'd never quite liked him. Probably because of this thing with Beth, living with her and never marrying her. But that might prove to be a blessing in disguise, now that this latest mess had come up.

"I understand you're involved in these teach-ins," he said.

"That's right," Bill said. "We think they're doing some good."

"Let me ask you something, Bill. You've done pretty well with this settlement house of yours. Wouldn't it be better if you just devoted your energies to that, instead of trying to stop the war too?"

"We think it's part of the same thing, Senator. Besides being immoral, the war's expensive. The money that's going for bombs and airplanes could be going for schools and hospitals."

"This Administration is building a lot of schools and hospitals."

"Not enough."

Hall's certitude annoyed Charles. These damn kids thought they knew it all. He decided to get down to business.

"Let me see whatever papers you have."

Hall handed some papers across the desk and Charles skimmed through them.

"Did you report for the physical?"

"No."

"Did you write them?"

"No."

"Do you realize you've already broken the law?"

"Yes."

Charles tossed the papers down. "Bill, I can't be your lawyer. But I've checked into this business, like I told Beth I would, and I can give you some preliminary advice."

"It's good of you."

"Let's understand each other," Charles said. "I'm doing this for Beth's sake. I don't want to see her hurt."

"Neither do I."

"Okay, let's get on with this. Tell me what your dealings have been with your draft board."

"I was deferred when I was in the Peace Corps. I guess I became 1-A when I got back, but my board wasn't drafting people who'd been in the Peace Corps. Then Johnson upped the draft calls, and I guess they changed their policy. Anyway, I got this notice."

"Which you ignored."

"Yes."

"Bill, do you want to go to prison?"

"No."

"Good. Let's talk about the alternatives."

166

"But I've got to say one thing at the outset, Senator. I don't want to go to prison, but I'll do that before I'll go into the army. And I'm not even sure I want to apply for conscientious objector status."

"Beth told me about that. Non-co-operation, is that what you call it? No commerce with the Devil?"

"Yes. People who choose non-co-operation simply ignore the draft."

"Until the FBI comes and hauls them off to jail, at which time it becomes a little hard to ignore."

"That's true."

"Well, if you choose non-co-operation, there's not much I can do for you."

"I'm not sure I'll do that," Bill said. "I'm not sure I've got the courage."

"Isn't it just a little other-worldly to pretend the system doesn't exist? From a practical point of view, isn't non-co-operation just playing into the government's hands?"

"I suppose so. From a practical point of view."

"Okay, let's talk about CO status. Are you against war in any form?"

Bill Hall frowned. "I don't know. I'm against this particular war."

"Would you have fought Hitler?"

"Probably. That's not the decision I face."

"No, but it's the kind of question you'll face if you go before your draft board seeking CO status. And they'll tell you you can't pick your wars, you've got to be against all wars to be a CO."

"I think there are just wars and unjust wars."

"Unhappily, the government tends to think any war it declares is by definition a just war. Okay. Do you believe in God?"

"Yes."

"That's good. Because the law says a 'belief in a Supreme Being' has to be the basis of your objection. But you've still waited damned late to apply for CO status."

"Maybe I should go to Canada."

"Do what?"

"Some guys are moving to Canada rather than be drafted."

"I hadn't heard that."

"The papers haven't picked it up yet. But that was a joke. I'm not going to Canada. Whatever happens, this is my country."

Charles felt troubled, uneasy. The idea of young men going to Canada or refusing to be drafted was new and disturbing to him. He thought back on his own military experience, a decade earlier. It had all been quite simple then. You went to college, then you did your military bit. Charles had spent two years at the Pentagon and it'd been a farce, but not an unpleasant time.

"Senator, if I'm tried, would it be here or back in Kansas?"

"Probably your lawyer could get it switched here, since you live here now."

"That'd be better. It'd shake my parents if I was tried at home."

"Who are your parents, Bill?"

"My father's a fairly prosperous farmer. A Republican. A Taft Republican, he'd say. He thought my joining the Peace Corps was wild-eyed radicalism."

"You know, it might not be a bad idea if you were tried back there. If your family's well known, it might help."

"No. I wouldn't do that to them."

It occurred to Charles that he was glad he was not representing Bill Hall. He wasn't exactly a model client.

"You understand, Bill, that even if you're granted CO status you still have to serve two years of alternative service, as a medic or in a hospital or something?"

"I understand. I know a fellow who's doing alternative service now."

"Who is he?"

"A kid named Tom Rodd who lives in Pittsburgh. The judge gave him a choice of five years in prison or two years as an orderly in a hospital."

"He was lucky."

"He's not so sure. One condition the judge put on it was that he couldn't take part in any demonstrations. Tom called me just before the White House demonstration. It was killing him not to be able to come. He told me he wasn't sure he could stand it another year."

"He's crazy if he doesn't."

"It's a matter of conscience, Senator. Tom has to live with his conscience and I have to live with mine and you have to live with yours."

"Do you think I should be having a hard time with mine these days?"

168

"I try not to judge other people, Senator. I'm having a hard enough time handling my own life."

"How many people are there like you and Rodd?"

"It's hard to say. I know of a few dozen who're facing charges now. There'll be more. There are an awful lot of people against this war."

"Bill, isn't it perhaps just a little presumptuous for young people who don't have a great deal of experience in foreign policy to announce that their government is wrong and a war is immoral?"

"Senator, I think it's presumptuous for the government to think it can send me off to kill innocent people."

"Some people think the issue is a little more complicated than that."

"I don't."

Charles saw no point in debating. He'd met other kids like this who thought every issue was black or white, right or wrong. But the world wasn't like that. Hell, he had his own doubts about Vietnam, but he didn't pretend it was an easy issue, that there wasn't merit to both sides of the argument. It was easy enough to take brave stands on principle when you were Bill's age, but it wasn't so easy when you found out how complicated the world was. His job was more difficult; his job was to study all the evidence and then make a judgment on what was best for the entire country, and the answer would more likely be gray than black or white. But that wasn't easy to explain to someone Bill's age, so he shrugged and gave Bill the name of a lawyer who'd agreed to take his case, then he shook the young man's hand and sent him on his way.

Dinner was good. They'd had some bad times that year, he knew that, the times when she resented his traveling and he resented her not accepting it . . . but this was one of the good times. The food was good and the waiters were polite and they got a little drunk and held hands across the table and the chef came out for their congratulations and the owner joined them for a final brandy.

Finally they were home and he watched her undress and walk naked to her dressing table to brush her hair. She had such a lovely body.

"Do you remember the time I counted the freckles on your back?"

"Could I forget?"

"I got to a hundred before I got distracted."

"Do I distract you?"

"Is the Pope a Catholic?"

"Don't change the subject."

"You distract me. Come to bed and I'll show you how much you distract me."

She slipped into bed and he began to touch her the way she liked most to be touched.

"Tonight was nice," he whispered.

"Ummm."

"There'll be more nights like this. All this traveling won't go on forever."

"Darling, make love, not speeches."

"Okay."

And it was good, very good, the kind that happened too rarely any more. She laughed aloud with pleasure when they finished, and curled his hair with her fingertips.

"Happy birthday."

"That wasn't bad for an old man, was it?"

"You've got a few years left."

"Were you worried?"

"Not any more."

"Don't worry. I'll be like Tolstoi, still wanting it three times a day when I'm eighty."

"Promises, promises."

She kissed him and rolled over and was soon asleep. He lay awake for a few minutes, all content, thinking that thirty-five wasn't a bad age, old for a baseball player but young for a politician, and he drifted to sleep promising himself to be better to Carol in the future, smiling at the thought of all the good days and good nights that were still to come.

6

"Will you sign the letter, Charles?"

Charles sank a little farther down into his chair. He felt trapped. "I don't know, Peter. I honestly don't know what to do."

Peter Wilson leaned forward intently. "We need you, Charles. We won't get any Southerners, but a couple of border-state names, you, maybe Gore, maybe Yarborough, would help a lot."

"How many do you have so far?" Charles asked.

"Fifteen for sure. Six or eight possibles."

"Is Bob signing? Or Ted?"

Peter jerked his hand impatiently. "You know how they are. They'll send their own letter. But we've got Bartlett and Metcalf and Young and Gruening and Morse and McGovern and . . ."

"Not exactly the power elite, is it?"

"It's a start," Peter Wilson said. "Listen, Charles, it's a very polite letter, a very modest request. All we're asking is that he continue his own bombing pause. I figure we're helping him, offsetting some of the Pentagon pressure."

"Don't expect any thank-you notes," Charles said. "When he gets this letter he'll blow his stack."

"Let him," Peter Wilson said grimly. *"We've got to stop this bombing."*

Peter began to pace about the office. Charles had never seen him so upset. Finally he stopped and managed a grin. "Charles, do you have anything to drink?"

171

"Sure," Charles said, and got up and poured them both some scotch. Two Senators, a hard decision, a quiet drink together. A ritual.

"Tell me how you feel, Peter," he said. "How far are you prepared to go with this thing?"

"I'll go all the way, Charles. How do I feel? I feel a kind of constant pain. I guess I feel guilt, because my country is committing this monstrous wrong and I can't seem to do anything about it. I watch the news every night and it almost drives me out of my mind. It's like I'm witnessing an endless atrocity right before my eyes and I'm helpless to stop it." He shut his eyes and held his drink against his forehead as if its coolness might ease his pain. "Do you feel any of that, Charles? Have you reached that point yet?"

Charles had listened to Peter with mixed emotions. He liked Peter Wilson, and it pained him to see Peter so distraught. Yet, at a deeper level of his mind, his instinct was to be annoyed, almost repelled by Peter's outburst—there was something bleeding-heartish, something *unmanly,* about his show of emotion. War was hard, they all knew that.

"I don't feel it that strongly, Pete," he said. "I'm just confused. Depressed. Worried."

"I know. I went through that six months ago, when the build-up started. I knew what was happening but I couldn't quite believe it. But, Charles, it grows on you. You'll keep thinking about it and one morning you'll wake up and you'll say, 'My God, this is insane!' And it is, you know. It's absolute madness."

"I just feel like I owe the President the benefit of the doubt. He's used up a lot of his political capital on his domestic program, and I hate to undercut him on foreign policy."

"Even if he's wrong and people are dying for it?"

"The thing is, Peter, if this war is wrong, then the best minds in this country have been wrong on foreign policy for twenty years, and I'm just not prepared to make that judgment."

"Charles, all I'm asking is that you sign a letter to the President asking him to continue his bombing halt."

"I'll think about it, Peter. But no promises."

Joe Clayton came to see him the next morning.

"I just don't think we can control the destiny of that little country,"

Charles said, after his secretary had brought them a second cup of coffee.

"Then I'd have to say you're wrong, Charles. We have the force necessary to do as we wish over there. We could level the country and make a parking lot of it."

"Okay, granting our power to prevail, *should* we prevail? Is their politics any of our business?"

"Perhaps that depends on whether you prefer democracy to Communism," Joe Clayton said. He looked tired, but his voice was sharp as ever.

"I don't think my preference for democracy is open to question."

"I didn't mean to imply that it was."

"But I do question whether Vietnam is ready for democracy."

"I'll grant that. But we're building democratic institutions in Vietnam. All we ask is a little time. Time for nation-building."

"Joe, isn't there a better chance for negotiations if we hold off on the bombings?"

"A bombing halt is a sign of weakness. You have to stand up to a bully. You know that, Charles. We'll get negotiations when the Communists are convinced we intend to stay the course, when they see that the game isn't worth the candle. That's why I hope you won't sign this letter. It just makes it harder on the President."

"We've got to get out of that war, Joe."

"We're getting out, Charles. Just give us a little more time. Trust us."

"Charles, old buddy, Ah wouldn't touch that letter with a ten-foot pole."

"You approve of the bombing, Rip?"

"Hell, no. It's crazy. The whole damn war's crazy. Good money after bad. But you try to tell the Big Possum that. He's got a hard-on for Uncle Ho."

"So what do we do?"

"We sit tight and hope he gets tired of zapping Chinks. 'Cause you know what, Chas-bo?"

"What?"

"He can zap Chinks to his heart's delight and there ain't nobody in this whole blue-eyed land that gives one happy fuck. Down where Ah come from, they're saying he ain't zapping enough of 'em."

"You're a cynic, Rip."

"A cynic? Nope, Ah'm a realist. Ah'm telling you how it is, pal, not how it ought to be. And Ah'll tell you something else. Your pal Pete Wilson has got to run this fall, and his ass is gonna be dragging if he don't watch out."

"Pete's following his conscience."

"He's liable to follow it right back to Pocatello, too."

Finally Charles talked to Al Kline. They'd never discussed the war before, because Charles didn't want the younger man to have a say in everything he did. It was too easy to let your staff do all your work for you. Charles had a half dozen colleagues he considered Senators in name only, pampered figureheads who had delegated all their power to this or that ambitious assistant. Al Kline was ambitious, so Charles thought it best to keep him at arm's length on some things, from time to time to remind him who was boss. But Al was also very bright, and when he came into Charles's office that afternoon, Charles decided he wanted to know what he thought about Pete Wilson's letter.

"Sit down, Al."

Kline perched on the edge of a chair, still coiled.

"I've got Pete Wilson waving this letter to Johnson in my face. Have you seen it?"

"Yes."

"What do you think?"

"About the letter? Or you signing it?"

"Either. Both."

"The letter's okay. But I don't think you ought to sign it."

"That's a bit of a paradox, isn't it?"

"It's a matter of your prestige. Wilson and that bunch will get fifteen signatures at the outside. They can't get Kennedy, they can't get Fulbright, they can't get Mansfield, they can't get Gore. What they've got is fifteen nobodies."

"I'm not exactly a powerhouse in this place."

"You can be. But not by aligning yourself with those people."

"Not even when they're right?"

"There's such a thing as being right too soon."

Charles almost laughed. This kid would go far.

As if he read Charles's thoughts, Kline said, "I'm not just being

174

cynical, Senator. I think the people who sign that letter are burning their bridges to Johnson."

Charles got up and began to pace about his office. It was time to make this damned decision, and he thought Al made more sense than anyone else he'd talked to. You didn't influence Johnson by grandstand plays and public letters.

"Okay, Al, here's what I'm going to do. I'm not going to sign that letter. A public letter just gets his back up more. Damn it, if you're going to do something, it's got to be something *effective*. The first thing I'm going to do is write him a private letter. Something thoughtful, something sympathetic, something he'll pay attention to. He'll listen to me. He knows how often I've gone out on a limb for him. And the next thing I'm going to do is in my speeches. Damn it, when I go back to the state, all I hear is that we ought to be bombing Hanoi. I've got to *educate* people. Make them see that negotiations are the only answer. When's my next speech?"

"To the Bowling Green Rotary, Friday week."

"Okay, give me a draft."

"Do you come out for a bombing halt?"

"Well, let's hold off on that. Just say we should pursue every avenue to peace, something like that. I've got to keep my *credibility*. That's all you've got in this game. I realize we've got to be tough—remember, the American eagle has arrows in one claw, but he's got the olive branch in the other. Put that in the speech."

Charles paced about, tossing out ideas and phrases for Al to take down. He was excited now. He'd start work on his letter to Johnson right away. And he'd make this speech a good one, the best thing he'd done, and he'd send a copy of it to the President too. That was the way to get results. To influence the system you worked inside the system. He didn't see why Pete Wilson couldn't understand that.

7

APRIL 1966

When Beth put down the telephone she gave Bill a bright smile.

"We have the nicest invitation," she said. "Lyndon B. Johnson has invited us to the White House this afternoon. Isn't that nice of Lyndon B. Johnson?"

"He's always thinking of us," Bill said. "What's the occasion?"

"Actually, it's a garden party. The guest of honor is the prime minister of . . . well, I forget exactly what country, but a very *significant* country, and Lyndon B. Johnson wants him to meet some of the younger set."

"Nothing formal, I hope."

"Oh, you know Lyndon B. Johnson. It's just sort of come as you are."

"That's swell. I'll call some people."

"Would you, dear? I would, you know, but I have an important engagement at the welfare department."

"What about our house guest? Do you think we ought to take him?"

"Oh, I think so. I think he's one of the most fascinating people I've met in ages. I think Lyndon and Lady Bird would simply *adore* him."

"We'll see if he wakes up," Bill said. "He may sleep till next week."

Their guest, who was sleeping on the sofa in the living room, was named Mel, or had been named Mel when they'd known him a couple of years earlier, before he went to California. Now he was back, a new man, and with new names. Usually he called himself Captain Trips, but after something Beth had said the night before he'd taken to calling himself the Man from Mars.

He'd turned up around dinnertime, needing a place to stay, talking a strange language, looking like nothing they'd ever seen before. His blond hair was shoulder length and he had a shaggy, Buffalo Bill mustache, and he was wearing a floppy hat with the brim pinned back and a suede jacket with fringe on it and a shiny silver shirt and strands of Indian beads around his neck and old patched jeans and a pair of scruffy moccasins. He said he now operated something called a "head shop" in someplace called "the Haight" and he kept babbling about Leary and Kesey and the Dead and the Diggers and good karma and bad vibrations and acid tests until Beth had thrown up her hands and said, "My God, it's like talking to a man from Mars!"

He liked that. He cackled like an old man and said, "A man from Mars . . . far out, far out . . . heh-heh-heh, just a simple dope-smoking boy from the Red Planet. . . . Oh, far out!" And after that he called himself the Man from Mars.

He had dinner with them, and after that he settled down on the sofa and talked about "the Haight," which his hosts finally figured out was a neighborhood in San Francisco.

"Mel, what do people do in the Haight?" Beth asked.

"Earth lady, you speak to the Man from Mars."

"Okay, Man from Mars, what do people do in the Haight?"

He pointed solemnly to a button that was pinned to his jacket, one that said, "Tune In/Turn On/Drop Out."

"That is the secret of the Red Planet," he said. "Make love, not war. Everybody's into love. Love and dope and acid."

"Acid?" Beth repeated.

"That's what they call LSD," Bill told her.

"Do you take LSD?" Beth asked.

The Man from Mars smiled at her, a dreamy, lopsided smile, and then he began to laugh, as if the question was the funniest thing he'd ever heard.

"What about politics?" Beth asked impatiently. "Do kids there demonstrate against the war?"

The Man from Mars was sobered by the question. "No, man. Like, politics is a downer. There's maybe a few political freaks left around Berkeley, but most people are into dope. Dope and love and acid."

"It must be like another world out there," Beth said.

The Man from Mars nodded solemnly and reached into his pocket and popped a small pink pill into his mouth. He smiled dreamily and stretched out on the sofa and was soon asleep and snoring loudly.

Now, fourteen hours later, he was still asleep and snoring loudly. "Let's let sleeping Martians lie," Bill said. "What's your hassle with the welfare department?"

"Oh, they caught Mrs. Hardy's boy friend in her apartment and they're threatening to cut her off. They've got their lovely little rules and nobody gives a damn if her children starve."

"Have fun."

"What about you?"

"Odds and ends. Paperwork. What time is the White House thing?"

"Three."

"Can you be back here?"

"I think so. It depends on those idiots at the welfare department."

"Courage." He kissed her and she slipped on her denim jacket and hurried out the door. Bill made some calls to people about the White House thing, then he sat down at the dining-room table and began filling out some reports for OEO. He hated paperwork but there was no one else to do it. Beth had no patience with details. And as he struggled with the complicated government forms, he couldn't help thinking: Who will do this when I'm gone?

It was not something you could keep from your mind. When he was with friends he could usually block it out, but when he was alone the reality of it would force its way back into his thoughts. Even now, as he sat here filling out poverty program forms and listening to the Man from Mars snore, people were trying to send him to prison.

He had talked to the lawyer Charles had suggested, a man named Segal, and he had agreed to fight the case in court. First he applied for CO status. He filled out his SSS Form 150 and attached a twenty-page handwritten essay that quoted St. Augustine and Gandhi and Camus and then two months later he went before his draft board. He was prepared to discuss the philosophy of non-violence, but instead he found himself being asked questions like "What would you do if someone was raping your sister?"

His CO application was rejected and he was ordered to report for induction. Segal advised him to report—not to accept induction, but to report. Maybe he would fail the physical. Maybe they'd screw up the paperwork or otherwise give him grounds for appeal. So one cold November morning he found himself with fifty other young men in a big flag-draped induction center where a gum-chewing sergeant was

178

calling out names. Each man, as his name was called, took a step forward and became a soldier. Except Bill, who stood fast. A captain appeared and took him to an office, where he declined to make any statement. Finally, after two hours, the captain said Bill could leave.

Then the real waiting began. "They might try you next month or next year," Segal said. "If the FBI comes around to ask you questions, that means they're getting close."

So Bill had learned to live with the realization that any day he might be ordered to stand trial and that after the trial he might be sent to prison for five years. It was not easy. The easiest thing was bitterness, and Bill was bitter sometimes, and Beth was too, but as the days passed he had learned to block out the bitterness and then he found that somehow his life was becoming better, richer. He learned to savor each day, each person, each experience. Sometimes a kind of beatitude filled him. He looked around him at the ugliness of the world—the ugliness of poverty, the ugliness of war—and he realized that the only answer to it was the goodness of individuals. So he waited, and he tried to be good, and there were times when he thought he was the happiest man on earth.

At noon he walked to the corner store for some milk and when he returned to Kennedy House he saw two men in dark suits standing on the sidewalk. One of them had a notebook in his hand and they seemed to be checking the address. He walked up behind them.

"Are you looking for me?" he said.

They turned around quickly—he half expected them to draw guns—but when they saw him they seemed to relax. Both looked the way he expected FBI men to look—lean, sharp-eyed, short-haired, bland. One was slightly taller than the other.

"We're Special Agents Walker and Tyson of the Federal Bureau of Investigation," the taller one said. He flashed a shiny badge that was attached to the inside of his wallet. "Are you William Hall?"

"That's right."

"And is this your place of residence?"

"Yes."

"We have a few questions to ask you, Mr. Hall," the taller one said. "I wonder if we could go inside?"

Bill thought a moment. He didn't know if Beth was back. He didn't know if the Man from Mars was still snoring on the sofa or popping pills or what. And his lawyer had warned him not to tell the FBI anything except what he'd already told, his name and residence.

"I think we can talk out here," he said. "I really don't have much to say."

"How long have you lived here?" the shorter one said. It was the first time he'd spoken.

"About two and a half years."

"And you plan to continue living here?"

"I hope to," Bill said. He thought it a mildly humorous reply, but no one smiled.

"Mr. Hall," the taller one said, "I wish you'd tell us a little about yourself, your background, and why you've decided to take this action you're taking."

Bill looked at the man's smooth, emotionless face. What was he supposed to do? Make a speech about children being napalmed? "My lawyer has advised me not to make any statement," he said.

"You don't have anything to be ashamed of, do you?" the shorter one said. Bill didn't respond. He'd been around a lot of cops in the last two years and he knew this game—the Mutt and Jeff routine, the good guy and the bad guy, one to scare you and the other to be your pal.

"I don't have anything to say," Bill told them.

"You know, we see a lot of fellows like you," said the taller one, the good guy. "By the time we see them, they've had time to think things through, and a lot of them decide the best thing is to go on into the army. Heck, most of them have enough education to get a desk job anyway. And I'll tell you something else. If you'll accept induction, even now, the government'll drop all charges, just like that." He snapped his fingers and gave Bill a tight, man-to-man smile. Bill suddenly realized that, however noble he might think himself, he was just a pain in the ass to scores of government people who didn't want to be bothered with processing him and investigating him and trying him and imprisoning him. Join the army, boy, and make everybody happy.

"Who are these earth people and why are they here?"

The voice of the Man from Mars boomed out of the doorway. Bill turned and saw him standing on the porch with his arms outstretched.

180

"What's that?" the shorter FBI man muttered. He took a step back and Bill saw the bulge of his shoulder holster under his coat.

"I am Captain Trips from the planet Mars," the apparition on the porch announced. "Take me to your leader."

"Does he live here?" the short one asked.

"No, no, he's just visiting," Bill said. "He's sort of an actor. Mel, go back inside."

"I come in peace, earth people."

"*Inside,* Mel," Bill pleaded, and with a final haughty stare the Man from Mars disappeared through the doorway.

"Mel what?" the shorter agent said.

"What?" Bill replied.

"You called him Mel. What's his last name?"

"I don't know," Bill lied. "Look, is there anything else?"

"No, not for now," the taller FBI man said after a moment. "Good-by."

"Good-by," Bill said. He stood on the steps and watched as they walked down the sidewalk and around the corner. They walked briskly and in perfect step, like two members of a drill team, and they never looked back.

The Man from Mars decided to go to the White House with them. He caused a mild commotion on Connecticut Avenue that afternoon —"dirty hippy," someone yelled—but he caused no commotion at all at the White House. When they went to meet the other demonstrators on the Ellipse, facing the back lawn of the White House, the Man from Mars sat down under a tree nearby and after a while he began to chant some kind of a Zen chant. A few tourists took pictures of him but he didn't seem to notice.

Bill began to circulate among the forty or fifty kids who were gathered behind the police barricades. It was not a bad turnout for such short notice. It was getting easier and easier to get people out. Bill thought the day would come when they would surround the whole White House with people chanting, "Stop the war, stop the war," and even Johnson couldn't ignore them.

A helicopter shot into view, hovered for a moment over the White House lawn, then began its gentle descent. The Marine Band began to play and four or five men came walking out of the White

House, one of them the President, coming out to greet the visiting prince or prime minister or whoever it was. From behind the police barricades on the Ellipse you could barely see the men shaking hands beside the helicopter, a hundred yards away, but the demonstrators began their chanting, not knowing if it could be heard over the loud music from the Marine Band:

"Hey, hey, LBJ,
How many kids did you kill today?"

Their voices rose louder and louder, some of the girls were almost hysterical, but the people exchanging greetings beside the helicopter gave no sign of noticing them. The whole thing made Bill sad. He came because it helped build the movement but he came without joy.

"Hey, hey, LBJ,
How many kids did you kill today?"

The people petition their President. Bill found that he was not chanting with the others, he was only watching them, particularly Beth, whose face was distorted by anger, who shook both fists as she screamed out her rage. He loved her and he feared for her. He loved her because she was here, because she was brave, and yet he feared that she did not belong in this life he had made for her.

"Okay, that's all, break it up, move on."

The park police were advancing on them. Getting arrested wasn't part of the plan, so the kids moved away from the barricades, away from the advancing policemen, across the Ellipse toward Seventeenth Street, tossing back one last chant over their shoulders:

"One, two, three, four,
We don't want your fucking war."

Some tourists were watching from the sidewalk, middle-aged men and women with cameras hung around their necks. Some had booed, and as the demonstrators raced past, a well-dressed woman with blonde, upswept hair stepped in Beth's path.

"They should send your kind back to Russia," she declared in a Southern accent. "Right back to Russia where you belong!"

Beth stopped and looked at the woman with interest, as if she had never seen a tourist before, as if indeed she were the tourist and the Southern lady the curiosity. Beth smiled her most engaging smile at the woman, and then, almost as an afterthought, gave her the finger, jabbing it under the woman's nose until she stepped backward in horror.

"Up yours, lady," she said cheerfully, and then she raced on after Bill.

8

SUMMER 1966

The calls began just after the Fourth of July. The first was from a doctor's wife who lived around the corner on Volta Place. Carol thought her a gossip and a bore, and she didn't pay much attention to her excited tale. But the next call was from a reporter's wife they knew, a woman Carol considered bright and well informed, and she too was upset by the new court decision and the impact it might have on the little Georgetown school their children attended. So Carol began to listen and ask questions and when the third call came—this one from a lawyer's wife whose son was Hugh's best friend—she was getting upset.

She told Charles about the calls that evening while they were having a drink.

"Have you heard about this new school integration decision? The one by the judge with the funny name?"

"Skelly Wright? I saw the stories in the *Post*. What about it?"

"Half the mothers in Georgetown called me about it this afternoon. It looks like Negro children from way over in Anacostia will be bussed to the Georgetown schools."

"They're still talking about a fifty-fifty ratio, aren't they?"

"Yes, but up until now we've had Negro children from middle-class families. Now they're talking about slum children."

"What you're saying, my little Alabama belle, is that you believe in integration wit' de good niggers but not wit' de *bad* niggers."

"What I'm saying," she said angrily, "is that I spent all afternoon

184

listening to stories about how slum children behave. About fights. About extortion of money. About disease and learning problems."

"So what do the mothers of Georgetown propose to do about this threat?"

"A lot of them are talking about putting their children in private schools."

Charles finished his gin and tonic, walked over to the bar, and poured himself another. He squeezed a half a lime into it and stirred it with the knife.

"Look, Carol, if any more distraught mothers call, you tell them that our kids are staying at Hyde, that we believe in public education, and we also believe in obeying court decisions. You and I are very fortunate people and we have an obligation to use whatever prestige or influence we have to help make this thing work. Okay?"

"Okay," Carol said uncertainly. "It's just that . . ."

"It's just that what?"

"It's just that even before this came up I was wondering if we ought to take the children out of Hyde. It's not a very good school, Charles. None of the D.C. schools are very good. There are never enough books and they don't have lab equipment or art supplies or anything. It's not like we couldn't afford private schools."

"Listen," he snapped. "I happen to be an authority on private schools. I attended the damn things all my life, from age six right on up. All I ever met were snotty little rich kids just like myself. You know where I learned words like 'wop' and 'kike' and 'dago'? In a fancy three-thousand-dollar-a-year prep school in Massachusetts. It took me ten years to unlearn all the prejudice I learned in the private schools I went to. My kids are going to attend public schools, and they're going to learn about poor people and Negro people and the way the world is, right from the start."

Carol fell silent, wondering if he might be right. She knew that she'd never gone to schools with Negroes, and perhaps that was why even today she didn't understand them, was a little afraid of them.

"Well," she said finally, "I guess it'd be pretty silly not even to give it a try."

"Right," he said. "Now, how about one more round before dinner?"

"Just a half for me," she said.

"Coming up." She watched as he mixed the drinks. She was glad

185

to see him in a good mood. He'd been so depressed, so withdrawn, these past few weeks. She guessed it was about Vietnam but they'd not talked about it. She'd found it wasn't wise for them to talk about Vietnam, because he was getting more and more against the war, and she still believed that the U.S. would have to stay until the war was won. She didn't want to argue with him tonight—while he was in a good mood there was something else she wanted to talk to him about.

"Charles, if the children stay in Hyde, I think we ought to arrange art lessons for Hugh outside of school."

"Art lessons? What for?"

"He's getting interested in drawing. Didn't you see those sketches of the horses he did at your mother's house?"

"I didn't pay much attention."

"He's really quite talented. He told me he'd like to take lessons."

"It seems like something he ought to be able to pick up on his own."

"He can't pick up painting on his own any more than Liza could pick up ballet on her own. He needs professional instruction."

"I don't know. I'm not sure it's something we ought to encourage."

"Not encourage? What *is* the matter with you? He has talent and he's trying to express himself and of course we should encourage him."

"I just don't see where it leads. His grandfather was a lawyer and his father's a lawyer and I don't think it's in the cards for him to be a Picasso."

Carol jumped to her feet. "Charles, you are absolutely impossible. Would to God he could be a Picasso."

"Where is he, anyway?"

"He's up in his room."

Charles looked out the french doors. "He's inside on an evening like this?" He went to the stairs. "Hey, Hugh," he called.

"Yes."

"Get your ball and your glove and we'll toss a few. Okay?"

There was a moment's pause. "I guess so."

"Okay then, come on." Charles slipped off his tie and walked out to the back yard. A minute later Hugh came down the stairs, head down, holding his baseball glove by its thumb.

Carol went into the kitchen to start dinner. She could see their

186

game of catch through the window and it didn't go very well. Hugh dropped most of the balls Charles threw to him and Carol could see Charles showing him how to hold his glove and how to bring his arm around and how to grip the ball. Hugh responded glumly, until finally she could see Charles speak to him sharply and see Hugh throw down his glove and walk away. Carol started to go out but she thought, No, this is something they'll just have to work out between themselves. And she thought too: Oh, God, give me strength, give me strength.

Molly's call disturbed Charles, even before they talked, because he'd never known her to place a long-distance call in her life. "A letter's ten times cheaper," she'd say, "and I don't reckon I've got anything to say that won't hold a day or two."

But this time she called, catching Charles at his desk on a mid-morning in late August.

"Charles?" She was shouting into the phone, clearly skeptical that the Bell System could transmit her voice from Kentucky to Washington, D.C., without a major effort on her part. "Charles? It's me, Molly. Can you hear me?"

"I can hear you fine, Molly. Why didn't you call collect?"

"How'd I know if you'd take a collect call from your poor relations?"

"I would. What's up?"

"Well, Eddie's home. That's my big news."

"He's home? Great. I thought he had another year to go."

"He did, but they let him out early." Her voice went down to a whisper: "Charles, he got hurt over there."

"What do you mean, Molly? Was he wounded?"

She hesitated. "Well, sort of. He wasn't hurt *physical*. But he's all upset. His nerves aren't right."

"What does he do?"

"He doesn't *do* anything. He sort of mopes around and watches TV a lot and goes for walks. And goes to church a lot, too. But you can't talk to him—he's way off on cloud nine."

"Is he getting any treatment?"

"He goes over to the VA hospital in Louisville once a week and they give him some pills but they don't do any good that I can see."

"Do you want me to talk to him? Is he there now?"

187

"He's out for a walk. But he wouldn't say anything on the phone anyway. What I wish you'd do is come by and see him the next time you're down here. He thinks you hung the moon, Charles."

"As a matter of fact, I'll be down this weekend," he said. He could arrange a trip easily enough. "I'll come by on Sunday afternoon."

He flew down on Saturday and spent the evening with his mother, talking about horse shows and marriages and grandchildren and deaths. She had been reading John O'Hara's new novel and when he asked her how it was she said, "Oh, I don't suppose he's the greatest writer in the world, but he seems to be the only one who cares about people of my age and class." On Sunday morning, after a huge breakfast of eggs and country ham, he started the hour's drive to Raleigh to see Molly. It was cloudy and looked like rain. He drove slowly, in his mother's Mercedes, listening to the summer's popular songs on the radio—"The Ballad of the Green Berets," "Paperback Writer"—and when he reached Molly's little bungalow it looked like it always did. The lawn needed mowing and the paint was peeling and her old Dodge was parked in the driveway looking like it didn't intend ever to move again. Molly met him at the door, hugged him, and led him inside. The living room was dark and for a moment Charles didn't see Eddie. The boy was slumped on the sofa watching a John Wayne movie on TV. He didn't look up until his mother spoke.

"Eddie. Charles is here to see you."

Eddie looked up and it took a moment for his eyes to settle on Charles, then another moment for any recognition to register in his face. When he pulled himself to his feet there was something awkward about the way he moved.

"Hi, good to see you," he mumbled, and gave Charles a limp handshake. Then he slumped back down on the sofa and turned back to the TV.

"Eddie," his mother cried, "Charles has come to *see* you." She clicked off the TV set and Eddie watched as John Wayne melted into a little white dot.

"I'll get the coffee," Molly said, and hurried into the kitchen.

"Well, how's it feel to be back?" Charles asked.

"Oh, good, real good to be back," Eddie said vaguely. "Back in the world. That's what the guys call the U.S. when they're over in 'Nam, the world."

188

"How was it?"

Eddie shook his head, as if the words he sought were beyond him. "Tough," he said finally. "It was pretty darn tough."

Molly brought the coffee in on a tray. It was steaming hot, but Eddie took his cup in both hands and emptied it while Charles and Molly were still blowing on theirs. The coffee seemed to pick him up.

"Eddie was glad to get home," his mother said. "He says the people in Vietnam didn't much like Americans."

"Is that right?" Charles said, hoping the boy would talk.

Eddie managed a lopsided grin. "It's almost funny," he said. "I mean, I went over there thinking we were saving those people from Communism and thinking we'd be heroes to them and we'd give the kids candy bars and they'd throw flowers at us and all that. Man, those people hate us. They think we're devils who sprang out of the ocean. We'd go into these little villages and they'd sell you a Coke for fifty cents; if you were real lucky it wouldn't have ground glass in it."

"Where'd they get Cokes in the first place?" Charles asked.

"You could get anything on the black market. You could buy a B-52 if you had the money. And there were plenty of sergeants and Saigon cowboys getting rich off it. Selling whiskey, selling uniforms, selling dope, selling anything."

"Was there a lot of drug use over there?" Charles asked.

"Could I have some more coffee, Mom?" Eddie asked. "I never got much into drugs," Eddie said when she was gone. "I blew some grass, everybody did that, but I was always afraid of the hard stuff. But you could always get anything you wanted. Some guys wouldn't go out on patrol unless they were stoned. Some weeks we'd have more ODs than KIAs." Eddie shook his head. "Listen, Charles, you want to go for a walk? I can't talk around Molly. It'd blow her mind if I told her how it was over there. But you ought to know."

Molly brought Eddie another cup of coffee and the boy gulped it down. Charles was coming to realize that Eddie was not the same boy he'd known before. They finished their coffee, then Eddie proposed a walk. Molly told him to put on his zipper jacket in case it got chilly. Then she stood on the back steps and watched them as they started across the field behind her house.

It still looked like rain. They followed a creek that ran toward some woods. The leaves were just beginning to turn.

"I didn't mean to be rude when you came in," Eddie said. "My nerves are all shot, and they give me these pills to calm me down and when I'm on them my mind sort of wanders sometimes."

"What kind of pills are they?"

"Some kind of downers. They pass out a lot of them to guys like me."

They came to a gate held shut by a metal hook. Eddie tried to unhook it, but his hands shook so that he couldn't. Charles opened the gate and, after they'd passed through, closed it again. He began to think they shouldn't walk too far, because he didn't know what these damned pills were Eddie was taking and he didn't really have any idea what sort of shape the boy was in.

Twenty yards inside the trees the creek joined another creek, and there was a sandy bank where they met.

"What say we sit down here?" Charles asked. "I'm getting too old for these long walks."

"Sure," Eddie said. "Fine." They sat down on the sand, so close to the creek that they could see minnows flashing just beneath its surface. Someone had left a red and yellow Fritos sack on the sand and Eddie stuffed it in his pocket. "People really make messes, don't they?" he said. Charles nodded and waited for Eddie to say whatever it was he wanted to say.

"The thing is, Charles," the boy said finally, "I wouldn't bore you with my opinions if it was just me. But I want to tell you how it was for all those guys, thousands of guys like me."

"Okay," Charles said. "I want to hear it."

"The Vietnamese hate us, you start with that. And they ought to hate us, the way we come in and burn down their villages and move them around. And we get to hating them soon enough. But the thing I'm trying to say is this. I don't care if they hate us, what really matters is what the war is doing to our own guys."

Eddie pulled a cigarette out of his shirt pocket, fumbled with it, lit it.

"I'm bitter, Charles. Not because I got my head messed up over there. I'm bitter because my government lied to me. My government made a damn fool of me. You gave me that song and dance about saving Asia from the Communists and I believed it and I went over there and found out it was a lie and people were getting killed and screwed up for no reason at all. What I'm trying to say, Charles, is

190

that there's an awful lot of guys who're awful bitter at the government. What we're saying is, 'Okay, brother, you fooled me once, but you'll never fool me again.' "

It had all come out in a rush and when he was finished Eddie sat smoking his cigarette. Charles scooped up some sand and let it slide slowly out of his hand.

"You're right," he said finally. "We did lie to you."

"I don't mean you personally," Eddie said. "Probably they fooled you too. I don't even know who it is that made up all the lies. I used to lie awake nights trying to figure out who wanted this crazy war. The only thing I could figure was the career people, the lifers. The sergeants who were cleaning up in the black market. The officers who were getting all kinds of promotions. Those bastards ate it up. My CO was living like a king. He had his house trailer with air conditioning and wall-to-wall carpeting and a stereo and a houseboy to wait on him. We always figured the houseboy was a VC spy."

"What'd you think of the VC?"

"They fight like bastards. We had this one VC surrounded, after we'd wasted all his buddies, and he kept shooting back till he ran out of ammunition and when we finally got him he was throwing rocks at us. A kid about seventeen."

"What about the South Vietnamese Army?"

Eddie leaned back on his elbows and laughed. "The Arvin? Listen, it's a wonder those guys don't win all the Olympics, because they're the fastest runners in the world. You just yell 'VC' and all those Arvins will run a mile in four minutes flat. It's hilarious, except that our guys are getting killed while the Arvin are running away."

Charles wasn't sure he wanted to hear any more. He thought they ought to get back. Then he had another idea.

"Eddie, I wonder if you'd like to come up to Washington and talk to some Senators and some government people I know. It'd all be private—I just don't think these people have ever talked to someone who's actually fighting the war."

Eddie looked frightened. "I'm not talking to anybody in Washington," he said.

"Okay. Maybe it wasn't such a hot idea."

But Eddie wasn't through. "You people in Washington made this war and now don't ask us to come explain it to you."

191

He jumped to his feet and towered over Charles. "God damn you," he cried, "you made us do it. Don't you see, you made us do it!"

He turned and started to run away, but after a few steps he threw himself down on the sand. After a while he began to talk.

"I'm sorry," he said. "I'm all upset. The thing is, there's something that happened to me over there I haven't told you. Haven't told anybody, not even the doctors. Sometimes I think it's driving me crazy, keeping it all to myself."

Eddie pulled himself up on the sand and sat with his knees up against his chest, staring across the creek into the young pine trees on the opposite bank.

"We were out on patrol, three of us," he began. "No, I'll have to back up. The first thing, we'd been losing a lot of men to booby traps and everybody was all on edge. So then there was this patrol, me and two other guys, and they should never been sent out together. There was this white guy from Georgia, a big tough guy named Kruger. And the other guy was this colored guy named Ball who was from Detroit or someplace like that. He was sort of the leader of the colored guys in our company and he and Kruger had already had a couple of run-ins.

"Well, they bitched at each other all morning, and I just tried to keep out of their way. So finally we stop to eat some C-rations and all the time we're eating Kruger is talking about what a great stud he is and all the stuff he always gets back home and all. Ball ignores him and Kruger makes like he's telling me about it, but what he was doing was trying to bug Ball, 'cause naturally he's talking about white girls and he figures Ball wishes he'd had some white girls. So Kruger keeps it up, about how he'd screwed this one and he'd screwed that one, and finally when we get up to leave, Ball just sort of whispers, 'she-yit'—you know how they say it.

"Well, Kruger has his M-16 under one arm and he kind of swings around and looks at Ball and says, 'You say something?' and Ball just looks him up and down, real cool like, and spits on the ground. Well, I thought they were going to shoot it out right then, except it was right then that we saw the two women coming down the road. And somehow, Charles, and I can't explain this, somehow all the hate between Kruger and Ball got . . . got *translated* into what happened next, with the women.

"It was a mother and her daughter. The mother was all wrinkled

192

up like a peanut, the way those women get, but the daughter was real pretty. About fourteen and probably didn't weigh ninety pounds.

"So Kruger, he charges out to the road and points his M-16 at them and starts asking to see their papers. The mother starts yelling, 'No VC, no VC,' and finally she pulls out some papers. Kruger looks them over, like he's the big intelligence expert, then he wads them up and throws them on the ground. 'They look suspicious to me,' he says. 'Better search 'em.' So he makes a big production of digging through these baskets and bundles they're carrying and he searches the mother and finally he starts to search the girl. Of course what he's really doing is feeling her up. She tried to stop him and the mother runs over and starts jabbering and grabbing at him.

"Kruger got mad. He hit the mother with his fist, so hard she fell down and didn't get up right away. Then he grabs the girl by the hair and jerks her hard. 'VC?' he yells and she starts shaking her head and crying and he slaps her a couple of times and then he turns around to us. Me and Ball had just been standing at the edge of the road, watching all this. I didn't like it but that damn Kruger was a madman and I didn't want any trouble. So now he looks at us and his face is all red and he says, 'I'm gonna take this VC suspect over there and question her in private. Any objections?' I didn't say anything, and Ball, he just gave a little shrug, like he couldn't care less what Kruger did. 'Course, we both knew what Kruger was gonna do. There were plenty of stories about rapes and all sort of stuff. Like I said, when you got out into the field, the war was just us against them, the round-eyes against the slant-eyes.

"So Kruger twists the girl's arm up behind her back and starts to walk her over to some trees and all the time she's yelling, 'Me virchin, me virchin,' which I guess meant she was a virgin, and about then the mother starts trying to get up.

"'Tie her up,' Ball said to me, and right then I saw that Kruger and Ball were going to rape that girl and maybe the mother too and if I wasn't careful they were liable to blow my head off. That may sound crazy, back here in the world, but over there it was like that.

"So I tied her up, and about that time, up in the woods, the girl starts screaming, terrible screams like Kruger was doing I don't know what to her, and then the screams stop, just a whimper now and then, except by then the mother had started screaming, until finally Ball stuffed a sock in her mouth.

"Pretty soon Kruger comes out of the trees, grinning and making a big production out of zipping up his pants, and he walks up to Ball and says, 'How 'bout you, you want some of that VC pussy?' and so Ball walks up there where the girl was and pretty soon we can hear her screaming again. I watched the road—I don't know what we'd've done if somebody had come along—and I swear that damn Kruger went over to the mother, who was sitting there with her arms tied up and a sock in her mouth, an ugly old shriveled-up peasant woman with tears running down her face, and he starts to do things to her.

"So finally Ball comes back and looks at me and says, 'Your turn now, Colonel.' They called me Colonel because I was from Kentucky. I swear to God the last thing I wanted to do was to rape that girl. I didn't want to touch her, not even look at her. But they'd done it and they wanted me guilty too and they'd've killed me in a minute if they'd thought I might turn them in. So I went up where she was, thinking I'd just pretend I'd done it. She was there on the ground with her hands tied and her clothes all torn off and there was blood on her legs and her face was all puffed up where they'd hit her. She wasn't crying then. She just looked at me like a kitten that thinks you're going to hurt it. I wanted to do something to help her. I thought maybe I'd give her a drink of water. So I knelt down beside her and sort of touched her face, pushed back the hair where it was stuck to her cheek, and all of a sudden she bit my hand.

"I went crazy. It doesn't make any sense, and it's no excuse, but I just plain went crazy. I hated her, hated her and Ball and Kruger and the army and the war and everything. I'd been in that damn country for eight months and I'd seen my buddies killed and torn up and I was scared and miserable and all of a sudden I was going to take it out on that girl. So I raped her. Not for pleasure, not even for sex, just out of pure hate. Raped her hard, so it hurt, raped her and screamed and cried and hit her in the face—I swear to God, I didn't know what I was doing. I was just blacked out and the next thing I knew her mother was scratching at my eyes.

"She'd wiggled loose somehow and run up there before Ball and Kruger could catch her. But they ran up fast and Kruger kicked her off me, kicked hell out of her, and then he smashed her with the butt of his M-16. By then I was up on my feet and the two women are there on the ground and I guess Ball and Kruger and I were all starting to think the same thing.

"We could've got in bad trouble if those women turned us in. There'd been some trouble the month before, where some guys had messed with some village women, made 'em do some stuff, and the province chief had complained to Saigon and there'd been a stink and it looked like one guy was gonna be court-martialed. So now we were all starting to cool off and we looked at those two women on the ground, the girl raped and both of 'em beat up pretty bad, and I knew damn well what those other two guys were thinking.

" 'Whatta you say?' Kruger asks Ball.

" 'Waste 'em,' Ball says. 'Two VC shot trying to escape.'

" 'Who does it?' Kruger asks. And Ball just shrugs and nods to me. 'Let the Colonel do it.'

"You get to be an animal over there but I wasn't that bad. I just said, 'I won't do it,' and waited to see what they'd do. I figured they might kill me, but probably not. Because if you killed an American over there there'd be an investigation but nobody worried much if you killed a slant-eye. Ball just shrugged and said we'd draw straws to see who did it. And it turned out that Ball drew the short straw.

"He told us to go down and watch the road. I felt like I was walking in a dream. It was the middle of the afternoon and the sun was blazing down and my face was bleeding where the old woman had scratched it. I felt like I was in hell—and when I thought about that I started to laugh because I guessed the Vietnamese were right and we Americans really were round-eyed devils who'd come out of the sea and turned their country into hell.

"I was still laughing when I heard the shots that killed them."

Charles sat staring at the ground. It was more than he could do to look at Eddie.

"What happened next, Eddie?"

"Nothing, as far as the women were concerned. Ball, the colored guy, got his leg blown off by a mine the next month. And I started having these sweats and nightmares until I wasn't good for anything. Finally they sent me to see the doctor and he sent me to another doctor and they decided my head was messed up so they discharged me."

"You've got to have psychiatric help."

Eddie nodded uncertainly. "The thing is, I've been afraid to tell anybody what happened. I mean, I trust you, but maybe some doctor would turn me in."

Charles shook his head. "A doctor won't turn you in."

195

There was a rumble of thunder, and they could feel the mist turning to rain. "We'd better start back," Charles said.

They got up and brushed the sand off their pants and started back the way they had come. When they came to the gate, Eddie kept his hands in his pockets while Charles opened and closed it.

"A thousand things like that happened over there," Eddie said. "Worse things happened every day. But those weren't me. If a village was bombed, that wasn't me. But that girl was me and I can't forget it."

When they reached Molly's house, Charles said he had to go for cigarettes. He had to get away from them because he thought he was about to crack, to start screaming and breaking things, and he thought that to drive might relax him. *You dirty sons of bitches,* he kept saying to himself. *You dirty sons of bitches.* And the worst of it was that his anger was at himself. The trouble was not generals who had behaved like generals, but Senators who had not behaved like Senators. Good God, how could he have kept quiet, gone along, tuned it out all these months? He thought of it and he cursed himself as he would never curse Johnson. But that was over now. He was angry now, ready to speak out, to show some courage, to make people understand what was happening. That was all it would take, enough people like himself speaking out. They were a minority now but it wouldn't take much to tip the balance. He drove out the highway for a half hour, and when he started back his anger had turned to determination. He was ready to fight now.

He wrote the speech himself, on the night he returned from Kentucky. His speech said all the obvious things—that the war was costing too much, that negotiations were the only answer—and it said them without recrimination, for he still hoped to oppose the war without breaking with Johnson.

As a courtesy, he sent an advance copy to the White House. Within an hour Joe Clayton was in his office, urging him to reconsider.

"I've been reconsidering for two years, Joe. My mind's made up."

"Charles, for your own sake . . ."

"Let's think about the country's sake, Joe."

"The country's interest isn't served by surrender."

"Surrender of what? It's insane."

"We're on the brink of victory, Charles."

196

"We've been on the brink of victory for too long."

"You don't believe me?"

"I believe you believe it. I don't believe it's so."

"We have access to documents . . ."

"I know, the famous captured documents. I read Joe Alsop."

"We can *win,* Charles. We *will* win if you people don't tie the President's hands."

Charles stood up; he was past taking that from Joe Clayton. "Don't try to put the blood on my hands," he said. "Maybe it has been, but not any more."

Clayton stood up, too, an elegant, intense man who was as sure the war was right as Charles was sure it was wrong.

"We're trying to save millions of people from enslavement," he said quietly. "I wish you could understand that."

"No, Joe, you're sending American boys to die for nothing. I wish *you* could understand that."

Joe Clayton left the office without another word.

Charles delivered the speech the next day at a luncheon meeting of the Kentucky State Society. This was a speech that had to be directed at the people who had elected him—a speech that would have been harder to deliver had there not been four years before he had to ask them to elect him again.

The next morning, he made page 3 of the Washington *Post,* page 78 of the New York *Times,* and the front page of the *Courier-Journal.* Soon the editorials would begin coming in. He expected three of the major Kentucky papers to support him and most of the smaller ones to oppose him. That was all right—he had four years to bring them around.

There was no immediate reaction from the White House. He saw Larry O'Brien that morning at a meeting in Mansfield's office and O'Brien was his usual genial self. That afternoon Rip Horton added his two cents' worth.

"Well, Mr. Snow White Dove, you still speaking to old backsliding hawks like me?"

"You're not a hawk, Rip. You're a buzzard."

"How's it coming? Are all them other doves billin' and cooin' and huggin' you to their feathery white bosoms?"

"More or less. Fulbright went out of his way to say something

197

nice. And McGovern and Morse called me. Welcomed me to the faith, you might say."

"How about Brother Bobby? Did he come hug and kiss you?"

"I can't say that he did. Matter of fact, I saw him in the hall this morning and he just nodded and kept on going."

"Ain't that strange?" Rip said. "And him such a peacenik."

Charles shrugged. "Maybe he thinks I said too little too late. Maybe he figures I'm not important enough to matter."

"Or maybe something else," Rip said.

"What?"

"Maybe he don't like the competition."

9

SEPTEMBER 1966

Carol had expected something worse—a bloody nose, perhaps—so when the first incident came it was almost a letdown.

She knew something was wrong as soon as Hugh came in from school. He didn't speak to her, just walked up to his room and shut the door. She waited fifteen minutes, then went to him. She found him lying on his bed, his face to the wall. When she asked what was wrong he didn't answer.

"Hugh, what *is* it?"

He looked up at her, his pale face pink-splotched with anger.

"Joe-boy stole my crayons," he cried. "He stole them right out of my desk."

Carol sat down on the edge of the bed and took his hand.

"Who is Joe-boy?"

"One of those new kids."

"Are you sure he meant to steal them? Maybe he just wanted to borrow them."

"He *stole* them. The ones Grandmother sent me. He took them out of my desk at lunchtime. I asked him to give them back and he just laughed and said I couldn't prove they were mine."

Carol stroked his hair. The immensity of the problem hit her all at once—her inflexible son had been thrown into a situation demanding limitless flexibility.

"This isn't the first thing," Hugh continued. "Those new kids stole another boy's scissors and a girl's hat and they're always asking people for money and they won't sit still and listen in class."

199

"What is Miss Cooper doing all this time?"

"She doesn't even know what's going on! She just keeps saying"—he mimicked bitterly—"'*Now let's all be little ladies and gentlemen.*' But, Mother, they're *not* ladies and gentlemen."

Carol fished into her pocket and found a bent Winston and a book of matches from the Jockey Club. She lit the cigarette and tossed the match into Hugh's wastebasket.

"Hugh, if they aren't ladies and gentlemen, it might be because they haven't had all the advantages you and your friends have. That's one reason they've been brought to your school, so they can learn from knowing children like you."

Hugh wasn't impressed. "All they do is steal and push people around and cause trouble."

Carol took a deep drag on the Winston—it was stale and the filter had a paperish taste—and knocked its ash into the wastebasket.

"Hugh, sometimes when people don't have as much as other people, they . . . they take things."

"That's *stealing*. That's not right."

"No, it's not right, but we have to try to understand people and why they do things."

"I don't want to understand those kids. I just want them to leave me alone."

"We'll talk to your father tonight," Carol said, and in a few minutes she persuaded him to come down for milk and cookies.

Charles was late getting home that night, and by the time he arrived Hugh had calmed down and didn't want to go through the story again. But Carol insisted, so the solemn, pajama-clad boy told his father all about the stolen crayons.

"Listen, son," Charles said when the boy finished, "here's what I want you to do. Tomorrow morning you go up to this Joe-boy and tell him to hand over your crayons or you're going to take them away from him."

"Charles!"

"Just let me handle this, Carol."

"Charles, some of these Negro children are two or three years behind in school—this Joe-boy might be three years older than Hugh and God knows how much bigger."

"That's not the point. He's got to learn to stand up for himself."

200

"He's got to learn to resolve differences without getting into free-for-alls."

Charles turned to her. "Listen, Carol, when I started in prep school there was an upperclassman who razzed me about my father being a crooked politician until finally I had to fight him. He had thirty pounds on me and he beat the shit out of me. But when the headmaster asked me what had happened I said I'd fallen down the stairs, and as soon as my face had healed up I fought the bastard again and that time it came out pretty even. But he was still wising off at me, so I told him we were going to have to fight again. By then he'd had enough, so he stuck out his hand and said we could be friends even if my old man was a crooked politician. I smashed that son of a bitch in the mouth and knocked out half his teeth and after that nobody ever messed with me again."

Carol looked from Charles, who was livid at the memory, to Hugh, who was staring at his father openmouthed. "Well, that's a lovely story," she said, "but you're not Hugh."

"The issue is the same."

Hugh began to cry.

"Charles, I think one of us should talk to his teacher. You do it if you want to." She knelt beside Hugh and put her arms around him.

"No, no, you do it. If I talk to his teacher it becomes a federal case. But he's going to have to learn to defend himself, that's all there is to it."

"Darling, say good night to your father," Carol said, and after father and son had exchanged hugs she took the boy up to bed.

Carol walked over to the school at noon the next day and found Hugh's teacher, Miss Cooper, alone in the classroom, grading papers. She was a slender, patrician woman in her mid-fifties who was from Virginia and had attended Smith. Carol thought Miss Cooper was a very good teacher—most of the teachers in Georgetown were.

They chatted for a few minutes before Carol came to the point.

"Miss Cooper, Hugh says another boy took his box of crayons from his desk and won't give them back."

Miss Cooper nodded sadly. "Did he name the other boy?"

"He said he was called Joe-boy."

"Yes, it would be Joe-boy," the teacher said. "I'll speak with him this afternoon."

Carol felt guilty for having complicated this woman's already difficult job. "It's not as if we can't afford to buy Hugh more crayons," she said absurdly. "But it upset him to have them taken from his desk."

"It's very difficult, Mrs. Pierce," the teacher said. "Frankly, for the time being it's best if the children don't bring anything to school that doesn't have their name on it."

"What can be done about all this?" Carol asked.

"I think we can get the stealing under control," Miss Cooper said. "Frankly, that isn't the worst problem."

"What *is?*" Carol asked. She was becoming upset. An elementary school seemed such a delicate, diminutive place, with its tiny lockers in the corridors and its tiny desks in each classroom, that it seemed incongruous, monstrous that it should be assailed by such huge problems.

"The worst problem is that some of these children, boys and girls ten and twelve years old, literally cannot read their own names. If I concentrate on them, children like Hugh become bored . . ."

"And vice versa," Carol said.

"Exactly. Mrs. Pierce, we had clinics this summer to try to prepare us for these problems, but I don't think any of us really appreciated just how difficult it would be."

"Is there anything my husband and I could do to help?"

"Yes, there is. Many of the Georgetown parents are still threatening to put their children in private schools."

"We'll both be glad to talk to other parents."

"It would help so much. We're desperate, Mrs. Pierce. We want so badly to make this work but some of us are beginning to fear it's just too much for us."

"We'll do all we can," Carol promised. "My husband is one hundred per cent committed to public education. We both are."

"There's so much to be done," the teacher said. "One problem is that there's no normal social relationship between the Georgetown children and the students from Anacostia. If some sort of after-school or Saturday program could be begun . . ."

"Of course," Carol said. "Hugh could have some of them to his house on Saturday afternoons or we could arrange trips on Sundays. Maybe Charles could get tickets to the Redskins games. Oh, there're a million things to do!"

Miss Cooper smiled, taking strength from Carol's enthusiasm, and

202

when Carol walked home she was brimming with ideas and excitement. She and Charles and the other parents could save this school. They could teach their children to grow up without the prejudices they'd been taught. There was so much they could do, right there in their own neighborhood. Too many people thought everything good had to flow from the hand of some government administrator, but this was a challenge for parents, people of good will, working together for their children's sake. They could have tutoring programs and weekend activities and a Parents' Council and all sorts of things. All that was required was imagination and plenty of hard work.

Carol savored the challenge. Her summer had been bad, bad at her job, bad at home, and perhaps if she and Charles could work together to help the school it would bring them close again, would make this fall a time when finally she would feel she was accomplishing something after months of frustration. Her job was all fouled up again. They had teamed her with Eddie Waters, the wisecracking weatherman, and to her amazement it had worked out fairly well. She and Eddie loathed each other, but that very fact had added zest to the show, and its ratings had soared, its advertisers multiplied.

Not that Carol was any happier. She kept asking for another job, reporting or making documentaries. But the answer was always the same: "You're doing great; let's leave well enough alone; don't worry your pretty little head," et cetera. She was sick of the show and sick of being treated like a nitwit. She had thought of quitting, but at least she'd gotten her salary up to twenty thousand dollars and it was hard to walk away from that.

And there was the other problem, the one she couldn't walk away from. Charles. All summer, particularly since he'd gone to Kentucky and seen Molly and Eddie, he'd been more and more distracted. She just couldn't reach him. He would nod and smile at what she said but he would have that faraway look, the one that meant he'd tuned her out completely. Or they would drive somewhere, alone together for twenty or thirty minutes, and he'd not speak a word. If he got home early enough in the evenings he would watch the news and that was the worst time. He'd watch the films from Vietnam—there was always some new, bloody battle being hailed as the latest victory—and he'd sit there, clutching his drink, just staring at the set, even through the commercials, oblivious to her and the children, sometimes laughing bitterly at the latest prediction of victory just around the corner.

About all they had left was sex, and even that wasn't much good any more. Even as they made love, even when they were that close, they were still apart. He took her out of habit, like he might wind an alarm clock, receiving pleasure, perhaps, but giving little. Once, as they began, she had thought wildly, I am being *screwed* by this *zombie!* She was sick of being used and ignored, and many nights she only pretended to make it. She felt guilty at first but he didn't seem to know or to care and it gave her a perverse pleasure to think she was cheating him, just as he was cheating her.

She tried to understand him. She knew he was agonized over the war and Bill Hall's trial and all the rest of it. But she still thought he owed her more than he was giving her. He could hate the war and still love her. That wasn't asking too much. But every night she saw herself losing him, saw him slipping away, and she was starting to feel a change in herself, feel herself growing hard, growing cold, ceasing to care. She hated it but she didn't know what to do about it.

She had no urge to seek affection—or revenge—with another man, although she was still the object of at least her share of passes at work and elsewhere. The episode with Hank the year before had left her shaken. She didn't trust her emotions. If Hank could upset her that much just by being in town for a weekend, what might happen if she became involved with someone who was available all the time? She had considered the possibility and rejected it. She didn't want a lover; she wanted her husband back.

But how? How to break through to him? That was one reason she found herself excited by the challenge at her children's school. She knew how much public education meant to Charles, and it was something they could work on together, a problem involving their own children, one with tangible victories to be won. The problems that had taken him away were so vast, so intangible—the war, the racial struggle, the urban mess—but here was a problem that was real, was on their very doorstep, and they could share it and perhaps it could bring them back together. She spent the afternoon in a state of high excitement; she had a dozen ideas for things they could do to help the school. The autumn afternoon was cool and fresh and she felt new energies welling up inside her. She made lists and she paced the floor, always with one eye on the clock. She could hardly wait for Charles to come home, so she could tell him all the new things that they could do together.

204

10

OCTOBER 1966

Bill had let his hopes rise in the last days before his trial. He had tried not to, had tried to be realistic, but his hopes had risen anyway, bright balloons sailing free, cut loose from his intellect. He had some cause to hope. He had a good lawyer, Segal, an old hand at civil liberties cases—"I'm the Clark Clifford of the underground," Segal would say, rubbing his broad belly, chewing on his cigar stub—and he had a good judge, too, Judge Meriweather, the liberal on the federal court in Richmond, the civil rights judge, the judge who had given light sentences in draft-resistance cases, who might consider a suspended sentence.

So Bill's hopes were high that morning as they drove down US-85 to Richmond, he and Beth and Segal in the lawyer's car, and some of their friends, Bill's character witnesses, following in another car. Segal was feeling good, humming to himself, proud of himself for getting the case before Meriweather, excited about some recent decisions by a California court, precedents that might win Bill the first suspended sentence in the D.C. area.

They arrived at the federal courthouse at twenty to nine and Segal went in to talk to the court clerk. Bill and the others waited in the corridor, talking nervously, looking at the little knots of people waiting for other trials in other courts. A plump, elderly man in a rumpled suit walked over to them.

"You Mr. Hall?" he asked.

"That's right," Bill said.

"I thought you was," the man said, and stuck out his hand. "I'm Arthur Jones, the chief bailiff. I don't reckon you and your friends'll be causing any trouble in the courtroom, will you?"

Bill smiled. "No, we won't cause any trouble."

"Didn't think you would," Jones said. "You can tell the ones who will." He grinned. "But we had one feller in here on one of these draft-dodger cases who gave us a heck of a time."

"How was that?" Bill said. Bill felt himself wanting to talk to this man. That was the worst of it, when hope seized you, you'd talk to anyone, grasping for tatters of encouragement.

The old man shook his head. "Oh, this feller, he was real far out, hair down his back, heck, I thought he was a girl the first time I seen him. He got up before his honor and said he was gonna be his own lawyer. He had him a Bible in one hand and a flower in the other and he made him a big speech like you never heard before."

"What happened?" Beth asked.

"Pardon?"

"To his case," Beth said.

"Oh, he got hisself five years," the bailiff said. "And when the sentence came down he pulls this Veet Cong flag out and starts waving it. Lordy, I don't know what they'd want to draft a feller like that for anyhow. Well, good luck to you, Mr. Hall. Don't you wave no Veet Cong flags at us."

The bailiff walked away, still grinning at the memory of the flag-waver.

Segal came out of the clerk's office and they saw at once that something was wrong. His face was white, the fire was gone out of him. It took him a few minutes to explain about the little girl, Judge Meriweather's daughter, who had been mauled by a neighbor's dog that morning while waiting for her school bus, who was now being given transfusions, and her father was of course at her bedside, could not be in court that day, and so Judge Walters was taking Judge Meriweather's cases. Segal knew Walters too, knew he definitely was not a good-guy judge, was not a civil liberties judge, and Segal had pleaded for a postponement. But Judge Walters had been adamant. He would try the Hall case, there would be no delay, motion denied!

Bill gasped when Judge Walters entered the courtroom, a tall, gaunt old man, stooped forward in his black robes, staring out at the courtroom until finally his eyes settled on Bill and Segal, a long, contemptuous look that brought Bill's hopes crashing back to earth. He felt his hands trembling. The courtroom began to blur; he sat transfixed at the defense table while the first legal motions shot back and forth, trying to keep hold of reality.

The trial soon reached its first turning point. Would there be a jury? The judge said no. The crisp young Assistant U. S. Attorney, Carr, said no, but Segal persisted, citing case after case. Segal was the outsider, the wandering Jew. The judge was kindly when he spoke to young Carr, but with Segal his voice reached depths of condescension. "I *know* the law, Mr. Siggle; you needn't lecture me on the law; my knowledge of the law perhaps even equals your own."

Bill tried to follow the arguments. To seek a jury trial had been his one important decision. At first he had told Segal he would be non-co-operative, would not even enter a plea, but the lawyer had talked him out of that. Don't surrender. Don't make it easy for the bastards. And Bill had agreed. The legalisms became so immensely complex. All he wanted to do was to follow his conscience, to be a moral man, to take his stand, but the law did not care about morality or conscience. There were labyrinths of legality to wander through, with always the hope of freedom at their end. But somehow, in those labyrinths, you lost hold of what had first made you set out on the journey.

Still, he had agreed to fight them in court. To make them do it. To make a bland young prosecutor named Carr present the case. To make twelve of his fellow citizens convict him. To put it on their consciences. To drain the government's resources. But that was a joke; he saw that now. The government's resources were endless. He looked at Beth, sitting in the front row, just behind the little wooden railing. Oh, God, help Beth, help Beth.

Somehow, they got the jury trial. The judge granted it disdainfully —to show his fairness, he said—but Bill wondered if it mattered now.

The jury was chosen quickly. There was no lengthy questioning of each one, like in the movies, only a few general questions put to them all. The only young person on the panel, a girl with long brown hair, was excused when she said, yes, someone in her family, her brother-in-law, worked for the FBI. The only black on the panel asked to be excused because his wife was sick. Soon the twelve were chosen and the trial began.

The government's case was simple. A thick manila envelope. The file on William Hall. The young prosecutor read from it. On such-and-such a date William Hall had appeared at such-and-such an induction center and refused induction. Segal's various objections got nowhere. The record stood; the manila envelope had spoken; the prosecution rested.

Defense witnesses. Bill's good character, high repute. Brother Apple, the black minister from Fourteenth Street. An OEO official who said, yes, Bill Hall had administered an outstanding anti-poverty program. A Georgetown University professor who testified to the sincerity of Bill's beliefs. The judge chose to question the professor. "You speak of morality, sir, but what happens to our country if all these high-minded young men decide they don't want to fight to defend our freedom? Answer me that, sir?" And the professor replied at length about individual conscience, a higher morality, Thoreau; he droned on until even Bill was bored.

Then the crunch. The defendant would like to speak in his own behalf.

"There is the question of intent, your honor," Segal insisted. "This young man acted out of conscientious belief, with no criminal intent, only to follow his beliefs, and it is the right of the jury to consider his intent when weighing his guilt or innocence."

"You do not deny that he broke the law?" Walters asked.

"I say he acted without criminal intent."

"Yet he broke the law when he refused induction?"

"I say he is a conscientious objector and should have been thus designated by his draft board."

"The draft board's decision is not under review here," Walters shot back.

"I assert that the jury may make the final judgment on the propriety of his classification."

"That is not a matter for the jury to decide," the judge said.

"The California case—"

"You have told us six times about the California decision," Walters broke in. "The California decision is not binding on this court."

The judge glowered. Bill saw that it was all over, it had been as bad as it could be, they had gotten the wrong judge and they had angered him and there was no hope now.

Just then Carr rose.

"Your honor, I would make no objection if your honor chose to let

Mr. Hall testify in his own behalf. My own view is that such testimony has no effect on the law of the case."

Even the judge was surprised. He frowned, blinked his eyes, stretched his lips tight.

"The decision rests, of course, with the court," he said.

"Of course," Carr said.

The judge pursed his lips.

"However, in light of the government's rather unusual statement, and my own desire to persuade Mr. Siggle of this court's fairness, the defendant may testify."

Three minutes later, Bill was on the stand.

"I suggest you keep your comments brief, young man," the judge instructed. "This trial has already gone on too long."

Bill took the oath. He saw Beth trying to smile at him; he saw the jury as a blur, twelve strangers in a wooden box; he heard Segal telling him to speak, to tell his story. Tell us your philosophy, in twenty-five words or less.

"I refused induction because I love my country," he said. "Somehow, this country is waging an illegal and immoral war, killing innocent people in a distant part of the world where we have no valid interests. I cannot in conscience make myself a part of that slaughter. My country asks me to choose between my conscience and my freedom. I must choose my conscience. I don't know what else to say."

Carr rose to cross-examine. "You did refuse induction, Mr. Hall?"

"Yes."

"And you were aware of the possible consequences?"

"Yes."

"You were prepared to pay the price for following your conscience?"

"If necessary, yes."

"No further questions."

Bill felt good as he left the stand. He might have said more, but he didn't think it would have mattered. He had made his point, and he doubted if the jury would have been impressed by oratory.

Carr's summation was brief and businesslike. Segal's was impassioned. The jury filed out at eleven o'clock and was back at eleven-thirty.

The jury foreman, a kindly-looking old man, stood up, glanced at Bill, then answered the judge's question.

"We find the defendant guilty as charged."

Bill sat motionless, staring at the jury foreman. He wished he could have met him somewhere else. He thought he could have made him understand. Bill felt no anger. He was glad it was finally over.

But Segal was on his feet again. "Your honor, I assume there will be the usual thirty-day postponement before sentencing?"

"Do you assume that, Mr. Siggle? I don't assume that. I think this case has dragged on long enough."

"There are of course affidavits we wish to file as to Mr. Hall's character and importance to his community."

"Mr. Siggle, I am willing to stipulate to Mr. Hall's fine character. We've already heard your character witnesses. I wish to proceed with the sentencing."

"Let me speak with my client, your honor."

The judge nodded and Segal leaned close to Bill. "I can probably get it delayed for thirty days if I insist," he whispered.

"Does it matter?"

"Not much. It'll still be Walters. Unless the son of a bitch should drop dead first."

"Do I go straight from here to prison?"

"No, we'll get a stay, pending appeal."

"Then let's get it over with," Bill said.

Segal rose. "Your honor, we are willing to proceed to sentencing. And at this time I'd like to petition your honor to grant Mr. Hall a suspended sentence, with the provision that he continue his settlement-house work as a form of alternative, civilian service."

"Mr. Siggle, I'm not conducting an employment agency."

"I realize that, your honor, but alternative service is an established concept, and well within your powers."

"Mr. Siggle, I've acquitted one or two draft dodgers, when the evidence required it, but I've never put one on probation."

"I suggest that now would be a good time to begin. Mr. Hall is clearly a man who has acted on moral grounds."

"Oh, bosh, Mr. Siggle. Mr. Hall is clearly a very clever young man. He lives in a big house in Washington with his girl friend and gets money from the government and doesn't have to account to anybody. So when he's asked to serve his country he becomes a Johnny-come-lately conscientious objector. I don't call that conscientious. I call that opportunism."

"Your honor," Segal protested, "I must submit that Mr. Hall is one of the least opportunistic young men I've ever known. He has worked with the poor, he served in the Peace Corps . . ."

"Yes, that too," the judge said. "Had himself a nice little junket at the taxpayers' expense."

"I submit that, given your honor's obvious attitude toward this defendant—"

"Stop right there, Mr. Siggle! You're getting very close to contempt of court. I know about you, sir, and the kind of people you represent."

"There are many precedents for leniency in cases of this nature. I think every fact calls for Mr. Hall to be given the lightest possible sentence."

Carr rose to his feet. "Your honor, if I might say one word?"

"Of course, Mr. Carr."

"The government makes no formal recommendation, but we would have no objection if your honor wished to be lenient with Mr. Hall."

Bill stared at Carr, a smooth, clean-cut young man with an American-flag pin in the lapel of his glen plaid suit. He felt a last atom of hope struggling inside him.

"Well, that is a most unusual comment," the judge said.

"My own observation, your honor," Carr said, "is that Mr. Hall is a sincere if misguided young man, and I am not unaware that other jurisdictions have shown leniency in cases of this nature."

Segal was on his feet again. "I applaud Mr. Carr's recommendation," he said, "and I urge your honor to give it serious consideration."

The judge frowned. "I will say this, Mr. Siggle, I have nothing against this defendant. But I am sentencing him because either federal judges must put some teeth in the draft law or the draft law can be torn up. I must do my duty. If the Court of Appeals chooses to reverse me, there will be no hard feelings. I couldn't care less."

The judge turned to Bill. "William Hall, have you anything more to say before I pass sentence on you?"

Bill hesitated. There was so much to be said. But it wouldn't matter. They were all playing out their roles—he and Segal and the judge and the prosecutor—the roles that their lives had prepared them to play, all of them believing in what they did, and whatever happened was inevitable, had been determined far back in the history of their lives and their nation. Nothing he could say would matter. Only what people did mattered now.

"No. Except to thank my lawyer and my friends, the people who have worked with me and believe in me. I take my strength from them."

The courtroom was silent. They all stared at the old judge.

"Mr. Hall, it is within my power to sentence you to five years in prison. However . . ."

However! Beth gasped.

"However, in view of Mr. Carr's statement, I am taking a more lenient course."

Bill stood straight. He was thinking of the pond on his father's farm where he had fished when he was a boy.

"I therefore sentence you, William Hall, to be committed to the custody of the Attorney General and confined in such institution as he may direct for a term of thirty-six months, unless sooner released by operation of law."

Beth's scream filled the courtroom.

The bailiffs moved toward her. The judge pounded his gavel.

"Get that woman out of here! Get her out! One more sound and you'll all be in contempt. It's my own fault, for this damnable leniency!"

Bill saw two bailiffs leading Beth out.

"I request a sixty-day stay of execution so the defense can appeal," Segal said.

"Granted," the judge snapped. "Appeal all you please. Court is adjourned!"

Bill turned, feeling weak, surprised to still be free, and raced after Beth. She was in the corridor, leaning against the wall and crying, with the two bailiffs standing nearby. Bill put his arms around her.

"Three years," she cried. *"Three years!"*

"There's still the appeal. And three years means I can be paroled in eighteen months."

"I can't stand it. *I can't stand it!"*

"We have to stand it," he told her. "Let's get out of here."

Segal caught up with them on the sidewalk. He put his arm around Bill. "I'm sorry, son," he said. "That was the worst travesty I've ever seen. And I've seen a few."

Bill tried to smile. "Well, you saved me two years."

"I didn't do that. Carr did that. I stayed behind and talked to him, to see if I could find out why."

212

"Did you?"

"He let drop that he was in law school with Beth's brother. My guess is that the Senator called him and asked him to do anything he could. And Carr was impressed by you, too. He said it was too bad about the little girl getting hurt and Judge Meriweather not being here. He said Meriweather would probably have given you a suspended sentence."

Bill began to laugh. For all his high-mindedness, it came down in the end to luck, luck and politics, the system operating as it always had.

"Yeah, that was a bit unfortunate, wasn't it?" he said, and their little group walked down the sidewalk to the parking lot to start the drive back to Washington.

11

Charles Pierce, bone-tired, growing more depressed by the minute, sat in the back seat of a Ford convertible waving at the occasional person who appeared on the sidewalks of this quiet Oregon town. The passers-by were few, and usually surprised to see the convertible and the waving men, for Peter Wilson's campaign worked on faith, not advance work, and no one had bothered to turn out a crowd. Most of the time, Charles looked above the townspeople and their little town at the majestic, snow-capped peaks that towered over them.

The sound of cheers jerked Charles's attention earthward. Cheers? Up ahead, in front of a movie house where a Disney film was showing, four high school kids, two boys and two girls, were cheering Peter Wilson's approach. One of the boys was waving a sign saying "Peace Now!!!" The four of them stepped up their cheers and applause as the little two-car motorcade drew near.

"Your people," Charles said to Pete Wilson. Pete was grinning and giving them the V-sign.

"Too bad they can't vote," Pete whispered back. The kids ran out into the street to touch Pete's outstretched hand. Then they began to trot along the side of the road, easily keeping up with the slow-moving convertibles.

"God bless 'em," Pete Wilson said.

Yeah, God bless 'em, Charles thought. Blessed are the little doves, let them come unto me, for such is the Kingdom of an ex-Senator.

Peter Wilson, his long face sadder than ever, fighting the good

214

fight, waving at shoppers who didn't wave back, trying to explain the war to people who didn't care, rejected by the Administration, barely renominated by his own party, running out of money, running scared against a good-looking, hard-lining TV-whiz opponent. Pete Wilson, lover of children, dogs, Mozart. Pete Wilson, moving through an indifferent world, trailed by a ragtag band of peacenik high school kids.

What am I doing here?

I am helping my friend.

Hypocrite! You are helping yourself. You are reminding yourself of the realities in the Age of Johnson. You are reminding yourself that it is the Peter Wilsons of the world who get defeated, and the Rip Hortons of the world who become chairmen of the Armed Services Committee.

Pete Wilson, decent, intelligent, doomed.

Up at the next corner, six or eight men were standing in front of an American Legion hall, drinking beer and watching the two oncoming cars. They waved two signs. One said "No Surrender," the other, "Wilson sells out GIs." The convertible came abreast of them. Boos, catcalls, curses.

"Wave to the sons of bitches," Charles told Pete Wilson. Charles smiled and waved and just then he saw the kids with the "Peace Now" sign trotting along the sidewalk, saw a man in a red and black mackinaw seize the sign from the sandy-haired boy who was carrying it and smash it to the ground. The sandy-haired boy tried to retrieve the sign and another man, bald, stocky, red-faced, knocked him down.

"Stop the car," Peter Wilson called to the college student who was driving.

"What do you think you're doing?" Charles asked.

"I can't stand by while they beat up my people."

"You can't get involved in sidewalk brawls," Charles said. "The kids can take care of themselves."

"I'm getting out," Pete insisted.

"The hell you are," Charles said. "Let's get going. We're late for the luncheon."

The scuffle seemed to be breaking up. Peter Wilson cursed, but told the driver to go on.

"I don't know what to do," he said. "Those Legionnaires didn't just happen to be there. It's organized. It happens in every town."

Charles nodded grimly. He was thinking that the Legionnaires were about all that was organized in his friend's campaign.

Carey's Diner. No one was out front to greet them. Inside, they eventually persuaded a waitress to tell them where the private dining room was, the one the Kiwanis used on Wednesdays, and the Democratic ladies were using today, trying to prop up the sagging campaign of Peter Wilson.

The luncheon began. Chitchat, chicken and peas, cheerful Democratic ladies, sullen-looking husbands. A tanned blonde with a deep voice tried to draw Charles into conversation. Charles talked to her—she was the best-looking of the lot—but only with half his mind. His mind was back at the airport where, a couple of hours earlier, he'd seen a real pro in action.

They'd arrived on separate planes, Nixon's a few minutes before Charles's. By the time Charles went in search of his hosts and his bags, Nixon was already talking into the TV cameras. Trim, well groomed, confident.

Tricky Dick, charming the boondocks press.

What did Mr. Nixon think of the San Francisco riots?

The smile faded. One clenched fist pounded the air for emphasis. "Let me just say this. We can't have mob rule in this country. The decent people of America, and there are many, many more of those, won't put up with it."

Did Mr. Nixon detect any trends as he traveled around the country on behalf of Republican candidates?

"Let me say this. I've noticed some new styles in the country. The skirts are shorter, the pants are tighter, and LBJ's coattails are going out of fashion."

Chuckles. Scribbles in little notebooks. The all-new 1966 Nixon.

An eager grin, an awkward wave, and the newest Nixon marched off, trailed by a young man in a dark suit who carried his bag. To Charles's surprise, Nixon walked straight toward him, hand outstretched.

"Charles? How've you been?"

They had met once, in the 1950s. Charles hadn't the slightest desire to renew the acquaintanceship. But he had no choice. That was part of the political game. The less you liked someone, the nicer you were to him.

216

"I'm fine. I hear you've been getting around a lot lately."

The quick grin, the narrow unsmiling eyes, the carefully chosen words. "Oh, I try to do my part. Well. I guess we're here in opposite corners, so to speak."

Of course. Nixon would be here to help Pete Wilson's opponent.

"I imagine so," Charles said. Irony? Just a touch. You could afford a touch of irony with a politician who'd lost his last two elections.

Nixon ignored it. "Wilson's in trouble," he confided. Impersonal. The old pro. "It's too bad. I hear he's a nice fellow."

A reporter came up. "Mr. Nixon," he said, "what do you think of Senator Wilson's criticisms of the war in Vietnam?"

A troubled expression. "Well, let me just say that while I would never question Senator Wilson's sincerity or his patriotism—and we all want peace, every American wants peace—I must in candor say that his criticisms and those of the other ultradoves can only encourage Hanoi and undercut the morale of our boys in the field."

The reporter scribbled, checked his watch, dashed for a phone booth.

Nixon smiled again. "Well, as I was saying, we're on opposite sides here, but I can remember being on the same side with your father, in many a fight, back in the old days. A fine man and a great Senator. Well, nice to see you."

The quick grin, a soft handshake, and Nixon walked briskly out to a waiting limousine. Charles picked up his bags, which had finally arrived, and wondered where the people were who were supposed to meet him. He sighed. He'd been in this state for fifteen minutes and already he was depressed.

But of course it got worse. His escort arrived, a few minutes later, two undergraduates in a green Volkswagen, and hauled him the thirty miles to meet Pete Wilson's two-car caravan to Carey's Diner, where now the chicken and peas had all been choked down, the chipped plates had been carried away, and Charles was rising to do his bit. For ten minutes he praised Pete Wilson. Pete Wilson the conservationist. Pete Wilson the friend of labor. Pete Wilson the consumer advocate. Pete Wilson who had brought jobs and dams and new post offices to the state. He praised Pete Wilson for everything he could think of, except of course the two things that were on everyone's mind, Vietnam and civil rights.

Because Pete Wilson would say all that for himself. In a year when doves were being shot down all over America, Pete Wilson would keep on calling the war unjust and immoral. What was it someone had called Mark Hatfield? The dove who ducked. Well, it was damned hard not to duck when your mail was running four to one against you, when you stood there day after day telling people truths they didn't want to hear, when your own Administration was fighting you, when you saw good men getting shot down in primary after primary for getting too far out front. It was damned hard not to back off, not to retreat to the weasel words about reasonable times and honorable settlements. Charles had done a little ducking himself. But Pete Wilson wouldn't duck. Pete Wilson would talk sense to the people. Like Adlai. Yeah.

As Charles neared the end of his introduction, he let loose with every trick he'd learned in three years of speechmaking. His voice rose, his fists pounded the air, his phrases rhapsodized . . . man of courage . . . man of vision . . . a fighter . . . a builder . . . my friend . . . great Senator . . . great American . . . *Pete Wilson!*

He knew what he wanted and they knew it too. He wanted them to get to their feet, to get their fat asses out of their folding chairs and give Pete Wilson a standing ovation. There was a moment's hesitation and he stared at them, challenged them, shamed them.

Up! On your feet, you sons of bitches. Up, damn you, up!

He won. They rose, cheering and applauding, and Pete came forward, eyes glistening, to shake Charles's hand and begin his speech. Charles walked back to his chair, enjoying the applause, pleased with himself, and as he sat down, the tanned blonde squeezed his hand in congratulations and held it longer than she needed to. Charles looked her over again, then turned his attention back to Pete Wilson.

Because Pete was blowing it. Charles had set him up, had gotten the audience excited the way you might get a woman excited, so that now all Pete had to do was ram it home, give it to them, give them patriotism and pie in the sky and whatever cheap thrills they yearned for, bring them over the edge for the climax they wanted. For politics and sex were hopelessly intermingled. The kids who jumped and cried for Elvis or the Beatles were not that different from the people who cheered and chanted for Barry or Jack or Bobby. They all wanted the same thing, wanted to escape reality, wanted the demon lover, the *deus ex machina* to swoop down from the sky and fulfill all their

218

fantasies, set to rest all their fears. Politicians, the younger ones at least, were supposed to be sex symbols.

Charles guessed his political success to date had been as much based on his good looks as on his good deeds, such as they were. Fine; he'd make the most of it. When he got old and gray he'd try to make the transition from sex symbol to father figure, but for the time being if the people wanted to be teased, aroused, seduced, why not give them what they asked for? Now and then, in the heat of passion, you might whisper a few words of truth into their ear.

But Pete Wilson would not seduce them. Pete Wilson would make a dull speech in a flat voice and soon the audience that Charles had aroused was lost, angry at this *coitus interruptus*.

It all seemed so hopeless.

Charles's father had once said he'd rather die in office that very day than be defeated and linger on as an ex-Senator. You saw ex-Senators around the Capitol occasionally, wandering like ghosts, men who seemed to have shrunk in stature, men who seemed more dead than alive. It was a terrible fate. Most Senators Charles knew would do almost anything to avoid it. But not Pete Wilson.

"Jesus Christ, I need a drink!"

"Look in the glove compartment," said the sun-tanned blonde, whose name was Marie something-or-other and who was president of the local Democratic women.

Charles looked, and found a bottle of Beefeater.

"Praise the Lord," Charles said. "What about ice?"

"There's a cooler in the back seat," Marie said, and gave him another of her lingering smiles. She was thirty-five or so, a pleasant, full-bodied woman, quick to laugh.

Charles poured himself a drink. He was in her Pontiac—somehow she had replaced the students in the Volkswagen—and he had two hours to kill before meeting Pete Wilson for dinner.

"You want one?" Charles asked.

Marie laughed merrily. "Oh, I don't drink," she said. "Like the old joke says, you don't have to drink and smoke to have a good time. Do you remember that one?"

Charles did indeed.

"A lot of politicians come to town," Marie said, "and having a bottle of something handy is a good way to be popular with most of 'em.

Most of 'em will even talk to an old widow woman like me, for a drink or two."

"You're a widow, Marie?"

"My late husband was on the county commission here. That's how I got into politics. I don't know much about the philosophies and all, but I like to meet new people all the time."

"How do you think it looks for Pete Wilson?"

Marie shook her head. "Lord, I just don't want to talk about it. I *love* Pete. But people just think he's gone overboard on this war thing and all this civil rights mess. And every time he opens his mouth he makes it worse."

"Let's don't talk about it."

"You want to go for a ride up in the mountains?"

"Marie, I'm tired, really tired, I'd rather just go somewhere and relax for a couple of hours."

"We could go to my house," she said. "Or back to your motel, either one."

So now it was "we." He looked at Marie again and approved of what he saw. A fine-looking woman, apparently available. Why not? Intellectually, he was willing. Physically, mentally, spiritually, he wasn't sure he was up to it.

"Maybe back to my motel," he said, "in case I get any calls."

She drove them to the motel and got out of the car without being asked, carrying the bottle in her purse, bringing the ice bucket, smiling.

"I guess I might come in for a few minutes," Marie said. "I was supposed to interview you for our Democratic newsletter."

"Sure," Charles said, but when they got inside she didn't interview him. Instead they talked about her.

Marie said she'd married her husband when she was seventeen and he was forty, a rich farmer and widower. "Lord, I hadn't the faintest notion what marriage was all about. I thought it was peaches and cream and going to church on Sunday. But Abe, that old goat, he only had one thing on his mind, he went after sex like it was going out of style. Lord, when I try to remember the first five years we were married, I don't think I ever got out of the bedroom. The funny thing was, just as I was getting interested, he was losing interest. Then we had the baby and it died and for a long while I was down on sex and marriage and life and everything. Then Abe had his stroke, and then there were all those years of nursing him. It was awful, going from being a wife to being a nurse. It'd been different if I'd really loved Abe, but I didn't. I was just chained to him, waiting for him to die."

Charles finished his drink and poured himself another, a short one. He was very tired. The thing he wanted to do most was to sleep, sleep for about twenty-four hours. "You sure you don't want one?" he asked Marie, who sat in the room's one chair while he stretched out across the bed.

"No, thanks. Abe drank a lot, and I used to watch him and think, Lord, if I ever started, I'd never stop. So I never started."

She gave him a big smile, and he tried to smile back at her.

"You poor boy, you're tired, aren't you?"

"Yeah."

"Lie down on your stomach and I'll rub your back."

"Do what?"

"Go ahead, don't be bashful. I'm the greatest back-rubber in six states. Go on, stretch out real comfortable."

Charles was too tired to argue. He loosened his tie and stretched out on the narrow motel bed and soon she was expertly massaging his back.

"How's that?"

"Good," Charles admitted. Soon he had forgotten all about Pete Wilson and the speech that afternoon and the speech to come that night, soon he was relaxed and content, poised somewhere between wakefulness and sleep.

"It'd be better if you took your shirt off," Marie whispered, but Charles didn't answer. He was asleep.

Marie kept up the massage for a minute, gradually slowing down, so as not to wake him. She got up and looked at him, his face profiled against the pillow, his arms crossed above his head, his breath coming slowly and gently.

"You boys," she said. "You boys are all the same."

At six Charles joined Pete and his advisers—a political science professor, a graduate student, an anti-war housewife—for dinner. They watched the evening news, which showed Pete trying to explain his open-housing position to a skeptical reporter, Pete frowning, stammering, getting into the legalities, seeming somehow evasive, then Pete's interview was followed by one of Nixon declaring, "We can't have mob rule in this country." To Charles, the contrast was devastating. He saw votes slipping away from Pete Wilson every time he spoke, like blood seeping from an open wound.

"You looked great, Pete," the political science professor declared. "Top drawer."

You poor bastard, you're living in a dream world.

Finally, the speech that night, three hundred people in an auditorium that would seat a thousand.

"We'd have had a better turnout," the poly sci professor told Charles, "except there's a big football game tonight."

Well, why didn't you reschedule the speech, you idiot? Or at least get a smaller hall?

Again, Charles introduced Pete, but without the fire he had aroused that noon. You couldn't get a standing ovation in a hall that was two thirds empty. Nor did Charles feel the spirit any more. He just did the best he could, then Pete made his speech, the same speech as that afternoon, and it was awful.

Pete insisted on taking Charles to the airport himself. On the way, they talked about the campaign.

"How'd it look to you?" Pete asked. "I get so involved, it's hard to make a judgment."

"Well, I'd like to see you open up a little, talk about the economy, not just the war." He tried to think of something positive to say. "Your people," he said, "your people are really dedicated."

Pete grinned. "Yeah, they're great, they're what's going to pull me through. You watch. The polls have been bad, but I can feel the tide beginning to turn."

My God, he believes it, he believes he's going to win.

At midnight they parted in the drafty little airport. It was like shaking hands with a corpse.

12

DECEMBER 1966

Carol called and asked to speak to Charles but, as often happened, she ended up talking to Al Kline.

"Al? I want to talk to Charles." She tried to keep the annoyance from her voice; she hated having to justify herself to her husband's assistant. "It's something about Beth."

Damn, Al Kline thought, but he only said, "What's the trouble?"

"I don't know exactly. A girl called here, looking for Beth, and said something about Bill leaving today and there being a . . . a *party* or something. I thought Charles would know."

"He's left for Chicago."

"I thought he left at noon."

"He caught an earlier flight."

"Damn. Well, I'll just call Bill directly, then."

Al Kline was thinking fast, wondering how much harm she could do if left to herself, wondering what the Senator's interests were and what his own interests were, caught in the same impossible equation that every Senate aide found himself caught in from time to time.

"I know a little about it," he said. "Bill has to turn himself in this afternoon . . ."

"Where?"

"At the Federal Building. And, yes, he and Beth are having some of their friends over."

"Then why has Charles gone off to make a speech?"

"He didn't know about it."

223

"Didn't *know* about it? You mean *you* knew and didn't *tell* him?"

"That's right."

"And you think you can play God like that?"

Lady, I don't play God; I play the right-hand man.

"Look, Mrs. Pierce, point one is there's nothing he could do there except get upset. Point two is Beth didn't *want* him there. I talked to her yesterday. She said, 'They live in a different world from us.' That's a direct quote."

"It doesn't matter what she *wants*. He's her *brother*. Her *family*. My God! I'll just have to go over there myself."

"I don't think you should."

"*You* don't think I *should?* Why, you presumptuous, arrogant—"

"Okay, I'll meet you there."

Carol couldn't keep from laughing. "You'll *meet* me there? You meet me there and I'll spit in your eye."

Carol slammed down the phone. Al Kline sighed and more gently lowered his receiver. As he did, Charles looked in the door.

"I'm off for the airport," he said. "Everything okay?"

"Sure," Al Kline said. "Have a nice trip."

Al did meet her there, but she didn't spit in his eye. She didn't like Al and she didn't think it was her fault. She guessed he resented her, saw her as a threat to his precious time with "the Senator." She had tried to be friendly. She had once very politely suggested that he call her Carol instead of Mrs. Pierce; he had frowned and after that he didn't call her anything. But Carol thought it was beneath her to squabble with him. If he showed up at Kennedy House she would be cool, cordial, proper.

Sure enough, he was standing on the sidewalk when she drove up, and he walked over while she parked her car.

"How did you know about this?" she asked.

"I've kept my hand in. I've tried to help Bill on some legal angles."

"Does Charles know about all this?"

"Some of it. He can't worry about everything."

They stopped in front of the old town house. They could hear music from within. "One thing you ought to know," Al said. "They were married a couple of days ago."

"*Married?* With him going to *prison?*"

"It was what she wanted."

224

Carol shook her head and pushed the front door open without knocking. Al followed her into the hallway. The twenty or thirty young people gathered in the living room didn't seem to notice them. Carol took off her coat and added it to the dozen others that were piled precariously on a chair by the stairs. Then she turned back to the living room, unsure of herself, not certain what she was doing here, yet sure that she had to be here.

She stood in the living-room doorway, waiting for someone to notice her, to greet her, but no one did. Carol was bewildered. All her life, parties had opened up to her, drawn her in, drawn warmth and gaiety from her, but these young people stood in their little groups speaking in whispers and listening to the music, a Dylan lament, as if she didn't exist. They didn't even seem alive.

"What's the matter with them?" she asked Al.

"Most of them are high as a kite," Al said. Carol was puzzled, because no one was drinking, and then she saw Bill coming across the room.

Bill was alive. There was pain and laughter and sorrow in his face, and when he reached her she threw her arms around him.

"Bill, I'm so . . . so sorry about everything."

"It'll all work out," he said. "Sometimes the hardest things are the best."

"It's so *unfair*."

Bill smiled. "No, the government is fair. It's insane, but very fair."

"I wish you'd told us you were getting married."

"I'm sorry about that. I had to do what Beth wanted. But after today there's so much you and Charles can do for her."

"Where is she?"

"She's upstairs. She'll be down in a minute."

"Bill, is there anything Charles can do? For you, I mean."

Bill shook his head. "He had Al check out some things, but it's really all cut and dried."

Carol saw him look away, and she turned and saw Beth at the head of the stairs. She was wearing a long white dress, a dress that might have been her grandmother's, with a full skirt and ruffles at the collar and cuffs. Her hair was long and loose around her shoulders. Carol thought how strange she looked, and waited for her to smile, to speak, to come down. But Beth just stood there, pale and lovely, staring into space.

225

Bill stepped to the foot of the stairs. "Beth, Carol is here."

She seemed not to hear, but after a moment she put one hand on the railing and began to descend.

Carol heard Al Kline mutter, "Enter Ophelia, stoned."

Only when she reached the bottom did Beth seem to come to life; she looked at Carol and smiled and extended her hands. When she spoke it was in a breathless, high-pitched voice—a debutante's voice, Carol thought. "Carol, it's so good of you to come," she said. "Have you met our friends? I do so want you to meet our friends."

"Beth, are you all right?"

"Of course," Beth said. "I'm here with Bill and my friends so of course I'm all right. Come on, now, and meet everybody."

She took Carol's hand and led her to a cluster of young men standing beside the stereo. "You've met Tim Carter, haven't you? He's Bill's assistant. Say hello, Tim."

"Hello," Tim said.

"And this is Skip, who's down from New York, and Junior, who's with SDS, and this is Brother Apple, who married us. Brother Apple, this is Carol, my brother's wife."

"The pleasure is mine, Mrs. Pierce," Brother Apple said gravely. He was a short, broad Negro in a black suit, and Carol saw that he was alive too, he had pain in his voice and sadness in his eyes.

"He had a *terrible* time marrying us," Beth went on in her singsong voice. "It was all my fault. I didn't want God in the ceremony. But you slipped God in there anyway, didn't you, Brother Apple?"

"Indeed I did, my child."

"It didn't matter," Beth said vaguely. "It was a lovely ceremony anyway. I'm so sorry you and Charles couldn't have been here."

She led Carol on from group to group, to meet young men and women who would nod vaguely and go on with their conversations; it was all eerie; Carol was frightened and a little angry.

"Beth, have these people been smoking marijuana? I thought I smelled it."

Beth nodded absently. "I guess so," she said. "Some may be doing acid. Did you want something? Tim would have . . ."

"I don't *want* anything," Carol cried. "I just . . ."

But Beth had deposited her with Brother Apple and gone back upstairs. She talked to the minister for a while, about Beth and Bill and the work they had done in the neighborhood, but they did not talk

226

about the thing that most concerned Carol, that Beth was acting so strange, seemed floating off in space somewhere.

Then she saw Al Kline having an argument with Tim Carter in the hallway.

". . . damn it, what's she on?"

"None of this is any of your fucking business."

"Answer me before I get mad." Al grabbed the younger man's collar and pushed him against the wall.

"Reds. She's on reds. What did you think?"

"You son of a bitch . . ."

"If you don't like her this way, mister, you ought to see her the other way."

Al Kline cursed, then released the boy and walked away. Carol grabbed his arm.

"Al, what in God's name is going on here?"

"What's going on? Most of these people are stoned and Beth's out of her head on pills and Bill's leaving for prison in ten minutes. That's what's going on."

Carol went upstairs to find Beth.

She found them in the bedroom. Bill was sitting on the edge of the bed with his face in his hands. Beth was in the bathroom. As Carol entered, she swallowed a pill and washed it down with water. Carol ran to her.

"Beth, you've got to quit taking those things."

Beth smiled at her. "Things? What things?"

"Charles and I want to help you. You could come stay with us."

"Oh, I'll be fine here with my friends. I'll have so much work to do now."

Carol turned to Bill. "For God's sake, isn't there anything you can do? Isn't there any way to get through to her?"

Bill shook his head. "You can't reach her now. But come see her tomorrow. She needs you. There's no more I can do."

"How can you leave her?" Carol cried.

"I have to live my life. I can't live two lives."

Tim Carter appeared in the doorway. "We've got to go," he said.

"Just one second, darling," Beth said. "I want to show Carol the beautiful poem I was reading last night. Wasn't that odd, that I'd be reading poetry? It was one of Shakespeare's sonnets, actually. Just a moment, it's here somewhere."

She was thumbing through a book of poetry while Bill looked on helplessly.

"Bill, we've got to go," Tim Carter said again.

Bill took Beth's arm. She turned and smiled at Carol. "I'll read it to you some other time," she said. "You'll come visit me, won't you?"

They walked down the stairs. Most of the people were waiting in the entrance hall and they said quiet farewells to Bill there. Only a few people followed Beth and Bill outside, where Tim Carter's VW bus was double-parked on S Street. Carol followed along, wanting to cry out in frustration, wishing Charles were here, yet knowing Al had been right, that Charles would only have made it worse.

Beth broke when they reached the sidewalk, as if the chill December wind had swept away all her defenses. One moment she was walking along holding Bill's arm, smiling, and the next minute her screams filled the air.

"You can't go you can't go we can go to Canada I have the money I won't let you go."

"Beth, I'm leaving now."

"No! *I won't let you go!*" She seized Bill's arm.

"Beth, please. I've got to go. I can't be late."

Still she held on, sobbing, her face against his chest. Tim Carter called to them from the car, "Damn it, we've got to *go*." He looked at Al Kline, who was standing beside Carol on the sidewalk. "You, mister, give him some help."

Al put his arms around Beth and loosened her grip on Bill. She seemed to have given up, but after Bill had kissed her and climbed into the VW, she began to scream again and to struggle to be free.

"Bill, *come back, come back!*" As the VW began to pull away, with Bill's face frozen at the window, she broke free from Al and began to run along the sidewalk. After a moment she stumbled and fell headlong. Carol started after her but Brother Apple had come out and he reached her first and helped her to her feet. Her lip was cut and blood had splattered onto her white dress. Carol tried to wipe the blood away but Beth pushed past her and stumbled into the house. Carol sank to her knees on the sidewalk. Everyone else had gone back inside except Al Kline. The street was quiet again. After a while Al helped Carol to her car and sat with her, holding her hand, until she had stopped crying and was able to drive on home.

13

The running away started in the early spring. The first time, Carol wasn't home, and the second time, Hugh just mumbled something about school letting out early. But the third time, Hugh's teacher called and said he had simply left school at lunchtime and not returned.

Carol was about to call the police when Hugh wandered in, a book in one hand, a bag of M & Ms in the other. Carol took him into the study and questioned him. He was casual at first—he'd just decided to go get an art book from the public library—but soon he fell into her arms.

"I hate school! I hate it. All those colored kids just yell and mess around and make so much racket that nobody can learn anything. I *can't* keep on going there!"

Carol went to the school the next afternoon and got Miss Cooper's permission to observe Hugh's class. For a moment, as she entered the classroom and saw the maps and the flag and the little slant-top desks, Carol felt a wave of nostalgia for long-forgotten schooldays. But her nostalgia soon faded. Carol's memories were of attentive children sitting ramrod straight, raising their hands for permission to speak, reciting their lessons proudly, accepting pleased smiles from placid teachers. Hugh's class was not like that.

About twenty of the thirty-odd students were Negro. Two of the Negro boys wandered about constantly, not causing any trouble, just wandering. One boy slept in the back of the room. Three Negro girls in the back row were reading a movie magazine. Miss Cooper, ignoring all this, was conducting a reading class for about ten children near the front of the room. Hugh joined this group but he was clearly bored. Most of the others were poor readers and Miss Cooper was drilling them on the ABC level. Hugh looked at Carol with a scornful, you-see-what-I-mean expression. Once the three girls with the movie magazine put it away and came over to Carol and shyly asked who she was and where she lived and how she kept her skin so pretty.

The only time Miss Cooper came close to seizing the class's attention was when she read them a story. The story, at least, was familiar to Carol. It was from the sort of Dick and Jane book that she'd used a quarter century before. The story concerned Bob and Sue who, with their parents, had gone camping—driving to a national park, pitching their tent beside a river, cooking over a campfire—an activity that mystified the Negro students.

"Hey, Miz Cooper, why them people live in a *tent?*"

"Man, they *really* poor."

"If they poor, how come they got that big *car?*"

"Mebbe they In-juns!"

"You dumb burrhead, they not In-juns, they *white* folks."

"If they not In-juns, why they live in that *tent?*"

"Hugh," Miss Cooper cried above the din, "can you tell us why these people are living in a tent?"

"Because they're on vacation," Hugh said dryly. "They've got a house in town but they want to go camping for a while."

"Man, you crazy! Nobody with a *house* gonna live in a *tent!*"

Miss Cooper tried to explain that Hugh was right, but her explanation was greeted by hoots of disbelief, although she struggled on until the tale of the camping trip was finished.

"Is it always like that?" Carol asked Miss Cooper when the school day ended. She was too shocked to be tactful.

"Oh, today wasn't bad at all," Miss Cooper said in her sad, Southern-soft voice. "They were quite awed by your presence today."

"But how can you teach children who won't even sit still?"

"You can't, obviously. The best we can do is to concentrate on those who want to learn. As for the others . . . well, it's just a holding operation, really."

"Are there any signs of improvement?" Carol asked. "Do you think that by next year . . ."

"Who knows? There's talk of bringing in more Negro teachers next year, and that might help. It won't matter for me."

"Why not?"

"I've decided to retire. I don't have to for another five years, but I'm not a good teacher any more." Miss Cooper paused. "I hate to end my career as a failure, but that seems to be the case."

Carol touched her hand. "You've been a wonderful teacher," she protested. "Everyone in Georgetown knows that."

Miss Cooper shook her head. "Being a wonderful teacher seems to depend a great deal on the context in which you teach."

Carol didn't know what to say. She couldn't help Miss Cooper and she wasn't at all sure she could help her son.

"I just don't know what to do about Hugh and this . . . this leaving school."

"Perhaps the best thing," Miss Cooper said, "would be for me to let him go read in the library when he gets too bored. Or perhaps he could go outside and sketch, now that spring's here."

"But he can't just sketch and read *forever*. He's got to *learn*."

Miss Cooper shook her head slowly. "Frankly, Mrs. Pierce, I'd suggest that you put Hugh in a private school next year. He's a bright, sensitive boy, and another year like this one might turn him against school entirely."

Carol looked out the window at the schoolyard. Hugh was sitting on a bench reading one of his art books. Past him, three little girls were playing hopscotch. A private school. It was so simple.

"The problem is his father," Carol said, half to herself. "He believes so strongly in public education."

"Yes," Miss Cooper said sympathetically. "Yes, I suppose we all do, don't we?"

Miss Cooper started giving Hugh library passes each afternoon, but he continued to leave school one or two days each week. He had a child's fierce and simple logic. School was a classroom and a teacher and lessons to learn. If his school didn't offer him those things, why should he waste his time sitting in the library? Nothing Carol said could change his mind. The school never complained and Carol never spoke to Miss Cooper again. Nor did she ever tell

Charles that their son was running away from school. Charles would be no help. He would rant at the boy or call the principal but he would not help the problem. Charles seemed to Carol to have an incredible blind spot where Hugh's education was concerned. He was ruled by instincts that he expressed in half-baked clichés. When-I-was-a-boy . . . Got-to-learn-to-defend-himself . . . Got-to-learn-to-live-with-all-kinds . . . blah blah blah. Carol was bitter. The Great American Male spouting clichés that had absolutely nothing to do with her son and his fears and his terrible vulnerability.

Charles had had his chance back in the fall, after the incident of Joe-boy and the stolen crayons. Oh, Charles had an answer for that one. Invite the boy over to play. Make friends with him. That was all right with Carol, for she was enthusiastic then, and so one warm, windy October Saturday afternoon father and son had driven to Anacostia and returned with Joe-boy Parker.

He seemed a nice enough boy. He was a year older than Hugh and at least twenty pounds heavier, although not nearly so verbal. He replied with cautious "Yessums" and "Nossirs" to their questions, until Carol realized that the child was petrified to be in this big house with the strange white people, and she began to do all she could to make him feel at home. She fixed their lunch and then Charles took them upstairs to play with Hugh's chemistry set. But Joe-boy wasn't interested in chemistry, and it was at that point that Charles unveiled his surprise for the afternoon.

He brought out a box the size of a hatbox and pulled from it four big, round, wine-colored objects—Carol stared at them in confusion.

"Boxing gloves!" Charles announced. "You ever boxed, Joe-boy?"

"Nossir."

"Well, it's time both you boys learned to box. Come on out back and I'll give you a lesson."

"Charles!"

"Just calm down, Carol."

"Joe-boy's parents didn't send him over here to be in a fight."

"This isn't a fight. This is boxing. Hell, look at those gloves—they're like pillows."

"You could have asked me . . ."

"I knew what you'd say. But Hugh's not so damn delicate as you think. You let me handle this."

Carol stood at the kitchen window and watched as the boxing lesson began. He marked off a little "ring" with four lawn chairs. He had the boys strip off their shirts. Joe-boy, bare-chested, was muscular, a rich, glowing black. Hugh, in his undershirt, seemed frail and hollow-chested and his arms were like little white sticks stuck into those fat, absurd boxing gloves. Charles spent fifteen minutes showing them the basics—how to jab with the left and cross with the right, how to block punches, how to dance in and out. Joe-boy frowned in concentration, a willing pupil. Hugh kept shaking his head, looking around the yard in desperation. But no help came. Carol stayed at the window, immobile, furious, helpless.

She laughed once. Charles was bent over, giving his lesson, and she thought of the Boys' Club slogan: "A man never stands so tall as when he stoops to help a boy." Well, here he was, Charles Pierce, U. S. Senator, liberal, leader of men, stooped over to help two small boys—help them learn to pound each other in the face. Lovely. Oh God Oh God Oh God. And they wonder why we have wars. You are all children, insane children, screwing up people's lives and screwing up the world and all the time thinking how wonderful you are.

Charles blew on a little red and white plastic whistle. "Okay, men, come out fighting."

But they didn't come out fighting, not right away. Hugh stayed in his "corner" looking frightened. Joe-boy shuffled to the center of the "ring" and then just stood there, looking from Hugh to Charles, waiting for further instructions.

"Come on, Hugh, move on out," Charles called, and his son stepped reluctantly forward, his hands held awkwardly at his waist.

"Get your guard up," Charles called, and Hugh raised his hands a few inches.

The boys stood a few feet apart, staring uncertainly at one another.

"Come on, mix it up. Let's see some hustle, Joe-boy."

Joe-boy, anxious to please, began to move in a slow, graceful circle around Hugh.

"That's it, that's it!" Charles yelled. "That's a regular Ali-shuffle. Now, where's that combination I showed you?"

Joe-boy began to feint and bob, then to jab with his left hand, one-two-three, before crossing with a flashing right that made Carol flinch. But Joe-boy's blows stopped a few inches short of Hugh's outstretched gloves.

"That's it, Joe-boy," Charles shouted. "But move in, let's have some contact."

Joe-boy stared at Charles in confusion. It seemed to Carol that it was slowly dawning on him that Charles really wanted him to *hit* Hugh. Joe-boy shook his head in disbelief, then returned to his graceful circling—to Carol, he was a tiger stalking a young deer. Her face was pressed against the window, her lips moved soundlessly.

Joe-boy's first blows were gentle, pats on Hugh's face.

"Get your guard up, Hugh, get your guard up!"

But Hugh's guard was gossamer, and Joe-boy's jabs and right crosses easily brushed past it. Joe-boy began to put more weight behind his punches. Carol saw the shock on Hugh's face when the first one stung him, insulted him. He kept on with his own feeble combinations but Joe-boy ignored them.

"Come on, mix it up," Charles was shouting. "Fight, Joe-boy, fight!"

Joe-boy's punches came faster. Snap. Snap. Snap. Hugh's face was getting red. Snap. Snap. Snap—then the right flashing hard against Hugh's ear and he was down on the grass.

"Get up, son, get up!"

Carol beat her fists hard against the window sill. Oh God make them stop make them stop.

Charles helped Hugh to his feet and pushed him back into the fight. Joe-boy shuffled forward. Snap. Snap. Snap—then the right again and Hugh pitched forward to his knees, his blood spurting into the grass.

"Stop it! Do you hear me? Stop it!" She was on her knees beside Hugh, holding a dishtowel to his nose.

Charles knelt down beside them. "An ice pack's the thing for that nose," he said. He took the boxing gloves off Hugh's hands and mussed the boy's hair. "You were damn good, son. You learned a lot today. If you can stand up to a big kid like Joe-boy you can stand up to anybody."

Hugh managed a faint smile. He had survived. He had pleased his father. He had seen the first glimpse of manhood. Charles helped the boy to his feet and took him over for the ceremonial handshake with Joe-boy.

Carol went into the house to get the ice pack. She felt sick.

Joe-boy came again two weeks later but there was no boxing that time. Carol had seen to that. Instead, there was a third boy along,

Calvin Hopkins, who was Hugh's only real friend among the Negro students. Calvin was wiry and bright-eyed and shared Hugh's love of drawing. It was a rainy afternoon and the boys played peacefully in Hugh's room for three hours. Not until the next day did Hugh notice that his silver dollar was gone.

The silver dollar had once belonged to Hugh's namesake, the first Senator Pierce, and it had been a gift from his grandmother.

"Joe-boy took it," the boy insisted. "I want it back."

"We don't know who took it," Charles said. "You had two guests."

"Calvin wouldn't steal," Hugh said bitterly. "Joe-boy took it."

"Well, it's gone now," Carol said, "and you might as well forget about it."

"Forget, hell," Charles snapped. "I want both those boys back here next Saturday. We'll get to the bottom of this."

"Oh, Charles, you're not Perry Mason and whoever took it certainly isn't going to confess to you."

"You don't know what they'll do," Charles said. "You can't let a kid get away with something like that. Besides, that dollar belonged to my father and it makes me mad as hell!"

So the next Saturday Charles had his confrontation. Stern father and three wide-eyed kids met in the study. Carol watched from the hallway. Serious matter. Question of personal honor. Taking wrong step on Road of Life. Owe it to yourself. Come forward, admit mistake. Blah blah blah. Carol was weary of the whole thing. She had enough problems already, without importing more from Anacostia.

But, inside the study, the drama played itself out. Joe-boy issued protestations of innocence. Calvin stared at his shoes, on the verge of tears. But no confessions. Charles ran through his let-us-gather-by-the-river routine a second time, but the deed remained unresolved and the afternoon ended on a tense, inconclusive note.

Calvin's mother called the next morning, furious.

"Just what does your husband mean, calling my son a thief?"

"Mrs. Hopkins, I assure you, my husband did *not* . . ."

"Calvin *said* he called him a thief!"

Carol tried to explain. A missing silver dollar. Old family relic. Naturally want to inquire. A misunderstanding. Carol's voice grew weaker. Why was she arguing with this woman? Why wasn't Charles here to enjoy the fruits of his labors?

She finally calmed Mrs. Hopkins, but Calvin never came to their house again, nor did Hugh mention him again. The series of Parents' Council meetings that fall met a similar fate. The Negro parents were ultrasensitive and the whites too often stung their sensitivities with references to "these children" doing this or that. In December an angry shouting match was set off when one white mother remarked impatiently, "Why, some of these children can barely speak English." The meetings did not resume after Christmas.

It was in January that Carol, cleaning out Hugh's room one morning, found the silver dollar in a crack in the floor behind his bed. She smiled and shook her head and flipped it in her palm a few times. That afternoon she took a long walk and tossed the coin into the B & O Canal.

So the running away in the spring was just another manifestation of the problem and Carol did not go to Charles with it. He had lost interest in the whole subject of Hugh's schooling. He clung as devoutly as ever to his clichés, but he had lost interest in the specifics. The real question that spring was whether Hugh would have to return to Hyde in the fall. The boy asked her that question often, and for the moment all Carol could say was, "We'll see, darling. Just try not to worry about it."

Carol's job, too, was much on her mind that spring. The movement that the local press would later dub the WSG Sisterhood began innocently enough one day when she had lunch with Sally McCann in the station cafeteria.

Sally was Ken Holton's secretary, a bright, lively young woman of twenty-five. "Oh boy, am I ever pee-oh'd," Sally began.

"At what?" Carol asked.

"At that bastard Ken Holton. Our beloved general manager. There was a job coming open in Publicity and I'd told him for months I wanted a shot at it. So this morning it turns out he's hired some guy fresh out of J-school, some kid who doesn't know his ass and'll still be starting at more than I make now. Damn Ken Holton!"

Carol stirred her strawberry milkshake with a red plastic straw. "I've been after him to let me produce a documentary on VISTA," she said. "But all I get is blah-blah-blah. Which, translated, means Ken Holton doesn't want women producers."

"He gave me all this garbage about how he couldn't do without me," Sally said. "You know what it really means? One, that he wants a pretty face outside his office. Two, if I got a promotion, all the secretaries would start thinking they could move up. He wants to keep the niggers in their places."

Carol nodded her agreement. "You know, the real Negroes—or I guess we're supposed to say blacks now, aren't we?—the real Negroes are doing pretty well around here."

"And you know why?" Sally asked. "Because they organized and raised hell. We ought to organize something."

"You and me?"

"All the women here. Get together. Sign a petition or something."

"How's Ken going to respond to that?"

"Oh, you know Ken. The big liberal. The smoothie. He'll try to charm us into submission. Let's call a meeting of women. What do you say?"

Carol drank the last of her milkshake and thought about the idea. It wasn't her instinct to rock the boat. And she wasn't sure how the management—the men—would respond. At best with ridicule; at worst people might be fired.

But Carol was fed up, sick of the way women were treated here and everywhere else. She hated it and she was ready to do something about it.

"I say let's do it," Carol said. "Let's start calling people today."

Sally beamed, and as they walked out of the dingy little cafeteria a minute later, Carol felt better than she had in months.

Their first meeting was held in an empty conference room a week later, during the lunch hour. About twenty women came, and they all had the same story to tell, of jobs denied and unequal salaries.

"They'll never make a woman a salesman," complained Fran Harris, who'd been the sales manager's assistant for a decade. "When I asked Sam to consider me, he just said, 'Fran, how would it be if you took some client to lunch and you reached for the check? How's a man gonna like that?' I told him I thought most men would like it fine."

"We've got to get the facts and and then get together behind a plan," Sally said.

"What about salaries?" Carol asked. "Bess, are women making as much money as men for the same jobs?"

Everyone looked at Bess Hampton, who had been the assistant director of personnel for twenty years. "Carol, I . . . I just can't give out that information," Bess said sadly. "We all know the pay scales are unequal, but I can't give out specifics."

"Well, we'll just go to Ken Holton and demand the salary information," Carol said.

"He won't give it to you," Bess said. "He'll say it's confidential."

"Well, look," Carol said. "Let's pool the information we have. I'll go through the phone directory and find out how many women work here and what jobs they're in. And we can compare notes on the salaries we know."

"I know what my boss makes," one secretary said. "I always deposit his check for him."

"Great," Carol said. "Let's meet again tomorrow. And let's be thinking about the demands we want to make."

"We don't want to be too belligerent," Bess cautioned.

"I'm belligerent," Sally declared. "I'm sick of men thinking all I can do is type and shake my ass."

"Don't we need a chairman or something?" Fran asked.

"You be the chairman, Carol," Fran said.

Carol hesitated. "I don't know. Maybe somebody else would be better. Sally or Fran." She didn't want to go through angry confrontations with Ken Holton and all the other men. Was it worth it? Was there really any hope of changing anything?

"No, it ought to be you," Sally said. "Look, let's be realistic. We don't know what we're getting into. But they're not going to retaliate against you because of who your husband is."

"Ha! He'd be on their side."

"Well, maybe they don't know that. Come on, Carol, do it."

"Okay," Carol said, grinning. "You bet I'll do it."

When Carol got back to her office she felt exhilarated, and she sat for a long time thinking. She was thinking less of what they had done that day than of all that she had not done for so many years. She had never before sat down with other women to discuss the forces that shaped their lives. She felt as if a new world had opened up before her. The implications of it were stunning—as the kids said, it blew her mind.

"I really don't understand it, Carol," Ken Holton said, puffing on his pipe. "I don't understand it at all."

238

"Will you meet with us?" Carol persisted.

"I suppose I can *meet* with this group," Ken said, "but I don't see what there is to meet *about*."

"The status of women at this station, Ken. The jobs we get. The salaries we make. The attitudes you in management have toward us."

"Is my attitude toward women in question, Carol?" A wry smile.

"What about Sally? A man as bright as she is would have been promoted years ago. But she's a pretty girl so all you see is a swell secretary for Ken Holton."

"What about you, Carol? Don't you prove my case? A woman with her own show?"

"Who's paid less than a man would be!"

"You don't know that for a fact."

"That's why we want the salary figures."

"I can't give out confidential, personal data like that."

"Besides, I'm sick of my show. I want to do documentaries."

"Could you travel, Carol? Could you work the hours?"

"Don't assume I can't."

"You have two children."

"So does my husband, and he travels plenty."

The little smile. The look of triumph. "But, Carol, you're the—"

"*Don't say it!* I *know* I'm the mother. And, incidentally, we're fed up with the station's maternity-leave policy."

Weary, reasonable. "It's to protect you women, Carol."

"Four months off without pay? Thanks loads."

"If it were my own wife . . ."

"It's not! It's working women who need the money. Four *weeks* off would be plenty."

A frown, a glimmer of impatience. "Carol, what *is* it you people want?"

"Equal pay for equal work. A fair chance at jobs we're qualified for."

"Carol, cruel as it may sound, it usually comes down to just that, qualifications. Or a lack of them."

"As defined by men for the benefit of other men."

Ken Holton fiddled with a thin gold fountain pen. "You know, Carol, I was thinking about that VISTA documentary. It's a good idea, if the costs can be kept down. Maybe you ought to go ahead with it. But I wonder if you'd have time for it and all these other . . . extracurricular activities, too."

Carol stared at him. For the first time, she was angry.

"Ken, are you saying you'll approve the documentary if I pull out of the women's group?"

"I didn't say that at all . . ."

"Because if you're saying that—as much as I want to do that documentary—you can take it and shove it—"

"Carol!"

"—up your left nostril. Because this isn't something you can buy off or brush off or laugh off. Now, will you be there tomorrow to meet with us?"

Bemused, tolerant. "You know, Carol, this is really an extraordinary conversation we've had. I feel as if I'd never known you before."

"Maybe you haven't. What about tomorrow?"

Ken Holton waved a hand absently. "Oh yes, I'll come. But I really don't know what's gotten into you girls."

The meeting was very polite. Carol gave a presentation, citing the facts and figures they'd assembled and citing some specific instances of sex bias. The station's department heads listened attentively, asked a few polite questions, and then Ken Holton made the classic response: give us time to study this.

The women, seeking results, were annoyed but could not refuse such a reasonable request. How long to study it? Ken Holton waved away the question. A month or two perhaps . . . much data to be assembled . . .

The two months became three, and management's study was still in progress. But the time was not wasted. The women's movement was spreading. And one day Carol and Sally had a most interesting talk with a woman lawyer Sally had met. To their amazement, they found the law was on their side.

It was just before the Fourth of July that Ken Holton called Carol into his office. She thought it was about the VISTA project—she'd been working with a writer on a script.

"Oh, Carol, about that report you gave us a while back, the one about women and their jobs."

"You've finished your study?"

"We looked it over pretty carefully."

240

"And?"

"And we don't really see anything to it."

"Don't see anything to it?"

"Carol, your statistics are all wrong. For instance, you say there are no female department heads, but Gail Wiley functions in effect as head of the accounting department."

"That's exactly the point. She does the work but doesn't have the title or the salary."

"The point is, Carol, that this report you gave me reflects a lot of frustrations but not a factual situation. That's understandable. Carol, everyone's frustrated. I'd like to be president of the network. But I'm not going to blame the fact that I'm not president of the network on my being brown-eyed or an Episcopalian or something like that."

"You *could* be president of the network someday, Ken," Carol said wearily. "You probably *will* be."

"Carol, we're liberal-minded people here. We have a good record on minority matters. We're leaders in the industry. And we have a lot of women, like yourself, in positions of trust."

He believes it, every word of it. Some of my best friends are Jews. We treat the niggers good down home.

Carol felt sad. She felt sorry for him, too.

"You really don't understand, do you, Ken?"

"I understand that I'm getting a lot of headaches for no good reason."

"But you don't understand that women are something besides lovely little children, that they're people who've been discriminated against all their lives, and mostly by goodhearted liberals like you."

"Carol, look at you. You have everything. A beautiful home. A successful husband. A good job . . ."

"You don't understand . . ."

"And yet you talk to me about discrimination. . . ."

"What about Sally? Making eight thousand while men with half her brains make twelve?"

"Why do you worry so about Sally?"

"Because she's a woman, damn it. Because she's my *sister*. Because both of us have put up with idiots like you all our lives."

"I don't have to take that, Carol."

"You may take worse than that before you're through. Did you know that you people are breaking the law?"

"What law?"

"The Civil Rights Act. Job discrimination on the basis of sex is illegal."

"We don't discriminate."

"When Fran Harris asked for a salesman's job, the sales manager told her he'd never hire a woman for that. I have her affidavit."

"Affidavit?"

"And you're violating FCC regulations too."

"Those are serious charges."

"We can prove them."

"Carol, what in God's name are you women up to?"

"You'll find out," Carol promised.

14

SPRING 1967

Tim Carter, a blue-jeaned, bushy-haired, surly intruder in the Senate sanctuary, was nonetheless whisked past the receptionist and the personal secretary and into Charles's own office when he hinted that the Senator's sister was in trouble.

Charles, his mind on the coming Easter weekend in Kentucky, rose to greet the young man, whose face was dimly familiar, but Tim Carter sought no handshake. Instead, he stopped in the center of the room, just stood there, his hands jammed into his hip pockets, his face angry.

"We met once," he said. "At Kennedy House."

"I remember," Charles said. And he did—this boy had been Bill Hall's second in command. "What can I do for you?"

"Nothing," Carter said. "But you might do something for Beth."

"What do you mean?"

"How long since you've seen her?"

"Christmas. Why?"

"How did she seem to you then?"

Charles thought: Cut out the questions, buster. But he said: "Depressed. Bill had just been gone a few weeks. She wouldn't take a drink, much less stay for dinner. It wasn't much of a visit. Why? What are you driving at?"

"Beth's into drugs. Deep in. I've done all I can. It's time you people did something."

"What kind of drugs?"

243

"How much do you know about them?"

"Not much."

Tim Carter shrugged. His hands were still in his hip pockets, his face was still angry. "Well, she started on Valium . . ."

"What's that?"

"A mild depressant. Little white pills. Except pretty soon she was eating them like peanuts. She was doing that by the time Bill left. Then she moved up to reds. She was on them when you saw her at Christmas. That's why she didn't take that drink you offered her."

"Why?"

"Because if you mix enough reds with enough booze it'll kill you."

"Where does she get them?"

"From doctors. From friends. They're not hard to get."

"What do they do to you?"

"Up to a point, they're something like booze. But you get hooked fast and if you stay hooked long enough they'll kill you, and if you get off, the withdrawal will make you wish they had."

Charles felt angry, sick. "Then why does she take the damned things?" he snapped.

Tim Carter looked at him coldly. "Maybe she's unhappy," he said.

"Damn it, lots of people are unhappy," Charles shot back. "I'm unhappy. But I'm not taking drugs."

Tim Carter folded his arms across his chest and looked at Charles with an expression of limitless distaste. "Maybe you're stronger than she is," he said finally. "Maybe you're a fucking tiger. She's not."

"Okay, mister, I'm not in love with you either. You've been with her. You could have helped her."

"Don't talk to me about helping her. I've been there, from the cold sweats to the convulsions. I didn't see you there."

Charles shuddered and dropped into his chair. "Sit down, Tim," he said.

"No, thanks."

"Where is she?"

"In New York. I can't reach her. And I can't drop everything to go look for her."

"I'll go. Where do I look?"

Tim Carter took a slip of paper from his shirt pocket and dropped it onto Charles's desk. "Try these places."

Charles slipped the paper into his pocket without looking at it.

244

"What do you hear from Bill?" he asked. Charles felt numb. He'd been meaning to call Beth but he'd put it off because he was annoyed at her—annoyed at the way she'd acted at Christmas, annoyed that he'd learned of her marriage second hand. So he'd waited. Let her come to him. The tough guy.

"Bill's all right," Tim Carter said in a crisp, none-of-your-fucking-business tone. "So long, Senator."

Charles opened his mouth but no words came. The young man marched out of the office, slamming the door behind him.

Charles and Al Kline caught the noon shuttle to New York the next day, Saturday. He asked Al along because he was a native New Yorker and all he himself knew of New York was a few dozen expensive hotels and bars and restaurants and theaters, and that wasn't Beth's New York, not according to the addresses he had. Al and Charles checked into the Plaza, then took a cab downtown.

Their first stop was a town house on West Eleventh Street. It was a nice block and it made Charles feel a little better. When the door opened, a burst of Beethoven flowed out, followed by a white-haired man who was wearing slippers and holding a copy of the *Saturday Review*. Yes, he said, his daughter and another girl had been by on Wednesday, but now they were gone and he really couldn't say where. He said he hoped nothing was the matter.

Their next stop was less elegant, a dirty tenement on a dirty block in the East Village. A boy with long stringy hair kept the chain lock fastened and claimed he'd never heard of any Beth Pierce.

"She may call herself Beth Hall," Charles said.

"Still don't know the chick," the boy muttered.

"She's from Washington," Al Kline said. "We're not cops. We're friends of hers."

A chubby, curly-haired girl peeked through the crack in the door. "You might try the *Other*," she said.

"The other what?" Charles said.

"The *Other*. It's a newspaper. She was by there the other day."

"How was she?" Charles pressed.

The girl's face darkened. "I think that was the day she went to the doctor," she said.

"What doctor?"

"I thought you were friends of hers," the girl said, and slammed the door.

They found the newspaper office but no one there would admit to knowing Beth. Someone suggested they try the "co-ordinating committee," which proved to be some offices on the top floor of a dingy building near the Bowery. They climbed five flights of steps to find a tiny, dark-eyed girl operating an ancient mimeograph machine.

"Hi," she said cheerfully. "You guys FBI?"

"Do we look like FBI?" Charles asked.

She looked them over thoughtfully. "Well, you're better dressed than the others," she said. "And he looks Jewish."

"It's just a disguise," Al said. "It's not my real nose."

The girl giggled and handed them two of the sheets she was running off. "Here, hot off the presses." The flyers urged people to withhold their income taxes as an anti-war protest.

"We're looking for a girl named Beth," Charles said. "From Washington."

The girl cut off the mimeograph machine and looked at them sharply.

"Why?"

"I'm her brother," Charles said. "I want to help her."

The girl's face puckered with pain. "She *needs* help," she said.

"Do you know where she is?"

The girl shook her head. "No, but I know where I'd try."

"Where?"

"At the Be-in tomorrow. Everybody'll be there."

"The what?"

"It's a kind of . . . demonstration," Al explained. "In Central Park."

"That's what these are for," the girl said, indicating the anti-war flyers. "You want to take some to pass out?"

"We'd better not," Al said.

"But thanks," Charles said. The girl turned back to the mimeograph machine and they started down the stairs.

That exhausted their leads. They walked over to Washington Square and sat on a park bench for a while, looking for Beth among the passers-by. Then they began to walk aimlessly through the narrow Village streets, now and then looking into a bar or coffeehouse where young people seemed to congregate. They passed the theater where *MacBird* was being staged—Charles had read about the controversy in the newspapers. They walked the streets until midnight, despite the light rain that had begun to fall, but Beth was not to be found and finally they caught a cab back to the Plaza.

After breakfast the next morning, Al suggested that they walk over and take a look at the Easter Parade. From the song Charles had a vague mental picture of elegant couples strolling in their finery, so he wasn't prepared for the reality of the event. Two thousand people jammed the intersection in front of St. Patrick's, pushing and shoving to get a view of two or three dozen wild-looking women wearing even wilder-looking hats. The point of the thing seemed to be for the horde of curiosity-seekers and photographers to decide what woman was wearing the most outlandish hat. The day's winner was clearly a tall, platinum-haired woman who was wearing a lush jungle of a hat topped by a birdcage with a live parrot inside.

Flashbulbs were flashing and the parrot was squawking and people were shoving and climbing lampposts to get a better view. The woman wearing the parrot kept yelling to the scrambling photographers, "Hey, you the one from the *Daily News?* Where's the one from the *Daily News?*"

"Irving Berlin lied to us," Charles said when they were out of the melee.

"They're good Democrats all," Al replied.

Charles laughed—Al's humor had been the one bright spot in the past twenty-four hours. In the office, they'd always maintained a formal Senator-and-aide relationship, but on this trip they'd loosened up.

"What is this thing?" Charles asked. "This Be-in. Or, as our right-wing friends would say, this so-called Be-in."

"It's billed as a medieval pageant."

"Ah, so. And exactly what does one do at a medieval pageant?"

"Whatever one pleases, I guess. They had one in San Francisco and people played flutes and flew kites and stuff like that."

"Let's duck in the Plaza for a drink," Charles said. "I never play a flute sober."

They lingered in the Oak Room for two bloody marys, then crossed to the Park. A lot of people were headed the same way, but it was not until they topped a small hill that they saw the panorama spread out across the Sheep Meadow.

"Jesus H. Christ," Charles whispered.

"I think I'll take off my tie," Al said.

Three or four thousand people were strung out across the meadow like tinsel on a cosmic Christmas tree. There was no focal point, no stage or bandstand, just people, people sitting, people standing, people wandering about. Charles and Al exchanged a glance, put their hands in their pockets, and began to move slowly through the crowd. There were other over-thirties in the throng—Charles spotted one white-haired gentleman in a tuxedo—but mostly there were kids. Kids in jeans and beads and Indian feathers, kids barefoot and in sandals and in hip boots, kids who looked like General Custer and kids who looked like Sitting Bull, kids with "Love" painted on their foreheads in Day-Glo letters and kids with "Make Love Not War" emblazoned across their shirts, kids with little American flags used to patch the seats of their pants, kids climbing trees and doing handstands and playing ring-around-the-rosy, kids with Rip Van Winkle beards and kids with shaved, holy-man heads, kids who looked like Gandhi and kids who looked like Jesus. Every kind of kid imaginable. But no Beth.

"Fantastic," Charles kept saying. "Fantastic."

Four girls ran up to them, young, pretty girls with long hair falling about their shoulders. They were ringing little gold bells and carrying a bushel basket full of daisies. They stuck daisies into Charles's and Al's buttonholes and tried to weave flowers into their hair.

"Hey, what's this for?" Charles asked, not quite comfortable.

"We love you," one of them said, a lovely girl with high cheekbones and honey-blonde hair that fell nearly to her waist.

"Why? Why do you love me?" Charles asked.

"Because you're a person."

Her reply seemed a non sequitur to Charles and he did not pursue it.

"Listen, I'm looking for a girl named Beth. From Washington. Do you know her? I think she's here somewhere."

The girls looked at one another, then shook their slender faces in reply.

"But we could look for her," the blonde girl said. She smiled and stepped forward to straighten the daisy in his lapel. He touched her face with his fingertips.

"Thank you," he said, and the girls laughed and jingled their bells and raced away.

248

"Dirty old man," Al Kline said.

"I don't understand it," Charles said. "Girls giving you flowers and saying they love you. Hell, my wife doesn't do that any more."

"These kids are different."

"I guess I'm just a fifties person. Nobody ever taught us to throw flowers at people."

Just then the banana bounced into view. It was three or four feet long and being held aloft by some boys and girls who chanted "Banana, banana" as they jogged along.

"A phallic symbol," Charles said.

"You're catching on," Al replied, as the banana people loped on across the meadow.

They kept on the move, looking for Beth, but the crowd had grown to five or six thousand and Charles was beginning to think it was hopeless. People kept giving them things. A girl in a sari with a tiny mirror on her forehead gave them jelly beans. A nun gave them sandwiches. A boy with a monkey offered them a drag on his joint. Charles waved him away, but Al took a puff.

"God damn," Charles said, "don't I have enough troubles without you smoking that stuff?"

Al feigned alarm. "You're not going to make a citizen's arrest, are you?"

Charles decided to drop it. "It's too bad we didn't bring something along we could give away," he said.

"We could have brought some of your old speeches," Al said.

The girls with the bells and daisies dashed by again, and Charles heard them saying, "Have you seen Beth from Washington? We must find Beth from Washington."

Charles and Al sat down on the grass to rest. Fifty yards away, two boys had stripped off their clothes and climbed a tree. People flew kites and burned incense and tossed Frisbees and turned somersaults and rolled in the mud in the middle of the meadow. There were gypsies and Indians and gurus and cowboys and one band of open-mouthed Hell's Angels. They even saw the lady from the Easter parade, the one with the parrot in her hat, but no one paid any attention to her.

Then the girls reappeared, bells ringing, daisy basket empty. "We found her," they said. "We found Beth."

"Where?"

The blonde girl pointed west across the meadow, where the afternoon sun touched the tallest buildings. "Over there," she said. "Under a tree. Almost to the street."

Charles raced across the meadow, zigging and zagging like a halfback in Bedlam.

She was sitting with her back against a tree and for a moment he didn't recognize her. She had lost weight and her clothes hung loose on her body. She sat against the tree, smoking a filter-tip cigarette, and she gave no sign that she saw Charles or the Be-in or anything at all. A skinny boy in a green sweat shirt lay near her on the grass, staring at the sky.

Charles fell to his knees beside her. "Beth, baby. Are you okay?"

She didn't answer, didn't even look his way. She just looked at her cigarette, which seemed about to burn her fingers.

"Beth, what's the matter?"

She rolled the cigarette between her fingers—it seemed to Charles that it must be burning her. He knocked it to the ground, then with a cry she threw her arms around him and began to sob. She felt brittle in his arms. Al Kline waited a dozen feet away and the boy in the green sweat shirt kept looking at the sky. Finally she stopped sobbing and turned her face to him.

"Your flowers are beautiful, Charles," she said. "I've never seen such beautiful flowers."

"You're beautiful," he whispered. "You're beautiful, and I'm going to take you to a place where you can rest."

She nodded slowly. "I need rest," she said. "I've been sick, Charles."

"Can you walk to the street?" he asked. "I'll help you."

As they arose, the girls with the daisies reappeared, their bells jingling softly, but Al spoke to them and they went away.

"Good-by, Nick," Beth called to the boy in the sweat shirt. "My brother's going to help me now."

The boy rolled over onto his side and smiled at her. "Be careful," he said. "Peace."

"Peace," she echoed, then she and Charles started toward the street. Al Kline ran ahead to find a cab. Soon the sounds of the flutes and bells faded behind them and they heard the honks and roars of automobiles.

"I had an abortion," Beth whispered. Charles shuddered—the word

250

called up images of screams, quack doctors, bellhops with wire clothes hangers, bloody deaths.

"It'll be all right," he told her.

"Children shouldn't be born into a world like this," she said.

"You need rest."

"I need Bill."

"It'll be all right," he repeated insanely.

He gave the cab driver an address in the East Sixties. Beth pressed against him while the cab driver listened to a talk show and muttered to himself. When they reached the East Side Beth opened her eyes and looked out at the people and the buildings.

"It's all shit, Charles," she whispered.

"Not all of it."

"Yes, all of it. Nothing means anything."

"Things are starting to change. Johnson will have to . . ."

"It's too late," she said, and they didn't talk any more.

The hospital was expensive and excellent. A handsome young doctor greeted them and two nurses who called Beth by name and took her off to her room.

The doctor left for a moment, then returned. "Could you come by about ten in the morning, Senator?" he asked. "Dr. Singer will want to talk to you."

"What have you done for her?"

"Just given her a sedative."

"What treatment does she need?"

"Dr. Singer will discuss all that personally," the young doctor insisted.

For a thousand dollars a week, you talked to Dr. Singer. He and Al Kline left the posh little hospital and stood in the soft dusk of the East Sixties.

"Now what?" Al asked.

"You do whatever you want to," Charles said. "I guess I'll have a few drinks and dinner somewhere."

"I've got some friends we could meet for dinner," Al said. "If you're up to it."

"I'm up to it," Charles said. "What the hell else have I got to do?"

Al shook his head. "I don't know. You could go see *MacBird*."

"I've seen *MacBird*," Charles said bitterly. "Come on, let's find a cab."

Charles wanted diversion that evening and he got it, more than he'd expected. Al's friend was named Jack Buchanan, a New York *Times* reporter recently returned from a year in Vietnam. They met him at Lola's, a place in the Village that Al said was a hangout for writers. Charles had been in Lola's only a few minutes when he decided that everyone there was drunk or angry or both. At the door, a formidable-looking woman barred their entry and declared she had no tables. Only when Al said they were meeting Jack Buchanan did the woman, who proved to be Lola herself, warm up a bit and escort them to Buchanan's table near the back of the restaurant.

Buchanan and two sports writers were sitting at the large round table arguing the relative merits of Joe DiMaggio and Ted Williams. When the debate quieted down, Al made the introductions. Charles shook hands and sat down warily. He was out of his element here, like a gunfighter in a strange saloon. But he soon saw that, except for Buchanan, no one here cared much about politics. Writers came and went all evening, but all they talked about was reviews and agents and paperback sales, and sometimes sports.

But Buchanan and Charles talked politics for a while. Buchanan began to tell Charles stories about Vietnam, angry stories of military fiascoes and diplomatic duplicity, but Charles had heard all those stories before and as soon as he could he changed the subject.

"Who are all these people?" he asked. "Writers?"

"Most of them are ad men and PR types," Buchanan said scornfully. "All the writers sit at two tables, this one and that one up by the bar."

He indicated a table where three men and a woman were engaged in animated conversation.

"Why two tables?"

"That one's for literary types," Buchanan explained. "This one's for journalistic types."

"Those people are literary types?"

"The tall one is a professional gambler who used to be a playwright. The bald one is a playwright who used to be a male prostitute. The one with the beard used to be a rodeo cowboy and he's just written his memoirs."

"Who's the woman?" He indicated a muscular woman who was shaking her fist at the bearded ex-cowboy.

"She used to be a lady wrestler and now she writes poetry."

252

"I'd like to read some of it," Charles said.

A pudgy young man in a red turtleneck sweater had come in and, amid many shouts and handshakes, made his way from the bar to the literary table.

"That's Billy Bob Beane, the magazine editor," Buchanan explained. "You ought to meet him. He'll come over after a while."

Sure enough, after finishing his drink and grabbing another at the bar, Billy Bob Beane approached their table.

"Jack, ya ole fart, when ya gunna write me that Veet-nam piece?"

"When are you going to read the last piece I sent you, Billy Bob? You've had the damn thing two months. Here, I want you to meet Senator Pierce."

Billy Bob Beane squinted in Charles's direction, grinned engagingly, and extended a plump hand.

"Lord-a-mercy," he declared. "I'se just thinkin' 'bout you the other day, Senator."

"Thinking what?" Charles asked.

"Thinkin' you oughta write sumpin' fer me."

"About what?" Charles asked.

Billy Bob Beane shut his eyes in contemplation. "About America," he said gravely. "A Senator Looks at America. A Senator Seeks the Soul of America. Hot damn, just look down deep into your heart and gimme ten thousand words on what you find there. Twenty thousand! Forty thousand, it don't matter! Just let 'er rip! Ain't that some idear?"

"I guess so," Charles said.

"I tell you, boy, it'd be the makin' of you. A prize winner. Make you famous. Yes, sir!"

"I'll think about it," Charles promised.

"Don't think 'bout it," Billy Bob Beane instructed, downing his drink and waving to a waiter for another. "*Do* it! Great piece. Yes, sir!"

He scratched his belly for emphasis and wandered back toward the literary table, mumbling about the soul of America.

"Is he serious?" Charles asked Buchanan.

"He's already forgotten about it," Buchanan said.

The two sports writers, who had been arguing about Bill Bradley, announced they were going outside for a smoke. As they left, a balding, overweight young man entered, was rebuffed at the literary table, and made his way to Buchanan's table.

"I shouldn't have come here," he said sadly. "I was just out for a walk and wandered in and I can see already it was a mistake."

"Oh, bullshit, Smathers, sit down," Buchanan ordered. "Not all writers hate reviewers. Hell, I like you. Didn't I tell you you remind me of Edmund Wilson? You're the only thirty-year-old man I know who looks like Edmund Wilson."

Smathers brightened at that, but only momentarily. "I shouldn't have come here," he repeated, but he sat down and ordered a drink.

The waiter brought Charles's and Al's abundant Italian dinner. While they were eating, they were joined by a young writer from Oklahoma. He was small and jug-eared and was wearing jeans and a plaid shirt. The young writer was drunk, but he seemed pleasant enough until he noticed Smathers.

"Fuck you, Smathers," he shouted across the table. "You chicken-shit bastard."

"I knew I shouldn't have come here," Smathers sighed.

"So my novel was a potboiler, was it? I ought to beat the piss out of you."

"Please be civilized," Smathers replied.

"Where are your books, Smathers?"

"One needn't write oneself," Smathers said, "in order to make judgments about—"

"Bullshit! You're like a virgin trying to explain a whorehouse. That's what critics are. Eunuchs in the great whorehouse of literature."

"That's not even original . . ."

"Fuck you, Smathers!"

"I *knew* I shouldn't have come here," Smathers said glumly, and signaled for a waiter to take his order.

"What was your novel about?" Charles asked the young Oklahoman, who'd seemed pleasant enough before he noticed Smathers.

"The past," the writer said. "It was about the past." He gulped at his Bourbon and soda and seemed to have forgotten Smathers.

Charles waited for details but none came. "Any particular period?" he asked finally. "Of the past, I mean?"

"Oh, sure," the young writer said absently. "It traced an Oklahoma family from 1850 to 1900. It was an epic."

"Would you rather write about the past than the present?" Charles asked.

"I only write about the past. I live in the past. I'd go crazy if I had to confront the 1960s all day long."

He had a dreamy look on his face, and Charles had a feeling that at any moment he might drift back into the nineteenth century.

"I don't feel that way," Charles said. "I don't give a damn about the past. I care about the present, the present and the future. The future is what's really exciting."

"And frustrating," the writer said. "The future is a carrot on a stick, always just beyond your grasp. I'll take the past; you can count on the past."

Charles decided they weren't getting anywhere. "How'd your book do?" he asked.

"Terribly," the writer said. "The critics called it irrelevant. Diffuse. Interminable. That dipshit over there"—he indicated Smathers, who was digging into his antipasto—"called it anachronistic. Hey, Smathers —fuck you!"

Smathers kept on eating. He was perspiring heavily—he did look rather like Edmund Wilson—and he kept patting his brow with his napkin. After a while the young writer got up and, without a word to anyone, wandered out of the restaurant, back into the past.

Charles began to talk politics with Jack Buchanan again, to talk about the "dump Johnson" movement that was struggling to be born, and Charles spoke bitterly about Johnson and the war. When Buchanan got up to go to the men's room, Al Kline leaned across the table and whispered to Charles.

"You've got to be careful what you say to him," Al said.

"Hell, I thought he was your old pal."

"He is, but he's a writer first. Writers are professional traitors."

Charles nodded, and they watched as a young man in a white suit and a psychedelic necktie entered the restaurant, accompanied by a willowy, fine-featured blonde.

"That's Zip Parker," Al whispered. "His first novel just sold to the movies for a hundred thou."

Zip Parker and the gorgeous blonde were about to join Buchanan's party. Parker had taken the girl's coat off and was hanging it on a hook on the wall when one of the waiters called to him:

"Don't use that one, Mr. Parker. Let me put it over here."

"I'll use any damn hook I please," the writer growled.

"That hook goes with the other table," the waiter insisted.

"Other table, other table," the writer mimicked. "What the hell's the matter with you?"

"What the hell's the matter with *you?*" demanded Lola, who had hurried over to defend the waiter.

"I'm sick of the cruddy service here," the writer said. "I spent two thousand dollars here last year and your waiters won't even let me hang my date's coat where I want to."

"Then go somewhere else," Lola shouted back at him. "Who needs your lousy money?"

"That's right," Zip Parker shot back. "Me and my friends made this dump famous and now you'll chase us out and get rich off tourists."

"I'll never get rich off deadbeats like you."

"Your food stinks!"

"Your writing stinks!"

"That's the last straw," Parker declared. "I'm through with this place. Come on, Karen."

The blonde looked annoyed. "If we go somewhere else," she said, "you'll just find something to complain about there."

"Then screw you, you bitch," the writer shouted, and stormed out of the restaurant, followed by all eyes and an excited burst of conversation.

The blonde shrugged and sat down in the chair next to Charles.

"Writers," she pouted. "Are you a writer?"

"No, I'm a politician."

Her face slipped from its pout into a stunning smile. "Goodness, you mean like a Mayor or something?"

"A Senator. My name's Charles Pierce."

"A Senator? Is that like Bobby Kennedy?"

"More or less."

"I used to live in Montana," she said. "There's a Senator from Montana, isn't there?"

"Two, as a matter of fact."

The waiter asked the girl what she wanted to drink. "An Americano, Henry," she said, and gave him the same breath-taking smile she had turned on Charles. She had long, fluffy-looking hair and wide-set blue eyes.

"I'm Karen Hill," she told Charles. "I don't know much about politics. You'll probably think I'm an awful dum-dum."

"No, I won't."

"I'm not, really. I mean, I made a hundred thousand dollars last year, so I can't be all dum-dum."

"Jesus, how'd you do that?"

"I'm a model."

"Do many models make that kind of money?"

"Four or five. Shrimp makes the most and probably I'm next."

"Tell me about modeling," Charles said. "I guess I'm a dum-dum on modeling."

"There's not really much to know. If you have the right bone structure and if you can keep from getting messed up, you can make a lot of money."

"How messed up?"

"Oh, with men and drugs and things. Lately the agencies have been bringing over all these Scandinavian girls—gorgeous creatures—but they don't speak the language or understand the culture and they get a little money and they go wild. They get mixed up with gangsters and Negroes and drugs and some end up as prostitutes and all sorts of terrible things. You see, there's a lot of insecurity to being a model. When those first wrinkles start showing, the agencies just say, 'Don't call us, dearie, we'll call you,' except they don't call. It's tough. Is politics like that?"

"It has its little insecurities," Charles said. He looked around them. Jack Buchanan and Al Kline were arguing about morality in government. Smathers was eating a piece of pie à la mode and saying he should leave. Lola was arguing with Billy Bob Beane about his bar bill. At the literary table the bearded ex-cowboy was shouting and waving his fist at the lady-wrestler-turned-poetess.

"Do you come here often?" Charles asked Karen Hill.

"No. Writers are such egomaniacs. They publish one book and they think they're Shakespeare. It's crazy."

"Who do you like? Actors?"

"Good Lord, no. They're worse than writers. I guess I like men who aren't so intellectual. Football players. Cowboys."

"How about politicians?"

She gave him the smile again. It was like looking into a *Vogue* cover—the eyes glistened, the just-open mouth trembled, the hair

257

seemed ruffled by a phantom breeze. "I like *you*," she said. "You're the only politician I know."

"Thanks," he said. "Can I get you another drink?"

"I've really got to go. I've got to be on location early tomorrow. The only thing they ask of us is that we look pretty, and if I don't get my sleep I'll be all puffy-eyed."

"I've got to go too."

"We could leave together," Karen said. "If we leave separately, they'll think we're rude, but if we leave together they'll think we're dashing off to bed and they won't be mad at us."

Just then there was a roar from the literary table.

"You fag bastard," the ex-cowboy boomed, jumping to his feet. He knocked over the table, seized his chair, and swung it at the playwright-turned-gambler, who was trying to defend himself with an empty wine bottle.

"Chauvinist pig!" the lady-wrestler-turned-poetess shrieked, leaping on the ex-cowboy's back and locking him in an expert full Nelson.

The ex-cowboy staggered around with the lady wrestler on his back, the playwright-turned-gambler had picked up his chair and was waving it above his head, and the people at nearby tables were scattering for cover.

"I think it's time to leave," Charles said. Karen nodded and he took her arm and led her safely past the melee to the door.

Outside, a light rain was falling. "And so we bid adieu to the wonderful world of literature," Charles said. "Is it always like that?"

"One night there was a duel," Karen said. "But mostly they just talk."

"Look, how about a nightcap? You pick the place."

"Well," she said, "maybe you could walk me home and we could have something there. I hate to be out alone at night. So many crazy things happen. I could survive a rape, but if some madman hit me in the face I'd be in trouble."

"Your place it is," he said, and she took his arm and led him across Washington Square.

It took three keys to unlock her front door. "Is it really all that dangerous?" he asked her when they were finally inside.

"You wouldn't believe it. They'll saw through bars and knock down walls and everything. It cost me three thousand dollars to make this place safe, and even then you're not sure."

The walls of her living room were covered with pictures of Karen, a gallery of Karen, somehow looking different in every pose—Karen shy, Karen arrogant, Karen giddy, Karen somber, Karen a schoolgirl, a secretary, a bride, a matron, a sophisticate, a siren, endless Karens, all desirable.

"The drinks are over there," she said. "Or do you smoke?"

Charles thought he must be the only man in America who hadn't smoked marijuana. "I guess I'll have a drink," he said. "I know what booze will do to me."

He opened a bottle of Cutty Sark and fixed his drink, then he joined her on a velvet-covered sofa.

"You live here by yourself?"

"Not usually. My roommate's in London."

"Is she a model too?"

"She's sort of an heiress. Her father used to be the Ambassador to Spain."

"Under which President?"

"Maybe Eisenhower, I'm not sure."

"What's she doing in London?"

"The last I heard, she was living with Mick Jagger."

"He's like a Beatle, isn't he?"

"Sort of, but sexier. Sudie got this mad crush on him and finally she flew to London and found out where he lived and rented a Bentley and parked outside his house until finally he invited her in. That was like a month ago."

She had taken a joint from a Chinese box on the coffee table and begun to smoke it. "This is awfully good," she said. "Sure you won't have just one teensie puff?"

"Maybe one puff. Since we're so secure here."

She scooted across the sofa to him. He took a drag, held it as long as he could, and waited. Nothing seemed to happen. She leaned close to him, smiling, watching his face. After a moment he kissed her.

It was a nice, leisurely kiss, not passionate but pleasant, an exploration, a question. When their mouths parted, she gave him a jaunty peck on the tip of his nose. He feared that answered the question.

"Tell me about politics," she said. "Before things get out of hand."

"Politics," he said, trying to refocus his mind. "Politics is how you

259

slice the pie. That's all, just people fighting over how you slice the pie."

"What about the war?" she said. "Are you against the war?"

"Yeah, I'm against the war."

"I don't understand it. Everybody's against it, but it just keeps on."

"Let's don't talk about it," he said. "Tell me about modeling. Is it fun?"

"For a while. It's a fantasy world. But when the fun wears off it's just bizarre, pardon the pun. I mean, last month they flew me out West to do a cigarette ad, Marlboro Country, or something like that. I was in a flowing white gown, riding along the edge of the Grand Canyon with the Lone Ranger. The honest-to-God real Lone Ranger, riding old Hi Yo Silver and everything. And all of a sudden it hit me, it just blew my mind. I mean, here I am, a normal American girl who went to high school and ran for cheerleader and worried about pimples and dug Elvis Presley and all that, so what in heaven's name am I doing riding along the edge of the Grand Canyon with the Lone Ranger? It's too much. The mind boggles. Am I making any sense to you?"

"Sure, you make sense," he said. "Politics gets to be like that. You think, My God, I'm just an ordinary fellow, what am I doing in the middle of all this chaos? People want you to solve all their problems and you can't even solve your own problems."

Karen frowned. Her face was like her pictures, always changing, always discovering itself, and now it was heartbreakingly sad. Or was her face simply a mirror, reflecting his mood, as she could effortlessly give a photographer the pose he wanted?

"I think I'd better kiss you again," he said.

"You probably shouldn't."

"You wouldn't like it?"

"It'd just lead to trouble."

"I was hoping it might lead to the other room."

She half smiled. "You're married, aren't you?"

"Sure."

"And I'll bet you're the faithful type. And you'd wake up tomorrow and hate yourself and say I clouded your mind with drugs."

"I wouldn't complain. Scout's honor."

"Am I right?"

260

"About what?"

"About you being the faithful type."

The moment had passed, so he put his feet up on her coffee table and took a sip of his neglected Cutty Sark. The moment might return. He hadn't played this game in many years, but he remembered all the basics—keep them talking, keep them happy, wear them down. Besides, he felt like talking.

"More or less," he told her. "An occasional slip, but essentially the faithful type."

"I think that's great. Really."

"It's just an accident. I meet plenty of women I'd love to go to bed with, but they're happily married or unavailable for one reason or another. It's just in the James Bond movies that every gorgeous babe you meet is dying to hop in bed with you."

"You must meet a lot who are."

"Oh, sure. But women who are that aggressive are usually screwed up one way or another. Women with messed-up lives who think they can screw their way back to happiness."

"Maybe they can," Karen said.

"I'm afraid of women like that. They might give you a great time one night, then decide to confess all to their husband the next night. You see, I think that being screwed up is a social disease, one you catch from screwed-up people. It's what the upper classes catch instead of VD. Am I being too crude?"

"You're not crude," she said.

"I guess men are more cynical about sex than women."

"I think women are far more cynical," Karen said. "Most married men I know are much more moral than most married women I know. You see, most women feel exploited—most women *are* exploited—so they think anything they want to do is justified. I think most of those quote happily married unquote women you meet are really a lot more available than you think, and it's your morality, not theirs, that gets in the way."

"You *are* a cynic."

"Am I? Sometime I'll tell you about models I've known who've married rich men and then gotten bored in Scarsdale and started coming into the city for a little midday fun. They have their little orgies and smooth their little skirts and catch the two twenty-five back to meet the kiddies when they come home from school. The thing you have to understand is that everything changed when they invented the Pill. If you don't have to get pregnant, then girls are no different from boys."

Charles shook his head. "It's a damned hard idea to grasp," he said. "Not for girls."

Her eyes were merry, amused, teasing.

"You know what?"

"What?"

"I'd sure like to go to bed with you."

"You don't think I'm a screwed-up woman who'd call your wife or blackmail you or something disastrous like that?"

"You may be the least screwed-up woman I've ever met."

She patted his hand. "It's tempting," she said. "But I'd better not."

"Why not?"

"Oh, you know, there's a boy. There's always a boy. I guess I'm going to marry him. It's funny, really. If I'd met you yesterday, I might have. But I got a sweet letter from him this morning, so I guess I won't."

It was past midnight and Charles was exhausted. He probably couldn't have made love if she'd wanted to. But she'd taken his mind off Beth and that was worth more to him than sex tonight. He thought he could at least have the last word, though.

"You see, it's your morality that's keeping us apart," he told her. "Not mine."

"Yes, but that's because I'm single, not because I'm a woman. Lovers are much more moral than married people. They have to be because that's all they have to keep them together."

Charles gave up on getting the last word. "Where is this boy of yours?" he asked.

"He has a ranch in California."

"A big ranch?"

"About the size of Rhode Island, I think it is."

Charles got to his feet. "I'd better go," he said. "So you can get your beauty sleep."

"You're sweet," she said. "But you look so tired. Why don't you just stay here, instead of worrying about a cab and all? In Sudie's room, I mean."

262

"Are you sure you trust me?"

"Well, Senators don't rape people, do they?"

"Only professionally."

"I trust you," she said, and five minutes later he was asleep, in Sudie's bed.

15

JULY 1967

Some days waking up was good. If you awoke before the bell went off, when the first light softened the bars and bricks, you might lie for a few moments and think you were anywhere. The hate would come back soon enough, as soon as the bell rang and men began to curse and groan, hacks began to shout, metal began to clank on metal, but for those few moments of dawn you were almost free.

Bill awoke thinking of Beth, wondering if her visit would come off, wondering how big a hassle it would cause. But he didn't want to think about that yet. He felt his anger flowing back, so he climbed out of his bunk and did things. Thirty push-ups. Get dressed. Straighten up the cell. Thirty more push-ups. That was the secret, to keep busy, not to brood, not to vegetate.

The cell door slid open and Bill stepped out into the corridor for the morning count. Mac fell in beside him. Mac was his Hell's Angels friend, a husky tattooed Southerner who was doing five for car theft. They'd almost had a fight the first time they met, but now they were pals; Mac was a useful link to the racist whites.

"Hey, man, this here's thuh day yore ole lady's s'pozed to come, ain't it?"

"Yeah," Bill said out of the side of his mouth.

"You think them mothah-fuggahs gonna try to screw you up?"

"Probably." It was true. He wasn't counting on Beth's visit. He hoped she wasn't either.

When the count broke up and they started down the corridor toward the dining hall, Bill moved away from Mac. He didn't want to talk this morning, he wanted to think. He'd been in this prison two months, he'd pushed the staff and they'd pushed back, and he had to decide how far he was willing to go. That was always the question, how far are you willing to go?

The COs were split on the question. Some said that once you had gone to prison to protest the war you had made your point and that, while there, you might as well co-operate, make it easy on yourself, and get out as fast as you could. Others said, no, you had to continue to resist in prison, even if it cost you extra months or years there. But resist how hard? Didn't you have to compromise at some point?

A thin young man fell in beside him in the chow line.

"You're Hall, aren't you?"

"Yes."

"I'm Watkins. Jim Watkins."

"You new here?"

"Yeah, but I know who you are. You're the guy who wouldn't clean his cell, right?"

"Yeah, that's me."

"Man, that's fantastic. Weren't you scared?"

Bill shrugged. He felt like an old soldier telling war tales.

"The thing is, Jim, they want to have a master-slave relationship, and we can't accept that. They said, 'Clean up your cell.' I said, 'If it's my cell, I'll keep it like I want it, if it's your cell, *you* clean it up.'"

"They threw you in the hole, didn't they?"

"For a couple of days. Then they backed down. Once they quit telling me to clean up my cell, I cleaned it up—but it was *my* decision."

"Far out," Jim said.

They came to the head of the line where a hack named Gibson was handing each man one knife, one fork, one spoon. Gibson stared hard at Bill and Bill stared back.

"I'm gonna be seeing you today, wise guy," Gibson whispered to Bill. Bill took the utensils and moved on past, making no reply.

"What'd that mean?" Jim Watkins asked.

"He doesn't like me," Bill said.

"Is he a badass?"

"Yeah."

They went through the line. Cons wearing clear plastic gloves

265

served them each one egg, one piece of toast, one carton of milk. Jim Watkins followed Bill past row after row of the dining hall's four-man tables until they settled at an empty one near the back wall.

"What're you here for?" Bill asked.

"Dope," the youth said. "Man, I got a zip-five sentence for being caught with two joints. *Two joints,* man! Ain't that a bitch?"

"Were you in college?"

"I'd dropped out. I'm a doper, man. I dig dope. I smoked dope 'fore I came here and I'll smoke dope after I leave here. I'll smoke it in here if I can."

"Are you into politics?"

Watkins took a bite of his egg. "This thing tastes like rubber. No, man. I mean, I went to a couple of peace rallies but it was mainly just looking for chicks. I don't know nothing about politics."

"You're in here because of politics," Bill said. "The old people who drink whiskey for kicks are locking up the young people who smoke dope for kicks, because they feel threatened by them."

"It don't make much sense, does it?" the boy said. "I mean, me being here for smoking dope when they're giving medals to guys for dropping bombs on villages and things."

That's right, baby, Bill thought. It was always a kick to watch them come around, to watch them make the link-up between their own personal grievances and the larger political realities. One thing you had to say for prison: for an organizer, it presented unlimited opportunities.

"What can you *do,* man?" Jim Watkins asked. "I mean, like, you know, to *resist* in a place like this?"

"There are issues you can organize around," Bill said. "The stinking food. The petty rules—all the keep-your-shirttail-in crap. The way paroles are handled. Everybody hates those things."

"Yeah, but whatta you *do?*"

"Lots of things. All the warden—any warden—wants is to keep order. He's a bureaucrat and he doesn't want any trouble. A hunger strike, a sit-down strike, even a petition, those things bug them. So we've got leverage too. Listen, when I was in Lewisburg, they shipped a friend of mine out without five minutes' warning. They needed a medical technician at some prison down South so they just shipped him out like a piece of furniture. Twelve of us, that night, started a hunger strike. And you know what we found out? That they

266

wanted us to start eating and to go back to work again worse than we did. They were scared that it'd make the papers."

Bill was exaggerating a little, but that was how it was when you told war tales. And it had been a victory of sorts, a moral victory.

"What're you gonna do here, man?"

"I don't know," Bill said. "I'm talking to people. There's a lot of bitterness about people working for fifty cents a day."

"Man, how do you get a raise in a place like this?"

"What if everybody stopped working one day?"

"Is that gonna happen?"

Bill shook his head. "I don't know," he said. "It could."

The bell rang and they got up and took their empty trays back. When they handed back their knives, their forks, their spoons, Gibson was still standing there.

"I'll be seeing you, sweetheart," he whispered to Bill.

Bill ignored him, although it wasn't easy, the hate was rising up inside him, the memory of Beth's last visit. Then he nodded good-by to the young doper and walked on down to the prison clinic to start his morning's work.

He nodded to the doctor and two nurses, then swept the place, mopped the hallway, then spent an hour folding sheets. It was a good job as prison jobs went. Sometimes he thought they'd only given it to him in hopes that he'd steal drugs from the clinic—plenty of the guys did. But Bill left the drugs alone and he searched his cell often to make sure they hadn't planted any there.

He worked steadily at his job, for his own sake. You had to keep your sanity. That was part of the equation of how far you pushed. Because if you pushed too hard you went to the hole, and he was not sure his sanity could survive two or three weeks in the hole.

Prison wasn't what you thought it would be. It wasn't even very bad, if you kept your nose clean—a lot of the COs said they wished it was worse, to feed their martyr complexes. When it was bad, it was bad in unexpected ways. You came in expecting loneliness, thinking you'd read good books and think noble thoughts for three years. But you soon found you'd go insane reading books. You were in a society, a warped, violent, menacing society, but a society nonetheless, and one you had to function in. So you learned about prison. What you could ask a man and what you couldn't. The racial taboos. The homosexual thing. Bill had come in, like most COs, worried by the stories of homosexual attacks. There was some of that but not much. The worst was when COs, or any young kids, got assigned to the "jungle dorms," the dorms for violent homosexuals, then there sometimes were rapes in the night, four or five men jumping one kid, the others just listening to the victim's screams until finally they died down. The next day the victim would be sewn up and probably sent away to another prison.

A few of the COs had been having homosexual relations. They argued that sex was normal and in prison homosexual sex was normal. Bill just tried to keep sex from his mind. It was another of the things that could drive you crazy.

They were an odd lot, the COs. Individualists, most of them, almost impossible to organize. One guy who'd sent his draft board a foot-long turd and gotten five years for sending obscene material through the mail. A Goldwater type who'd refused to pay taxes to support a no-win war. A small colony of Jehovah's Witnesses, who didn't seem to mind prison at all; they got cakes from home and letters from their girls. They also got paroles after eighteen months, while COs were serving three years or more for the same offenses. Only a few of the COs were really political—Bill hadn't been really political until he got to prison and discovered it was either resist or lose all self-respect. His best friend here was Hal Stowers, one of the Minnesota Nine who'd been sentenced for raiding draft-board offices. They were both thinking about the idea of a work strike; that might be the fall offensive.

"Hall!"

He turned. It was Gibson, scowling at him from the doorway.

"Come on."

"To where?"

"You don't ask questions. Just foller me."

Bill shrugged and followed the hack down the corridor. Soon he realized that Gibson was leading him to the warden's office. The warden had a name—Hemphill—but no one ever used it. He was just The Warden. He was a tough, wiry little man who'd seen too many Jimmy Cagney movies. Bill didn't mind him. At least he didn't give you a lot of liberal bullshit like the warden at his first prison.

"Sit down," Gibson said. "He'll call you when he's ready for you."

Bill sat down on the wooden bench. Gibson marched on down the corridor and disappeared. That was one of the warden's tricks, to let people stew awhile on a hard bench to soften them up. He sat down and thought about Beth's visit. Then he made himself stop thinking about it.

Nan came by and smiled at him. Nan was a secretary in the records office, a plain, shy girl who'd been friendly toward the COs, apparently because her boy friend was in Vietnam. She looked up and down the corridor, saw that it was empty, and spoke to him.

"I hear some people are mad at you," she whispered.

"'Cause I'm so good-looking?"

The girl blushed. Bill decided she was probably a virgin.

"No, because you're trying to organize a strike or something."

"Me? All I'm trying to do is dig a tunnel out of this place."

They heard steps coming toward them. She reached out and touched his shoulder. "Be careful," she said, and hurried off.

He watched her legs as she walked away. They were thin but nicely tapered. His shoulder was still warm where she had touched it. He shut his eyes and thought of what Nan had said.

Probably the warden had heard about the strike plan. Probably that was why he was here. That was one of the risks of trying to organize in prison. Informers were everywhere. Everyone was trying to survive. One way was to have a weapon, one way was to have money; one way was to be strong or to have a lover who was strong enough to protect you; and one way was to have scraps of information you could trade to the hacks for favors. Who had ratted? Maybe Watkins, that doper at breakfast.

From where he sat, Bill could see in the assistant warden's office across the corridor. No one was inside. In a wastebasket, he saw a New York *Times*. He stiffened; he almost jumped from the bench. He wanted that newspaper desperately. Perhaps the worst thing about this place was the total isolation from the outside world. You got news of the war, news of the Movement, second hand and weeks late. Each night the men in each cell block decided by a democratic vote what TV programs to watch, and each night "I Love Lucy" won out over the news. He wanted that *Times* the way an alcoholic would have wanted a bottle of whiskey.

His eyes swept the corridor. Still empty. It wouldn't take five seconds to grab the paper, stick it under his shirt, and return to the bench. It was almost too easy. That worried him. Had they set him up? No, you paranoid fool, grab the damn paper while you can. He started to rise from the bench . . .

"The warden will see you now," the warden's secretary said from the doorway.

Bill followed her into the office. His head cleared. He almost laughed. Five seconds more and the bitch would have caught him with his hand in the wastebasket: "Anti-War Leader Caught Stealing Newspaper; Gets Five Years in Hole."

The warden's office was huge.

"Sit down," the warden barked. Bill sat. The warden chewed on a cigar stub as he looked Bill over. Bill stared back. He was past being scared. He could take the hole; he'd written off his good time, so there was nothing more to fear. Resist.

"I hear you're organizing some kind of a strike," the warden said.

Zap! Hit 'em between the eyes. But he shouldn't have said "some kind of"; that showed uncertainty, maybe fear.

Bill said nothing.

"Well?"

"Well, what?"

"Well, are you organizing a strike?" He was getting mad. Bill was enjoying the scene. This was the best thing since somebody had slipped him some bennies the week before.

"I'm talking to people about conditions here," he said. "It's outrageous that men work all day for fifty cents."

"So you plan to make them stop working?"

"I can't make anybody do anything. But if you pay men slave wages you'd better expect the slaves to rebel."

"If you stir them up."

"I don't stir anybody up. I just talk to people. I've got that right."

"You've got no right to cause trouble. I could put you in segregation right now with the information I've got."

"Go ahead."

"By God, I ought to."

"People will still protest, whether I'm in the hole or not."

The warden stared at Bill angrily. Bill could see him calculating, could see the wheels turning. He guessed the odds on the hole were about fifty-fifty. The warden hated his ass, that was for sure. But there were other factors. What if Bill's friends started a hunger strike in protest? What if it made the papers?

"I understand your wife visits you this afternoon," the warden said.

Bill nodded. Subtle bastard. Playing his trump?

"Visitation is a privilege, you know."

"I know the rules."

"Look, Hall, you've got a bad attitude. I didn't send you to prison, but I've got to take care of you while you're here. I play fair with people who play fair with me."

"Then do something about the pay people receive here."

"That's set by the legislature."

"Then ask them to change it."

"What good would that do?"

"What harm would it do? It'd be a sign of good faith."

The warden waved his hand. "I'll think about it," he said. "It'd be fine with me if they wanted to pay you people more. If a man works, I say pay him all you can."

"They'd work better for better pay."

"Hall, you're a smart fellow and there's no use for us to cross swords. I want us all to get along here."

"So do I," Bill said. He was thinking that the warden was scared, was weaker than he'd thought. Or was he just buying time? That could be it. They might ship him out of here the next day, send him on the Tour, the Prison-a-Month circuit.

The warden stood up, Jimmy Cagney again. "Don't tangle with me, Hall. You'll be better off that way. Treat me square and I'll treat you square."

He pushed a buzzer and a moment later a hack appeared to take Bill back to his cell. Bill had missed lunch but he didn't mind; it was good to skip meals occasionally, to keep yourself ready for hunger strikes.

Gibson came at three and got him. He didn't know why Gibson hated him. Politics, probably. Gibson had worn a Wallace button on his uniform one day. They marched silently toward the visiting room.

"Get your ass in there, boy," Gibson snapped. Bill felt the hate filling him. He didn't want to go through this again. He wanted to smash this bastard, just once, in his ugly sneering face. But Beth was waiting. Waiting only yards away, needing him. Bill stepped into the little room.

"Okay, strip."

"You've got no right—" He bit off the sentence.

"You eat shit," the hack said. "The rules say any prisoner can be searched before and after a visit."

And they did. Except the rules were almost always ignored, or limited to a quick pat-down. But Gibson had another game.

"Now get them clothes off."

Bill stared at him. One word on his part would be enough to cancel the visit. He could have killed the bastard. But Beth was waiting. He began to take his uniform off.

"Turn around," Gibson said when he was naked. Bill turned around.

"Bend over and spread those cheeks."

Bill did as he was told. You son of a bitch, I'll get you if it takes the rest of my life.

He flinched as something cold poked his rectum.

"Hot damn, thought maybe you hadda machine gun hid up thar," Gibson cracked. "Okay, get them stinking clothes back on."

A minute later, Bill was dressed and was facing Beth through a glass partition.

She looked better. Thin, tired, but better. She'd been to see him the first time, that winter, and it hadn't gone well and after that the drug thing had begun. He'd heard about that indirectly, then there'd been the letter from Carol that said she was getting treatment.

"Hi," she said. They had to speak loudly because their voices had to pass through the little wire mesh opening in the glass.

"How are you?" he asked.

"Not too bad." She smiled and looked years younger, almost like he remembered her from the Peace Corps days. "I've been working mornings for Charles."

"What do you do?"

"Oh, answer letters. A little casework. Help people with their Social Security benefits."

"It sounds interesting."

"I've got a lot more respect for Charles now that I've seen what the Senate's like. And what the mail is like. He may not get re-elected next time, just for what little he's said about the war."

He tried to seem interested. Her reality was so far from his now that they might have lived on separate planets. Had he really once

272

slept with this girl, once loved her? All he could feel now was a fear of hurting her.

"How about Kennedy House?" he asked.

"I go by a couple of afternoons a week. Tim's got everything under control. He really doesn't need me. And I'm not sure I'm up to the hassles."

She told him some of the Kennedy House gossip. About marriages, divorces, affairs, imprisonments. About how acid was everywhere now. About the Movement and the big march planned for the fall and the rumors that some Movement leaders were going to be indicted.

"Tell me about you," she said.

"I'm all right. I'm meeting some good people. Hal Stowers is here, one of the Minnesota Nine."

"There was a story in the paper, that some of them were being punished for something."

"That was last month. That's when they sent Hal here. They tried to organize an inmates' council."

"Bill, you won't do anything like that, will you?" She leaned forward, her face almost touching the glass.

"I might, Beth."

"Bill, listen, I heard that the Parole Board might start letting COs out after eighteen months."

"I doubt it."

"I'm trying to check it out."

"Beth, I've got a three-year sentence and there's no use in either of us thinking I'll be out before that."

"Bill, you might be out in another eight or nine months."

"Don't expect that. Please."

"You'll help, won't you? You'll keep out of . . . you know, trouble?"

"I can't promise that."

"But you must, you must! What good does it do to make trouble in there? The only thing that's important is to get you out of there."

He hated to upset her but it was important that she understand.

"Beth, the way it's put to you here, sometimes, is a choice between your freedom and your self-respect. The way to get a parole is to grovel but it's just not worth it."

"Anything's worth it, to get you out, to have you back!"

The clock showed five minutes more of visiting time.

"The thing is, Beth, you change in here. I came in a pacifist. I won't leave here a pacifist."

"I just want you to get out," she said. She was starting to cry.

"We've got to resist, Beth, wherever we are." He put his hand against the glass, inches from hers. He smiled at her. "Don't let the bastards get you down."

"If you'll just stay out of trouble," she said. "If they get these new parole regulations . . ."

"They teach you to hate, Beth. There are murderers and psychotics and black militants in here who don't hate any more than I do. It's just directed at different targets."

"I love you, Bill."

"I love you," he said, wondering what the words meant. Wondering if he ought to tell her to forget about him. But if she wanted words he would give them; words were cheap.

"Don't worry about me," he told her. "The warden here wants me out as bad as you do."

She smiled and that made him feel better. "It's you who's got to take care of herself."

"I'm off drugs," she said. "Maybe a little grass but nothing more than that."

"You shouldn't even smoke grass," he said. "There are people in here for smoking a joint or two. It's not worth it."

"Nothing's worth anything any more."

A buzzer sounded, meaning there was only a minute more.

"You're still staying with Charles and Carol, aren't you?"

She nodded.

"That's good. Just take it easy."

"I'm so much better," she said. "I've got this great doctor."

"Do what he says."

"I miss you so."

"I miss you. I love you."

The buzzer sounded again and the guard started forward.

Beth pressed her face against the round wire mesh circle. He hated that, hated this struggling to overcome barriers that couldn't be overcome. But he pressed his face against the wire, too, in a cold, eerie kiss, and then she was gone.

274

Gibson was waiting at the door.

"Come on, wise guy. Get in there and strip down."

Bill walked into the little room and took his clothes off. He wasn't even angry now, just relieved, and his only thought was of how much work still waited to be done.

16

SEPTEMBER 1967

The fight over the school had simmered all summer. Charles of course was adamant. Hugh would return to Hyde. He was doing fine, the school was getting better, blah blah blah. Carol finally stopped arguing. Sometimes it seemed as if all they did was argue any more; it was their only means of communication. Oh, they had their moments. Sunday mornings were nice sometimes. The phone didn't ring so much then and Charles would charge around the kitchen in his pajamas, a dishtowel slung over his shoulder, frying bacon and fixing pancakes, taking a boyish joy from getting everything ready at the exact right moment. After that he would read the funnies to Liza, then he might watch the interview shows or, if there was no one he wanted to see, putter in the yard for a while. On weekday evenings when he was home he would settle in and watch an hour of the news, both Cronkite and Huntley-Brinkley, often with Liza nestled in his lap.

Liza didn't understand the news, but the commercials fascinated her, dramatic little vignettes about people with bad breath and bad teeth and bad stomachs, people who worried that their underarms stank or their private parts stank or their living rooms stank, women whose washes weren't white and whose floors weren't bright, people whose false teeth were loose or stained or feared they were, people with runny noses and stopped-up bowels, people with cracks between their toes and dandruff in their hair, people with chapped hands and sore backs and weak legs and tired blood, women with too much

276

breast or too little, women whose tummies sagged, men whose muscles ached and hair thinned and feet hurt. . . . Night after night, Liza Pierce discovered this America, a land of sick, stinking, neurotic people, nestled in her father's arms, as he waited silently for the news from another country where people were dying.

They sent Hugh off for August to a camp in North Carolina. Just before Labor Day they drove down to get him, not talking much—what was there to talk about any more?—but they were cheered when they saw Hugh, tanned and five pounds heavier, excited about the medals he had won in the swimming meet. Their enthusiasm dimmed a bit when the camp director pulled them aside and spent a half hour telling Charles that some kooks in Washington were trying to pass a camp-safety bill and that his camp was already safe, safer than most homes, never had a serious accident yet and this was just some nuts trying to make trouble. Charles was sick of being lobbied every time he turned around, but he heard the man out because Hugh might want to come back here the next year.

Hugh, emboldened by a month on his own, brought up the school question on the drive home.

"You know, Dad, I don't want to go back there this year. To Hyde, I mean. A couple of the other guys are switching to private schools and that's what I want to do."

"Son, I thought that was settled. You're going back to Hyde. Heck, after this month in camp you'll be the toughest kid in school."

"I *can't* go back there, Dad. I *can't!*"

Carol shut her eyes, vowing to say nothing.

"Sure you can. Hey, how about a lunch break? You look like you could eat a horse. Or at least a HoJo Special."

But it wasn't settled. Carol listened to the boy's arguments all the next week, winced at his tears, felt like a stranger caught between this father and son. She argued with Charles about it once but got nowhere and finally she gave up, just gave up. Somehow, it would have to work itself out.

It worked itself out at 3:00 A.M. on the morning before school opened.

Carol heard the screams first. They seemed to fill the house. She leaped out of bed, and Charles was just behind her. They found him kneeling on the floor beside his bed, red-faced, out of control.

"I can't go back there I can't go back there I can't go back there!"

They knelt on the floor beside him. Charles put one hand on the boy's shoulder.

"Son, calm down, just calm down."

"I won't. I can't. I won't go back to Hyde. Please don't make me. Please, please, oh, God, don't make me."

"Now look, Hugh, it's all settled. Just calm down."

The boy started to scream, a wild animal sound, and Carol took him in her arms.

"Now, Hugh, just relax," Charles began.

"You shut up!" Carol screamed. "Just shut up, you son of a bitch. Leave this child alone! Just go away!"

"Damn it, Carol . . ."

"God damn you, shut up! He's not going back to that school if I have to take him and we'll go away together."

"Carol, you're acting like a—"

She hit him in the face with her fist and began to cry, still holding the boy in her arms. Charles got up and left the room. It took her thirty minutes to calm Hugh with her kisses and her promises, and when he was finally asleep she went back to their bedroom. She meant it. She would leave.

He was lying on the bed staring up at the ceiling. She thought he had been crying but she wasn't sure.

"He can go to a private school," he said. "We'll check it out in the morning."

"Okay," she said.

She got into bed. She thought of kissing him, thanking him—for him, it was a lot; it was as close as she had ever known him to come to saying he had been wrong—but all her emotions were gone, left behind in the other bedroom. In a minute she was asleep.

So Hugh enrolled in a private school. She won that battle. And, surprisingly, she was winning some battles on her other front, at the station.

Their lawyer, their tough lady lawyer, had said, "File your charges first, then negotiate."

So they filed their complaint with the EEOC. It was the biggest step they had taken, and the signing of the complaint was a great ceremony. The station had quit giving them conference rooms to meet in, so they walked down the street to an Episcopal church one day in late September and met with their lawyer there. They had maintained total secrecy. The men knew something was up—Ken Holton had tried to worm it out of Carol—but they never knew what until it hit them. When the last signature was written, cheers filled the church. Then the lawyer climbed into a waiting cab to deliver the complaint to the EEOC, and messengers left to deliver press releases to all the city's newspapers and radio and television stations—including one to their own boss, Ken Holton. The revolution had gone public.

After the initial controversy died down, they entered what Carol called the Paranoia Phase. Whenever Ken Holton left his office, even for coffee, he locked his door, presumably so Sally or one of the other women wouldn't rifle his files. He began cutting off his extension phones before taking certain calls from New York. Locks appeared on drawers and filing cabinets. One day the New York lawyers appeared, sleek men in expensive suits, for a mysterious conference with Ken. A few days later the first of the EEOC investigators appeared and took away with him the salary data that had been denied to the women. Ken Holton was livid that week.

But there were results. Two new female reporters were hired, both of them black; that was one of the tricks management had learned, that if they hired a black woman they got a check mark in two categories at once. But others benefited too, Carol among them. After her VISTA documentary was shown, and well received, Ken Holton finally let her become the station's first full-time woman producer.

And yet once the first flush of excitement was past, Carol knew she had won a hollow victory. She had won without caring; she cared for the other women but she no longer cared for herself. The first documentary had been fun, and the second one too, but after that they were just hard work, filled with hassles with writers and cameramen and a million other people. Soon she was wondering how long she would keep on with it. The main thing that kept her going was knowing that Ken Holton would laugh at her, say he'd known all along she wasn't up to the hard work of being a producer.

She could have done it if she'd had to, if she'd needed the money, but she didn't, they didn't. One of life's little ironies was that, even as Charles opposed the war, the wartime boom was making him rich, or richer. All their stocks were soaring; they had more money than they could ever spend. So she kept going out of pride, wondering how long she could stand it. It was just too much, the hassles at work, then the hassles at home. Life with Charles was just so *grim* now—that was the only word for it. There were still the occasional good times, good parties, good sex, but they were separated by barren miles of his silence, his brooding, his sudden anger at the smallest things. She took her comfort in the children, but they were growing up, needing her less, busy with their schools and their friends. Only the war went on, morning after morning in the papers, night after night on TV, always on Charles's mind, always inside him like a cancer. She no longer knew what she thought about the war. She had quit talking to people about it at parties because everybody else hated it and she was sick of arguing about it. All she knew for certain was that the war was changing her husband before her eyes, that somehow it was ruining her marriage—that her husband wept for villages destroyed ten thousand miles away but was blind to what was being destroyed in his own home.

He had shown some interest in what she was doing at the station; part pride, she thought, and part amusement. She hadn't said much about it—he didn't bore her with his Senate tales much any more, so she didn't bore him with her TV tales—but they discussed it at dinner on the night the newspaper stories about the EEOC complaint appeared.

"Well, you guys have really done it," he said. He was feeling good. The kids were in bed and he'd had three gin and tonics before dinner and they were well into a bottle of Montrachet. "Five Senators must have come up to me and asked what this was all about."

"What did you tell them?"

"I told them, 'Hell, I don't know what it's all about, my wife never tells me anything.' What *is* it all about?"

"Maybe you shouldn't get me started."

"It looks like you're already started, according to the front page of the *Post*. Go ahead, enlighten your poor dim-witted husband."

"Well, in a word, it's about sexism. Discrimination because of sex."

"Like women not being drafted?"

"Like women not getting equal pay for equal work."

"There are reasons. Women have a habit of quitting and having babies. You lose your investment."

"I know women who've worked twenty years and never had babies

280

and are still underpaid. And I know men who change jobs every three years and always get a promotion. Is that fair?"

"Maybe not. I guess not. Tell me about the EEOC thing."

She told him about the EEOC and the FCC and their statistics and their legal issues. He liked that. He was attuned to statistics and legal issues.

"That's great," he told her. "If you've got the law on your side, go to it. But I still think there are some difficult areas."

"Such as?"

"Well, would it be realistic to think your station could have a woman as its general manager?"

"Why not? I could do a great job."

"There are questions of temperament, training, experience . . ."

"Which women by definition lack. Is that it? Charles, on sex, you're like Senator Eastland on race."

"Thanks."

"I've been through this same conversation a hundred times with Ken Holton and he never understood a word I said and I'm afraid your thought patterns are exactly like his."

She thought of stopping the conversation there, but didn't. "Charles, do you ever try to put yourself in someone else's place. Someone really different from yourself? A Negro, maybe?"

"I've tried. When we went to the Indian reservation—I tried to think of Hugh and Liza growing up like those kids. It wasn't much fun."

"Well, sometime try to imagine being a woman, Charles. A woman with some sense. A woman who wants to work and have some kind of a life of her own, some kind of self-respect. Try to imagine being a woman with a job, who's competitive, who wants to show how good she is, and all the time having to pretend to be sweet and feminine so the men won't call her a bitch or a ball-breaker or all those things they call women who threaten them."

"Carol, I think . . ."

"Just wait a minute. Try to imagine that ninety per cent of what people judge you by is your looks. Try to imagine spending an hour every day trying to make yourself prettier than you are, worrying about the circles under your eyes and the lines in your face. Try to imagine having a husband who thinks the highest compliment he can pay you is to say, 'You look great.' I could be deaf and dumb and it wouldn't matter to you as long as I *looked* great."

"Carol . . ."

"Just be quiet. Try to imagine having to deal with men all day who never listen to you, just stare at your body and think filthy things about you and make dirty jokes behind your back. Do you think you'd like that, Charles?"

"Do you think I'm all that insensitive, Carol? I understand. At least I try to. But it's just that women . . ."

"Are women. Not people, just women."

He put his elbows on the table and leaned forward. "It's hard to change the way you think, Carol."

"Charles, the thing is, this is 1967, and you're an intelligent person, and we've all learned a lot in the last few years. In the fifties we discovered that Negroes weren't happy. And then Kennedy went to West Virginia and discovered that there were poor people in America and now we've got a war on poverty. And we've learned about the war—we all know a lot more about the Pentagon and the generals than we did a few years ago, don't we? And some people are beginning to figure out that maybe homosexuals are people too. And all I'm saying to you is that you ought to discover that women are discriminated against, in every tiny part of their lives, and you ought to try to understand it. Things are happening, Charles. The war isn't everything."

He shook his head. "What can I say? I know I'm preoccupied, I know I'm a son of a bitch sometimes. Sometimes I wonder why the hell I'm not living a normal life like I always wanted to live. Look, how would you like it if we started going out to dinner more often, Rive Gauche or the Jockey Club or . . ."

She put her head in her hands. "Charles, Charles, you don't understand at all, do you?"

"I guess not. But keep trying if you want to."

"Did you like your dinner tonight?"

"Sure, it was great. I've always said you were the greatest cook in the world. I just thought . . ."

"That I'd rather eat at Rive Gauche, I know. No, Charles. But think what's going to happen in a few minutes. We'll finish this stimulating discussion and then you'll go back to your study or to the TV or to the telephone or whatever, and I'll clear off the table and do the dishes and clean up the kitchen while you attend to the affairs of state."

"I help with the dishes sometimes."

"Yes, about once a month when we've had a party and you're in a hurry to get me up to bed."

"I'm just a fucking animal, aren't I?"

"No, you're just a typical American male."

"Thanks again."

"You're welcome. Now, let's break this up, before anyone's feelings get hurt."

She started to rise. He jumped to his feet.

"Don't get up," he said. "Finish your wine. I'll do the dishes."

"Charles, really . . ."

"I'm serious. You're dead right. I ought to do my share. You just sit there and finish your wine and I'll take care of everything."

So she sat, while he stacked the plates and balanced them precariously on one arm and grabbed the empty wine bottle with his free hand and marched into the kitchen. She winced when she heard the clatter of the plates on the drainboard—he'd surely break something—but she was afraid to say anything. In a minute he came back for the glasses and the napkins.

"Does all the leftover stuff go down the disposal?"

"Yes. All except the biggest bones. And the silverware."

"Got it," he said, and returned to the kitchen. She heard the sound of water running, cupboard doors slamming, pots rattling. She blew out the candles, started to go to him, then sat back down. She finished her wine and stared out the barred windows at their dogwood tree, washed in moonlight. She heard the sound of a dish breaking and Charles's loud "God damn it!" After a while she began to laugh, although it wasn't really funny. At least he was trying. She'd gotten through to him, just this once. This would pass, too, like all his brave resolves passed after a few days or weeks. He'd never change the way he thought, not enough to matter. He wouldn't change and she wouldn't stop changing, and she sat alone at her table, listening to the clatter in the kitchen, wondering how it all would end.

17

OCTOBER 1967

"Naturally you think I'm a silly old woman."

"I don't think that at all, Mother," Charles said, and signaled Walter to refill their glasses.

"Of course you do," Emily Pierce insisted. "I'd certainly think it, in your place. Here she is, fifty-six years old, a grandmother, a woman with friends and money and freedom, and now the poor old fool wants to *fall in love*. Absolutely insane."

"Love makes the world go round," Charles said. They were sitting in his living room, waiting for their dinner guests to arrive.

"Don't be flip," his mother said sharply. "The thing you realize as you grow older is that you never really understand the generation ahead of you. Your parents. If *my* mother had done this at my age, I'd have surely had her carted off to the state farm. At least *my* children are enlightened. You liberals understand these things, don't you? Or do you? The worst prudes I've known have been liberals. Well, no matter."

"If you want to marry again, that's great." He was tuning her out now. He had spent the afternoon marching in the hot sun in another world and he wasn't ready to cope with his mother's views on sex, politics, or anything else. Agree with her. It's her night, agree with her.

"It's not *great*, Charles. You should pick your adjectives more carefully. But it's *human*, to be lonely, to want companionship. You lose a lot with age, beauty and health and passion, but you don't

284

lose the need to be cared about. Plus the social aspects of it. A widow, even a rich one, is a nuisance socially. In our society you need a man. And there are men available, believe me. More than you might imagine. But you must consider their motives and most of them just won't wash."

"Howard is impeccable."

"That's a good adjective. Yes, Howard *is* impeccable. After marriage to Hugh Pierce, almost any other man would be a step down. But Howard is a peer, you must give him that, however objectionable you find his politics. Even your father respected Howard."

"He always said that Senators came and went but newspaper columnists go on forever."

"Walter, just a little more champagne, please," his mother said, and the old Negro hurried over with the bottle. She had brought him with her from the farm, where he had served the Pierce family for thirty years.

"Howard has his journalistic distinction," Emily Pierce continued, "and he had his social position even before that. His family is quite distinguished."

"I seem to recall hearing about that," Charles said. His mother, if she caught his irony, ignored it. In truth, Howard Chamberlin rarely let an hour go by without reminding you of his family tree. My cousins, the Biddles, and all that. No grubby police reporter, he!

"He is a gentleman in a profession that seems to attract precious few of them," Emily Pierce continued. "I sometimes wonder how he feels about marrying a woman who has a son in the Senate and a son-in-law in prison."

She meant it as a joke but he didn't find it funny. He wondered how much champagne she'd had. "Don't ever say that in front of Beth," he told her.

"I don't say anything in front of Beth, you know that. Beth and I live on different planets. I don't understand Beth and she doesn't understand me."

"You could try."

"I *have* tried, thank you. I have *tried* to understand how a young woman with her background, with her education, with the values she was exposed to, could turn away from everything she was taught to hold dear. I *don't* understand it and I *won't* apologize for it. I think the mistake was made a long time ago, when we let her go East to school, or when we let her join that Peace Corps. Those Kennedys came in with all their pretty talk and all their big ideas and all they did was to undermine respect for authority."

Oh, you and Howard Chamberlin will make a lovely couple; maybe you can write some of his columns for him.

"If I might ask, where *is* Beth?"

"I don't know. Maybe she ran into some friends. She'll be along."

Actually, he knew where Beth was. That was his little secret for the evening. Beth would miss her mother's engagement party because she was in the D.C. jail.

"It's terribly rude of her," his mother said.

Charles drank his champagne and didn't answer. Good God, what a night for a party. It was the wrong people on the wrong night of the wrong season. This was no season for bringing people together. He had been to too many parties that summer that ended in bitter words, tears, broken friendships, angry departures. The passions that were ripping the country apart reached now even into the dining rooms of Georgetown and Spring Valley. He and Carol had all but stopped going out. But tonight it would come to them.

"Hi," Carol said from the doorway. "Am I late?"

"You're right on time," Charles said. "And you look tremendous." Or was he supposed to say that?

"Thank you," she said, smiling at him. "Let me just take a quick peek in the kitchen." She disappeared down the hall, and was back moments later.

"Everything's under control," she announced.

"Charles," his mother said, "do we have cigars for the men after dinner?"

Charles caught it. After ten years he was attuned to his wife and mother. If Carol announced that everything was under control, his mother would seek something that wasn't under control. It was female instinct; they actually liked each other.

"Cigars, brandy, and dueling pistols," he said.

"Oh, let's not play that boys-in-the-study, girls-in-the-bedroom game tonight," Carol said.

The daughter-in-law strikes back.

"Well, I'm just old-fashioned enough to think Washington's tra-

286

ditions should be preserved, even in an era of rebellion. *Especially* in an era of rebellion."

"I just hate that idea that women are ninnies to be shunted off while—"

There was a knock at the door and a moment later Walter ushered in Howard Chamberlin.

He was a tall, imposing man of sixty, with a long nose and quick gray eyes. Charles's memories of him went back twenty years, to Sunday afternoons when he would come by to drink Bourbon and talk politics with the Senator.

"My dear," the columnist said, taking Emily Pierce's hand and bending to kiss her cheek.

Charles watched with mixed emotions. He guessed he had some instinctive Oedipal hang-up; he didn't want any man marrying his mother. And yet he had to concede that, politics aside, Chamberlin was about as eligible a sixty-year-old man as could be found in America. Damn you, who do you want her to marry, Dr. Spock?

Chamberlin gave Carol an identical kiss, then extended his hand to Charles. "My boy, you are so fortunate, to be surrounded by such elegant women."

"I certainly am," Charles said carefully. No sarcasm. Be humble. If you can't manage that, be quiet.

He waved for more champagne and settled back as Howard Chamberlin began to talk nonstop, about the decline of Georgetown, about a new Hungarian restaurant in Chicago, about his forthcoming trip to Spain, about the advance reviews on his latest book. Emily Pierce listened contentedly. She really does look happy, her son thought. I'll be happy too, if I don't have to entertain this bastard more than once a year.

A moment later Rip Horton and his wife Cissy arrived. Rip and Cissy had been Emily Pierce's idea, "to have some more of you young people," and also because Chamberlin considered Rip a rising Southern statesman.

The columnist and the young statesman pumped one another's hands. "How'd, that's a mighty fine column you had on Hubert this mawning," Rip declared.

"Hubert's come a long way in the past three years," Chamberlin said. "We can all be proud of him."

The women exchanged compliments too: Emily's dress, Carol's

new drapes, Cissy's gold bracelet. Cissy fascinated Charles. She was petite, exquisitely built, expensively dressed, and a total bitch. She hid her bitchiness behind a syrupy Southern drawl, but if you listened closely there was a barb in every sentence.

"What y'all gonna do?" Rip was asking. "Move old Charles out of here after you get married?"

"Oh, isn't this y'all's house?" Cissy asked Carol.

"Technically it's Mother's," Charles put in quickly. "But I don't think she'll evict us."

"Not at all," Emily Pierce said. "Howard is taking an apartment at the Watergate, and I hope to persuade him to spend summers in Kentucky."

"And I hope to persuade Emily to travel more," Chamberlin said. "The General has promised us an audience if I'll bring her over next spring. Then she could stay in Paris while I visit Saigon."

"Going back to the front again, How'd?" Rip asked. Charles watched Rip, looking for traces of irony. In private, Rip had a devastating imitation of "General" Chamberlin delivering marching orders to "his" troops.

"Got to get back once more before it's all over," Chamberlin said. "Westy tells me the VC won't last out the winter."

"Haven't they been saying that for a long time?" Carol asked. Charles listened to her with interest; she'd been coming around on Vietnam, slowly, painfully, but steadily.

"Well, people say a lot of things, my dear," Howard Chamberlin said. "It could have been over a long time ago except for the Communists' ruthless disregard of human life. They're down to their sixteen-year-olds now."

"Well, we're down to our eighteen-year-olds, aren't we?" Carol said. "I mean, we're losing a lot of young people too, aren't we?"

"People do die in wars," Chamberlin said patiently. "But the kill ratio remains highly favorable to our side."

"It's not so favorable if one of the dead people is your own son, though," Carol insisted.

"I do believe you've been listening to your dovish husband," the columnist said.

"I just read a book by Bernard Fall," Carol said. "There was all this history I'd never known about. That war's been going on for twenty years. It may never stop. And if it goes on a few more years,

288

my own son might have to fight there. And I won't have that, Howard. I'd take him to Canada before I'd let him be killed halfway around the world."

"Ah do think it'd be difficult for Charles's career, if y'all went off to Canada," Cissy injected.

"I'm not talking about Charles's career," Carol said. "I'm talking about *my son.*"

"Well, let's not get all upset about it tonight," Emily Pierce said.

"Carol dear, the point is really moot," Chamberlin said. "The war will be over within a year, and on terms that will assure that neither your son nor any other American boys will have to fight the Communists again in our time."

Charles bit his lip, said nothing, and the conversation turned to his mother's horse farm.

But you could not escape Vietnam for long. Vietnam was always there that season, hanging in the air, drifting under doors, perched on shoulders like an albatross. It came back to them at dinner, when Rip asked an innocent question.

"Where'd you get that red nose, Chas? Been out on the links this aftahnoon while all yore fellow doves was marchin'?"

Charles thought it over. It was his house and he had listened to Howard Chamberlin's bullshit and Rip Horton's pieties for an hour and he was sick of it.

"No, as a matter of fact, Rip, I got my sunburned nose marching to the Pentagon with my fellow doves."

"Fascinating," Howard Chamberlin said.

"An' yew wun't arrested?" Cissy asked. "Ah hud on thuh radio there was *thousands* arrested!"

"Hundreds, maybe," Charles said. "But not me. You had to try pretty hard to be arrested."

"And you didn't make that effort, Charles?" Chamberlin asked.

"No. I thought I made my point by being there. But plenty of kids felt that, to make *their* point, they had to commit civil disobedience."

"Ah *really* don't undahstand it," Cissy said. "Ah mean, what is thuh *point* of marchin' around a big old building and gettin' yourself arrested?"

Charles knew what the point was, but he doubted that he could explain it to Cissy.

"Is that where Beth is?" his mother asked. "At the Pentagon? Or under arrest?"

"I guess so," he admitted. Now he was sorry he had said anything. He should have learned that lesson by now. Any discussion of the war inevitably got out of hand. "Late this afternoon Beth and I got up to within thirty feet or so of where the soldiers were lined up on the Pentagon steps. We could see the girls on the front row putting flowers into the rifle barrels. I said I thought that was as close as I wanted to get. Beth said she was going up to the front and that was the last I saw of her."

"Charles," Howard Chamberlin said, "I wonder if you'd tell us why you were there? And what it was like. As a reporter who missed the event, I'm curious."

"I was there for two reasons, Howard. The first was personal. A few nights ago on the news they started talking about the government's preparations for the march. The paratroopers being airlifted in from Bragg. The loaded weapons. The helicopters. They made it sound like the Battle of the Bulge. Up to then, I'd hardly thought about the march, much less planned to go. But the next morning I read another of the saber-rattling stories about troops and guns and I realized that Johnson was trying to intimidate people, to scare them away from a perfectly peaceful, legal march. And I took it personally. I thought to myself, That son of a bitch . . ."

"Charles!" his mother said.

". . . That son of a bitch is trying to scare me. And the more I thought about it, the madder I got. Then Beth asked me if I wanted to go with her and I decided to go. I asked Carol if she wanted to go, and the kids too."

"I wouldn't go," Carol said. "I was afraid for the children. I wish we had gone now, all of us."

"I do too," he said. "There were a lot of people there with their children."

"Hippie people?" Cissy asked.

"There were hippies, sure, thousands of them. But there were plenty of what we'd call ordinary people. I remember standing there in the Pentagon parking lot and cheering all the groups that marched in carrying their banners. There was even a bunch of guys from UVA, my old school, and, believe me, if the fraternity boys are marching on the Pentagon, Johnson's in trouble."

290

"They haven't the faintest understanding of this conflict," Chamberlin said. "They are fools, being manipulated by clever people who . . ."

"They understand that it's their lives being used to test your theories or Joe Clayton's theories or whosever theories they are," Charles replied.

"Freedom and totalitarianism aren't theories," Chamberlin said. "They're facts."

"Well, a lot of people see the facts differently."

"Granted," Chamberlin said. "But to get back to you, Charles, what was your second reason for marching today?"

"The second reason was political. The only thing that can stop Johnson now is a mass movement. He won't listen to the Senate and he won't listen to his own advisers and so . . ."

He was the first to see Beth standing in the doorway. In a moment the others saw her too, and even in the candlelight they could see her half-closed eye and swollen lip. Carol rushed to her. Emily Pierce half rose, then sank back down in her chair. Charles dipped his napkin in his water glass and went to wipe the blood from her mouth, but Beth stopped him.

"No," she said. "Let everyone see it."

Carol handed Beth a water goblet. "Drink this," she said. "Please."

"What happened?" Charles asked.

Beth leaned against the doorway, holding the water glass in both hands. "It happened after dark," she said. "After all the reporters and photographers had gone. About fifty of us sat down on the Pentagon parking lot. We were going to spend the night. The soldiers told us to leave and when we didn't they charged into us, people who were just sitting there, and began beating everyone with their nightsticks, just beating people down like dogs."

She stopped and sipped some more water. "But I got away. I didn't want to miss Mother's party."

"Weren't yew *scared?*" Cissy asked.

"God damn you, shut up!" Charles shouted.

"Hold on, old buddy," Rip Horton said.

"You shut up too," Carol cried. "This child has been beaten and . . ."

"She's hardly a child," Howard Chamberlin said.

"That's right," Beth said. "If you want to talk about children, let's talk about the children in Vietnam."

"Let's not talk about anything now," Chamberlin said. "Beth is upset and the hour is late and perhaps we'd all best go home and . . ."

"That's right," Beth said. "Go home and forget about everything. Maybe you'll go home and write one of your lovely columns about kill ratios and the ruthless Communists. Let me tell you something, Mr. Chamberlin. I think you're sick. I think you're all sick and you're all as guilty as Johnson is and I hope you all rot in hell!"

Howard Chamberlin remained perfectly calm. "Someday, my dear," he began, "when you are older, I think you will see . . ."

"Oh, *shut up!*" Beth cried, and hurled the water goblet at him. It grazed Chamberlin's forehead, then crashed against the sideboard. Carol screamed and Beth ran from the room.

"I'm all right," Howard Chamberlin whispered. There was a cut on his forehead and a tiny trickle of blood running down the side of his nose. "Don't worry about me, I'm all right."

Charles viewed his wounded guest coldly. Maybe Lyndon would give him the Purple Heart.

"Well, Ah reckon the party's over," Rip Horton said, finishing his wine and rising.

Charles heard the front door slam. He saw his mother sitting very straight in her chair, tears welling in her eyes.

"I reckon it is, Rip," he said, then he hurried out of the house to find his sister.

BOOK III

A LAND OF DREAMS

Ah, love, let us be true
To one another! for the world, which seems
To lie before us like a land of dreams,
So various, so beautiful, so new
Hath really neither joy, nor love, nor light,
Nor certitude, nor peace, nor help for pain;
And we are here as on a darkling plain
Swept with confused alarms of struggle and flight
Where ignorant armies clash by night.

Matthew Arnold, *Dover Beach*

1

SPRING 1968

The idea started with Al Kline.

Al was one of those bright young men who are found at the right hand of all powerful and potentially powerful politicians—the Kennedys seemed to have dozens of them, and Charles counted himself lucky just to have one. Al was part of a network of young Capitol Hill aides who met often to talk over the politics and policies of their bosses. And all that long, bitter winter, one topic dominated their talk: the possibility of ousting the President of the United States.

As talk of a "dump Johnson" movement surfaced, the politicians and the newspaper columnists greeted it with derision. But the younger men had a different sense of the nation's mood. They *knew* Johnson was vulnerable. They saw only one problem: they lacked a candidate.

Bob Kennedy had turned them down, then McGovern, and time was running out. Al Kline had urged that his boss be considered, but the others were unpersuaded. Senator Pierce was too young, too little known. So, finally, the "dump Johnson" movement found its candidate in Eugene McCarthy.

But Al had another idea, one he took to Charles in the first week of the new year. It was an audacious idea, but he thought he understood Charles's mixture of anger, frustration, and pride, knew how to play it, and so it was with some confidence that he laid out his plan.

"What it comes to is this, Senator. McCarthy's going into New

Hampshire, Wisconsin, Oregon, and probably a couple of others. Fine. He's going to do better than all the self-styled experts think. But there are plenty of other primaries he won't enter. Particularly in the South and the Border States. What I'm saying is the track's wide open for an attractive Southern anti-war liberal to run in some of those primaries—I'm thinking particularly of Tennessee and Kentucky—and give Johnson fits."

Charles studied the young man across from him before he answered. Al was smart—Al *looked* smart, Jewish-smart, too smart to ever get himself elected to anything, for politicians are well advised to look handsome, to look boyish, to look bumbling, to look almost any way but smart. But Al didn't want to be a politician, only to advise one, to control one if possible. Charles understood that, resented it a little, and accepted it as the price you paid to have smart people around you. For Al was priceless. He had a nose for issues, had gotten in with Nader early in the game, had put Charles on top of the pure-milk controversy and that had led to plenty of headlines, to Charles's first "Meet the Press" appearance and to the first important bill with his name on it. He wondered how much longer he could keep Al. He was too bright to be a Senate aide much longer; he'd want to go into private practice soon. Theirs was a standard, quite satisfactory political relationship: you use me, I use you.

He knew what Al wanted to use him for now. He had seen this conversation coming. He wasn't *that* dumb. He'd known Al would end up here, across the desk from him, with a plan that would take Charles farther than he wanted to go. Al couldn't understand the pressures. No one could.

"Fine," he said, laughing, stalling. "Who's your attractive, Southern, et cetera, candidate?"

"You."

"You're out of your mind."

"No, I'm not."

"You want *me* to run for President?"

"I want you to enter some primaries and give people a chance to vote against Johnson."

"I can't see it. It's crazy."

"If you win primaries it's not crazy."

"What makes you think I can win any primaries?"

"Because Johnson is a paper tiger. If you don't believe it, walk out

296

that door and ask the first ten people you meet on the street what they think about Johnson. Eight of them will say they're sick of the bastard. Listen, don't believe that stuff the columnists write. McCarthy's going to win some primaries and you can too."

"Which means?"

"Which means that either Johnson will be scared into stopping the war, which is good, or he'll withdraw, which is better."

"In which case Bobby'd move in like gangbusters."

"Maybe so. But you'd still go to Chicago with some delegates, which gets you the kind of publicity money can't buy. Listen, Senator, let's face it, right now you're back in the pack with a lot of other guys named Joe who want to be President someday—Tydings, Mondale, Harris, Bayh, McGovern, et cetera, et cetera."

"I never said I wanted to be President."

"Are you saying you *don't?*"

"I ain't saying."

"Let's assume you do. There's '72 to think about, and '76, and maybe the vice-presidency this year, if things broke right."

"Damn it, I don't want to be Vice-President. All I want to do, honestly, is to do something to stop this damned war."

"Okay, then, enter the primaries. That's the *only* way. You can win Kentucky and some others too. What have you got to lose? Johnson's not doing you any favors these days. Why not hit the bastard where it hurts?"

Like you're hitting *me* where it hurts, Charles thought. He was confused, pained. He hadn't wanted to face this. Why me? Why in God's name me?

"Incidentally," Al said, "if you want flattery, you'd make a hell of a lot more attractive candidate than McCarthy."

"He quotes poetry."

"I've got my Bartlett's. You can quote poetry too. So what do you say?"

"I'll think about it," Charles promised. "Now get the hell out of here."

The trouble was, the more he thought about it, the more sense it made. He wouldn't really be running for *President,* any fool could see that. But he would be running against Johnson, against the war—he would be doing *something.* He'd done all the rest that winter. He'd made speeches; he'd attended peace rallies and raised money for anti-war candidates; he'd cast a vote against appropriations for Vietnam. But it didn't seem to matter. The hawk columnists denounced him, his hate mail tripled, the White House cut off his patronage, but the war went on. The only way to stop the war was at the polls.

Bob should do it, of course. Bob had the money and the name and the troops. Charles had all winter read those carefully planted articles about Bob's agony, Bob as Hamlet, Bob not wanting to split the party. Bullshit. The party was already split. Bob just didn't want to risk screwing up a sure-thing nomination in '72. But soon his anger at Kennedy became anger at himself. All the same arguments applied, if on a smaller scale. The moral imperatives were the same. Either you had the courage of your convictions or you didn't.

He sought advice from the few people he trusted. He talked to Pat O'Neal, who told him that his break with Johnson was already endangering his re-election and that this madness would guarantee his defeat. That turned him off for a day or two.

But Al Kline kept hammering at him. He repeated his arguments and he brought others to bolster them, students and clergymen and Vietnam veterans and peace activists and rich doves who dangled money. Then Al played his trump. He sent Beth to see him.

"You promised," she cried at the end of a long, painful talk. "You promised to do all you could and people are still dying every day and all we're asking is that you enter some elections. Is that so much?"

"No, it's not so much."

"Then why are you *waiting?*"

"I'm not sure it'd do any good."

"Charles, if you don't, I'll never forgive you."

He could feel it getting closer.

"And do you know what's worse? You'll never forgive yourself."

He nodded, smiled at her, loved her. "Okay," he said. "Okay." She hugged him and he knew that this was right. Pat O'Neal might call it madness but Pat still thought the world was sane. Charles knew now that the world was mad and that this particular act of madness held out the only hope of sanity left in his cluttered life.

That wasn't the end of it, of course. Negotiations came next.

He went to McCarthy first. McCarthy had begun his much-

298

ridiculed New Hampshire campaign. Charles had never cared for McCarthy but he had to admire him now.

McCarthy was vague, enigmatic. He didn't discourage Charles but he didn't encourage him either. Charles understood. To McCarthy, he was a potential rival for publicity, manpower, money. At the end of a long, meandering talk, McCarthy mumbled something about "the imperatives of conscience" and Charles chose to take that as a kind of blessing.

Bobby was next. Bobby encouraged him. Bobby frowned and knitted his brow and said, Yeah, sure, do it. Charles understood that too. Bobby saw McCarthy cutting into his national constituency, locking up people and money while he hesitated, and from his vantage point any success Charles might have would only detract from McCarthy's momentum. The equation was intangible, uncertain, but most politics is intangible and uncertain, tilts and balances and expectations. From Bobby's vantage point, any delegates Charles won would be fair game later, if it came to that. Charles was no threat to him, they both understood that, and he would be an easier man to deal with than Gene McCarthy would ever be.

So he did it, not sure it was wise, sure it was necessary. On a rainy Monday morning in mid-February he stood before a roomful of skeptical Washington newsmen, with Carol at his side and Beth watching nervously from the back of the room, and announced that he would enter the presidential primaries in Tennessee, Kentucky, and perhaps some other states.

When he had made his statement, the reporters asked the questions he had expected—"Are you a *serious* candidate for President?" "Do you have an arrangement with Senator Kennedy?" "Do you think you're *qualified* to be President?"—and he gave them the answers he'd rehearsed. When it was over, Beth cried and Carol smiled and the reporters filed out indifferently to call their offices.

His announcement made page 13 of the next morning's New York *Times,* won a mildly enthusiastic note in the next week's *New Republic,* and inspired Joe Alsop to a frenzied column about "the liberal death wish." A couple of hundred encouraging telegrams arrived at his office, but not much money.

Running for President, Tennessee, mid-March, 1968:

The plane takes off before dawn from the Louisville airport. Beth sleeps, the little plane rises and dips in the morning mists, and Al briefs Charles on the day's events, names to remember, points to stress, feuds to avoid. Finally Al runs out of names and Charles relaxes, looking down at the rolling hills, the pickup trucks moving along dirt roads, the lights of Clarksville, finally the suburbs of Nashville, just coming to life.

He feels the sensation coming, resists, then accepts it. He feels godlike. The feeling always comes when he is poised above a new city, knowing that faces are upturned to him, hands outstretched to him. He could soar from city to city and always there were new people, new cheers, new trust. It was strange, so strange; it made you both more and less than you were; it set you apart from people and brought you closer too; it brought pride and humility, courage and fear, love and hate. They laughed in Washington and it made you hate them more, but out here there were people who believed in you, needed you, and you drew strength from them. Whatever happened, it was worth it.

7:30 A.M. Earthbound, mortal again. The Nashville co-ordinator, a bearded Vanderbilt professor, brimming with questions, warnings. Quick handshakes in the terminal. Questions from a friendly, sleepy reporter. Out to the waiting station wagon, driven by the professor's talkative wife. Squeezed into the back seat between Al and the professor. More briefing on the way to the Du Pont plant. The beard bothers Charles.

7:50 A.M. Outside the plant gate, hand outstretched, as the eight o'clock shift files in.

"Hello. I'm Charles Pierce . . . running in the presidential primary . . ."

"You're who?"

". . . Charles Pierce . . . appreciate your support . . ."

"This is Wallace country, mister."

"Charles Pierce . . . running for . . ."

"You the one was in that flood?"

". . . Pierce . . . running . . ."

"I'm for you, brother. Peace."

". . . appreciate . . ."

"You gonna do something about them niggers?"

". . . Charles Pierce . . . appreciate your . . ."

"Running for *what?*"

300

He loses count. Fifty hands shaken? A hundred? He remembers the four or five who were friendly, and he remembers more those who gave him a cold, resentful stare. There ought to be a better way to run for President than standing outside plant gates accosting strangers. But no one had found it yet.

9:00 A.M. The professor's old frame house near the Vanderbilt campus. Thirty or forty volunteers, coffee, questions, hope mingled with despair. These people had started the decade with Kefauver and Gore; now Kefauver was dead and Gore was in trouble and there was talk that Wallace could carry the state in the fall. Charles gives an optimistic account of his campaigns. He tells of the appeals for him to enter the Arizona and North Carolina primaries.

"What if the Governor enters the race here?" a woman asks.

"Let him. We've tried to pre-empt him, but if we're not afraid to take on Johnson, we're sure not afraid of the Governor."

A graduate student asks how Charles expects Senator McCarthy to do in New Hampshire that day.

"I talked to his people last night and I think he's going to do damn well."

After the questions, Charles circulates, shakes more hands, tries to remember names. People try to corner him, get him aside, share their grievances. The women are worst. The women always feud. "Senator, we have a terrible problem in West Nashville because, well, frankly, even though she's one of my best friends . . ." He nods gravely and urges unity.

11:00 A.M. The office of the editor of the Nashville *Tennessean*. The editor is sleepy-eyed, shrewd, a Kennedy man. They discuss the Gore problem. Will Albert help out? Perhaps not, if the Governor gets in the race. Albert has problems—getting re-elected in 1970. The editor ticks off names, county chairmen, mayors, friendly reporters. He urges a meeting with a local Negro leader named Good Jelly Brown. He suggests ways to appeal to the farmers and the Wallace people—a hillbilly band at Charles's rallies might help. His secretary brings in coffee and sandwiches. Al takes notes.

1:00 P.M. A change in schedule. The editor insists that Charles's news conference be postponed an hour, too late for his competitor's deadline. Charles readily agrees. The *Banner* has been knifing him ever since he first set foot in the state. Its eighty-year-old publisher wrote a front-page editorial, a kind of prose poem, declaring that

Charles was a fool or a traitor or both. In the *Banner's* cartoons, Charles is an emaciated, goggle-eyed puppet, manipulated by a shaggy-haired creature labeled "Bobby." The *Tennessean* has countered with a noble-featured Charles dressed as David, slingshot in hand, crying "Stop!" to a Goliath labeled "The War." Charles can't decide which cartoon is more ridiculous.

He goes back to his hotel suite to spend an hour on the phone. His first call is to Rip Horton.

"How's it going, old hoss? You setting the woods on fire?"

"Things aren't bad, Rip. What's new there?"

They chitchat awhile. He calls Rip every day or two when he's on the road, not because he likes or even trusts him, but because Rip knows so damn much. Wherever you were, you feared that somewhere else someone was about to do you in. The politics of paranoia.

The banter continues awhile, then Rip plays his card for the day.

"Say, pal, Ah hear there's some folks been calling 'round, asking 'bout yore in-laws. Or should Ah say out-laws?"

"Tennessee folks?"

"That's what Ah hear."

"What's up, Rip?"

"Beats me, pal. But Ah'll say this, there's folks down there what play a mean game."

He finishes with Rip and, uneasy, makes a half dozen calls but finds out no more. Bill Hall's imprisonment is a matter of record, but no paper has yet used it against him. The other calls relax him a little. The phone is an extension of himself now, a link to all the actors in his little drama, a stimulant that keeps him going. If things were good, you called people you could brag to; if things were bad, you called those you could count on for encouragement. There was always one more reporter to gossip with, one more ally to bolster, one more adversary to keep off guard, one more contributor to flatter, one more plot to spin out over the long-distance wires. He kept mental lists of people to call, as a child hoards old toys for a rainy day.

He makes a final, quick call to Carol and the kids, touches that base briefly, then hurries off for the news conference.

2:00 P.M. The hotel's conference room. TV lights. Angry reporters who've been kept waiting an hour. The *Banner's* man jumps up first.

"How do you feel, Senator, about men who won't fight for their country?"

He stays calm. The talk with Rip had at least prepared him for this. "If they act out of conscience, and are prepared to pay the consequences, I respect them."

He waits for the other shoe to drop. *"Isn't it true, Senator, that your own sister's husband . . . ?"* But it doesn't drop. The *Banner's* man scribbles, smirks, shuts up. The rest of the news conference goes well. But Charles leaves shaken. *Beth. What would it do to Beth?*

3:00 P.M. Back in the hotel room. More phone calls. Through the bedroom door, he sees Beth meeting with six girls, six of her campus organizers. Sweet Beth, the old Beth again, full of hope, full of strength, believing in him.

Beth brings in her organizers for a handshake. One is a tiny, dimpled girl named Claudia, no more than eighteen. Charles comments on the tiny American flag pin she wears on her blouse.

"We're patriotic too," she says. "But last week I was canvassing in East Nashville and this man came to the door and got furious and ripped my flag off my sweater and said I wasn't fit to wear it."

"Then what happened?" Charles asks.

"I thanked him and went on to the next house."

He squeezes her hand, then the organizers hurry off to another meeting.

4:00 P.M. A short drive across the tracks to Good Jelly Brown's café, a rambling, asbestos-sided building in a tumble-down Negro neighborhood. Good Jelly Brown meets them at the door, shakes hands slowly, takes them to a table in the back of the room. He offers them barbecue and beer; Charles settles for coffee. Good Jelly Brown is big, very black, courtly. He wears a starched white shirt, bow tie, and old shoes with slits in the side to relieve his corns. He was once a bootlegger who sold his wares in jelly jars; hence his nickname.

"I'm running to give the people a chance to vote against the war," Charles says. "The war is hurting poor people worst of all."

"The poor is hurting, all right," Good Jelly says.

"Let me tell you about Senator Pierce's record," Al says, and ticks off the anti-poverty votes, the open-housing votes, the civil rights votes.

The Negro nods appreciatively. "Good," he says. "Good." He asks questions, good questions, about open housing, about the FEPC.

"You gentlemen lawyers?" he asks. "My son, he's gonna be a lawyer."

"Would he like to work on my campaign here?" Charles asks.

"Wouldn't be good for my boy to *work* for you," Good Jelly says. "We got to be more *private*. If the Governor gets in the race, I'll have his posters all over these walls. But you gonna get the votes."

"We don't think he'll get in," Al says.

"I suspect he will," Good Jelly Brown says. "I hear that Mr. Johnson called him from Washington last night an' *told* him to."

Al and Charles exchange a surprised glance.

"I know a boy who works in the Governor's Mansion," Brown adds.

"Whatever happens," Charles says, "we'll appreciate any help you can give us."

"We know who our friends is," Good Jelly says. "We got to know that much to live."

More handshakes, then the two white men step from the dim café into the bright March afternoon.

"You just got yourself four hundred votes," Al says.

"What about that bit about the Governor?"

"I don't know."

"Find out," Charles says, pointing to a pay phone on the corner. Al hurries to it, returns in a minute to report that the Governor has just announced his entry into the primary.

6:00 P.M. A reception at a rich dove's mansion in Belle Meade. Champagne and checkbooks. A Quaker lady hugs Charles and promises him a thousand dollars. Just then he sees her, fifteen feet away, smiling at him over her champagne glass, a *Vogue* cover come to life—that unforgettable face, but what the hell is her name? He agonizes. Karen. Of course, Karen. "God bless you," he tells the Quaker lady and hurries to her.

"Is it really you?"

"Little me," she says, smiling, glowing, her face lovelier each instant than the last.

"What are you doing here?"

"Oh, making a documentary for some company. GENESCO? They bought Tiffany's. It's nice to get out of New York. It's almost spring here."

304

"What happened to your boy?" he asked. "The one with the ranch as big as Rhode Island?"

"He got away. Eluded me."

"Too bad."

"Not really. Oh, you're wearing your hair longer. Ummm, I like it."

"Ummm. I like you."

The smile again, then a frown. "Don't look now, but you're wanted."

"Where are you staying?"

"Some big hotel downtown. The Stonewall Jackson?"

"The Andrew Jackson. That's where I am."

"I'm in the penthouse. Maybe you could tippie-toe up for a drink later."

"It'd be late. Maybe midnight."

"I'll be up," she says, and slips away as his hostess approaches with another rich dove in tow. A dove in the hand is worth . . . how much?

8:00 P.M. Four thousand dollars richer, bone-tired, scribbling in the margin of his speech as Al speeds east on West End Avenue, slumped in the death seat, his eyes starting to close, his mind wandering, trying to summon up some enthusiasm for the rally ahead, chain-smoking (Salems this week; they seem to hurt his throat a little less), wondering if he's overscheduled, wondering if this rally will be a flop like the one in Bowling Green, wondering if he cares. Then the car jerks to a stop, the kids are waiting at the curb with cheers, V-signs, outstretched hands, hand-lettered signs, behind them he sees some workingmen and blacks, he handshakes his way slowly through the crowd, and he feels his strength returning, a wave that begins in the gut, fills the chest, revives the voice, carries him up onto the stage where somehow he is alive again, the candidate again, alert, confident, soaring, delivering with passion a speech he has delivered a hundred times before.

He finishes and takes questions. The first two go well enough and he is about to recognize a big man at the back of the hall when he sees Al signaling to him. *Cut it off! Cut it off!* He frowns but cuts it off, the band begins to play again, and he moves into the crowd for more handshakes until Al grabs his arm and steers him out to the car.

"What was that for?" he asks. "It was going good."

Al reaches into his pocket and hands him a flyer.

305

"That big guy who wanted to ask the question had just got there with this, hot off the press."

Al turns on the car light and he reads the crudely printed flyer. "Does Kennedy stand-in Charles Pierce support draft dodgers while real Americans are murdered by Communists?" it begins. "Ask Appeaser Pierce what his brother-in-law did to Serve his Country." It was signed "Nashvillians for Victory in Vietnam."

"Has Beth seen this?"

"I don't think so."

"I'll talk to her. Not tonight. Cool it tonight. Maybe tomorrow."

"Okay."

Al flips on the radio, a country-music station, and Charles slumps down in the seat, passion drained, weariness returning.

10:00 P.M. The first drink down, warmth spreading, shoes off, feet up on the coffee table, watching the reports from New Hampshire. Fantastic. Beth keeps pacing the floor, cursing the commercials. Al is getting drunk.

"I knew the bastard could be beat," he mutters. "I knew it."

"It's not over yet," Charles says. "He can still be nominated."

"He'll quit," Al says. "He's a coward and he'll quit."

"Don't bet on it," Charles says. "Anyway, this means Bobby's in."

"He wouldn't," Beth says. "He's waited too late. He's lost it."

"It's never too late for Bobby. He'll get in this week. He may come South."

"To hell with him," Beth says. "He had his chance. He didn't have the guts."

Cronkite says McCarthy is up to 47 per cent. The phone keeps ringing. The *Tennessean* calls, wanting a comment on New Hampshire. Charles praises McCarthy, declines comment on Kennedy. He puts down the phone, depressed again.

"Beth, Bobby's going to need good people. If you want to go work for him, go ahead. He's the only one with a Chinaman's chance of beating Johnson. You too, Al. I'll keep on where I'm committed, but you guys do what you want to do."

Beth jumps to her feet. "Are you out of your mind? You're going to win primaries and we're going to help you."

"I'm just being realistic, Beth."

"Screw realistic," she says, and sinks down beside him on the sofa.

306

"You're the one, Charles. Pierce for President. Grass in the Rose Garden, right?"

"Right," he says, and squeezes her hand, but the gloom continues, the old questions return.

Why me?—that was the first question. Why an ordinary, screwed-up, half-educated bastard like me to save America? Let them find themselves a Galahad, a man on a white horse, Bobby if he's what they want. If they want their sons to march off and die for the greater glory of the Pentagon, why beat your brains out arguing with them night after night? Did it matter? Did any of it matter? No matter what happened in the primaries, wouldn't Johnson still be nominated? So it would be Johnson against Nixon in the fall, and then what choice did he have? He'd have to back Johnson, war or no. So where did that leave him now? Tilting with windmills. Digging his own grave. God, how had they gotten into this mess? The war was a mess, a fine Democratic mess. The convention would be a mess, you could see it coming, Daley versus the kids. And the election would be a mess. Good God, would Nixon be President? Had the country come to that? What had happened to them? Who did you blame? Johnson? Kennedy? Truman? Fate? Capitalism? Human nature? He didn't know, he didn't know anything except to try to do what was right, and being right didn't seem to count for much any more.

Midnight. He tells Beth and Al he's going for a walk, but he walks only as far as the elevator, rides to the top floor, to a pink and white bridal suite where a *Vogue* cover waits, eyes gently mocking, hands soft, mouth warm, and for a time, finally, he finds the escape he longs for.

He was in Louisville when the first word came of the shooting. He hurried to a phone and called Carol in Washington.

"I can catch the next plane and be home by ten," he told her.

"Why do that?"

"Why? Because the whole damn city might blow."

"I'm not worried."

"I am."

"Charles, if you want to see me and the children, fine, come see us, but come because of *us,* not because of some catastrophe."

"Let's don't argue now."

"I'm not arguing. I'm just telling you that we're fine and if you have business to do there, do it."

"I do have a fund-raising breakfast in the morning."

He also had plans to see Karen in the afternoon.

"Fine, raise your funds."

"I'll check in with you," he said. "Maybe nothing will happen."

But the next afternoon looting and burning began and he caught the three o'clock plane home.

Washington was burning. When his plane circled over the city, he saw a dozen pillars of smoke rising through its green April flush. He thought of a movie, some epic, Troy in flames. But this was no movie, this was Washington. For an instant he imagined the flames spreading endlessly, all-consuming, the last judgment.

At home the phone kept ringing, friends from the suburbs were calling. Come stay with us. What if they burn Georgetown, burn the city? Charles wavered, thinking of the children, but Carol was angry, adamant. This was her home and this was where she would stay, so they stayed, watching TV and waiting for Armageddon.

Saturday was quiet, the quietest day he had ever known in Washington. National Guardsmen were on the streets, the curfew began at six, and at dusk they sat on their front steps watching the empty, silent street, hearing birds they had never heard before, seeing the city as it would never be again. They had planned a dinner party that night, and they sat up late drinking two bottles of the Montrachet they'd meant for their guests. He told her of the primaries, Tennessee lost to the Governor's strength and the draft-dodger thing, Kentucky narrowly won, Arizona looking improbably good, North Carolina surprisingly bad.

Carol listened without interest. Where were her smiles, her old enthusiasms? She had campaigned twice in Kentucky, hadn't liked it, and not campaigned again.

"I've got a little problem too," she said eventually. "Not as cosmic as yours, but all my own."

"What's that?"

"Oh, the station, my job, my checkered career, what else?"

"Now what?" he asked, and poured himself more Montrachet. Her job, her ups and downs, no longer interested him. It was only an annoyance. He didn't understand what she wanted, why she fought so many fights for so little gain.

"Ken Holton wants me out," she said. "He's wanted me out ever since I organized the women, and now he thinks he's got an excuse."

"Being?" He put down the wine and poured himself a drink. He thought of some phone calls he ought to make.

"You," she said. "You're the excuse. Now that you're running for President he says you're controversial so I'm controversial. I think maybe he's getting pressure from the Johnson people, not that he needs any. But he says if I'm producing news shows there's a question of bias. What if Muriel and Ethel came and said they wanted to produce news shows?"

"That's idiotic. You're not me. To hell with them. Fuck 'em."

Fuck 'em. A fine, all-American, soul-cleansing phrase. He used it a hundred times a day. The columnists? The unions? The Administration? His snickering Senate pals? The patriots who heckled him? The editors who wouldn't cover him? Fuck 'em! Fuck 'em all! That was the true motto of American politics, no matter what pieties they engraved on the coins.

"I know it's idiotic," she said, "but he's talking about me producing a kiddy show or a cooking show or something, and if I fight it, it'll be the lawyers and the arguments again, and the thing is, I'm tired, just too tired to fight back."

"So quit. Come campaigning with me in Arizona next week. Fun in the sun."

"I've got another plan. Fun elsewhere."

"What's that?"

"You might not like it so much. Do you want to talk about it?"

"Why not?"

"Well, for one thing, the moment I start the phone'll ring, and for another you're getting that glassy-eyed look that you get when you drink whiskey before dinner and wine with dinner and more whiskey after dinner."

"I'm still rational."

"Do you have to drink so much?"

"Yeah, I do have to drink so much. By some miraculous process, it destroys the brain cells but preserves the sanity. Short-term gains. Now, what is it you want to talk about?"

"I drove out in Virginia Sunday, to this little village called Gilead.

It's beautiful and you can see the Blue Ridge Mountains off in the distance, and there're farms and hills and horses and everything."

"Do you want to return to nature?"

"I looked at this tremendous old house that's for rent, on five acres, just outside the village. Cheap. We could rent it and use it on weekends and summers. It's just an hour's drive. It's quiet and there's a stream and the kids could run loose and we could have a horse and there wouldn't be riots and National Guardsmen on every street corner."

"How cheap?"

"Three hundred a month."

"A good house?"

"Big and old and elegant. A huge study for you with a view of the mountains. Old, wide flooring. Five fireplaces, even one in the master bedroom."

"Sex by the flickering flames . . ."

"And a stable . . ."

"Sex in the hayloft . . ."

"Oh, shut *up!* So what do you think?"

"It's okay with me. After I'm elected it'll be the Virginia White House."

Carol smiled at him, pleased. At least he'd listened, even shown some interest. Perhaps the assassination had taken his mind off politics, made him think for a little while of his family.

"Who killed him?" she asked. "The Klan?"

"Some nut," he said. "You watch, when they catch him it'll be some nut."

"But there's got to be a reason. At least a Klansman would have a reason."

"The reason is that this great land produces the world's finest nuts, like we produce Chevrolets and Coca-Cola. American know-how. Listen, just between us, there's a secret nut factory deep in the Everglades. The CIA pays for it and RAND provides the staff and scientifically selected nuts go through a six-week training course and when they graduate each nut gets a rifle and a list."

"I wish you wouldn't joke about it."

"Who's joking?"

"They showed some of his speeches on TV. The 'I have a dream'

310

speech. I couldn't stop crying. It was the most beautiful speech I ever heard."

"He can keep his dream now. Dead men keep their dreams."

"He was such a *good* man."

"Too good for this screwed-up country."

He poured himself a final drink and sat staring at the floor, thinking of his wife. He didn't know what he thought of her any more. He knew they both had changed and how little he understood her now. He knew that little was spontaneous between them any more; now each remark had to be plotted several moves in advance, like a chess game. He wished she had been willing to share politics with him, to care about it as he had, but she had been unwilling to enter into his world, and they had drifted further and further apart, until there was little left except habit and convenience and of course the children. He wondered if he and Carol would stay married if not for the children; he didn't know.

Carol thought of Charles. She thought the two months of campaigning had been good for him. For two years she had watched the war overpower him, watched his frustration sap his vitality, watched it make him moody and bitter and short-tempered. But in these past two months, as he raced from state to state, as at last he *did* something, she had seen him come alive again, seen the energy and enthusiasm that she remembered from years past. Not that it helped *them,* but it helped *him,* and she was glad for him, as she might be glad to learn that a sick friend was getting better. She wondered if this would last. Perhaps, if Bobby could be nominated and elected and the nation began to get well again. . . . But she didn't count on that. She didn't count on anything any more. She thought she was just marking time, waiting to see what happened. She had little hope that she and Charles would ever be close again, really close, the way they once had been. She felt less love for him now than affection, compassion, sadness. She thought him immature—that was his fatal flaw. She saw much to admire in him, but she thought that at bottom he was irredeemably the American man/boy, cherishing his dreams of sun-kissed girls, fast cars, clever quips, easy answers. She thought herself stronger than he. Charles expected too much from life. He had been prepared for conflict but not for sorrow, and when he had confronted the sorrow of the world, the sorrow of the universe, he had been overwhelmed by it. She wished she could help him, protect him, win him back, but it never worked. Too much had happened and they were too far apart.

After a while they went up to bed, hand in hand, he pleased that she was leaving her job, she pleased about the house in the country. It had been one of their better evenings.

2

JUNE 1968

"Ummm. I think I'll nibble your ear."

"My what?"

"Your *ear,* damn it. I like your ears. They're like potato chips, thin and delicate and sort of curved around."

"They're funny-looking. That's why I wear my hair the way I do. They're my flaw. My Achilles' tendon."

"Achilles' *heel."*

"I'm *so* sleepy."

"Do you love me?"

"Charles, *please.* Not at this hour. Let's order breakfast."

"Let's talk. Would you marry me?"

"You're already married."

"Suppose I wasn't."

"But you *are.* You have a wife named Carol and two lovely children whose names I forget. Tell me about Carol."

"What about her?"

"Is she beautiful?"

"Not beautiful. Very pretty."

"Nice?"

"Nicer than I am."

"You're nice."

"To you. But not really. Carol likes people more than I do. I'm in the wrong business for liking people."

"I think you're nice."

"Nice enough to marry?"

"Can't we just have fun? Fun and maybe breakfast?"

"We have fun."

"That's what I mean. Isn't that enough? I'm practically your *camp follower,* and isn't that enough without you talking about *marriage?*"

"Don't you want to be married?"

"Not to you. You'd hate me in a week."

"Why?"

"Because we're so *different.* You're the serious type and I like to have fun."

"I might like some fun myself. You know something? I'm rich. I've got money I never see. When the good people of Kentucky retire me from my present employment, I could practice law and be a rich son of a bitch. I could spend half my time in France or Acapulco or someplace."

"Don't you see, darling, you're *serious.* You'd be miserable in Acapulco. You don't *know* the kind of people who go there."

"Okay, New York."

"You'd hate it too. You're the Washington type, a world-saver. Don't you see, Charles? You don't mean any of these things you say about me. You'd never leave your wife because you'd die if you thought you hurt your children. I'm your fantasy life. You're upset about the war and about your sister and I'm a tasty little morsel who takes your mind off your troubles. One day one of us will get tired of it and that'll be that."

"You're so damned realistic."

"We working girls have to be."

"But you never answered my question."

"Which question?"

"Do you love me?"

"Don't you understand? People like you and I don't *love* people. We *enjoy* people. You have to choose, because once you start loving people you're sure to stop enjoying them."

"How can you know so much without being married?"

"I have a lively imagination. Like right now, I'm imagining a thick slice of country ham with rib-eye gravy—is that what you call it?—and a big glob of grits all soaked in butter."

"Karen, what happens to people like you?"

"Sometimes they starve to death."

314

"I'm serious. What'll you be doing ten years from now?"

"Lying about my age, for one thing."

"Damn it, answer me."

"Oh, Charles, who knows? I'll just go on being beautiful as long as I can, and after that I'll be rich."

"You don't get involved, do you?"

"Most people don't. That's what you don't understand. The people who go to Acapulco—do you think *they* worry about the war? Or the fashion editors I work with. Do you think they lose sleep over Vietnam? Not unless there's a new hemline coming out of Saigon. Now, what about breakfast—that's something I care about."

"Suppose instead of breakfast we made love?"

"Maybe we could do both if we hurried," she said. "Room service is pretty slow."

They did, then she went off for some shopping. Charles took a shower, started to dress, then turned on the TV to get the final returns from California. That was when he heard the news.

Bobby. Now Bobby. Bobby with his brains spilled out on the floor of a Los Angeles hotel. It was too horrible. Charles paced the floor, poured a drink, sank into a chair, wept. The kids. What would happen to all those kids? What would happen to America? Charles thought of America and saw only madness, mayhem, monsters. Now Bobby. Would he live or die? Good God, don't let him live like a vegetable, let him die the way he'd want to.

Bobby. He saw the shock of hair, the grin, the stooped way of walking. He wished he'd known him better. They'd been too much alike to be friends. But Charles thought he understood Bobby. They'd been through the same process. They'd started as insiders and somehow the madness of their time had made them outsiders. He wished they'd had a chance to talk about it.

Karen returned. Lunch came and wasn't eaten. More news bulletins. He felt adrift. He called home and talked to Carol without knowing what he was saying. He lost sense of time.

"Weren't you two sort of . . . *rivals?*" Karen asked once.

He laughed at that, his first laugh of the day.

"Rivals?" he said. "No, we weren't rivals. He was going to make it and I wasn't."

He knew what was coming. Hubert against Nixon. Which meant Nixon. Which meant . . . what?

315

What is happening to America?

He was sitting in a stupor sometime before dawn when Mankiewicz came on the screen and said Bob was dead.

He cried out, lurched to his feet, threw his glass across the room. He felt hate, rage, destruction. He picked up a chair and smashed it against the wall. Someone was shouting in the next room. He shouted back and began to beat on the wall with his fist. Karen took his arm.

"Darling, don't. Please. Your hand is bleeding."

"He's dead."

"Please come and sit down."

"This country is all fucked up, do you understand?"

"You can still do good things."

"No. Not me. I've had it. I give up. Screw it. I'm going to Acapulco and let Hubert Humphrey save America. Let's fly down tomorrow. Today. Rent a villa. Drink rum and screw and dance the rhumba. Gather ye rosebuds while ye may. Don't you see, Karen, it's too late for Bobby but it's not too late for me. What do you say?"

"I say please come to bed and get some sleep and then we'll talk about it."

She took a towel and wrapped it around his bleeding knuckles. He sat on the edge of the bed staring at the towel. His face had an unfocused, desperate look that frightened her. He had always been so disciplined.

"I don't think I can sleep," he said.

"I'll hold you and keep you warm."

He touched her hand. "You're nice," he said. "It's not just that you're so damned beautiful, you're really nice."

"Thank you."

"In the end, that's all you ask of people, that they be nice."

"Come to bed, darling, come to Karen."

"Sweet Karen," he said. "Sweet Karen, my fantasy with whom I could live happily ever after in Acapulco."

"Crazy Charles," she said, and held him close and in a moment he was sleeping.

Karen was still asleep when he awoke at noon. He packed his things quickly. He started to leave her a note but he decided she'd understand. She usually understood more than he did. So he only blew her a kiss from the doorway as he left for the airport.

316

At home, an invitation to the funeral awaited him. He didn't want to go, but Carol insisted that he should and after a while he saw that she was right. That was what frightened him most; he didn't know what was right any more.

3

JULY 1968

Carol spent the morning working in her gardens. The day was hot and cloudless, and she wore a floppy old straw hat to protect her from the sun. She weeded the flower gardens around the house, then she sprayed for potato bugs in the vegetable garden down by the barn. Her heads of Bibb lettuce were huge, and at noon she picked one and carried it back up to the house to make a salad for lunch. She put on three eggs to boil, and water for iced tea. The children would be home soon from their swim at a neighbor's pool. Carol had been invited to swim, too, but she'd decided she'd rather work in her gardens.

Such was the rhythm of Carol's life in their new summer home, and she loved it. Already she was thinking they should buy a place out here. They could take an apartment in the Watergate for the nights Charles had to be in Washington. Carol didn't care if she never saw Washington again. Out here, only an hour from the District, was like a different world. Carol didn't even read the papers or watch the news any more. She'd given that up when Bobby died. All she wanted was a peaceful, quiet life for herself and the children, and this little village seemed as good a place as any for it.

The front screen slammed and Hugh and Liza raced in from their swim, their shouts echoing through the old stone house. They loved it here—the swimming, the riding, the fishing, the woods to explore. When Carol asked them if they'd like to live and go to school out here, Hugh had said, "I'd like to go to school anywhere where there's no colored kids causing trouble," and Liza had nodded fierce agreement.

Just as she served lunch the phone rang. It was Charles, calling from New York.

"How's it going?" she asked, as she always did.

"Oh, so-so. Nickels and dimes."

She guessed it wasn't going well. He and the other anti-war people were trying to hold uncommitted delegates away from Humphrey. Some were rallying behind McCarthy, and a few, liberal Southerners mainly, were pledging themselves to Charles's candidacy.

"How's it with you?" he asked.

"Great," she said. "You know, the corn is as high as an elephant's eye. And the peas will be ready by this weekend. What's chances of you joining us?"

"I don't know. I think I've got to go to the Coast. We're trying to hold the California delegation together."

"We'd like to see you."

"I know, I know. I'll try. Are the kids there?"

So he talked to the children, to Hugh about the twelve-inch bass he had caught, to Liza about her learning to swim under water, and when the talk was over the kids finished their salad and agreed to rest for an hour.

Carol went out to the screened-in porch and stretched out on the chaise to read a paperback book on organic gardening. It was cool on the porch. Huge oak trees sheltered it from the sun, and birds sang in their branches. Carol was lulled by their music, content. She thought she could see the rest of her life stretching out before her. Not a perfect life, but not a bad life either. It was a compromise, of course. When Carol was a girl her mother had told her that everyone eventually has to compromise with life. Carol hadn't believed it then, hadn't believed it for many years, but now she guessed it was true. Her compromise was her marriage. She had dreamed of the perfect marriage, the team working together. Now she knew that politics would always draw Charles away from her. She accepted that. She would make a separate peace. She would have her life, Charles would have his, and now and again they would intersect. Poor Charles. He hadn't wanted this either. She could remember how he'd vowed that politics would never break up his family. But somehow he'd gotten caught up in it, in the whirlwind of his times, and there

319

was no turning back. She respected him. He was doing what he thought he had to do. So was she.

In the late afternoon Jane Firestone called and asked Carol to come over for a swim and a drink. Carol agreed and, after a moment's hesitation, slipped into her bikini. She'd lost four or five pounds, working in the garden and riding every day, and she thought she looked good.

There were seven or eight people at the Firestones' pool, and a dozen kids. The Firestones were Carol's favorite people in Gilead. Carol had met Jane at the post office early in June. They shared a love of gardening, had children about the same age, and now they usually talked or visited at least once a day. Jane was blonde, vivacious, and fortyish. Pete Firestone was older, white-haired, charming, a lawyer in Washington.

Carol didn't catch the names of the others at poolside—a doctor and his wife, a writer, and an architect and his wife—but they all chatted easily over their gin and tonics. No one ever mentioned politics or the war out here. Carol guessed a lot of these people were Republicans, but the subject never came up. They talked, instead, about horses, children, resorts, gardens, tennis, the weather. It wasn't like Washington. These people liked her for herself, not because of her husband. No one asked much about Charles. These people were living the good life and they weren't much concerned with politicians.

Carol saw the doctor staring at her legs. When he saw her looking back at him, he grinned and raised his glass in a silent toast. Carol blushed, got up, and went for a swim. She'd have to remember to stay away from the good doctor. That was one thing she didn't need, not here, not now.

The Firestones invited her for dinner, but she declined. She'd promised the kids they'd grill hamburgers and then catch fireflies at dusk.

At home, as she started the fire, she heard angry shouts from the Scruggses' house, across the road. That happened a lot. Mrs. Scruggs lived in a run-down old farmhouse with her five children. Her ex-husband came around sometimes and there'd been a couple of fights between him and her present boy friend. Carol felt sorry for Mrs. Scruggs. The woman wasn't much older than Carol and she lived on welfare and all she'd known all her life was hillbilly men who drank too much and drove too fast and never had a dime. Carol wondered how much all the Great Society hoopla had helped the Scruggs family. Not very much, she imagined.

She and the children ate their hamburgers amid the Scruggs family's shouts, then they dashed about the yard catching fireflies. When it was dark, and their Mason jar was full, they let them go, a shower of yellow sparks rising toward the stars, then Carol herded the children up to bed.

When they were asleep, she sat on the dark porch for a while. The Scruggses had quit yelling and the night was quiet except for crickets and an occasional passing car. She thought of having a drink but decided she'd rather have a dish of ice cream. She'd just finished it when the phone rang. It was Hank, who said he was back in Washington for three weeks before leaving again for Vietnam.

4

AUGUST 1968

Charles slowed the car as he neared the stop light in Leesburg. He glanced at a girl on the sidewalk, then past her at the Confederate soldier on the courthouse lawn. When the light turned green and he turned onto Route 15, he thought he felt the car pulling to the right. There was a service station at the edge of town and he started to stop. But he didn't, because the owner was a Wallace man and Charles didn't think he could stand to talk to him today. He didn't want to argue, didn't want any delays, just wanted to go home. So he drove past the station, driving slowly, not sure that either he or the car could stand any sudden jolts, and after another mile he turned down the narrow road that led to Gilead.

He hadn't seen Carol and the children for two weeks. He'd been on the road, in the Southwest, in California, speaking to state caucuses, pleading with uncommitted delegates, trying to lure votes away from Humphrey. But it was no use; Hubert had it locked up. And of course the liberals were fighting among themselves. There'd been a "stop Humphrey" meeting scheduled in Chicago the next day but it had been called off at the last moment. Charles had gotten the news at the airport in Los Angeles. There wasn't time to call Carol, only to dash through the terminal to catch the next plane for Washington. So now he was headed home, two days earlier than he'd expected, about to surprise his family and get a few days' rest before he went out again.

The road to Gilead twisted between rich green fields. He passed a

322

faded red barn with rust-colored pigs rooting in the mud beside it. He coasted down a long hill and felt a jolt as the car crossed the old wooden bridge at the bottom. The car jerked to the right, he heard a loud flap-flap-flap, and he pulled the car off the road and got out.

The right front was flat. Charles groaned, cursed, and opened the trunk to get out the spare. Then he changed his mind and slammed the trunk shut. Better to walk on home and call someone to change the tire. He could be there in fifteen minutes, still in time for dinner, and after that he could play with the kids and then have some time for Carol after the kids were in bed. He needed to talk to her. He wanted to tell her it was almost over, Chicago would be the end of it, and after that things would get better for them. It had been a tough year for everyone and she'd been damn good about it and after the convention he'd make it up to her. Maybe they could take the kids and spend a month in Europe. Or not take the kids. Whatever she wanted.

He opened a gate and walked across the field that adjoined their house. He waved at some boys who were fishing in a pond. He circled around some cows, then entered the grove of trees beside their house. He could hear voices ahead and he grinned at the thought of emerging from the trees to surprise Carol and the kids.

Then, as he reached the hedge beside the driveway, he saw Carol and the man standing on the porch, twenty feet away.

Carol was crying. The man, who was wearing an army colonel's summer uniform, put his hand on her arm. Charles gasped and stepped back into the trees.

"I'm sorry, Hank," Carol said. She wiped her eyes and tried to smile. "You've made me so happy and now I'm acting like a little fool."

"It's all right," the man said.

Hank. Charles tried to remember. Some old school friend of Carol's. She'd mentioned him a few years before. Charles stood transfixed.

"I just can't stand for it to end," she said.

"Good things always end," Hank said. "Only bad things never end."

"Like that damned war," Carol said, and began to cry again. "It took my husband away from me and now it's taking you."

"It's my duty. I believe in it."

"I know," she said. "I know." She sat down on the top step and took his hand and he sat down beside her.

"I can't let you go until I tell you how much this has meant to me," Carol said. "Hank, I haven't been loved in so long. I'd forgotten what it was like to be loved, how good it is, how alive you feel. I'd been frozen in ice and now you've loved me and warmed me and brought me back to life. I never thought I'd feel this way again. And now you're going away."

She buried her face in her hands. Hank took one of her hands in his and kissed it and she looked at him and tried to smile again.

"You've got so much," he said. "There's no way to have everything."

"I used to think I could," she said. "A million years ago, when I was a silly little girl, I thought I could have everything. And I did for a few years, when I was first married. But then everything changed. The world changed and Charles changed and finally I changed too. I got hard and cold and I quit caring. I guess I do have a lot, Hank, everything except love. And I guess that's all I really want."

"Not many people have love," Hank said. "I had it for a while with the woman I married, but I wanted something else, adventure or war or my glorious self-image or whatever you want to call it. So I let her go. I gave up on loving one woman and just loved a lot of women, all I could. Maybe that was best for me, for what I am. Then I found you again and had something beautiful for a few days and maybe that's the last time I'll ever have it."

"Don't go back there," Carol cried. "You could be killed and it's not worth it."

"I believe in it," he said. "Not the way I did five years ago. Not the great crusade. It's different now. It gets to be personal. Just you and Charlie, that little guy on the other side. You respect Charlie. He's a tough little bastard and he believes in what he's doing just as much as you do. But you're going to kill him. Either that or he's going to kill you. Even if you can't win, you've got to keep on trying."

"Oh, God, that's what Charles would say, about what he's doing. All you men killing yourselves in wars you can't win."

"There are different kinds of winning."

"I know. I'm sorry. We all do what we think is right, and what we think is right is so different. I guess I couldn't love a man who

324

didn't do what he thought was right. But it's so awful, loving people and then losing them."

"I've got to go, Carol."

"Yes, you'll go and I'll pick up my children and fix their dinner and then Charles will call from wherever he is and finally another day will be over and I'll be alone again."

Hank got up and picked up his overnight bag and after a moment Carol rose and they walked toward his car, hand in hand. Charles stepped back deeper into the trees. He had watched them dumbly, as if he had stumbled into a movie that was somehow about his life. For an instant he felt an urge to leap out, to confront them, but he knew that was insane. He was the intruder here. Whatever he was to do or say must come later, when he could think again. So he watched.

Hank put his bag in the back seat of his rented car. Carol watched him. Her eyes were red from crying. But when he turned to face her again she summoned up the kind of glowing, joyous smile that Charles remembered from a dozen years before. The smile seemed to fill her, to transform her. She raised herself on tiptoes, spread her arms wide, and kissed him quickly. Then she stepped back.

"Thank you for loving me, Hank, for making me so happy. Thank you and now please go quickly."

Hank got into the car and started the engine. He looked at her once, almost spoke, then slipped the car into gear and rolled forward along the gravel drive. Carol stood watching, one hand at her breast, the other raised in farewell, until his car turned onto the road and disappeared. Then she started back to the house. The house faced west, toward the mountains, and the shadows from the big oak trees by the road reached almost to the front of it. Carol moved through the shadows, walking slowly, her head down, her hands clasped together at her waist, and as she climbed the front steps she started to cry again.

Charles almost followed her into the house. But part of him knew that anything he said now would be wrong. After a minute he turned away from the house and walked back across the field toward his car. The boys at the pond called to him and held up a string of fish but he didn't answer them.

I haven't been loved in so long.

He jacked up the car and changed the tire, not noticing until he finished that he'd cut his knuckle. He drove west, toward the mountains. The highway rose, twisted, and began to drop as it neared the river. He saw the lights of a truck stop ahead and decided to have the flat fixed. It was stupid to drive without a spare. The attendant said the tire would be ready in a half hour. Charles nodded and walked next door to the Linger Longer Lodge.

It was a big, family-style place with fish and deer heads mounted on pine-paneled walls. It had a nice din to it—hillbilly music poured from the jukebox and two young men in work clothes were playing the pinball machines beside the door. A picture window looked down to the Shenandoah, a hundred feet below. Charles took a table by the window and asked the waitress to bring him a hamburger and a beer.

I haven't been loved in so long.

His wife had taken a lover. He started with that. But he knew it was only the starting place. He had tried, as he drove along the highway, to blame her, to hate her, to plan fitting revenges for this injustice. But it didn't work. He had seen her unhappiness and, mirrored in it, his own failures. If his wife was that unhappy, he had been a miserable failure as a husband. The logic was irresistible, and he remained a logical man. This new reality churned in his mind and he felt himself changing, he felt his illusions slipping away. He had told himself for years that his career was all-important and that all the sacrifices he asked of her were justified. He had blinded himself to her unhappiness. He had shut her out of his life and pretended that it would all work out. Now he knew how wrong he had been. He had seen her that evening as he had known her years before, loved and loving, and he had seen the damage he had done to her, to them. He thought of his parents and their marriage and of the promises he had made to himself when he married Carol. But he had broken those promises, one by one. He saw himself now as she must see him. She had wanted love and he had offered her celebrity.

The waitress said something as she brought his hamburger and beer. He nodded without hearing and she handed him a bottle of ketchup from the next table. He drank some beer and left the hamburger untouched.

He had lost her. He had destroyed the happiness they had once had. He had been a fool—the realization maddened him, he wanted to cry out in rage. But instead he sat quietly, looking out into the night, seeing his grim face reflected in the window. He shook his head hope-

326

lessly. He was thirty-eight years old, he was sitting in a little hillbilly tavern by the edge of a river, and it seemed like the end of the line. He had screwed up his career; he had screwed up his marriage, and he didn't know where he went from here.

He looked out at the dark, surging Shenandoah and thought: Maybe I ought to jump in there and be done with it.

But the thought angered him. That was bullshit, romantic bullshit. You're not some moon-struck kid who throws himself into a river. You're a guy whose business is solving problems and now you've got a dandy one to work on. To wit, you're a stupid son of a bitch and your wife doesn't give a damn for you. So what's your solution? He took a bite of his hamburger and his pragmatist's mind began to work again.

You could do nothing. That was one alternative. Let it pass. She plays her games and you play yours.

Except you can't do nothing. It was like having cancer and doing nothing. Do nothing and your marriage dies a slow, terrible death.

Or was it dead already?

Probably. Why not admit it? Call it quits, and let both of you start over. Let her marry her Hank or whoever could make her happy. You still have Karen, a phone call away, or if not her there were plenty of others. Admit your mistake and try again. Plenty of people did. It would be tough on the kids, but no tougher than the past few years had been. Hell, given this Hank thing, you'd be pretty strong in court. You could get the kids summers and every other Christmas or something. In a few years they'd be going off to school and you wouldn't see much of them anyway. In time you'd remarry and have more kids and you'd love them just as much.

Then he thought of Liza, he saw her smiling at him, and the vision tore his heart. My God, my God, if I hurt that child I'd kill myself.

So divorce was bullshit too. Another illusion, the illusion of an easy out. There were no easy outs, not halfway through your life. If you can't make Carol happy, you can't make any woman happy. Karen? Karen was right; Karen was fantasy, make-believe. Carol was reality. Carol who had loved you, had borne your children, had put up with your madness longer than you had any right to expect. Carol who was older and wiser and sadder now, a woman now, not the jaunty girl you married, Carol who still was all you wanted and more than you deserved.

He wanted her back.

Yes, of course. He had lost her but he could win her back. He felt a surge of excitement. It wouldn't be easy. It would take time. But he could do it. There was too much between them to be swept away by one affair. She was still his. He could make it up to her. He would do all the things he had not done, listen to her, compliment her, care about her. They could fall in love again. The challenge thrilled him. His life had been out of control. He had been mad—politics had been his madness as alcohol might be another man's—and blind to his madness. But now he saw it, understood it, could conquer it.

A plan began to take shape in his mind. There would be no confrontation—a confrontation now might bring down the whole fragile house of cards. No, he would go home as if he knew nothing and he would win her back. Deeds, not words, mattered now. He would change. He would concentrate on his marriage all the energies he'd so long squandered on hopeless political battles. As his plan took shape a sense of immense well-being swept over him. He had new goals now, the only goals that mattered.

He was anxious to begin, but not tonight. Tonight he would rest. He paid his bill, picked up his tire, and drove to a motel. The next morning at nine, relaxed, confident, he called Carol and told her he'd be home in an hour.

When he stopped the car in front of the house the three of them were on the porch. Liza raced out to meet him.

"Daddy, Daddy, pick me up!"

He lifted his daughter high against the morning sky and for a moment he was drunk with the sound of her laughter.

"Daddy, I've been riding every day and I can dive backwards off the board at the Firestones' pool and Mama says maybe I can have a record player for my birthday."

"That's great, Liza. That's tremendous."

He took her hand and walked to greet the others. Hugh stood watching him. Hugh would not rush out. Liza forgave everything; Hugh forgave nothing. Sometimes he thought the boy hated him.

"How are you, Hugh?"

"Okay."

"Catching any fish?"

"I caught four yesterday."

328

"We'll do some fishing while I'm home."

"Will you have time?"

"I'll make time," Charles said.

He turned to Carol. She raised her face to him and he kissed her lightly on the mouth.

"How are you?"

"Fine."

"You look fine. That's a great tan."

"Thank you." She smiled at him and went into the house. He saw it her way now, saw it was a role she played. Your husband comes home and you greet him and smile at him and forget him, just as he's forgotten you. He'll spend a few days and you'll talk a few times and make love a few times and then he'll leave and you can return to your real life, your private life, your children, your friends.

She was right. She was frozen. But the other Carol was still there, waiting to be released. He wondered how long it'd take. No matter—whatever it took, he'd do it.

"You want to see my tree house?" Hugh asked.

"There's not time now, Hugh," Carol called. "You're both late for your swimming lesson. Charles, why don't you put your things away and we'll have lunch when I get back. We weren't expecting you today. How long are you here for?"

"Right up to the convention."

She looked surprised. "That's nice," she said.

She herded the kids into her car, the station wagon, and drove off. Charles went into the house and walked up the stairs to their bedroom. The house was cool; it was always cool, even on the hottest days. He put on sneakers and Bermudas and a polo shirt she'd given him two or three years before and he'd never worn. Then he went down to the kitchen and poured himself a glass of iced tea and waited for her to return.

He glanced for a moment at a copy of *Time* he found on the back porch. He'd all but quit reading the news magazines. They only told him things he already knew, things he didn't want to know, and things he didn't believe. He'd quit reading most of the newspaper columnists too. They all wrote such shit. They'd been wrong about Vietnam, wrong about Johnson, wrong about McCarthy, wrong about everything. How could men be so wrong and stay in business?

He shrugged. He'd been wrong about a few things himself, as

wrong as Joe Alsop ever was. Let he who is without sin cancel the first subscription. He heard the station wagon on the driveway and walked out to meet Carol.

"How does your garden grow?"

"With silver bells and cockleshells."

"Show me," he said. "What are those yellow things there?"

"Lilies."

"What's that clump of stuff there?"

"It's called baby's breath."

"It all looks great," he said. "How about the vegetable garden?"

"Come on and I'll show you."

He took her hand and they walked down to the vegetable garden she had planted beside the barn. Her hand was loose in his, passive. He let it go when they got to the garden.

"My God, that lettuce is as big as basketballs. And the corn's fantastic."

"The weeds are fantastic. It takes an hour a day to keep up with them."

"Maybe I could help you."

"You, weed my garden? What's gotten into you? Sunstroke, maybe?"

"Maybe I'd like to try the simple life."

"It's pretty simple."

"I might like it."

"I like it," she said. "Wait a minute and I'll pick some lettuce for lunch." She took a straw basket from the barn and picked a dozen of the biggest, greenest leaves of lettuce.

"Is that Bibb lettuce?" he asked.

"This is iceberg," she told him. "That's the Bibb over there."

They started back to the house and he offered to carry the basket for her.

"It's not heavy," she said. "How does it look for the convention?"

"Dismal. But I'm not the guy to ask. I'm just a little fish about to be swallowed up by the big fish. I don't even know if I'll go."

"You'll go."

"I don't know. I'm pretty sick of the whole thing."

"You'll go."

The phone was ringing in the kitchen.

"That'll be Al Kline," she said. "He called twice last night and once this morning. How come he didn't know where you were? He knows everything, doesn't he?"

"Not everything," Charles said, and picked up the phone.

"Senator, where have you been?"

"What's on your mind, Al?"

"Things are breaking in Florida. If you'll go down there you can pick up four or five delegates."

"You go. I'm on vacation."

"Senator, this is serious."

"*I'm* serious. You talk to them. And don't call me, I'll call you. Tomorrow morning. Okay?"

He put down the phone and turned back to Carol, who was slicing tomatoes for their salad. "How about some wine with lunch?"

"Okay," she said. For an instant he was angry at her indifference. She'd tuned him out; she didn't care if he was here or not. They'd been through this before and always before he'd met her coolness with his own. But not now. He would keep on trying.

"Tell me what you've been doing," he said.

"Nothing exciting. Working in the garden. Trying to keep the children amused."

He wouldn't let her get by with that. He asked more questions, he feigned interest, and soon he had her talking about the people she'd met in Gilead, the parties she'd been to, the gossip she'd heard. When they finished lunch he cleared off the dishes and rinsed them in the sink.

"How long till the kids get back?"

"An hour or so."

"Want to take a walk?"

"It's awfully hot."

"Come on, show me the old homestead."

They walked down by the creek. She showed him the spot where Hugh fished and they crossed a field where wildflowers grew. He picked some and gave them to her.

"Happy birthday," he said.

"Thank you. You haven't given me flowers in a long time."

"Like ten years, maybe?"

"Maybe."

"I think I gave you some on our first anniversary."

"I seem to recall that."

"Well, better late than never."

"I guess so," she said. "We'd better go back now, the children will be coming home."

The phone rang in the late afternoon and Carol answered it.

"It's Jane Firestone," she told Charles. "She wants us to come for a swim and to stay for dinner. Would you like to?"

He didn't want to, but he said, "If you'd like to."

"Let's do," she said.

The Firestones lived on a farm a few miles outside Gilead. They'd restored the old stone farmhouse and built a pool beside it, facing the mountains. Pete Firestone was a corporation lawyer, bright and pleasant and Republican, and he mixed a good martini. The four of them sat at poolside, drinking and watching the children swim.

"Just out for the weekend, Senator?" Pete Firestone asked.

"No, for a couple of weeks," Charles said. "Until I leave for Chicago."

"Goodness, we've never seen that much of you before," Jane Firestone said. It had taken Charles about three minutes to figure out that she loathed him.

"The past few months have been pretty hectic," he said.

"Well, how will it turn out?" Firestone asked. "Does Humphrey have it?"

"It looks that way."

"What about McGovern?" Firestone asked. "The columnists are calling him a stalking horse for Teddy."

"I wouldn't call him that. He wants to give Bobby's delegates a place to go."

"Couldn't they have gone to McCarthy?" Jane Firestone asked. "Or to you?"

"They could have but they didn't," Charles said.

"What will you be doing this week?" Firestone asked. "A lot of last-minute telephoning?"

"No, just enjoying my family. Eating my wife's delicious salads. Taking it easy."

"He picked me wildflowers today," Carol said. He wondered if she was being sarcastic. He wondered, too, how much Jane Firestone knew.

"How romantic," Jane said. "I didn't think Senators had time to be romantic."

332

Fuck you, sister, Charles thought. But he let it pass. He was going to have to let a lot pass. "Usually they don't," he said.

"How about another martini?" Firestone asked.

"Great," Charles said. "How about you, Carol?"

They got off politics after a while. They talked about the children and the local schools and the next production of the Gilead Players. Jane was starring in *Born Yesterday* and Charles asked her about it until she warmed up a little. Pete grilled steaks and after dinner they watched the sun drop behind the Blue Ridge. It was not an unpleasant evening. Carol seemed to enjoy herself and that was what mattered.

When they went to bed that night he turned to her.

"I've enjoyed today," he said.

"It's been nice."

"Carol, I want to make you happy."

"I'm happy."

"Happier, then."

"That'd be nice."

She'd tuned him out again. She'd been cheerful and charming with the Firestones but now, with him, she was frozen again.

I haven't been loved in so long.

Time, he told himself. It'll take time, time, time.

He guessed she was waiting for what should come next, what always came next at this point. But not tonight. There'd been too much of that when she didn't want it, when it meant nothing. He didn't want that any more.

"It can still be like it used to be," he said.

"Okay," she said, her voice muffled by the pillow. "Good night."

"Good night," he said, and rolled over and went to sleep.

He took the children fishing the next morning. They caught a half dozen perch and he cleaned them and fried them for lunch. After lunch the children took naps and Carol went out to work in her garden. He went out and watched her.

"It's awful hot for you to be working out here."

"The work's got to be done."

"Can I help?"

She stood up and wiped the sweat off her face. "Not with this," she said. "It'd take too long to explain everything. But there is one thing I want done."

"What's that?"

"See that fence?"

"Sure. What about it?"

"I want to move it."

"Move it?"

"If it was ten feet farther back I'd have room for a new garden—the sun would be just right—and it'd give the children more room to play, too. The owner said he didn't mind."

"Carol, that fence has been there forever. Let it be. Anyway, it'd cost a fortune to get somebody to move it."

"I thought maybe you could do it. I mean, you said you wanted to help. And Hugh and the other boys play ball out here and that's left field and it's too shallow or something."

Naturally she'd bring Hugh into it. What kind of father wouldn't go out in the August sun and move a fence so his boy could have a proper place to play ball? Charles was exasperated. This was typical—crazy make-work that didn't need doing. He was about to tell her so but she had knelt back down in the garden.

I haven't been loved in so long.

Okay, pal. Moving fences is part of the game. If she wants it, do it. What else have you got to do? Write your acceptance speech?

"Okay," he said. "I guess it'd be good exercise."

"You don't have to do it if you don't want to. Maybe Hugh and I could do it."

"Oh, good God, Carol, I'll do it. I want to do it. Please let me do it."

"Don't be sarcastic."

He worked from two till almost dark, shirtless, sweating, struggling with a shovel and a posthole digger to pull up the posts and dig new holes ten feet farther back. It was an old split-rail fence and if he dug the new holes in just the right spot the crossbars would slip back into place. After a while it got to be a challenge, to measure the distances exactly right and to get the damned thing done perfectly. Carol brought beer out to him and watched him for a while, looking pleased. It was just a fence to him but to her it was one link in an intricate plan that involved gardens and trees and terraces and cobblestone

334

walks. When finally he fitted the last rail into place she helped him put away the tools.

"It's perfect," she said. "Now I can plant a row of boxwoods there, just inside the fence."

"It does make the yard look bigger."

"This can be a beautiful yard, when I get everything done. It just takes time."

"Carol, we're just renting the place, remember?"

"We really ought to buy it. I got them to agree that our rent would count against the purchase price if we do. I think they'll sell for sixty thousand."

"Carol, I just haven't thought that far ahead."

"You've got to think ahead," she said. "You get cleaned up now and I'll get dinner ready."

The children were spending the night with friends. Carol fried chicken and made a salad and he opened a bottle of their best wine. Dinner was pleasant and he was pleased, pleased with the way things were coming together. After dinner, as Carol talked about all the improvements she would make on this house, he decided to play another trump.

"I guess we could buy this place," he said. "It's pleasant here. It's as good a place to live as any."

"And it'd be a good investment," she said. "Prices are booming around here."

"That's what we're after," he said. "Good investments."

That night, when they slipped into bed, he thought, What the hell, let's don't carry this thing too far.

"Would you like to make love?"

"If you do."

He froze for a moment. He thought he deserved better than that after his day's labors. To hell with her. She was impossible.

I haven't been loved in so long.

He relaxed. It was an honest enough answer.

"I guess I'm pretty tired," he said. "Good night."

"Good night."

He was almost asleep when he felt her hand.

"Charles?"

"Hmmm?"

"Maybe if you're not too tired . . ."

He smiled in the darkness and put his arms around her.

"Never too tired," he said.

It was nice; not spectacular but good, a small success, and soon they were asleep, their toes touching lightly at the foot of the bed.

It came slowly. The days passed and each one was better than the one before. It wasn't perfect. There were occasional flare-ups, the old clash of wills over small, stupid issues. But he was learning to concede points, and the bad moments passed quickly and were lost in the good ones. Soon his role ceased to be a role; it became a habit, then a pleasure. He liked pleasing her, liked watching her slowly thaw, liked seeing her smile and laugh and talk to him the way she had years before. Soon they were turning down invitations to go out because it was better to be together, to swim, to ride, to listen to records, to linger over drinks and dinner. He didn't delude himself that the battle was won. He thought his victory a fragile, tentative one, but a victory nonetheless, a beginning, something to build on.

And there was politics, never entirely out of his mind. He called Al Kline each day, but Al's reports seemed more and more distant, unreal. He thought of not going to Chicago. Chicago would be hell, sheer hell, anyone could see that. Who needs it? He could find an excuse not to go. He could release his delegates with a single phone call. Nobody would miss him. The party could destroy itself without his help. So why bother?

But he had obligations. He was a delegate and a candidate, however minor. People had worked for him and were counting on him; he couldn't just dump them overboard because he'd rather be with his family. And that was not all. Part of him wanted to go, was drawn by the drama ahead. And of course there was ego, the lure of the network cameras and the national audience he might never address again.

He had decisions to make. He had seventy-nine or eighty or eighty-one delegates—the number changed daily—and he would be put in nomination, would have his little footnote in the history books. Or would he? It looked as if he would go in with his eighty-odd delegates, and McGovern with maybe two hundred, and McCarthy with four or five hundred. That wasn't a majority, but perhaps a miracle would occur, perhaps if Hubert blundered somehow it might be possible to stop him. If they got together, united. But behind whom? Charles knew he damn well wasn't going to be the candidate, but perhaps if

336

he threw his delegates behind one of the others, it might start something. That was another decision he would have to make.

And there was Beth, gone again, somewhere. But he knew she'd be in Chicago, drawn to it just as he was, and he would find her and talk to her and now that he was getting his own life straightened out he could do more for her. Maybe she could come back to the farm and stay until Bill got out of prison. He wanted to help her, make her happy, make them all happy.

And then it was his last day.

The four of them rode in the morning and after lunch, after the kids were down for their naps, he and Carol made love. They hadn't planned it; they just went to the bedroom to change and it happened.

"These last few days have been so wonderful," she said when they'd finished.

"There'll be more like this. Lots more."

"I'm just afraid you'll get to Chicago and be nominated for something."

"Not bloody likely."

"Something always happens. One more speech or one more campaign or something."

"Not any more. Listen, Carol, there's something I ought to tell you. I'd been saving it, but now's as good a time as any. I'm not going to run again two years from now. Probably I wouldn't win if I did, but that's not the point. The point is I don't need it any more. I can practice law and enjoy my family and be happy as a hog."

She shook her head sadly. "Don't get my hopes up, Charles. Not if you don't mean it."

"I mean it."

"Forgive me if I don't believe it until I see it."

"Okay."

"Where would you practice law?"

"In Washington. We could buy this place and keep an apartment in town."

"That'd be wonderful."

"Strawberry fields forever."

She smiled and ran her hand across his chest.

"Look, Carol, I know things haven't been right between us for a long time and I know it was my fault. But I'm coming out of it now and I'm going to make things right again."

"It wasn't all your fault. I was selfish sometimes and I let my feelings be hurt when I didn't need to."

"Let's don't think about the past now, only about the future."

She pressed against him and they made love again and when it was over he held her close, his heart pounding, thinking, *My God, how much I love this girl.*

After dinner that night they sat on the back porch talking with the children. Hugh, who at various times had wanted to be an artist, a deep-sea fisherman, and a nuclear scientist, now was saying he wanted to be a lawyer.

"Just like the old man, huh?" Charles said.

"I'm afraid the real influence is a new TV series about a crusading young attorney," Carol said.

"It's not always like that, son."

"Why not?" Hugh asked. "There was this one show about a landlord who wouldn't do anything about the rats in his buildings but then the lawyers took him to court and the tenants didn't have to pay any rent until he fixed everything up."

"There's some of that," Charles said. "Maybe by the time you come along there'll be a lot more of that."

"I'm going to be a doctor," Liza said.

"Girls can't be doctors," Hugh declared.

"Oh, God," Carol cried.

"Sure they can," Charles said. "Some of the best doctors are women."

"Mama says in Russia more of the doctors are women than men," Liza said.

"That's right," Charles told her. "You'd make a great doctor, Liza. You can take care of your old broken-down mother and father in their declining years."

But Hugh had hurt her feelings, and it was to her father that Liza looked for comfort.

"Daddy, let's you and me go catch fireflies," she said.

"Sure, baby," he said. "Maybe these other guys can put the dishes away."

He opened the screen door for her and they walked into the yard hand in hand. Scores of fireflies glittered in the dusk, dipping above the grass, hovering beside the lilac bushes. Liza raced after them, barefoot, wearing a blue and white polka-dot dress. She paused, with one bright firefly a tantalizing foot above her head, and slowly raised her hands as if in prayer.

"I've got one, Daddy, I've got one."

"Let him go, darling. Let him go and catch another one."

She held her hand palm upward until the firefly's yellow light rose into the air. Then, with a happy cry, she raced off again. Charles sank into the grass and watched her. He stretched out his hands to her, trembling a little, wanting to hold her, wanting more to see her run free and joyous through the evening, through life. He was overcome by his own happiness. He thought this was what it was all about, finally, just this, watching a barefoot girl in a polka-dot dress chasing fireflies in the summer dusk.

5

AUGUST 1968

When his cab reached the hotel on Sunday afternoon the sidewalk was crowded with delegates and curiosity-seekers and police. A girl in jeans was marching back and forth on the sidewalk carrying a black-draped picture of Bob Kennedy with "He Died for Your Sins" written under it. A policeman at the hotel entrance demanded to see his identification. When Charles finally got to his suite, Al Kline was waiting impatiently.

"I need to brief you on the Texas challenge and the Vietnam plank, then there's a million people lined up to see you."

"Such as?"

"Rip Horton. Pat O'Neal. Joe Clayton."

"Sounds like Old Home Week."

"And about half the Kentucky delegation, wanting you to release them."

"You don't mean they want to vote for somebody else?"

"They seem to think Hubert is the wave of the future."

"Tough shit for them. Okay, you've got fifteen minutes, then I've got something else to do."

"Oh, my God, what?"

"I'm going to take a walk."

"Senator, I tell you, these people have been waiting all week."

Charles looked at his watch. "They can wait a couple more hours. I'll be back by five."

Al shook his head. "Senator, maybe there's one little thing you could tell me before you take your stroll."

340

"What's that?"

"What the hell you're going to do this week."

"Al, I'm going to try to do what's right."

"What's right," Al repeated. "And could you possibly give me any clues as to what that might be?"

"I'm not sure yet," Charles admitted. "I guess that's what I'll be doing this week, trying to find out."

There were two or three thousand kids in the park when he got there, some sleeping, some sitting around under trees talking, some gathered around a boy with fuzzy hair who was singing a wild, incomprehensible song. Charles walked the length of the park. He passed some Yippies who had signs saying "Vote Pig in '68." He stopped for a minute and listened to a boy and a girl arguing about whether or not they should defy the curfew in the park that night. It all seemed peaceful enough. Charles crisscrossed the park until ten minutes to five, then started back to the hotel. Beth wasn't there, or if she was, he hadn't found her.

Rip Horton was his first caller.

"Chas-bo, we gotta save the party."

"I've been trying, Rip."

"You been out riding your white horse, but that ain't saving the party. Look, Hubert's in, right?"

"Probably."

"And down where Ah come from, Hubert's about as popular as a turd in a punch bowl, right? And if he can't carry the South he can't beat Nixon, right?"

"So?"

"So the only way Hubert's got a Chinaman's chance is to do some right smart ticket-balancing, that's how I see it."

Charles poured them both a drink. He saw Rip's game now and he didn't have much patience for it. "Look, Rip, we went through this four years ago. You want to be Vice-President. Okay, fine. But as long as you support the war, I can't support you. If Hubert gets it, let's have a dove for Vice-President."

"A dove like you, maybe?"

"No, not me. Like McCarthy or Teddy."

"Charles, the thing you gotta understand is, Ah'm a dove. Hell, so's Hubert, far as that goes."

"I'd somehow failed to notice that."

"Listen, if Hubert got elected, he'd have that war over so fast it'd make your head spin."

"Rip, how can you sit there and say that with a straight face?"

"You know why Hubert's talking all that hawk talk?"

"Maybe he believes it."

"You know better'n that. Hubert's scared shitless that if he don't toe the line Big Daddy's gonna swoop down from the Big Ranch in the Sky and let hisself be nominated again. But once Hubert gets nominated, he'll sprout little white feathers and start billing and cooing all over the blessed U. S. of A."

"Okay, Rip, let's assume that you and Hubert are closet doves. What can I do for you?"

"You can tell all your dove pals what a fine feller Rip Horton'd be for V.P."

"What'll you do for us, Rip? Support the Texas challenge? Support the peace plank?"

"Ah can't do none of that yet, Charles. Ah gotta walk a thin line right now. But once Ah get in . . ."

"It's now or never, Rip. It's time for people to stand up and be counted. If you won't, I can't help you."

"Is that it, Charles?"

"That's it."

"Ah'm sorry to hear it."

"I'm sorry too."

Rip got up from the sofa. "Well, ain't nothing wrong with having a drink with an old pal."

"Any time, Rip. Finish your drink."

"No, Ah reckon Ah better mosey on." He started to the door, then turned back. "Say, Charles, Ah heard a rumor you might not be with us much longer."

"Yeah?"

"Yeah. They was saying you might hang it up after '70."

"You hear a lot of rumors these days."

"Well, can't say as Ah'd blame you. A feller could make a heap of money practicing law in Washington. Least, he could if all his old Senate pals would help him out now and then."

"So long, Rip."

"See you, pal."

342

Beth sat in the park, waiting for the police to come.

She was sitting with some kids around a campfire, one of a score of campfires that blazed across the park. The police warning had come over the loudspeaker and they had only minutes left.

"They could have let us use the park," a girl said.

"No, they couldn't," said the boy who called himself the Hawk. "That would have been too smart."

The Hawk was one of the crazies who'd been around the park all week, a razor-thin young man with a sharp nose and deep-set, intense eyes. He had reddish hair worn in a pony tail, and he also had some good grass that he had been circulating around their campfire.

"It's going to be bad," one boy said grimly.

"No," said the Hawk in his coldest voice, "it's going to be beautiful. The pigs split a few heads and we destroy the Democratic Party."

Oh, shut up, Beth thought. I'd rather have my head split than listen to any more of your damned revolutionary rhetoric.

But she didn't say it, because she knew enough about this boy, this Hawk, to know he'd earned the right to speak. She knew he was from a wealthy family, and that he'd been in Mississippi, and with SDS in Newark—and she'd also heard that in the past year he'd dropped so much acid that he'd messed up his head for keeps. But there were plenty of people around who were talking revolution who hadn't messed up their heads, people who were convinced that Armageddon was at hand, that this was the decisive year, that you started with Tet and then came Columbia and then Paris and now the showdown in Chicago that could start the revolution the students and workers had almost brought off in France. That was why the hard-core revolutionaries were here, not to protest the war but, should their fantasies come true, to bring down the government.

Beth thought that was a lot of crap. She knew how powerful the government was—she had learned that when it had so effortlessly taken Bill from her—and she knew it was not about to be toppled by a few dozen freaks and crazies and would-be revolutionaries. Beth understood those people, in a way she loved them, but she did not share their fantasies and she had not come to Chicago to make a revolution. She had come, rather, because her friends would be there, and because she hated the government too much to let it scare her away.

She had reached Chicago by a roundabout route, by a journey

that had begun that spring when she helped Charles on his primary campaigns, not because she believed he could win, but because she loved him and because he had pleaded with her to give the system one more chance. So she had. She had worked hard and stayed clean and then, in June, everything had come apart. First, Bobby's death. She had worked for Charles but it was Bobby they had counted on, all of them, somehow to overcome the odds and win the nomination and . . . and then he was dead and that little fantasy was over. And after it came the realization that Humphrey would be nominated, that they who had worked for the peace candidates had been fools, that the system would give them Humphrey against Nixon, which meant that the system was corrupt beyond redemption. Finally, at the depth of her depression, she had gone to the prison farm to see Bill, only to learn that he was in solitary for organizing a work stoppage, that he had lost his good time, that his chance for an early parole was gone.

All those things, one after another, had been too much. She had left Washington and gone to New York and the drugs had begun again and one night her friends had held her down while she screamed until dawn and after that she had known she must leave New York and must leave the drugs too and she had caught a ride with some kids who were going to East Lansing for the SDS convention. The ride out had been fun, smoking grass and digging the little towns they passed, but the convention had been heavy, with fights and confrontations until finally the whole thing fell apart, with two rival factions each claiming to be the one true SDS. Beth had wandered through it for a few days, high on grass, grooving on it, and then on the last day she had met Chuck.

"Screw politics; I'm going back to the farm." Those were the first words she heard him speak, words not spoken to anyone in particular, just a farewell to politics.

"Where is your farm?" she'd asked him, because she liked his face, because he had a gentle manner that reminded her of Bill.

"In Oregon," he said. "You ready to go?"

They laughed at that, and they talked awhile, and she did go, because she liked him, because she had nothing better to do, because it sounded peaceful, and finally because of that other, the thing she had resisted so long but now she knew was coming. So they went to the farm in Oregon and they were lovers and Chuck was good and gentle and she was glad. She felt alive again. For six weeks she was up at dawn and she would work in the garden and cook and fix up the cabin and in the evenings they would sit on the porch and smoke and watch the sun go down over the mountains. She almost forgot the world outside, yet when August came she knew she must go to Chicago.

Chuck tried to talk her out of it, but when he saw that her mind was made up he offered her his van, but she said no, she'd hitchhike, it wasn't any trouble, although in truth she didn't like hitchhiking, but she couldn't take the van because she wasn't sure she'd ever return. It had been wonderful, but she had another life waiting, she had Bill waiting, and after Chicago she would have to go back to Washington.

So she had come to Chicago, not because she wanted to but because she had to, and now she was sitting by a campfire with some crazies who were talking revolution, waiting for the police to come. Someone passed some hash to her and she smoked deeply and soon she felt herself rising, all of their little circle rising up and up in the dark sky, and she didn't know who she was or where she was, she was soaring through the universe, and the other campfires in the park were stars that twinkled to her from a million miles away.

She was still high when the police came at midnight, and what happened was like a dream. The freaks threw rocks at the police at first, but then the tear gas started and they began to retreat to the street.

"Don't run," Beth shouted to people. "Walk, don't run."

But too many of the kids didn't understand and when they began to run the cops broke ranks and chased after them, catching stragglers, beating them down.

When they got to the street they found more police, police everywhere. Beth thought she saw an opening but a cop stepped from the shadows and clubbed her in the small of the back. She fell to her knees and he was about to hit her again when a flashbulb went off. The cop turned to chase the photographer, who stopped after a dozen yards and raised his hands and yelled, "Press, press." The cop clubbed him across the jaw and smashed his camera. All around her, Beth saw kids running and screaming and being beaten. Somehow she scrambled past them and escaped up a dark ghetto street. She hid in a doorway and listened to the screams and sirens in the distance. It had been worse than she'd expected. The cops had gone crazy and she hadn't expected that. Beth sat in the doorway, her high gone, her back throbbing, knowing now just how bad it was going to be.

Charles's talk with Pat O'Neal was difficult for both of them. They were on opposite sides now. Pat was working for Humphrey. Charles wouldn't have expected anything else. Pat was a party man.

"Believe me, Charles, I'm not here because we need your vote. We don't need it, not for anything. I'm here because I'm worried about you. I want you back where you belong, back with the party."

"If Hubert would just give some ground on the Vietnam plank."

"He's given ground, all he can."

"It's not enough. He's fuzzed it up but it's still the Johnson policy."

"Charles, are you going to support the ticket in the fall?"

"I don't know yet."

"Is Nixon what you want?"

"That's what we'll get unless Hubert repudiates the war."

"Charles, some of us have worked for the party a long time, good years and bad, because we believe that by and large it'll do what's best for America. Maybe it's not always right, but it's the best there is. And it's not easy for us to see people splitting the party because they can't get their way on every little issue."

"This isn't a little issue."

Pat O'Neal walked over to the window. Down in the park some kids were chanting, "Dump the Hump, dump the Hump."

"Is *that* what you want? Are *those* your people?"

"They believe what I believe, about the war."

"The war, the war, the war. Damn it, the war isn't everything."

"Yes, it is, Pat. It is everything."

Pat O'Neal ground out his Lucky and lit another one.

"We've been through a lot, Charles."

"I know how much I owe you, Pat."

"Then let me tell you exactly what I think. Do you know what you're doing? You people are destroying the Democratic Party!"

"And you people are destroying America."

They looked at each other for a moment. "You could have made it, Charles," Pat O'Neal said. "You could have gone all the way. But you went crazy."

Charles looked at the older man and felt only sadness. "Maybe so," he said. "Maybe so."

346

Beth was gassed the second night but somehow she stumbled out of the park without being beaten or arrested. But she saw enough to know it was worse that night. There were more cops and more kids and more beatings and there weren't many photographers around to take pictures.

The young man who called himself the Hawk was arrested that night. He had known all day they had a tail on him—he accepted the honor as his due—and when the police charge began three plainclothesmen grabbed him quickly and hustled him to a patrol car. At the precinct house they threw him into a cell and it was not until the next morning that the beating began. It was an expert job, with fists and nightsticks used mainly on the body, on the places that didn't show, but the beating was not without passion, for these men knew who the Hawk was, knew who his father was too. The three detectives hated the young man for his wealth, or more precisely for his rejection of his wealth, and so they beat him carefully, almost lovingly, until at length he cracked and began to scream and curse them and then of course they beat him some more, until hot coffee poured on his face would no longer revive him, at which point they tossed him back into his cell and went to lunch.

"Charles, *please* come home."
"I can't yet. I still have things to do."
"What *can* you do? Can you make them stop beating people?"
"People are trying. Maybe something can be done."
"It's insane. *Please* come home."
"I can't yet. I'm sorry."
"Liza wants to talk to you."
"Hi, Daddy."
"Hi, sweetheart. You being a good girl?"
"We wish you'd come home, Daddy."
"I will soon, baby. I promise."

Beth didn't want to return to the park the third night. It wasn't the police she feared, it was the hate that was in the air, everywhere, like tear gas; she thought that if you breathed too deeply it would kill you. Yet she went, drawn there by something stronger than her fear, and she joined the people gathered around the cross. The clergymen had come to protest the violence and now they were at the

347

heart of it, huddled around their cross with four hundred kids, waiting for the police. The clergymen prayed and the kids put on their wet handkerchiefs for the gas and their Vaseline for the Mace and there was a final, eerie silence before the first tear gas canisters crashed through the trees. Suddenly there was chaos, with people screaming and running through the clouds of tear gas toward the woods. Ahead of Beth, a young clergyman fell to the ground, clawing at his eyes.

"Don't rub them," she yelled at him.

"I can't see," he cried. "I can't see."

Beth pulled him after her. There were more police at the street and one of them began firing his revolver into the air.

"Oh, God," the blinded clergyman kept moaning. Beth got him to a subway entrance where some of the other clergymen had taken refuge. Then she went back to the street and met some kids who said everyone was going to Grant Park, across from the Hilton, and she joined them and eventually there were two or three thousand of them at Grant Park and the police watched them but left them alone. They could see people watching from the windows of the Hilton and they began to chant, "Join us, join us," and soon some McGovern and McCarthy people did come across to the park. Then someone yelled, "If you're with us, blink your lights," and lights began to blink on and off, scores of them, all across the huge hotel.

Beth wondered if Charles was up there somewhere. She guessed she should have phoned him but she wasn't sure what good it would do either of them. What was there left to say?

When the cries of "Join us" began, Al said he was going down.

"I should go," Charles said. "My sister may be down there."

"You won't find her in the dark," Al said. "Get some rest."

Charles nodded. "I've got McGovern in the morning," he said. Al left and Charles watched a little longer from the window. When people started blinking their lights, he started to blink his, but it seemed such bullshit. If you wanted to help those kids, you should be down there with them, not blinking your lights in your seventy-dollar hotel suite. After a few minutes he put his lights out and went to bed.

He saw McGovern first thing the next morning. The invitation had been for breakfast but he'd declined. This wasn't social, this was politics, and he wanted to get it over with.

348

McGovern was waiting for him in his shirt sleeves, with one aide, one of the Kennedy men, a tough-looking man, his bartender's face ravaged by the strain of the past months.

"We need your help, Charles," McGovern said.

"How does it look?"

"It doesn't look good. But something could still happen."

"If we can pick up some more delegates," the aide said, "it might start things moving."

"I've polled my delegates," Charles said. "If I release them, you'll get most of them."

"Forty-three, we figure," the aide said.

"Something like that," Charles agreed.

"Are you willing to release them?" McGovern asked.

"We know what you'd be giving up," the aide injected. "We wouldn't forget it."

"Yes, I'll release them."

"When?" the aide said.

"Right now."

"Charles," McGovern said, "if there's anything at all I can do for you . . ."

"Maybe you could make me Secretary of State," Charles said.

McGovern smiled his stiff smile at that, but the aide didn't. He was staring hard at Charles and Charles knew what he was thinking: Get it nailed down before the bastard changes his mind.

"I'll draft a statement," the aide said. He hurried into the next room and in a moment they heard a typewriter clacking.

"This is a big thing for you to do," McGovern said. "I know how hard you worked for those delegates."

"Maybe it'll help."

"Would you like to make a seconding speech? It'd be good exposure."

"If you like. I don't care."

They were silent for a moment while the typewriter clattered in the next room. "That must be some statement he's writing," Charles said. They grinned good-fellow grins at that, but their minds were somewhere else. McGovern was making mental calculations, trying to figure how these new delegates might fit into his total equation, what new leverage they might give him, what fence-sitters they might

349

bring down on his side, how his hundred-to-one shot might be improved to, say, ninety to one.

Charles was thinking about McGovern, thinking that McGovern was tougher than he was. For he was pulling out and McGovern was going ahead. Politics was a process of elimination and he was being eliminated, self-eliminated but eliminated all the same. You found out about yourself in politics and he'd found that he lacked some essential ingredient, call it ambition or toughness or ruthlessness. He wished McGovern well. He hoped he could juggle his ambition and his family and his conscience to his satisfaction. Charles couldn't.

The aide came back with the statement. Charles looked it over. "It's fine," he said.

"I need to make some calls," McGovern said. "Could you come back around noon and we could have the press in?"

"Sure," Charles said. "Noon's fine."

He went back to his own suite, where Al Kline was waiting nervously. "Now will you please tell me what's happening?" Al began.

"Sure. I just told McGovern I'd release my delegates."

"Oh, my God," Al said, and sank down onto the sofa. Charles felt sorry for him; poor Al, he'd backed the wrong horse.

"I'm pulling out, Al."

"How far out?"

"All the way. It's no go for '70. If you want to bail out before that, feel free."

"You haven't told people about '70 yet, have you?"

"No, but they'll start to figure it out."

"I wish you wouldn't say anything. You might change your mind."

"I won't change my mind."

"Look, I know things don't look so great for '70, but maybe if you pulled back on the war and campaigned hard for Hubert . . ."

"You don't understand, Al. I'm not quitting because I'm afraid of losing. I'm quitting because I'm afraid of winning."

Al stared at his shoes. "No, I don't understand."

"Al, to play this game you've got to believe in it. You've got to believe that because you tell all those lies and wade through all that shit and screw up your life something happens, something changes."

"Things change."

"Do they?"

"You're copping out, you know."

"Sure I'm copping out, but don't get too smug about it. Five years from now you'll have an office downtown and corporations for clients. Maybe we can be partners."

"Go to hell."

"Wait and see."

Al fell silent. Charles made some phone calls, then he took the elevator down to the lobby and walked out to the street. It was still early, still cool, and he decided to walk over to the park. Not many people were out, a few cops, a few kids, a couple of sanitation trucks trying to restore the city's dignity. When he got to the park a few kids had returned there, curled up in their sleeping bags or sitting on the grass talking. He walked about the park, still thinking he might find Beth. A few signs of the last night's battle were still there: picnic benches that had been a futile barricade, tear gas canisters, shoes scattered about, a pair of glasses, a lot of trash. But a calm had settled, if only temporarily, over the battlefield, and as Charles walked he felt the same uneasy calm settling over himself. He felt as if he had put down a great burden. He had passed the point of no return. He guessed that what he had done was unprecedented in American politics. He had given up something for nothing. That made no sense. A politician always got his quid pro quo. That was as basic as breathing in and out. But Charles wasn't a politician any more. He wasn't sure just what he was, a madman or a statesman or a burned-out case, but he wasn't a politician. He was free now, free to think of his family and himself and whatever peace he could salvage from the wreckage of his political career. He walked across the park and he saw the kids, kids with bandages on their heads, kids with terror in their eyes, and he was sorry for them but he knew he was leaving them now, going off to fight more limited battles. Perhaps he was a cop-out but if so there was nothing to be done about it. He thought he had come to grips with himself and his limitations. He saw kids staring at him as he walked by, probably thinking him a plainclothesman, and he looked back at them without guilt. He was doing the best he could and he felt good about it, he felt at peace.

Once the debate started, Joe Clayton paced the convention floor, a tall man towering over the little knots of delegates he passed, stopping to encourage his allies, pausing now and then to listen to the speakers, pleased with Muskie's statement, furious at Sorensen's.

Joe Clayton was tired. He'd gone sleepless for three nights, readying the Administration's forces for the Vietnam debate. The meetings with Hubert were the worst. He'd coaxed him and encouraged him and pressured him and still he was worried. Not about the vote, they'd win that, but the doves had scored a victory just by getting this debate, getting it on national television, another forum for their lies. The pressure was mounting on Hubert and Joe Clayton didn't trust Hubert. Hubert was too soft; he agreed with everyone. They had him on record, of course, a thousand times over, but he was slippery like all politicians and who could say what he'd do after he was nominated? Joe Clayton was sick of politicians. With half the world at stake they smiled and double-talked and read their polls. He'd trusted LBJ, trusted him and sweated blood for him, given up his marriage and his career for him, shown him what had to be done if the world was to be free, and then when the going got tough LBJ had let him down, let them all down, panicked and pulled out when he could be here, right now, being renominated and re-elected and going on to finish the job they'd started. Left them with Hubert, who agreed with everyone and might do anything, might let it all go down the drain after five years of blood and toil, at the very moment when victory was within their grasp. Sometimes Joe Clayton thought Nixon might be better. He'd read everything Nixon had said on Southeast Asia and he thought perhaps Nixon could be trusted if anyone could. But could anyone? So many of them had turned yellow, Kennedy men and Johnson men who'd talked a good game once but now had crossed over, who now were going to stand up before the TV cameras and say their mea culpas, begging for absolution. So now Joe Clayton was left, almost alone, making this last stand, doing what could be done but despairing for the months ahead, helping Hubert and wondering if he wanted Hubert to win or lose. Sometimes Joe Clayton wanted out. His health was bad, his stomach had been acting up again, he needed rest, a quiet year or two. He couldn't go back to his old job, the dove professors would have their little revenge there, but there were other schools, other jobs. He could get all the money he needed from a publisher and then he could write his book, the story of America facing its greatest test, of those who had met the challenge and those who had not.

But how would his book end? That was the agonizing question. With victory or dishonor? He didn't know, couldn't know until the election was over, until power had passed to the new man. There even were rumors that LBJ might still appear, might let himself be nominated, perhaps that had been his plan all along. But Joe Clayton didn't believe those rumors. He believed that LBJ had deserted them, quit their cause, left them with Hubert whom he didn't trust or with Nixon whom he didn't trust either but for whom there might be hope. Joe Clayton had briefed Nixon after his nomination, the standard courtesy briefing, and he'd been impressed. The man had presence and a keen mind. Joe Clayton had left the meeting thinking this was a man he could work with. Freedom was not a partisan matter, and if Nixon became President he'd want the best minds around him, the men who didn't buckle under pressure, the men who were best when the going was toughest. So perhaps there was still some hope. For those who believed as Joe Clayton believed, there was always some faint light at the end of the tunnel.

Although the young man called the Hawk had a father who no longer cared what happened to him, he also had a sister who did care, a woman of sufficient wealth and influence that by early afternoon she had learned of his whereabouts and arrived at the precinct house with her lawyer to secure his release.

"Get me to a doctor," was all the young man would say as they helped him from the police station, and after he had seen a doctor his sister said he must come to her estate for the rest he needed. But the young man was only angered by the suggestion. He cursed his sister and demanded that she give him money. She cried and pleaded and in the end she was glad to see him go, for she was accustomed to the hate in his eyes but now there was something worse than hate.

So the Hawk took her money and caught a cab to the ghetto where he quickly made a purchase, one that was vital to his plans now, and then he caught another cab back to the park. He arrived at the park in time to see a wedge of police charge into a crowd of peaceful people, people who had a permit to demonstrate, charge in with the clubs swinging and beat down everyone in their path. The Hawk watched with ever rising excitement. For he knew the pigs had gone crazy now, blood-crazy, and as he wandered through the park later that evening he felt the desperation they had left in their wake and he welcomed it and yearned to shape it to his own ends.

He moved through the dusk seeking out the few people he trusted,

353

SDS veterans, people who would be going underground after Chicago, and, gasping for breath, he told them his plan, told them the time had come to bring it all down, that if the pigs wanted war they must give them war, that the final battle must begin, here and now. But the others only shook their heads, told the Hawk that he'd freaked out, that he looked bad and he ought to get out of town, that they'd already won, already gotten what they wanted, and the thing he urged would only bring down force that could destroy them all. Trembling, blood oozing from beneath his bandages, the young man cursed them for their cowardice, cursed them and moved on through the night, looking for those who shared his vision and his hate, until finally he knew there would be no others, that what must be done he would have to do alone.

Charles decided not to go to the convention hall that night. It was a long way to go to watch Hubert be nominated. He and Al stayed in his suite talking and drinking and looking at television occasionally. They watched from the window when people began to gather in the street below. First the Poor People's mule train, then the kids who soon filled the intersection, penned in by police. Nothing seemed to be happening and Charles was about to pour another drink when the police attacked.

Beth saw them come and heard the screams and knew that this would not be like the park, there was no escape here. They were surrounded, packed into the intersection, and the police cut through them at will, this way and that, cutting people down. Beth was with a dozen other people who were trapped against the wall of a hotel and beaten to the sidewalk. She was hit on the wrist and on the neck and finally on the head and she blacked out. When she came to she crawled away from the others and vomited onto the pavement, blood dripping down from her head. She heard a crash and saw some cops pushing people through a plate-glass window. She looked for a way to escape and saw none. She saw four cops coming toward her and she tried to get up, stumbled, and just then a white-haired man grabbed her arm and began to pull her toward the hotel. She thought he was arresting her but he waved a key at the cops guarding the entrance to the hotel. "She's with me," he said. "She's my daughter." In the elevator he took out his handkerchief and was mopping the blood from

354

her face when she passed out again. When she came to she was lying on the floor of a hotel room that was now a first-aid station. The white-haired man was gone and she never found out who he was.

Charles and Al were frozen for a moment, unable to believe what they were seeing. Then Al began to curse. "I've got to get down there," he said. He dashed from the room, leaving Charles staring at the street.

Charles didn't want to go down there. He knew there was nothing he could do, nothing anyone could do. He watched the battle beneath him and he thought the most terrible thing was how inevitable it had been. It had been building for twenty years, twenty years of racism and anti-Communism and superpatriotism, twenty years when the best people had thought they could do right at home only by doing wrong abroad, twenty years of madness that now had erupted in this street. It had to come, it had to be Chicago, it had to be the Demo-crats. He shared the guilt. If he had been right for two years he had been wrong for twenty, he and his father and all of them. He had been part of it and now his punishment was to stand here and watch it helplessly, knowing that the final tragedy was that when the battle was over, when all the blood had flowed, everything would be the same, those in power would have kept their power, would have learned nothing and forgotten nothing.

Al returned, trembling with rage.

"What happened?"

"I never got out of the lobby. The bastards wouldn't let me out. It was full of gas and they were beating people right there, right on the floor of the God damn lobby. There was one kid—"

"I don't want to hear about it."

"We'll get those bastards," Al said. "We got Johnson and we'll get Daley and Humphrey and all the rest of them."

"Here, have a drink."

The fighting in the street had stopped and they sat for a while and talked. Al talked about working for a fourth party, a new party. When the television showed the balloting beginning, Charles got up.

"Let's go somewhere," he said. "There must be something we can do."

"They've set up a first-aid station in McCarthy's press office," Al said. "We could go down there."

"Okay," Charles said. "Let's go."

The suite was filled with the wounded. Medics were using strips of sheets to bind up bloodied heads and others were treating those who'd been gassed and Maced. He walked through the rooms, talking to kids, shaking their hands, trying to encourage them, saying things he didn't believe any more, and he was about to leave when he noticed the girl sitting on the floor in a little room at the back, tearing sheets into strips. Her back was to him but when she turned her head Charles saw her profile and ran to her.

"Beth!"

She had a bandage on her head and a huge bruise on her arm but she seemed all right; she rose and embraced him.

"I looked for you," he said. "Where were you?"

"I've been all over," she said. "I've been hard to find."

"How bad are you hurt?"

"Not bad. Some stitches, but I'll be all right. I survived. That's the important thing, we all survived."

"Come up to my room," Charles said. "You can sleep there and tomorrow you can fly back to Washington with me."

"I don't know. I don't know what I'm going to do."

"Just spend a couple of months in the country with us. No strings."

"Maybe for a while," she said. "I need time to get my head straight."

"Right now you need rest. Come on up to my room."

"No, I've got to stay and help the medics. We're almost out of sheets. Maybe you could bring the sheets from your room."

When he had left, she sat back down on the floor and began tearing sheets into bandages again. Her head hurt but a kind of peace had settled over her. The worst was over now. They had survived. Perhaps it would be good to go to the country with Charles and rest and think about the future, about Bill and politics and everything. It would be good to ride and swim and take walks in the woods and get to know Charles's children. The thought warmed her. She had survived the worst and somehow it would all get better now.

The next morning Charles and Beth were having breakfast when Al came in and told them about the march. It would be peaceful, he said, mostly delegates and writers and clergymen who would try to march to the convention hall.

"I'm going," Al said. "It's the least I can do."

"I'll go too," Beth said.

Charles frowned at the development. "We've already got reservations on the eleven o'clock flight," he said. "Carol's expecting us."

"You go on," Beth said. "I can catch an afternoon flight."

Charles bit his lip in annoyance and decided it was better to keep Carol waiting than to leave Beth behind. "No," he said. "I'll go too. My last hurrah."

The march was slow getting started, like all marches. Everyone had his own plan. A bearded writer kept yelling for everyone to follow him, but others insisted that they wait because it was rumored that McCarthy might come. Charles gave a halfhearted interview to a hung-over reporter, then stood in the street talking to Beth and Al and wishing he hadn't come. It was hot as hell and he'd missed the first plane and now it looked like he'd miss the second one. But finally they started. He marched in the front row with some delegates and a famous actor and a black singer and a couple of writers. As they moved up Michigan Avenue he began to feel better, began to think the gesture a good one. A dozen policemen walked beside them, but they were helpful, even friendly; they knew these were VIPs and they knew, more importantly, that the real battle was over and they'd won it. The marchers were singing and Charles was enjoying himself when he saw the National Guardsmen ahead, blocking the next intersection.

The march stopped a dozen feet from the row of National Guardsmen. A Guard colonel approached them, and a police sergeant who said his name was Monaghan. The bearded writer stepped forward but Charles thought the writer wouldn't know how to handle these men, so he walked over to the colonel and the police sergeant and introduced himself.

"You can't go any farther," the colonel said.

"Why not?" Charles said.

"Security," the colonel said. "We've got orders from the Secret Service."

"You better tell your people to turn back," the police sergeant said. "We don't want trouble here."

357

Charles looked at the sergeant. He looked like he meant business. Charles could see it was no use, these men weren't budging, but he didn't feel like giving up right away. He thought he'd play out the string.

"This is a peaceful march," he said. "A lot of these people are delegates to the convention."

"I don't care who they are," the sergeant said. "We've got our orders."

"Is there someone here from the Secret Service?" Charles asked.

"Now look, mister . . ." the sergeant said, and it went on like that for a minute, back and forth, with the other marchers pressing forward and the young National Guardsmen shifting nervously in the street, their rifles at the ready.

The sidewalks were lined with people, blacks from the neighborhood who feared more trouble, reporters, plainclothesmen, curiosity-seekers. The Hawk stood behind a big Negro woman, watching over her shoulder, his vision blurred, trying to focus on the scene in the street, thinking, yes, this was the time, the moment he'd waited for, yes, let it come here, now, in the ghetto, let it begin. He knew the consequences, he wondered for an instant if this was right. But finally he was overcome by his pain and his vision and his hate. The cops and the marchers argued in the intersection as he slowly reached for his gun.

Three subsequent investigations attested to the confusion of the next few seconds. Charles heard Beth scream, "Watch out!" saw the police sergeant grab for his gun, saw the Guardsmen start to break ranks. Confused, he spread his arms wide. "Wait a minute," he cried. "Let's calm down." Then he heard the shot, felt the pain, saw the golden sun spinning, tumbling, turning blood-red in the sky above him. After that there was only an instant's vision of a girl in a polka-dot dress, racing after fireflies in the summer dusk.

Then darkness.

6

JANUARY 1969

Beth awoke, alone in the cold room.

She slipped on her jacket and her boots and rubbed her hands together for warmth. She went to the window, pulled back the torn shade, and looked out. The morning sky was overcast, and soldiers lined the street.

She started water for coffee, then put on a Stones album and listened to it while she waited for the water to boil. Somehow, the chaotic music calmed her. When the water was ready she poured it into a chipped mug and spooned in the instant coffee.

She sat on the bed for a moment, sipping the coffee and looking around the small apartment. She didn't know whose it was. It was just an apartment near the Capitol that people used when they were in Washington. She'd been there over the weekend and hadn't gone out except to eat. She didn't expect to be back again this night, so she got a broom from the closet and swept the floor and knocked some cobwebs down from the ceiling. When she finished, she turned over the Stones record and sat back down on the bed and lit a joint. It calmed her a little. She looked around the apartment, her little sanctuary, and thought that it was like a lot of apartments she'd been in since Chicago. Cheap furniture. Two posters on the walls, one of Ho and the one of Huey Newton sitting in the wicker chair. And one other picture, pinned to the back of the door, the *Life* cover of Bobby Kennedy they'd carried just after he died, the one that showed him running along the beach in California with his dog beside him, running along beside the blue water as if he'd run on like that forever.

She stared at the picture and suddenly it seemed to come to life, he seemed really to be moving, running, growing smaller in the distance. Beth blinked her eyes and finished the joint, thinking about Bobby. She'd thought a lot about him that winter. She thought that his death had been the worst of all the terrible things that had happened. She had loved Charles and what had happened to him had been tragic—in that last year there had been so much tragedy, all the tragedies had blended together and become one, become life, reality—but Bobby's death was the one that had hurt her most, deepest, longest.

From the window she could see a clock above a bank. It was just past nine, still early, what she had come to Washington to do could not be done until the afternoon. She thought of it and began to pace the floor, then reached into her knapsack and pulled out a vial of reds. She swallowed two, and after that she began to feel better, began to lose her fear, and she tried to think what she would do for the next few hours. She guessed she'd eat a good lunch somewhere. That was all she could think to do.

There was a knock at the door.

Beth froze. The door was locked. She wouldn't answer it. They'd go away. But the damn music was playing. Idiot! She stood in the middle of the room, waiting.

"Beth? Are you in there?"

A woman. A voice she knew. Whose? From which life?

"Beth! It's Sharilee."

She relaxed and opened the door.

Sharilee looked prosperous with her pants suit and her suede coat and the big diamond ring on her finger, but her face was still proud and angry, the way it'd been when she was a young civil rights worker and Beth had first known her.

"How'd you find me?"

"It wasn't hard."

"I'm serious. Nobody knows where I am."

"Honey, I've been representing some of your freak friends. And since they don't pay me money, I can at least get a little information from them. Now, how about inviting me in?"

"Sure, come in, sit down. You want some coffee?"

360

"No, thanks. But I wish you'd turn that noise down."

Beth cut off the stereo and sat down on the bed. Sharilee took the room's only chair.

"You . . . you went to law school, didn't you?"

"That's right. And I got married. I met him in law school. His name's Roland Carter and we've got a little boy, six months old."

"You're the only success story I know. Everybody else I know is messed up."

"I've been lucky."

"Are you . . . you know, practicing?"

"I'm into public-interest law. *Pro bono*. Which translates as no money. I defend tenants and welfare mothers and freaks and radicals, the whole bit."

"That's great."

"It's a pain in the ass. But it's got to be done. Things have been bad and they're going to get worse."

"I know. Half the kids I know went underground after Chicago, and there'll be more charges after today."

"That's why I'm here. Four of us are starting a public-interest law firm. We've got some foundation money. And we've got a job for you."

"For me? What do you need, a horrible example?"

"You're not up for anything, are you?"

Beth shook her head. "It's crazy. I'm in the middle of everything and everybody else gets busted but they always miss me. I'm like Wonder Woman with her magic bracelets. The bullets all bounce away. Evil cannot touch me."

"What we need is somebody to run the office. Screen clients. Do some legwork. A million things. You'd be perfect."

"No, I wouldn't. I'm a high-risk employee. Anyway, after today I may not be available."

"You're not going out there with those crazies today, are you? That's madness, sheer madness."

"Is it?" Beth said vaguely. She felt herself pulling away from Sharilee.

"You're damn right it's crazy! You can't beat them in the streets."

"You fought in the streets once."

"It was different then. Now the only way we have a prayer is in the courts. You know that. Look, the Chicago people are going to be indicted and we'll be working on the case and we'll need a hell of a lot of research and . . . Are you *listening* to me?"

"Sure."

"What did I say?"

"Chicago. Fight in the courts. Research."

"What are you on?"

"Reds, mostly."

"God damn, Beth! I get so sick of this. How can we ever win if our people keep shooting that shit into their heads? If you want to kill yourself why don't you use a gun?"

Beth shrugged and stared at the picture of Bobby. It seemed to shimmer, and he faded farther and farther into the distance.

"Listen, I'm not your mama. I can't tie you up. But if you go out there and get busted today it won't be fun and games. They've got federal charges waiting for those crazies today."

Beth wished she could make her understand. "Sharilee, do you remember what Thoreau said?"

"No, I don't remember what Thoreau said."

"He was in jail and a friend of his came to see him and he said, 'What are you doing in there?' And Thoreau looked at him and said, 'What are you doing out there?' "

"I'm not into parables, Beth. I'm working like hell trying to help people. We need you. You need us. You think about it and come see me tomorrow if you want the job. Here's the address."

She handed Beth a card. Beth slipped it into her pocket. "Thanks," she said. "I do appreciate it."

"Don't thank me. Help me."

"I can help another way. How's your law firm fixed for money?"

"We've got enough for the first year. Everybody draws a hundred a week. Lawyers, secretaries, everybody."

Beth pulled a checkbook and a ballpoint pen from her knapsack. She wrote a check and handed it to Sharilee.

"That's a contribution to the cause."

Sharilee looked at the check and tossed it aside. "Jokes I don't need."

"It's no joke. Cash it. A grant from the Beth Foundation."

"Are you serious?"

"Sure. I'm an heiress, remember? My stocks keep splitting."

Sharilee picked up the check and put it in her purse. "I'll take the

362

money, Beth, but it's you I want. I want you helping us, the way you helped me a long time ago when I was a dumb little pickaninny fresh from the cotton fields. Let me help you, Beth, please let me help you."

Beth slumped down on the bed and began to cry. Sharilee sat beside her and stroked her hair. "What can I do?" Beth whispered. "You went one way, Sharilee, and I went another way and now my friends are those freaks who'll be out there today and how can I walk away from them?"

"Fight the way you can win," Sharilee said. "Those people are lost but you're not."

Beth looked at her, wishing she could make her understand. "Sharilee, did you ever do acid?"

"Not on your life."

"Everything is different afterward. You forget all the rules they've taught you. You're sort of . . . born again."

Sharilee looked angry. "You're only born once, lady."

Beth searched for the right words. "Those kids in Chicago, and the ones today, they've done acid. That's why they're not afraid of the cops. The cops just don't *exist*."

"They exist, believe me."

"Sharilee, I've had the war *inside my head*. Do you understand? Bombs exploding and people dying *inside my head*. You see *everything*."

"People aren't supposed to see everything, child. There's too much bad to see. Now you come talk to me tomorrow about that job, okay?"

Beth sat up and tried to smile. "I'll think about it."

"Good," Sharilee said, and got up. "How's your brother?"

"I don't know. About the same, I guess."

"Tomorrow, Beth. You can start a new life tomorrow."

Beth hugged her and let her out the door. Then she leaned against the door for a minute thinking, her mind in pain, not wanting to face a new decision. She had her plan. She was deep into her own world and now Sharilee wanted to pull her back into the other world. After a while she put the Stones record back on and took another red and lay down on the bed, thinking about everything, thinking about nothing.

A little after ten, she got herself together and went out to catch a cab. People were already streaming toward the Capitol. There were police everywhere. Beth felt them staring at her. Two cabs passed by her before one stopped. When she tossed her knapsack in the back seat, the driver eyed her suspiciously.

"You got money, sister?"

Beth showed him a ten-dollar bill. "I've got money. Let's go."

She still had plenty of time, so she had him take her by Kennedy House. It was boarded up now, the way it had been five years before when she and Bill first went there. She'd heard the story second hand. There'd been a controversy, complaints from a Georgia Congressman who controlled OEO's appropriation, a long hassle, with OEO defending them at first, then giving ground, cutting back their grant, finally withdrawing it. Beth walked up the sidewalk and looked in the window. The living room was cluttered with trash and beer cans. It was as if all that they had done had never happened.

Beth ran back to the cab and told the driver to take her to the Watergate.

Carol opened the door and stared at her.

Carol had put on weight and her face was lined and her hair was streaked with gray.

"Beth! We didn't know where you were. Come in."

Beth followed her into the apartment. The living room overlooked the Potomac.

"I came for the Inaugural," Beth said.

Carol looked at her. "Are you all right? Can I get you anything? Coffee?"

"I'm all right," Beth said. "How're you? How's Charles?"

Carol sat down on the long green sofa, opposite Beth. "He's about the same. The first operation didn't do much good and they want to try another one, when he's stronger. They don't know much about spines, really. Would you like to see him now?"

"Where is he?"

"In the bedroom. The bedroom window faces the city. He sits up now, during the days, and I always think he's happiest there, by the window. You can see the monuments from there. I don't know what he can understand, but . . ."

She buried her face in her hands. Beth stood up, felt a rush, felt herself fading in and out, and breathed deeply, trying to clear her head. It passed, and she walked into the bedroom.

He was sitting in a wheel chair in the dark bedroom, silhouetted against the window. He wore pajamas and a robe, and had a blanket across his legs. Past him, Beth could see the Lincoln Memorial and the Washington Monument and the leafless trees of the Mall. She went and stood beside him and put her face close to his.

"Charles. It's Beth. I've come to see you."

His eyes stayed fixed on the city.

"I don't know if you can hear me but it's going to be all right. We're all going to keep on. And we need you, we need you to get well and . . ."

She stopped. The screaming in her mind was so loud that she thought he must hear it. She bit her lip, tried to calm herself. He sat motionless in the wheel chair, his face toward the city. She touched his hand and kissed him quickly on the cheek. Then she hurried back to the living room.

Carol was smoking a cigarette. She'd brushed her hair and she looked a little better.

"I don't see how you stand it."

"There're three of us now. Molly's here and we have a professional nurse who's here at night. And the doctor comes by every afternoon. We manage."

"Where are the children?"

"I sent them off to school. I see them on weekends."

"Wouldn't it be easier on everybody if he was in a hospital and the children could be home with you?"

"I'm trying to do what's right, not just what's easiest. When the children are older, and can understand the choice I faced, I want them to think I did the right thing."

"But how long can you . . . ?"

"I don't *know!*" She ground out one cigarette and lit another. "I'm sorry. It's just that my mother was here last week and we went through this a thousand times. 'Send him off somewhere. Send him to Walter Reed.' But I won't *do* that. I won't have him among strangers, not so long as I'm capable of caring for him. If he knows anything, I want him to know he's here with us. I just can't *desert* him, Beth. He's my husband and he needs me. He never needed me before but he needs me now."

Beth lit one of Carol's cigarettes. "It's too much," she said. "Just too much."

"It comes down to duty," Carol said. "All my life people have done things for me and now it's my time to do something for someone else. My mother thinks I'm crazy. But sometimes you have to do what you believe is right. It's like you and politics, Beth. You keep on doing what you think is right, don't you?"

"Yes," Beth said. "I guess so."

"You're like Charles. He cared so much. Sometimes it almost killed me, how much he cared. But he was changing, right at the end, right before Chicago. He'd been through that cycle that people go through, four or five years of trying to save the world, then figuring out that the world can't be saved and the best you can do is to save yourself. He'd come back to us, those last two weeks in the country. It was the nicest thing that ever happened to me." Carol paused and ran her fingers through her hair. "I'm sorry. I'm rambling again. I tend to ramble these days."

"That's all right."

"How about you, Beth? Are you ready to pull back and live your own life for a while?"

"I don't know. There's so much to be done and somebody has to do it."

"But not the same people, all the time. It wears people down. It kills people. Give yourself some rest."

Beth didn't know what to say. She wanted to go. She could face her own problems, but these were too much for her.

There was a television set in the corner. The picture was on but the sound was down. They could see pictures of the crowd at the Capitol and the politicians on the platform. Johnson. Humphrey. Nixon. Nixon put his left hand on a Bible, raised his right hand, and his lips moved soundlessly. Then he stepped before the microphone to begin his speech.

"Want some comic relief?" Carol asked. She went over and turned up the sound.

". . . We see the hope of tomorrow in the youth of today. I know America's youth. I believe in them. We can be proud that they are better educated, more committed, more passionately driven . . ."

366

"I'm sorry, I can't take it," Beth said. She turned off the television. "I've got to go."

"Stay a few more minutes," Carol said.

"Just a few. Can I use your bathroom?"

Carol pointed her toward the guest bathroom. Beth washed her face, then slipped the vial from her pocket and took two more reds. She looked in the medicine cabinet and saw a bottle of sleeping pills and another of Valium, with Carol's name on the prescription. Another doper. Welcome to the club.

"I talked to your mother this morning," Carol said.

"How is she?"

"Fine. She and Howard are going to the Inaugural Ball tonight. She was all aglow."

Beth slipped one of Carol's cigarettes from the pack and lit it. Her hands shook a little.

"Are you all right, Beth?"

"I'm fine. I just forgot to have breakfast."

"I'll fix you a sandwich."

"No, I've really got to go."

"How's Bill? When does he come home?"

"I think he gets out this spring. It's all messed up."

"You must be excited."

"I don't know what'll happen. It's been so long and so much has changed. He's changed and I've changed and . . . I don't think I'm right for him any more. I don't think I'm good enough for him."

"You'll get back together. I know you will. You need each other."

"I don't know what I need any more."

"Can you come back tonight and have dinner with me?"

"I don't think so. I don't know where I'll be tonight."

"Are you going to stay in Washington?"

Beth didn't want to answer any more questions. She was sick of questions, a world of questions.

"I don't know. I've been offered a job here. I think I'll go back to New York."

"Let me tell you something, Beth. Charles is going to get better. I *know* he is."

"Do the doctors . . . ?"

"No, no. All they do is mumble maybe and if and perhaps. . . .

367

If all I had was the doctors, I'd kill myself. But I have . . . well, call it faith, if that's not too corny."

"It's not," Beth said. "Everybody has to have faith."

"Beth, I know you have your friends and your own life, but there's something I'd like to suggest, just for you to think about."

"What?"

"Molly has to go back to Kentucky next week and I'll have the extra room and if you'd like to come stay with me . . . with us . . . I'd like to have you."

Carol's words seemed to come from a long way off. Beth looked at her and tried to think. She knew that for a long time she had not cared for Carol, had thought her frivolous, had made her a symbol of all that she had left behind, but this was a different Carol whom she felt calling to her, drawing her close. She felt a surge of love for Carol, but it was followed by something else, a sense that no, this is not your place, your world, your place is out there in the streets where the war still raged.

"I don't ask it for *me*," Carol said. "People feel sorry for me but they don't understand. I won't tell you I'm happy, Beth, but I feel *good*. I think that what I'm doing is right, and that makes up for a lot."

"I understand," Beth said.

"Would you like to do it? I think we could help each other. I really do."

Beth went to her and took her hands. "I don't know what to do," she said. "But I'll think about it. And whatever happens, I want you to know . . . well, I'm trying to say that I love you for what you're doing. And there's not much I love any more."

Carol held her close for a moment. "Thank you, Beth."

"I do have to go now," Beth said. "The parade will start pretty soon."

"The paper said they're expecting trouble. All those police and soldiers. My God, won't this ever end?"

"I don't know," Beth said.

She took a cab to Seventeenth Street. The driver was a young black who kept looking back at her and asking if she was all right. When she got out, Beth gave him the four or five dollars she had in her pocket.

368

"You take it," she said. "I don't need it."

She walked across the Ellipse to the place where Pennsylvania Avenue met Fifteenth Street. A dozen blocks down the wide avenue, at the foot of Capitol Hill, she could see the motorcade moving toward her. At its front was a V-shaped wedge of motorcycle cops, an arrow pointed at her, and behind them bands and soldiers and finally the long line of black limousines.

The sight of the motorcade made her blood run fast, made her forget Carol, reminded her of why she was here and what she must do. No matter what anyone thought; she knew what she must do.

What are you doing in there?
What are you doing out there?

All she asked now was an instant's confrontation, one moment to let him know how she hated him and all he stood for, to make him see her face to face, to make him know that all his police and soldiers could not protect him from the people. She would have her moment, for Bill, for all the boys in prison and all the boys dead in Vietnam, for all the others, and after that she didn't care what happened; she just didn't care any more.

What are you doing in there?
What are you doing out there?

Beth waited.

At the other end of the avenue, the motorcade moved forward slowly, like a glacier.

Police and paratroopers lined the curbs. Behind them, thousands cheered the marching soldiers and the slowly moving bombproof limousines. Boy Scouts passed out tiny American flags and people waved them as they cheered. Little bands of demonstrators chanted and jeered from the fringes of the crowd. They threw rocks and bottles and coins at the limousines. The Secret Service men who jogged beside the limousines tried to fend the objects away, and policemen knifed into the crowd to arrest those troublemakers they could catch. But there were more of them at every corner.

The motorcade moved up Pennsylvania Avenue, toward the White House.

369

Beth watched it come.

From where she stood, she could see the crazies who'd gathered at Thirteenth Street, in front of the National Theater. The police tried to hold them back, but they kept regrouping, chanting, throwing bottles at the police, breaking store windows. They were the hard core, freakdom's kamikaze, making their last stand. Beth thought of joining them. But she would not. Let them draw the police. She was on her own today, on her own private kamikaze mission. All around her, people cheered and waved their little flags. Beth barely noticed them.

The motorcade moved on.

As it passed the crazies at Thirteenth Street, there was a new barrage. Bottles, beer cans, stones, a firecracker, a smoke bomb. A dozen Secret Service men fought to fend them off. The police charged the kids. A silver object, the size of a baseball, flew through the air at Nixon's car. A Secret Service man leaped high and batted it away. The limousines jerked forward, picking up speed.

Beth was ready now. The motorcade shimmered, dissolved, became an advancing army, with her alone to challenge it.

> *What are you doing in there?*
> *What are you doing out there?*

The first motorcycles had reached the corner, were turning onto Fifteenth Street. She hadn't known there'd be so many of them, an army of police, the ring of Secret Service men, the helicopters hovering overhead. But she would get through. She was invisible, an apparition who would materialize beside Nixon's car, beating on its windows, shouting at the little man inside. She wondered how he felt now, inside that limousine. She would make him know that he lived in a prison too, as real as Bill's, as real as death.

The Marine Band marched by, playing "Hail to the Chief." The limousine was sixty feet away, fifty. She inched toward the front of the crowd, toward the young paratrooper who was the first obstacle in her path. She looked at people who did not look at her, wondering who they were, where they had come from. Nothing registered. These were not her people, this was not her country. Where was her country? In the past? In the future? Or never to be? She stood beside a young black woman who was wearing a Nixon button and cheering. Beth looked at her and thought of Sharilee, the job, the new life she

370

had promised. Suddenly her certainty crumbled, became confusion. Her thoughts tumbled, raged out of control. Was she mad or sane? She whispered a kind of prayer. She heard shouts inside her mind, louder than the band and the motorcycles, the voices of the men she had loved, the men who once had told her what was right and wrong, her father, Charles, Bill, calling to her . . . stop . . . go on . . . yes . . . no . . . The limousine was almost abreast of her, her body grew taut, the voices called louder . . .

She turned her face from the limousine and cast one last, parting glance at the Ellipse, at the long expanse of grass that swept toward the Washington Monument. . . . That would endure. . . . She would return to this someday. . . .

What are you doing in there?
What are you doing out there?

Then she saw him.

He was alone, walking across the Ellipse, his back to her, but she knew him at once, knew that tousled hair, knew that slight stoop, knew it was he.

He was there. He wasn't dead. He'd come back, of course, he'd come back to lead them again, he needed her, he needed her and Sharilee and Carol and Charles and all of them. She cried out his name but he didn't hear her, he just kept walking, away from the crowd and the noise and the soldiers, going his own way, going to find those who had helped him before and would help him now, now when they needed him most. Beth screamed, turned, pushed through the crowd, began to run after him, across the street, across the grass, running after him, calling his name, Bobby Bobby Bobby, wait for me, I'm coming, I'll help, there's still time and there's hope, yes, there's still hope, we can make it right again, we can do it, yes, we can do it, all of us, wait, wait for me . . . She ran faster and faster, flying across the grass, her arms outstretched to him, her eyes filled with tears, crying out his name, running on and on toward the open sky, running, crying, hoping, joyous, free.